W9-CAW-235

The

SCHOOLMASTER'S DAUGHTER

The

SCHOOLMASTER'S
DAUGHTER

JOHN SMOLENS

PEGASUS BOOKS
NEW YORK

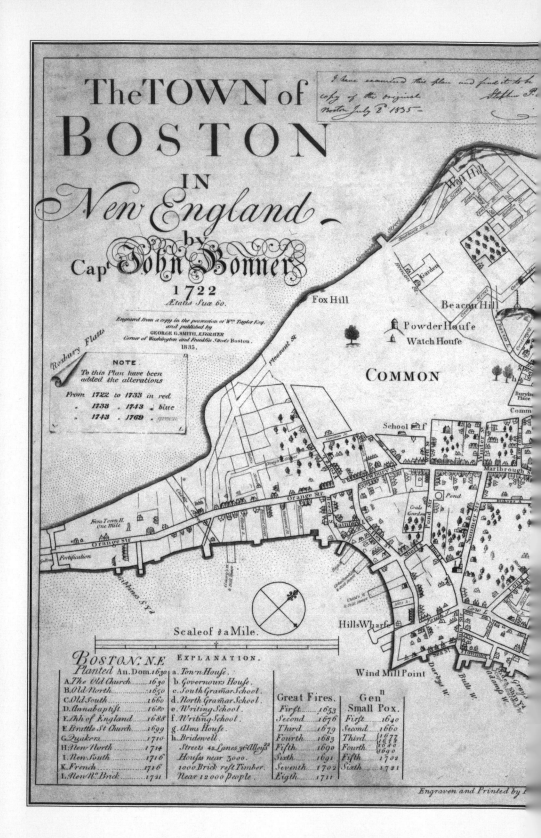

The TOWN of BOSTON

IN

New England

by

Capt John Bonner

1722

Ætatis Suæ 60.

Engraved from a copy in the possession of Wm Taylor Esq.
and published by
GEORGE G. SMITH, ENGRAVER,
Corner of Washington and Franklin Streets, Boston.
1835.

I have examined this plan and find it to be a
copy of the original
Boston July 8. 1835 —

NOTE.

To this Plan have been
added the alterations

From 1722 to 1733 in red
" 1733 . 1743 . blue
" 1743 . 1769 . green

Roxbury Flatts

Fox Hill

Wolf Hill

Garden

Beacon Hill

PowderHouse

Watch House

COMMON

School

Marlbrough

Pond

Coals Garden

Orange Str

Pleasant St

From Town H.
One Mile

Fortification

Orange Str

HillsWharf

Wind Mill Point

Scale of ¼ a Mile.

EXPLANATION.

BOSTON: N.E.
Planted An. Dom. 1630.

				Great Fires.		Gen Small Pox.	
A	The Old Church	1630	a. Town House.	First	1653	First	1640
B	Old North	1650	b. Governours House.	Second	1676	Second	1660
C	Old South	1660	c. South Gramar School.	Third	1679	Third	1677
D	Annabaptist	1680	d. North Gramar School.	Fourth	1683		1678
E	Chh of England	1688	e. Writing School.	Fifth	1690	Fourth	1689
F	Brattle St Church	1699	f. Writing School.	Sixth	1691		1690
G	Quakers	1710	g. Alms House.	Seventh	1702	Fifth	1702
H	New North	1714	h. Bridewell	Eigth	1711	Sixth	1721
I	New South	1716	Streets 42 Lanes 36 Alleys 22				
K	French	1716	Houses near 3000.				
L	New N. Brick	1721	1000 Brick rest Timber.				
			Near 12000 People.				

Engraven and Printed by

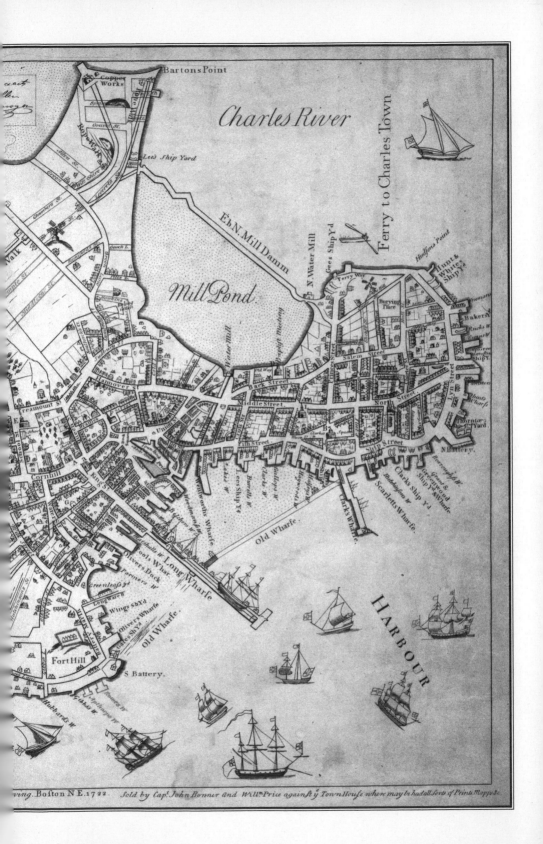

Charles River

Bartons Point

Copper Works

Grav'd St.

Lee's Ship Yard

Eb N. Mill Damm

Mill Pond

N. Water Mill

Gee's Ship Yd

Ferry to Charles Town

Hudson's Point

Hunt & White's Ships

Water mill

Burying Place

Salem Street

Bakers

Rucks

Charter Street

Back Street

Middle Street

Lyn Street

Hanover St.

Tremount

Cornhill

King's

Union Street

N Battery

Clarks Ship Yd.

Greenwood Ship Yd. & Salvate

Charks Ship Yd.

Scarletts Wharfe.

Old Wharfe

Clarks Wharfe.

Old Wharfe

Long Wharfe

Olivers Dock

Greenleaff's

Long Wharf

Wings sh Yd

Olivers Wharfe

Gees Sh Yd

Old Wharfe

Fort Hill

S Battery.

Hubbards W.

HARBOUR

THE SCHOOLMASTER'S DAUGHTER

Pegasus Books LLC
80 Broad Street, 5th Floor
New York, NY 10004

First Pegasus Books cloth edition 2011

Interior design by Maria Fernandez

ISBN: 978-1-60598-252-6

10 9 8 7 6 5 4 3 2 1

Printed in the United States of America
Distributed by W. W. Norton & Company, Inc.

In memory of my wife,
Patricia Anne Miles Smolens

War's begun—and school's done.

John Lovell, Headmaster
The Latin School, Boston
April 19, 1775

PART ONE

April: The Alarm

In the fall of 1774 and the winter of 1775, I was one of upwards of thirty, chiefly mechanics, who formed ourselves into a committee for the purpose of watching the movements of the British soldiers, and gaining every intelligence of the movements of the Tories. We held our meetings at the Green Dragon Tavern. We were so careful that time we met, every person swore upon the Bible that they would not discover any of our transactions but to Messrs. Adams, Doctors Warren, Church, and one or two more.

—Paul Revere, Boston

I soon received intelligence from Boston that the enemy were all in motion, and were certainly preparing to come out into the country.

—Reverend Jonas Clark, Lexington

I

A Small Incident

ON A TUESDAY EVENING, ABIGAIL LOVELL HAD JUST ENTERED Dock Square when the music of waterfront commerce, shopkeeps and fishmongers hawking their goods, was broken up by the sound of running footsteps, a shout, and then a collision. Twilight made it difficult to see: a boy sprawled on the cobblestones, two redcoats standing over him. Bostonians gathered round, fearfully silent now. Abigail pushed through the crowd and found that it was her younger brother, Benjamin, on the ground. One of the British soldiers had his rapier drawn.

"And why are you in such a hurry?" the sergeant demanded, holding the tip of his blade within an inch of Benjamin's throat.

"Begging your pardon, sir," Benjamin said. "It's my fault."

Every day, such incidents in Boston: the occupier and the occupied.

Abigail recognized the other soldier, a Corporal Hubert Lumley, who billeted with a neighbor on School Street. "Sergeant Munroe," Lumley said. "I suggest it's nothing intentional on the boy's part. Merely an accident. And I recognize him. He's the schoolmaster's son, and as you see he's—"

"I am to see *what,* Corporal?" Munroe turned to Lumley, angered by his impertinence.

Lumley was perhaps the same age as Abigail, in his early twenties. He was dark-haired and the shorter of the two soldiers, but seemed to have considerable self-possession, enough that Sergeant Munroe appeared thwarted, and he returned his attention to Benjamin. "The schoolmaster's son, you say? On your feet, lad."

Careful of the sergeant's sword, Benjamin got up off the cobblestones, his britches smeared with butcher's blood, fish guts, straw, and manure, standing with his back to Abigail. He was seventeen; tall, lean, yet with inordinately broad shoulders, the result of rowing in the harbor. His tricorn lay at his feet.

"Your hat?" Lumley said.

Benjamin nodded.

"Well," Munroe said, pouting, "aren't you going to retrieve it?"

Reluctantly, Benjamin picked up the tricorn, which Lumley snatched away. He began to inspect the inside of the crown.

"And where are you going in such a hurry?" Munroe asked Benjamin.

"Home, sir. I was just—"

"Sergeant," Abigail said, stepping forward. Both soldiers appeared startled that she would even think of intruding. "Please, sir. The corporal is correct. This is my brother, Benjamin Lovell, and he was indeed on his way home. We live on School Street, but a few doors from Corporal Lumley's billet."

Her brother nodded slowly, wary of the sword which was still pointed at his neck. Incredulous, the sergeant touched the steel tip to Benjamin's skin, just above the Adam's apple.

"*Sergeant.*" A voice to Abigail's left, and then, as the crowd parted, an officer approached, causing Munroe and Lumley to stiffen. "No need for *that.*"

4

Reluctantly, Munroe lowered his arm, holding the sword at his side. "Of course, Colonel Cleaveland."

Lumley seemed to comprehend the delicacy of the moment, and he looked up from the hat in his hands. "And you might be . . . Mistress Abigail Lovell?" he said.

Several of the people in the crowd snickered.

"Yes, I am Abigail Lovell. And our father is the headmaster at the Latin School, and, well, he's quick to employ discipline with his ferule. Late for dinner customarily brings two whacks, one for each palm." She gazed about at the crowd, drawing them into the conspiracy. "But, of course, you understand this all really has to do with fishing."

Munroe looked as though he'd heard enough prattle, but Colonel Cleaveland seemed mildly interested. "How so, Miss?" he asked.

"Well, sir. On such a spring evening young men must needs go fishing down to the harbor, but my brother will not be allowed to venture forth until he has eaten a proper supper."

There were more snickers: *Fishing, indeed.*

"Or perhaps if the tide's out," she offered. "They might row across the Back Bay to go digging in the clam beds."

And there were consenting murmurs and nods. *Aye. In beds.*

The colonel studied the crowd, his gaze deliberate, suspicious. Taller than the other two soldiers, he was a different cut of Brit. Blond hair smoothed back and tied in a neat queue with a fine ribbon. Deep blue eyes, a clean-shaven jaw. "This is not about fishing, young lady," he announced for everyone's benefit. "But order. These two soldiers patrol the streets of Boston in an effort to maintain order."

"But, sir—" she began.

"Do not confuse the issue," he said, looking at her now, and his eyes became, reluctantly, she thought, genuinely curious. And she herself suffered a moment of reluctance, much as when she would stare at herself in the looking-glass, to find silky brown tresses spilling over her shoulders, a rather long jaw, eyes large-lidded, and a mouth that she thought too wide. It was her friend, Rachel Revere, who often said, *you are too critical in your self-regard. I note the way men look upon you.* "Mistress Lovell, is it? You do recognize the necessity of such street patrols?"

Abigail said nothing, merely staring back at him. Sometimes, with men, silence was best. In the presence of their occupiers Bostonians often dissembled, frequently conspired, and it often led to sorrow, shame, and even bloodshed. But Abigail's last resort was silence. Look a man in the eye and speak not.

The colonel studied her with a cold, deliberate eye. Did he take this reticence for a bold challenge, or was he merely admiring the way strands of her dark hair drifted across her cheek?

After a moment, Lumley said, "Begging your permission, sir." And when Colonel Cleaveland nodded his approval, reluctantly, it seemed, Lumley took a small step toward Abigail. "Your father, Schoolmaster Lovell," he said as he considered Benjamin's tricorn once more, as though here he would discover the secret, the true threat. "If I am not mistaken, he is an outspoken Tory, loyal to the king?"

"He is that, sir," Abigail said.

"But then your brother," Lumley said, looking up at her suddenly. "Your other brother, your *older* brother, that would be—"

"Yes, James Lovell, he is the usher, the assistant headmaster at my father's school."

"Also loyal to the crown?" Lumley asked, and when she did not reply he smiled indulgently. "I think not. No, in fact, *he* has quite the reputation and has been known to deliver some of the most fervent speeches on matters of taxation, liberty, and . . . your provincials' notions of independence." Abigail was about to speak, but Lumley raised his free hand. "I expected to find a missive tucked inside this hat," he said. "Boys frequently run through these crowded streets, acting as couriers for the likes of Samuel Adams and Dr. Warren and their patriotic mob. But—" he held out Benjamin's hat. "There be no damning evidence here."

"Boston boys are given to running," Abigail offered.

Colonel Cleaveland asked, "And why do they run?"

"It's in their nature."

"Their *nature*?" Munroe said. He was clearly put out that Lumley had taken possession of the moment, as well as the hat, and now he gazed at Abigail, his eyes drifting down the length of her. With some of them, there was that, too. "Corporal, perhaps you're searching in the wrong place."

"You are insulting, sir." Abigail stared back at the sergeant until he looked away.

The Bostonians, gathered around them like water surrounding a peninsula, showed their appreciation with snorts and laughter. This *was* bold—bold and raw, like the salt wind that scoured this city.

Lumley considered the crowd, recognizing how often such ribald humor had suddenly turned to aggression, here in the city streets, where cobblestones and bricks could easily be taken up against the occupiers. To quiet them, he said loudly, "Perhaps we should inspect everyone's hat. And shawl. And pockets. Secrets— you're all bearing secrets, are you not?"

The crowd quickly turned sullen, and seemed to press forward slightly, poised.

"I assure you," Abigail said quickly, sensing that this incident might easily get out of hand. "My brother—both my brothers wish you no harm." All three soldiers considered her now. "Gentlemen, are not we all British subjects here?"

There was absolute silence in Dock Square, for no one had an answer.

"Subjects," Lumley said finally. "Quite right. We're all sub-jects." Impatiently, he returned the hat to Benjamin, as though to hold it another moment would result in an irreparable contami-nation. He then took a step backward, a gesture that seemed to suggest that the danger had passed, the worst was over, and they best get on about their business.

Abigail looked at Munroe then. He appeared to have no choice but to go along, and he stiffened with resentment—he was the soldier of rank on this patrol, before Colonel Cleaveland had intruded. Reluctantly, he sheathed his rapier. "Well, boy," he said to Benjamin, "we will be on patrol throughout the night, so don't let us catch you out and about—"

"Escort your sister home now," Colonel Cleaveland said, with the slightest bow toward Abigail, and for a moment he seemed to recognize the absurdity, perhaps even the humor of such an incident. "You'll not want to let your chowder get cold."

"Thanking you kindly, Colonel," Abigail said as she took her brother's arm. "We must make our haste for dinner, Benjamin, lest we invoke the wrath of our father."

Laughter then as the crowd began to break up. Something to take home, or to the grog shop: a Boston girl, her younger brother, and three lobsterbacks in the evening shadows of Dock Square. There was a moment when it could have become something dangerous, something inevitable. Such encounters often led to incarceration, fines, or both. How many Bostonians languished in British prisons under false or trumped-up charges? It was a seemingly small incident such as this that had led to the Bloody Massacre five years earlier.

Occupied and occupier.

"Good evening, then," Abigail said.

Corporal Lumley touched the brim of his hat.

However, Sergeant Munroe seemed unable to respond. He still gripped the handle of his sword, as though eager to draw it from his scabbard once more.

The crowd parted, allowing Abigail to cross the square toward Fanueil Hall, holding Benjamin close to her side. "That was brilliant," she whispered. "Not putting anything in your hat."

"What would I carry?" he asked as they skirted a small pond of muddy water.

"You're not carrying a letter?"

Abigail was five years older than Benjamin, and clutching his upper arm she guided him through the crowded streets, as she had since they were small children, until he suddenly took her by the hand and pulled her down an alley. Boston was a warren of narrow lanes, crooked alleys, and Benjamin employed them constantly. They turned a corner and negotiated their way through a bleating flock of sheep which was being herded toward King Street.

"Mind your step," Benjamin said.

"Benjamin, we do not have to enter our own house by the summer kitchen."

"Front doors are for Father's Tory associates," he said. "Besides, I'm not going home."

Most houses had room for vegetable gardens and livestock, and many were backed by a barn or stable. There were the sounds—and the odor—of animals everywhere: chickens, cows, horses, swine, goats, not to mention seagulls wheeling overhead. When they were clear of the sheep, Benjamin and Abigail reached a passageway cluttered with rain barrels standing between the blackened clapboard walls of two houses. He led his sister down this damp, mossy nook until they were in a tight courtyard, which was nearly dark. Overhead garments hung from clotheslines, fluttering in the salty breeze that came off the harbor.

"Turn around," he demanded as he released her arm.

She glared at him. "And have you play one of your impish pranks? No."

"As you wish." He began to unfasten his belt buckle, and then reached down inside the front of his loosened britches. "Here," he said, handing her an envelope.

"Warm," she said. "Good thing those two soldiers didn't decide to search you more thoroughly. You'd be taking your dinner aboard the prison ship anchored in the harbor."

"I need you to deliver it," he said. "I haven't time."

"No fishing tonight?" Holding up the envelope, she said, "Who is this from?"

"You needn't know that. It's safer not to—"

The envelope was fastened with a wax seal. "Nor should I even know the contents."

"No, no, you shouldn't. Look, it's just a sign, a signal that you're the legitimate courier."

"And what am I supposed to—"

"You hand over this letter and you'll receive another."

"Another letter?"

"Without this you get nothing."

"This is a rare precaution."

"It is, yes. But you have noticed the redcoats today?"

"There's much activity," she said. "They're gathering on the Common."

"In full field gear."

"A drill? They often parade on the Common. Or do you think this is it?"

"We've known that they would march out from Boston soon. There have been so many signs, preparations—"

"But General Gage," she said with a quick smile; "he *does* like his decoys."

"True."

"Where am I to deliver this letter?"

He removed his tricorn and curled the brim.

"Benjamin?"

He wouldn't look at her. "Province House."

"The governor general's mansion—isn't *that* just fine."

He put his hat back on his head and stared at her.

"And I give this to . . . General Gage himself?"

"You take it to the carriage house," he said. "There's a groom named Seth. Deliver it to no one but Seth."

"Have you ever done this before, taken something to Province House?"

"I just go where I'm told," he said, "but, no, I've never gone to the governor's house before. Tonight I think you'll have a

better chance of getting through, especially after what happened earlier." He shook his head. "Besides, there's something
else I must do. Listen, go immediately to Province House. I'm
told Seth has just come back from Barbados. Missing an ear.
Sorry to ask you to do this. With the redcoats gathering at the
Commons, street patrols will be stopping runners everywhere
tonight."

"As I told the colonel, Benjamin, boys run. Boston women
walk. And I walk wherever I want in this city—even if it's to
Province House." She smiled, but her brother did not, and she
suddenly understood that he was nervous, perhaps even afraid.
"And after I give this letter to the groom?"

"You will be given a reply—which you must take straight
away to James."

"So he can encode it."

"Probably. Then he'll determine what's to be done with it."
Benjamin looked impatiently up the alley. "I must go."

"Father will be upset. It appears we will both miss our
supper."

"Father is always upset."

"Usually, at least."

Benjamin looked at her then, and it was there in his eyes,
if only momentarily: he was again the boy who not many
years earlier would come to his sister's bed, frightened by a
reprimand, or a nightmare. On such nights she would draw
him to her beneath the warmth of the counterpane and hold
him tight.

"Where are you going, Benjamin?"

"Can't say. You understand."

"I do. But I worry—I worry that you'll . . ."

"Disappear."

"Dear Benjamin, you have been finishing my sentences since
we were children."

"We both have."

It was true. When they had been very small, no one in the family could understand what Benjamin was saying, except Abigail, and they all looked to her for an interpretation.

"It's Ezra," he said. "You've not heard from him?"

"No," she said. "Not since he left Boston two months ago. I am beginning to wonder—"

"If he means to disappear. From you." She stared at her brother, afraid, exposed. "You chose him, Abigail. So you run the risk, but I don't think he's disappeared because he doesn't love you."

"Sometimes in such matters, in matters of the heart, we have no choice."

"I suppose not."

He started up the alley, but paused and turned around. It was almost dark now and she could barely see his face. He pulled his hat down snug on his head, causing his long hair to curl out over his ears. "I think it's beginning finally, tonight."

She went to him, taking ahold of his hand. He looked down, and she almost thought he was going to walk home with her to dinner, hand in hand, like they did when they were younger. Gently, though she knew he didn't want to, he pulled his hand free. He turned and ran, his familiar loping strides, the sound of his boots reverberating down that narrow cavern of weathered clapboards.

There was no choice now.

Choices had been made, for all of them.

II

Sympathetic Ink

PROVINCE HOUSE HAD A WELL-TENDED ORCHARD AND GARDEN, and sentries stood guard on the wide front steps. Abigail walked around to the back of the property, where the carriage house gates opened onto Governor's Alley. Inside the wrought iron fence she saw a boy of about ten, beating a row of horse blankets on a clothesline with a stick. When she motioned to him, he came to the gate.

"Do you know a groom named Seth?" she asked.

"He's my father, Ma'am."

"I wish to speak to him." He gazed through the bars at her and didn't move. "Please tell him I have something for him."

The boy ran across the yard and entered the carriage house, which itself was a handsome building, with a fine cupola. A moment later, a man came out and walked toward the gate. He had no hair, and his round forehead shone in the faint light. On the right side of his head there was just a small nub of flesh where there should have been an ear. "You have something for me?" For a man with such broad shoulders, he had a voice that was high and quite musical. His accent was Caribbean, which was heard frequently in the port of Boston.

"Your name is Seth?"

He nodded.

"I'm to deliver a letter."

"James Lovell sent you?"

"Yes, he's my brother."

Seth opened the gate, allowing Abigail to slip inside.

"You should not have come until it is completely dark," he said.

"Odd. I'm usually admonished for refusing to *not* stay indoors at night. Or perhaps you would have me taken for the sort of woman who sells her wares in the dark?"

"I speak not of your honor, Mistress, but of necessity." He studied her with a bold eye, which made her uncomfortable, but then he whispered urgently, "Boston is in such a state, what with hangings, executions, and tarrings, that we all may be required to make sacrifices, no?" He bowed his head, as though requesting forgiveness.

"Indeed. This is so."

He smiled then, revealing broken yellow teeth, and then with great haste and an air of formality he led her up the cobblestone drive to the carriage house, which they entered by a side door. It was a clean, orderly stable, smelling of horses and hay, and they went into a small office, where there was an oil lamp on a desk. From her shawl she removed the letter Benjamin had given her and handed it to Seth.

"Sit, please," he said, gesturing toward a desk chair.

Abigail didn't move. To sit would seem to place her at a disadvantage. Other than her brothers, no one could be entirely trusted.

"Very well," Seth said. "You can stand here, if you prefer. All the easier to flee for the gate, if you lose your nerve. Some do, you know. The British have made us all wary. Fear is their greatest weapon." He stared at her once more, his dark eyes earnest and even greedy, and then he tucked the letter in his pocket, saying, "It may take a while, but I will be back."

She watched as he went out into the courtyard and entered Province House by a back door. In one window she could see an enormous chandelier with dozens of lit candles, their glow casting an oblong of light down across the cobblestones, making them seem polished.

There were so many letters. They were the whispered voice, the unspoken language of Boston, the only means of genuine communication since the city had fallen under the yoke of General Gage's military occupation. The British had been a heavy presence in Boston for as long as Abigail could remember. Before she was ten she had witnessed her first hanging at the Great Elm in the Common, and since then public floggings and executions were all too frequent. Gage was perceived as being even-handed as he meted out punishments for his men as often as for the colonists. Tensions increased five years ago, when on a wintry night in March British soldiers opened fire on a crowd of Bostonians gathered in front of the Customs House on King Street. Five people died and numerous others were wounded, yet at the trial the commanding officer, Captain Preston, had been absolved of any culpability. The Bloody Massacre, as it was often called (though the British referred to it as the Boston Riot), was commemorated every March 5th by enormous crowds gathering to hear Whig speeches, this year's being given by her brother James.

As the situation became increasingly intolerable, more troops were shipped over from England. There were some fifteen thousand Bostonians, and perhaps three thousand British soldiers, many of them billeted in homes against the will of their owners. The sense of confinement on the Boston peninsula only contributed to the tenor and frequency of altercations. Yankee rum was plentiful and cheap, and there was a great tendency toward drunken disorder amongst the Regulars. Boston being a seaport, the situation was further complicated by the availability of easy women. Daily incidents occurred in the streets, in the taverns, and particularly in waterfront establishments, which were infested with idle sailors since General Gage had ordered the port closed, as a form of reprimand for the colonials' unwillingness to bow to a series of edicts and acts regarding taxation. That winter, even William Dawes, jocular Billy Dawes, had knocked down a soldier in the street in response to an insult made to his pretty wife.

Indeed, all of Boston was waiting, expecting the situation to break open any day, especially since the series of powder alarms which had taken place the previous fall. It started when General Gage began a campaign to secure the gunpowder throughout New England. A sound strategy, perhaps, taking weaponry away from a discontented people on the brink of revolt, but ultimately the plan only succeeded in exacerbating the situation. In September, he sent the first of several military expeditions out from the city. There were only two ways off the Boston peninsula, and before daylight a Lieutenant-Colonel Maddison led his men out Long Wharf, where they boarded some dozen longboats, which were then rowed across the harbor and up the Mystic River. They landed at a place called Temple's Farm and marched about a mile to the Quarry Hill powder house. This stone tower, which housed several hundred barrels of gunpowder, belonged to the towns in the province (one of Benjamin Franklin's new lightning rods rose up from its conical, shingled roof). It was a tidy operation, the mission carried off without any mishaps, and nary a shot fired; by midday the soldiers returned to Boston with the largest supply of gunpowder in the region, plus two brass field pieces.

But Gage was forever underestimating what he often called the "Country People." Early on the day of the raid, they were caught unawares by the British deployment, but soon church bells tolled, and an elaborate system of alarm went into effect, riders sprinting on horseback deep into the countryside to give warning. After the

British soldiers marched back into Boston, rumors rolled through the province like ocean swells in a nor'easter. There was talk of shootings, of people wounded and killed; the British men-of-war in the harbor were bombarding Boston (which was not true). War had finally, inevitably broken out. Within hours, thousands of men collected in villages and towns throughout New England and, armed with muskets and cartridge boxes and provisioned with hastily prepared wallets of food, marched toward Boston.

By the following day, several thousand country people were collected on Cambridge Common, their anger fueled by newspapers which printed a letter (always, the letters) from William Brattle to General Gage, suggesting the raid upon the provincial powder house on Quarry Hill. William Brattle was one of the wealthiest, most flagrant Tories in Massachusetts. Four generations of Brattles had resided in a mansion with mall and garden which ran down to the banks of the Charles River. It was a brutally hot day and Whig leaders, such as Dr. Joseph Warren, persuaded most of those gathered on the Common to lay down their arms, so the mob was primarily equipt with stones and cudgels when they marched on Brattle's house. Brattle fled, taking refuge on Castle Island in Boston Harbor. (Though he subsequently wrote a letter of apology, which was published in the newspapers, he had yet to dare return to his house.) The crowd then swarmed the residence of a Tory barrister, Jonathan Sewall, where windows were broken and the house ransacked. They weren't through. Benjamin Hallowell, Customs Commissioner, was accosted, escaping Cambridge on horseback, pistol in hand. Hundreds chased him all the way to Boston Neck, where his horse collapsed and died of exhaustion. Hallowell barely made it behind the safety of the British sentries who stood guard at the gates to the city.

Throughout the winter, the rift only became more pronounced as both sides awaited the inevitable moment when the smoldering tensions would be sparked to violence. The judicial system was rendered ineffectual; juries could not be sequestered and hastily printed handbills were nailed to the doors of attorneys, threatening death to anyone who attempted to conduct business in a court of law.

General Gage attempted several subsequent raids in search of gunpowder and weaponry—north to Salem and Portsmouth, New Hampshire—but they failed to quiet the colonials. The alarm system worked, and with each attempt it proved even more efficient. Through the winter months it was not uncommon to hear stories of men and women working over fires, in barns, in stables, or even in the open air of the dooryard, melting down tankards and plates, and pouring the molten pewter into bullet molds. Metal of all kinds was sought—even organ pipes ripped out of a church across the harbor in Charlestown.

At least a half hour had passed when Seth returned to the carriage house. He handed Abigail two letters, both sealed with a red wax. "This," he said, tapping one of the letters, "must be encrypted by your brother immediately, and then taken to Dr. Warren's surgery. The other here, the other is a fake."

"All right."

He led her out of the carriage house, toward the back of the Province House. "Now it is dark. I'll let you out a side door, and you must go quickly."

When they reached the courtyard, there was a shadow that blocked the light from the chandelier in the house—it was a woman at the window, peering out into the night, a very elegant woman, wearing a dress of red satin. She wore a gold silk shawl about her shoulders and her hair, piled up on her head, was wrapped in a blue turban. It was the general's American wife, Margaret Kemble Gage; her elegance and her penchant for Turkish-styled garments were legendary—she had sat for a portrait by John Singleton Copley. There were rumors that she was sympathetic to Whig cause.

"Mistress," Seth whispered.

The woman gazed down at Abigail for a moment. There was no change in her expression. She held a small fan, which she began to flutter beneath her chin.

"Mistress Lovell, *please.*"

Abigail curtseyed, and then the woman turned away from the window and disappeared into the vast room.

Boston was such a small peninsula, its nights now illuminated by hundreds of streetlamps, smelling of burning oil, and it was only a matter of minutes before Abigail approached her brother's house. But when she turned a corner she saw two soldiers standing beneath the next streetlamp—Sergeant Munroe, accompanied by Corporal Lumley. She had no choice but to continue on toward them slowly.

"Rather late for you to be out and about," the sergeant said.

He'd been drinking. In fact, they both had been, though Lumley seemed in fuller possession of his faculties.

"It is curious," Lumley said, not unpleasantly. "A young woman, out alone."

"Evening, sirs," Abigail said.

"Not long ago, Sergeant Munroe, Miss Lovell was in a hurry to get home in time for her dinner with her brother."

"And where you be headed now, Miss Lovell?" the sergeant asked, leaning toward her slightly, as though compensating for a sudden tilt of the earth.

Before she could answer, Lumley said, "I believe she has two brothers, and one lives back this way—James, who is a terribly outspoken supporter of the Whigs."

"James," Munroe said. "Of course."

Abigail straightened her back as though to proceed, and said, "I'm going to visit my brother and his wife, who is expecting. Now, if you don't mind—"

Lumley stepped in her way, and then taking hold of her by the shoulders maneuvered her out of the lamplight and only stopped when he had her pushed up against the shingled wall of a house. The smell of rum came off him like an insult.

"*Sir,*" she said.

He said nothing, and Munroe, standing next to him, only glanced up and down the street to see that no one was approaching. Lumley's hands still clutched her shoulders more firmly as she began to resist his grasp.

"What would she be bringing to her brother, do you suppose?" Munroe said as he stepped closer, also reeking of liquor. "Begging your pardon, truly I am," he whispered.

He ran his hands up her sides and then over her breasts. Abigail tried to turn away but her shoulders were pinned to the wall behind her. Munroe fondled her thoroughly until he found what he was looking for and then removed his hands. "If you please, Miss Lovell, you will hand over that letter, or I shall retrieve it myself."

Lumley let go of her shoulders. "Should we do her the honor of turning our backs?"

"Certainly," Munroe said. "We are gentlemen, after all."

Both soldiers did an exaggerated about-face.

Abigail untied her shawl and unbuttoned the top of her dress. She removed the letter, and then set everything to right. "Here," she said.

The two soldiers turned around and she held out the envelope to them, which Lumley took. Munroe looked put out, but Lumley said, "Shall I open it, sir?"

"Yes, of course."

Lumley broke the wax seal and removed a sheet of paper, which he unfolded as he turned toward the nearest streetlamp. He didn't say anything.

"Well?" Munroe demanded.

"It appears—" Lumley glanced up at Abigail, angrily. "It be a recipe, sir."

"For what?"

"'Quahog pie,' it says here," Lumley said. "'Two quarts of fresh quahogs, finely chopped. Onions, diced potatoes——'"

Munroe grabbed the letter away and held it up close to his face. "I haven't got me spectacles," he said. He moved his lips as he read, and then he gazed across the top of the paper at Abigail. "Why, it's a recipe."

"I told you that, sir," Lumley said.

As Munroe folded up the sheet of paper, he said, "It's in code, in'it?"

Lumley gently removed the letter from the sergeant's fingers. "Perhaps it is, sir."

"We should take you in, Miss. Give this missive a proper examination and see what you're really up to."

"I said I was on my way to my brother's, to visit his wife who is expecting."

"Yes, another bold young patriot about to enter the world," Munroe said, leaning close, until his sour breath was warm on her face. "That's one way to build an army, right, Love?"

Lumley stepped closer as well, but it seemed in an effort to deflect Munroe. "May I inquire, Miss, why you concealed the letter?"

"Sir, one never knows who one might encounter here on the streets, at night. To carry an envelope in hand only invites curiosity."

Lumley nodded. "Of course."

"I say we take her in," Munroe said. He placed a hand on her upper arm.

Abigail tried to pull herself free, but stopped when Lumley cleared his throat. "Sir."

"What?"

"Un*hand* me!" she said, trying to yank her arm free of his grasp.

Munroe only gripped her arm more tightly, and he clearly seemed to enjoy seeing her struggle. His eyes darted about, frequently falling upon her breasts. Earlier he had put his saber point to Benjamin's neck, and now he seemed determined to make up for being thwarted. "I like your spirit, girl," he breathed, his face nearly pressed to hers. "You want to put up a fight, eh? That makes for good sport!"

"I *will* scream," Abigail said, "if you don't release me *at once,* I will—"

"Might I suggest, Sergeant," Lumley said with remarkable calm, "that we confiscate the letter and let the young woman pass?"

Munroe seemed angered by such distraction. "I want to conduct a thorough search," he said, pulling Abigail hard against him. "This mistress bears more than a letter, I think."

"But we have the letter," Lumley said.

"Corporal, I'll wager it's in code. Look at this one—sly as she is comely."

"Perhaps, sir," Lumley said. "But we must determine that. If it is, we know where the girl resides." Gently, he removed Munroe's hand from Abigail. "And if it proves to be an innocent recipe, then we won't have to explain to the schoolmaster why we have detained his daughter. Mr. Lovell is, after all, most loyal to the king, as everyone knows."

Munroe tried to take hold of Abigail's arm again, and for a moment there was the slightest test of strength between the two soldiers. Both their faces were hovering over Abigail's as they tugged at her, until finally, Munroe relented, and he stalked out into the street.

Lumley remained in the shadows with Abigail. "I'm truly sorry for this imposition, Mistress Lovell."

"This has been more than an imposition, Corporal. I should report it. You've been drinking, both of you."

Lumley only lowered his eyes.

When he looked up at her, he said, "Report us? I think not." Then, with surprising kindness, he said, "Rather, I think you'll just continue on to your brother's and pay your visit to his pregnant wife, and this will all be forgotten, for the time being." This time his bow was exaggerated, and then he walked down the street with Munroe as if nothing had happened.

Abigail remained with her back pressed against the wall, gasping for air. Her limbs shook, and then she discovered that the sleeve of her dress was torn and her elbow was bloodied where it had scraped against the shingles. She touched the burning skin and oddly the sight of blood on her fingers helped to calm her.

James's wife Nancy answered the door and stepped outside onto the stoop, holding a covered chamber pot by the handle. "Abigail, please go in. I must needs get rid of this at once."

"You shouldn't be, in your condition—"

Though Nancy was only a few years older than Abigail, her brow seemed pinched with worry, and her hair was without luster, dry as straw. It was as though she had aged rapidly to catch up with her husband, who was more than a decade her senior. She was a good seven months along and stood with her back arched and her legs spread for balance.

"When his diarrhea is this bad, I've little choice, have I?" Gingerly, she made her way down the steps. "Quiet as you go, I just managed to get the children bedded down."

"Of course."

Abigail watched her sister-in-law walk to the corner of the house and turn into the alley which led to the privy. Then she stepped inside the house and, as she closed the door, she heard coughing. She went down the hall and knocked on the study door. "Jemmy?"

He coughed again, and said, "Abigail, come in."

She opened the door and found James seated at his desk, scratching away with a quill. Though it was a warm night, the fireplace was blazing and the windows were shuttered. When he looked up, she could see beads of sweat at the edge of his wig.

"It's bad tonight," she said, going to his desk. "You should be in bed, Jemmy."

He glanced up, irritated. But she was the only one he allowed to use his childhood nickname, and his eyes softened. "There's much afoot, and you'll have me sleep through it?" He studied her a moment, his eyes curious and perhaps alarmed, and then said, "Are you all right? You look—"

"I have something for you," Abigail said. She turned her back to her brother and lifted up her skirts, so she could remove the other letter from her pantaloons. After smoothing her skirt down, she placed the envelope on the desk. "From Province House."

He put his quill in the ink well but ignored the envelope, as though he didn't want to acknowledge its existence.

"Jemmy, something's happening tonight—the soldiers are about, and they're not headed for the taverns but fitted out for a march." Abigail suddenly felt weak, and she sat in the straight-back chair facing the desk.

"It's been coming, we've known that." He picked up a glass jar and sprinkled sand on the letter he'd been writing. "And now, now it's begun. General Gage has many flaws and weaknesses, one of them his inability to do anything in secret. We've seen all sorts of signs. Last weekend it was observed that numerous longboats were being repaired on the beach below the Common. Then we hear word that the grenadiers and light infantry are to stand down from duty. This was intended to deceive us? And we've had word of officers, dressed as civilians, venturing out of Boston. They've been seen as far west as Worcester. For weeks there have been all sorts of reports of these 'civilians' turning up in roadhouses asking questions about the country, distances, terrain. Maps—they need maps." He carefully folded up the letter he'd been writing and tucked it inside an envelope; the skin on his frail hands was the same color as the parchment. "Perhaps our greatest weapon is the countryside. Thousands of redcoats bottled up here on Boston peninsula, and they haven't a decent map! They don't know the land out there at all. There are soldiers—I hear as many as seven or eight hundred—marching out tonight, and they have little idea of where they're going. At least until recently. We believe they finally have a map, an accurate one." He took up one of the candles on the desk, tilted it, dripping red wax to seal the envelope.

"If it's accurate," Abigail said, "someone gave it to them."

"True," her brother said. "It's certainly not the result of their reconnaissance. No, this is the real concern: they got it from one of us."

"They've done this before, marched out into the country in search of arms and powder—but, Jemmy, eight hundred men?"

"Yes, this time it will be different. But with each foray, we're more prepared."

"Where are they marching to this time?"

He didn't seem to hear her. "We've set up our own government, the Provincial Congress, the Committee of Safety—committees, so many committees." With a finger he tapped the pile of letters on the side of the desk. "These committees create paper—and a bureaucracy to generate it. That's my role, I'm afraid, to sit here in my study, *assisted* by my damned chamber *pot,* and scribble . . . letters and more letters. But every government needs an army. We're going to establish an army and we've begun to collect supplies. This, more than anything, has led Parliament in London to declare that we are already in rebellion, though a shot has yet to be fired."

"Jemmy, you talk as though you might—"

"Others will stand in the field, and I envy them."

"Tonight," she said, and he nodded. "Do you know where?"

"Wish I did, with certainty. We have—we have only conjecture and theory." He picked up the letter she had brought. "Tell me, who gave you this letter at Province House?"

"A groom named Seth."

"Good."

"And there was a woman—"

"You spoke with her?"

"No. I only saw her in the window. I believe it was Mrs. Gage—"

"His beautiful wife from Pennsylvania?" James's smile was brief.

"The letter was from her, I believe," Abigail said.

"You're certain?"

"No, not certain." Then she said, "You've received letters from her before."

He stared up at her, the candle light dancing in his eyes. "You never saw her. Do you understand, you never *saw* her."

For a moment, she felt like she was a girl, back when her older brother was a third parent, often correcting her, reprimanding her behavior. But this was something else. "No, James, I never saw her."

"Right, then." James had a way of disposing of business, and then moving on; all very efficient. He looked down, broke the seal on the envelope, and removed a single sheet of paper, folded once.

"May I see?"

He glanced up and at first she thought he was going to say no, but then he nodded his head. She went around the desk and stood at his side. He opened the letter and spread it out on the desk. Abigail leaned down, placing a hand on her brother's shoulder.

> *My Dearest Samantha,*
>
> *I have been much remiss in conveying to you this simple recipe, which you requested when last we met. Please accept my apologies.*
>
> *7-8 quarts quahogs or oysters, finely cubed*
> *2 white onions, chopped*

Celery
Parsley
6 eggs
Salt pork
¾ lb. Butter
Crumbled bread for crust(4 qt.)
flour
Milk, 2 pint (if cream, somewhat less)
Salt & pepper
White wine, touch (if not for Sabbath dinner)

Bake time depends on the quahogs 1 hr. at least. Or till fork doesn't pull. Quahogs must be tender, fresh. Preferably taken from Back Bay or Cambridge marshes. Avoid digging in Noddle's Island beds unless you want your pie seasoned with the urine of grazing livestock.

In your hands, I am assured that this pie will make a fine repast.
Yours Sincerely, Louisa B.

"It's the same," Abigail said. "Same recipe as in the other letter."

"Seth gave you two?"

"Yes."

"And?"

She cleared her throat. "On the way here, two soldiers on patrol stopped me."

"Did they now? And?"

"Quite rude. They'd been drinking, of course."

James turned and gazed up at her. "Boston rum is so cheap, they can't resist."

She took her hand off his shoulder, went around the desk, and settled in the chair so she could stare into the fire again. Something soothing about the dance of flames upon the logs, the heat on her face.

"Along with our uncharted countryside," he said, "Boston rum and whores may be our best defense."

"Women. Indefensible women, James. This is our defense?"

He didn't answer immediately. "I do worry about you, Abigail, walking the streets of Boston alone, particularly at night."

"Yes, *yes,* Jemmy, but please don't start," she said. "You. And mother. And father. All singing the same tune about why a woman should remain sheltered. But I often slip out of the house when they're occupied. Would you have me locked up in my room?"

"No, of course not."

"Should all Bostonians stay shuttered away, cowering in their houses?" She turned from the fire and faced him then.

"No, Abigail," he said quietly, as though reprimanded. He could not quite look at her. "How? How rude?"

She didn't answer; she could not.

"I'm sorry. Sometimes I wish you were not so . . ."

"So what?"

"Pretty. And—"

"And?"

"Bold."

"Is that what I am?"

"In a word, yes," he said. "If you were otherwise, you wouldn't be you, but it might be safer."

"James, no one in Boston is safe."

For a moment he seemed at a loss for what to do. "This, this all becomes so . . ." He glanced at her, helpless. It lasted only a moment. He was their older brother, like a third parent when they were growing up. Rarely did he reveal this, uncertainty and apprehension. "It becomes personal."

"So we must put that aside."

"Yes. And we must attend to the matter at hand."

James opened a side drawer and removed a bottle and a rag. He dampened the rag with the yellowish liquid, and then carefully daubed at the paper. Abigail got up and leaned over the desk. She drew the lantern closer to her brother's work and watched as new lines appeared on the letter, scrawled in a different hand, rounder and more elegant.

"Sympathetic ink," she whispered.

"Yes." He was suddenly buoyant, invigorated by the discovery.

"The recipe," she said. "That's the hand of some servant or cook. But this other, this is from the lady. So many numbers."

"Troops."

"Leaving Boston tonight."

"You've always been too bright for your own good, and—"

"And. There's another *and?*"

"Bright, and naughty."

"You're one to talk about naughty."

"It's true I strayed in my youth, but I'm married now, with children and responsibilities. But that doesn't mean I can't see you as men see you—"

"And how exactly do they see me?"

"You really don't know, do you?" He leaned back, fixing her with an assessing eye. "They see this slender, lithe beauty—but not frail, no, and with a fine carriage."

"Carriage—Jemmy, please."

"Bosom, then, if you prefer. A full bosom." He smiled quickly. "Don't blush—you asked how men see you. And then there's the long dark hair, the way it catches the light and tumbles down over your shoulders. Even when you wear it up, men can only imagine how it would look undone."

"Now you're trying to make me blush."

"Not yet, Abigail." He hesitated, and she realized that he was reluctant to continue. But then he cleared his throat and pushed on, a bit of color coming to his pale cheeks. "It's your eyes. They're large, deep and soulful. Intelligent. But they also hold—I'm not sure how to put it, and I'm rarely at a loss for words—this sense of inquiry. You gaze at someone and sometimes it seems that you're seeking them out, reaching right inside them."

"And this is 'naughty'?"

"Some young men, yes, this is how they will respond. You're the daughter of a schoolmaster—you're supposed to be educated, to possess poise, and you do. But you're also supposed to be demure, even a bit dowdy. And that you most definitely are not."

Abigail couldn't look at her brother any longer, so she turned to the fire. They were silent for some time. He was getting close to something she thought she could conceal. "You've always been able to do this," she said finally, still gazing at the burning logs. And then she turned to him and began, "Jemmy, I have to tell you—"

But he held up his hand as he leaned forward and placed his elbows on his desk. "Hold it, hold on to it here." Gently, he rapped his fist against his chest. "We must all bear our fears and sorrows quietly, because our situation is about to become very hard, unlike anything we've seen before—and Lord knows, Boston has been under the king's heel for years. We'll all have to contribute, some in ways that we can't imagine. Rather than think of ourselves, we must act."

"I know," she whispered. "You're talking about sacrifice."

"I am."

"We're going to have to make sacrifices. It's why we're here."

"With these coming difficult times, Abigail, I would take a more active role—but, regrettably, I will remain here at my desk, with a chamber pot close by." James removed the quill from its well and began to make notes on a separate sheet of paper. He worked for several minutes, the only sound in the room the crackle of the logs on the fire and the scratch of his pen. At times he moved his lips, which reminded Abigail of their father, who often silently mouthed the words he read from one of his Latin tomes.

When James was finished, he leaned back in his chair. He now appeared weak, exhausted. "You're going to have to go directly to Dr. Warren's surgery," he said. "No encrypted letters. There's no time for that. I hate to send you out on the streets again."

"No, Jemmy. Just tell me."

He looked up at her. "Listen carefully."

She loved Boston at night. Despite her parents' warnings, she often managed to get out of the house. Hurrying to Dr. Warren's, she kept mostly to the alleys, where the shadows were heavy and she was more likely to encounter stray cats, dogs, and pigs, rummaging for food. When she did have to use the streets, she encountered few Bostonians, only redcoats, bearing haversacks, and bayoneted rifles, hurrying toward the Common, as though lured by a piper's silent flute.

We are all British, Father said frequently. Announced, rather (he never really left his classroom, even at the dinner table). And he often noted that General Gage was widely perceived to be a man of decency, one who was often more inclined to impose restrictions on his own Regulars than on the "Bostoneers" (as the redcoats often called them).

At the bottom of it, many colonials still hoped that at some point the king's men would simply come to their senses and acknowledge that there was no point in dividing them. They were all British. They were, like the Lovells, a family divided. And all families, which possessed love, respect, and honor, had the ability to heal themselves. Did they not?

It will never happen. Ezra had said this many times. They will never treat us as equals, never. The purpose of the colonies is simply to provide. Provide for England.

Ezra had been apprenticed to Dr. Church for several years. He often answered the door when Abigail visited the doctor's office. He frequently delivered prescriptions to the house, as Abigail's parents were often in need of elixirs and potions. Perhaps, when she was still in her teens, Abigail had ignored him because she was afraid of him, of what he might become to her. He seemed, in her presence, to gaze too long at her, while at other times he couldn't bring himself to look at her at all. Though he was tall, with broad shoulders, he looked crushed by some invisible weight when he was near her. But that's the way boys were: awkward, nervous, distressingly incomplete. Better to simply ignore them.

But one summer afternoon when she was twenty-one, he entered the dooryard by the back gate, a package for her mother in hand. Abigail had just stepped out of the chicken coop, a half dozen eggs cradled in her apron pocket. She bid him good day, and then, to avoid having to talk to him, she stepped back inside the coop. To her surprise, he stopped in the open doorway, blocking the light.

"You need more?" he said.

"Beg your pardon?"

"Eggs. You need more?"

She leaned over the bins, alarming the hens. "Six. I have six, but Mother's recipe calls for eight." She was lying—to the doctor's apprentice, she was lying. With both hands she shifted the straw about, though she knew there were no other eggs to be found. "But these hens seem unwilling to cooperate today."

He said nothing. She was keenly aware of him, standing behind her. Why hadn't he simply gone on to the house to deliver his package?

"Mother has been anxious for you to deliver her medication," she said.

But he still remained in the doorway, silent. There was only the sound of her hands rummaging through straw and the chatter of chickens, alarmed that these two large beasts had disturbed the peace of their darkened house. Occupied and occupier.

"It must be hard," he said at last. His voice was different now, as though they had been having an entirely different conversation and he was trying to commiserate with her plight.

She began to turn, but hesitated, and asked, "Excuse me?"

"Here, in your house," he said. "It must be difficult . . . to get along, I mean."

Abigail straightened up, her skin flooding with heat. As she removed her hands from the straw her fingers brushed against something smooth, round, and very warm: a freshly laid egg.

"You are a divided family," he said. "It can't be easy, for any of you."

She kept her back to him for a long moment, unable to speak.

Finally, he stepped out of the doorway, admitting light to the henhouse. "I'm sorry, I should deliver—" He started across the dooryard. A swirling breeze coming off the harbor caused his blond hair to whip furiously about his head. He had a wide, straight back, and his stride was long and determined.

"Wait." Abigail picked up the fresh egg and stepped out into the sunlight. He paused and turned, watching her walk toward him. "I'll take her the medicine," she said, taking the package from his hand. "And this is for your trouble." She placed the warm egg in his palm, and then walked on toward the kitchen door without looking back.

So it began and she thought of it, how she felt about him at first, as though it were an egg, its perfect ovoid shape, the shell hard and protective, yet fragile. They carried it together, it seemed, nestled in the palm of their union, a delicate secret. Love proved to be a kind of conspiracy. They met in streets and squares while she was ostensibly on errands; at dockside they looked over the day's catch together. But soon enough there were trysts after sundown. She would claim she was only going into the North End to visit with Rachel, who was more than happy to be complicit, providing the alibi so that Abigail and Ezra could meet in one of their chosen darkened corners of Boston. She had kissed boys certainly, but previously it had always been a form of teasing, a game. Rachel, who was five years older and just beginning to be courted by the older silversmith widower Paul Revere, said bluntly and with her snorting laugh that it was about time Abigail went into heat. Rachel found all matters of sex intoxicating and hilarious. Most Boston girls your age, she would say, already have a brood of chickens huddled about them. Often Ezra would wait for Abigail after dark. Claiming that she wanted to visit Rachel, Abigail would leave the house and walk up School Street, past King's Chapel, across the burying ground, to the bushes along the brick wall surrounding the granary courtyard. There, in the shadows, she and Ezra would hold each other, his whispered breath warm on her neck, while his hands. . . .

The thought of the sergeant's rough hands clutching her breasts struck through her, causing her to walk faster, almost at a run, breathing long and deep through her mouth as she repeatedly glanced over her shoulder. Nothing like Ezra's hands, tender, loving. . . .

Abigail had not seen Ezra since January, when suddenly, without explanation, he had quit Boston. She tried not to think on it, but it was impossible to put aside.

One of Dr. Warren's apprentices answered the door, and he led her up the stairs to Dr. Warren's office. Dr. Warren was seated at a polished mahogany table with Dr. Church, and they got to their feet and greeted her cordially. Dr. Warren was a widower and he had a large house across the Neck in Roxbury where his four children were cared for by various family members. Here in the city, his rooms were sufficient for his medical practice. He had wavy blond hair and pale blue eyes, and, as always, his cheeks bore a high flush. Dr. Benjamin Church was more somber, and his straight black hair held a fine gloss in the candlelight. His eye had a tendency to dwell, lingering upon Abigail's face.

"A glass of wine?" Dr. Warren asked, nodding toward the decanter on the table.

"No, thank you, Doctor. My brother has sent me."

"How is James's health tonight?" Warren asked.

"It has been better."

"Encourage him to come and see me, will you?" Dr. Warren offered her a chair at the table, but Abigail shook her head. "You bear a letter from him?"

Dr. Church had moved to a window, hands clasped behind his back. He was often reticent in Abigail's company, since two years ago when Ezra Hammond, one of his apprentices, had begun to court her. Since then, Dr. Church had seemed careful around her, distant, and yet she was always aware of his presence. When she wasn't looking, she felt that he was watching her, and now she suspected that rather than gazing down into the street, he was actually observing her reflection in the glass.

"No, there is no letter tonight," she said. "My brother said there wasn't time."

"Just as well," Dr. Warren said. "James has a reputation for missives that are impossible to decipher. But then he's a schoolmaster's son." He could be polite to a fault, and he seemed now to cut himself short—there wasn't time for pleasantries this evening. He raised a hand and with his fingers gently massaged his jaw. For the briefest moment, he seemed to be in considerable pain, but then he said, "So then, Abigail, what have you to tell us?"

"There was a report, from Province House," she said. Dr. Church turned away from the window now. "As most Bostonians know, General Gage has a sizable force gathering on the Commons, an estimated eight hundred grenadiers and light infantry. The letter says they will cross the Back Bay by longboat."

"By water," Benjamin Church said. "You're sure of that?"

"Yes," she said. "The troops will disembark somewhere between the Cambridge marshes and Lechmere Point, and then they'll march out through Cambridge and Metonomy to Lexington and Concord. Their objective is to secure weapons, ammunition, powder, and cannon stored there. They are also to seize Mr. Adams and Mr. Hancock, who are currently stopping at Concord."

Neither doctor spoke for a moment, until Warren looked at Church and said, "This confirms the other reports we've received. If nothing else, our system of observation is alert and responsive to the movement of our British brethren."

"Yes." Church turned back to the window. "It's as we expected."

"Now that we know how they're leaving Boston," Dr. Warren said, "we'll send Dawes and Revere."

Both doctors were members of the Committee of Safety and the Parliamentary Congress. Warren was famous (or notorious, in the view of the Tories) for his eloquence. For years he had produced a constant barrage of articles, broadsides, and speeches, issued on behalf of the cause of liberty in the colonies. In March he gave a speech commemorating the fifth anniversary of the Boston Massacre. Old South Meetinghouse was packed, and there were dozens of British officers seated directly in front of the pulpit. Warren delivered a rousing speech in a white toga while the lobsterbacks expressed their displeasure by rolling and clicking lead shot in their hands like dice. As the doctor concluded his speech, some of them shouted *"Fie! Fie!"*—which was misunderstood by the huge crowd as *"Fire! Fire!"* A riot broke out as everyone tried to evacuate the building. In the street a detachment of armed soldiers happened to be passing by (by design or coincidence, no one could say), and there was a confrontation between them and the Bostonians, most of whom had cudgels of various sorts which they'd kept hidden beneath their coats. A fight was barely averted.

Church glanced away from the window. "We'll send both Dawes and Revere?"

"Yes," Dr. Warren said. "No doubt Gage already has soldiers out there, watching the roads. At least one express has to get through to Concord and Lexington. I'll go send my runners to fetch them."

Warren left the room, closing the door behind him. Abigail turned and went to the other window. Down in the street, several redcoats marched by.

"This is a larger expedition than before," she said.

"I'm afraid it is." As Church approached her, she continued to stare out the window. "How did your brother come by this information from Province House?"

Abigail watched his reflection in the mirror. "By letter."

"You saw it, the letter?" He stood behind her, off to the right as though he wished to accommodate her as she gazed at his reflection.

"I did."

"And the source, it's reliable?"

She turned around, which seemed to at first surprise him, but then his eyes softened and he appeared relieved. "What are you asking me, Doctor?"

"It's only that General Gage is himself well versed in subterfuge."

"The letter came from Province House," Abigail said. "It was given to me."

"By whom?"

"By an intermediary, Doctor. So perhaps it was from General Gage? Or perhaps from Mrs. Gage, who is, after all, an American, and is often suspected of sympathizing with the Whigs." She took a step closer to Church. "Or maybe *I* wrote the letter, and it's full of misinformation? Maybe the British troops aren't headed for Lexington and Concord at all? Instead, they could be going south, or is it north? Perhaps they're boarding ships that will take them to Gloucester or Newburyport—"

"Abigail, please—"

"Or perhaps the ships will take them down the coast to New York, where they'll sever us New England upstarts from the rest of the colonies. Wouldn't that be an ambitious yet sensible plan?"

Church unclasped his hands and raised them as though to protect himself. "Really, Abigail, I only—"

"No, Doctor, let's think this all the way through. You suspect something? There's *so* much suspicion—no one's to be trusted. Maybe *I* am not to be trusted, even by my own brother. Maybe this is a question of *my* loyalty." She moved closer still, causing him to lean back slightly. "Because everyone knows about the Lovell family—reputable educators, father and son, but look how divided they are in their allegiances."

He placed his hands on her shoulders, gently, and then he said, "I must apologize, Abigail. I mean to make no inference—"

She turned her head, glancing at the hand on her right shoulder, and then looked back up at him. Embarrassed, he removed his hands as though he had committed some heinous crime and walked back to the other window.

"It's just that we—we are overly wary and cautious," he said. "It's the nature of things now, particularly since we are forced to have His Majesty's army live among us. I think it very brave of you to venture into the streets on a night such as this."

"You have no idea," she said with a sigh, calming down. "The redcoat patrols . . . they show no respect."

"This, I suspect, is what makes matters so difficult," Church continued. He seemed not to hear her; he seemed not to want to hear what she'd just said. "Why? Because so many Bostonians are obligated to bivouac soldiers in their homes. Provide them a bed and food and drink—and the Lord knows what else—without any say as to what or how many soldiers will live under one's own roof."

"And all for no compensation, regardless of their circumstance."

"Exactly," he said. "Other than the privilege of accommodating the king's men."

She thought of Munroe and Lumley, their hands, and said, "There has been enough accommodation for the king's men."

He seemed nervous, standing at the window. "I am sorry. I wish there was something that could be done."

"There is." She waited, but he would not turn from the window. "You could tell me what happened to Ezra. You do know, don't you?"

"Well, I can't say. I shouldn't say." After a moment, he added, "I realize how hurtful to you this has been, his sudden—"

"Do you? Do you, Doctor? He suddenly comes to me in a hurry one night and says he's leaving Boston. No explanation about where he's going, when he'll be back, and now he's been gone more than three months."

"I wish I could tell you—"

"But you can't? You know, but you can't?"

"I can't." Dr. Church looked around, slowly. "I'm sorry."

"Ezra is your apprentice. Surely he would not leave without your permission."

Dr. Church considered her for a long moment, until they both suddenly looked toward the door. There were footsteps out on the stairs, and then Dr. Warren reentered the office. Abigail realized that she was blushing, but Warren was too preoccupied to notice.

"So," he said, "that is done. I have sent for express riders."

Down in the street there was a familiar cadence, running footsteps. Abigail looked out the window and caught sight of her brother Benjamin just as he sprinted around the corner. "You've sent my brother Benjamin," she said, "to fetch Mr. Revere?"

"No, another boy's on that mission," Dr. Warren said. Again, his hand tenderly rubbed the side of his face, just beneath the left ear. "I sent Benjamin for Mr. Dawes, who is already preparing to leave the city." Abigail thought his faint smile was intended to be reassuring. "They're as good as we've got, your brothers," he said. "James's fierce pen and Benjamin's swift feet."

"And with this we're to rid ourselves of the king's men?" she asked.

Dr. Church went to the table and poured himself a glass of wine. "And with your help, as well," he said, though he wasn't smiling. "How can we lose?"

III

Into the Country

BENJAMIN HAD BEEN INSTRUCTED BY DR. WARREN TO GO TO THE
Green Dragon Tavern, where he would find William Dawes, the
tanner. Dawes was already drunk. Or pretending to be—it was
always hard to tell. Most likely he'd had a few bowls of flip, for
he reeked of the sweet concoction. After they left the establish-
ment, he let Benjamin help him climb on his horse and then take
the reins as they walked through the city toward Boston Neck.
Dawes was tall and lanky, with a long nose and the expression of
a half-wit, and he rocked from side to side in his saddle.

"Where are we going if we get through the gate?" Benjamin
asked.

Dawes slumped forward until his head rested against the
horse's mane. "You are to take me only as far as the gatehouse,
understand?"

"But I always accompany you through the gates—"

"I know, but tonight is different. I will give you a coin for your
trouble, which the guard will find quite a distraction. I know the

soldiers that stand duty at the Neck, and not one of them can see past the glimmer of a coin." When Benjamin did not respond, Dawes said, "You understand?"

It seemed Benjamin was always being asked to understand. To understand was to be told no. By his father, his mother, Abigail, and James. And now, when Dawes asked a second time, reluctantly Benjamin nodded his head.

Of course, it wasn't fair. They had gotten through the gates together so many times. Dawes was a convincing thespian, an accomplished smuggler. He would assume different costumes, sometimes a farmer, sometimes a tanner, sometimes a farrier. Often drunk, real or pretend. When they brought gold out of Boston, to be delivered to his wife who had removed to her family's farm with their small children, the coins were covered in cloth and sewn on to his jacket as buttons. Dawes was fearless. He would smuggle anything, coins, a lamb shank, butts of beer. By water, by land, and often right through the city gates at the Neck. Guards could be tricked, they could be bribed.

But Dawes's greatest feat—his legend, which was now whispered about by the Bostonians—were the cannon. It took months, several trips a week, to take two stolen British cannon, piece by piece, out of Boston. Beginning in January, he and Benjamin dismantled the cannon Dawes kept hidden in his tanner's shed. The wheels were laid in the bottom of a wagon, loaded with hides. One barrel was concealed beneath bales of hay, the other a boatload of seaweed. Other, smaller parts were buried in bushels of oysters or boxes of cod. Once, a firing pin, tied to a leather strap which was then wrapped about Benjamin's waist, had been hung down into his breeches, the steel bumping against his inner thigh as he walked out the Neck alongside Dawes's horse, which had more parts sewn into the underside of his saddlebags. Dawes was adept at fashioning leather pouches that would fit beneath their clothing. The trick, he would tell Benjamin, was to walk as though you weren't carrying the weight, as though heavy steel, cold in the winter air, wasn't pressed against your skin.

Since his youth, Benjamin had loved cannons. There was the fearsome noise when they fired, jarring the earth and belching smoke, followed by the terrible whistling of the projectile as it hurtled toward its target—which brought a distant, spectacular explosion. Countless times Benjamin had watched the redcoats conduct artillery drills on the Common or Fort Hill or the North Battery. With other Boston lads, he observed the intricacies of loading and firing a cannon, the methods of cleaning the sundry parts, the specifics of design. But he'd never actually gotten his hands on a cannon until the last time he and Dawes had traveled to Concord. It was a miserable night as they rode the wagon through a driving sleet, with steam rising off the backs of the team as it labored through the icy mud. Finally, at dawn, they arrived at Colonel Barrett's farm across the river from Concord village. Several men were in the barn, their tall lantern shadows thrown up on the stalls as they considered the pieces of cannon which lay spread out on tarps, awaiting assembly.

There was bread, cheese, and whiskey. There was laughter among the men. Colonel Barrett, commander of the Concord militia, presided over their activities much like a preacher before his congregation. One minute he would chastise them for not taking care in their handling of the parts, while the next he would slap his girth, thrust his hips, and crow about the day when they would give Tommy Gage a bit of his own cock.

Benjamin was given the task of climbing into the back of the wagon with a pitchfork and digging out the three crates, bound up in old sailcloth and concealed beneath the pile of seaweed. Dawes and the colonel's men removed the crates and laid them on the ground. It was a solemn moment, silent with anticipation. Dawes opened each crate and the men leaned in closer. No one moved, no one spoke. Finally, Dawes reached into one of the crates and then stood up, holding a cannonball in his hands. There was something tender, even loving in the way he cradled the leaden orb in his hands.

"Ben," he said, looking up. "We've made many a journey together, and I think you should do the honors."

The other men gazed up at him, some smiling, though a few of the younger fellows were clearly envious.

"Come on down now," Dawes said.

Benjamin jumped off the back of the wagon. Dawes walked toward him and handed the ball over, gently, as though it were alive, a new-born living creature.

In his hands the ball's surface was rough. There were nicks and ridges beneath his fingers, which made him think of a face, a lead face, with nose and eyes and perhaps even dimpled cheeks. The other men stared at him expectantly.

"Round shot, solid iron," he said, and then he paused and gazed down at the ball, as if to make sure that it was really there, in his hands. And looking up at them again, he said, "I believe this is . . . an eight-pounder."

There was a moment when they seemed confounded—until Colonel Barrett snorted, and then he laughed. "Right you are, Lad! It's an eight-pounder! Why, I'll bet you even know about assembling such a gun."

"I have watched the redcoats do so many times, sir."

"Then, please, Benjamin, show my boys here, because these bumpkins have no idea where to start."

"Well, sir. First, we must assemble the carriage, and—"

"Hear that, lads?" The colonel shouted. "We start by assembling the carriage!" He slapped his belly, while the others laughed, too.

They worked into the morning, and by the time the sun had risen above Punkatasset Hill there were two eight-pound cannon standing in Colonel Barrett's barn. The whiskey was passed around one last time, until the jug was empty. They stood about, gazing dumbly at the fruit of their labors, until Dawes said, "Would be lovely to roll them outside and set off a round—as a form of practice."

"Aye," another said. "To make sure they are in proper operating condition."

Colonel Barrett ran a hand lovingly along one of the cannon barrels, but then said, "No, you don't want to go wasting precious powder, and you don't want to alert all of Concord to that fact that we have these guns at all." He eyed each of the men sternly. "You're not to breathe a word about them, understand?"

They nodded like reprimanded schoolboys.

"Good," the colonel said. "Now you want take them apart again and hide them. Some parts can go up in the hayloft, and I think the large pieces should be wrapped in canvas and buried out there in the woods beyond the fields." They looked at him, incredulous. "So get to it, boys," he said, striding out the barn doors. "And I'll see if my wife has enough eggs for breakfast."

When the doctor's apprentice announced that Paul Revere had arrived, Warren and Church accompanied Abigail downstairs and out the back door. Revere was in the alley, his arms folded, a shoulder leaning against the brick wall of the house. He was a different sort of man than Warren and Church, possessing little of their gentlemanly refinement—and not seeming to care. Swarthy and thickly built, he had muscular hands and forearms from wielding the silversmith's tools.

"It's certain now," Warren said. "We've already sent Dawes out by the Neck, so you must cross the water, Paul. It will be dangerous—you'll be in sight of the troops, and we've heard that they've anchored the *Somerset* in the mouth of the Charles."

"I've already arranged for a horse with Deacon Larkin over to Charlestown." Removing his tricorn, Revere gazed up at the sky. "It's about ten o'clock, and a clear night. The moon'll be up later, so I must be away."

"God's speed," Church said.

Revere didn't acknowledge Church's comment, but was staring at Dr. Warren, who again was rubbing his jaw. "The new teeth I made you," Revere said, "still bothering you?"

"They are well fitted, Paul," Warren said. "I know. I'm a physician. Such things take time."

"If they continue to bother you," Revere said, "I'll have to adjust the wires."

"For that I will prescribe an ample portion of rum for myself," Warren said, and then to Abigail, he added, "My dear friend, Mr. Revere, a man of many talents. The finest silversmith in the colonies, but he also makes the best false teeth in Boston. And just to spite me, he refuses to say from what animal he extracted my two new teeth."

"I can't recall with certainty," Revere said. "But I believe my supplier said that for weeks he'd been tracking a feisty bobcat."

He and Warren laughed, and then the doctor said, "Perhaps you could accompany Miss Lovell as far as her home?"

"Of course," Revere said.

Warren smiled at her. "You can be his decoy, Abigail."

"If you encounter redcoats," Church added, "they will be distracted from this brute by your sublime beauty."

"They won't even notice me." Revere stepped forward and took her gently by the arm. "I'll be as invisible as her brother's ink."

Both doctors bowed graciously toward her, and then Church went back into the house, while Warren remained in the alley a moment longer, watching them as they walked out into the street, arm in arm.

They saw few British soldiers. Revere suspected it was because they had orders to be at the Common by ten to begin the embarkation—it would take several hours to ferry so many soldiers across the Charles, and he'd heard that they'd already begun to encounter delays. "Word is that the expedition is being led by a lieutenant colonel named Smith," Revere said. "He's very fat, very slow—the perfect man for the job."

When they turned a corner and entered School Street, they saw a pair of redcoats up ahead, rushing toward them hastily. Revere, who had kept his hand on Abigail's upper arm, pulled back so as to slow their pace as they strolled toward the two men. "These two must be late for the dance."

"Or they recognize you."

They walked on slowly, and as they neared the soldiers Abigail said, "The boy left the door to the summer kitchen ajar, and of course some hens were lured inside by the smells coming from simmering pots, and they caused all sorts of havoc, so that Mother was absolutely furious, demanding that father reprimand the stupid lad with the switch."

"A lesson he'll long remember next time he sits down to his fried eggs." Revere touched the brim of his tricorn as they passed the soldiers, adding, "Evening, gentlemen."

They merely nodded as they marched down the street, and then turned the corner in the direction of the Common.

"Mr. Revere, I'm not the one who needs an escort tonight," Abigail said when they stopped before her house. "Should I accompany you farther?"

"Thank you, no," Revere said. "It would only mean you'd have to walk back home alone." He began to turn away, but then faced her again. "If you don't mind my asking, when you visited Dr. Warren's did you bear a letter?"

"No letter. My brother James didn't think there was time."

"So you conveyed information . . ." he hesitated. "To Doctor Warren."

"Those were my brother's instructions."

Revere merely stared at her. "So you spoke to both doctors?"

"Yes."

"I see." Again he seemed hesitant. "Might I ask you a favor?"

She nodded. "Of course."

"You've been such a good friend to Rachel. It's a large brood we have in that small house, and she has only my mother there to help her. Might you look in on her, if I don't return to Boston soon?"

"She's like a sister to me. I will visit her as often as I can."

"I'm most grateful," he said, as he touched the brim of his hat in farewell. "You've been a wonderful escort on this fine spring evening, Abigail." He set off quickly in the direction of the North End.

They crossed the Neck, which connected Boston to the mainland. Dawes liked to call it walking on water. It was merely a strand not a hundred yards wide; when there was a storm surge the road was often flooded, rendering Boston an island. To the left, there was a vast salt marsh, and across the water a few lights could be seen on Dorchester Hill; to the right, water lapped against a pale beach, strewn with wrack lines of seaweed.

When they could see the guards' lantern up ahead, Dawes said, "No matter what happens at the gate, you are to return to the city."

"But I always go through with you, sir."

"Tonight I must ride hard. There's very likely to be British patrols on the roads tonight and I must travel light."

"You're going to give the alarm. I could go to Concord. I can walk."

Dawes didn't answer.

"I can go to Concord, where the cannon are. That's why the redcoats are marching out, isn't it, to secure armaments, and to capture Mr. Hancock and Mr. Adams?"

"No, Dr. Warren said you are to report back to him."

The air was heavy with the smell of salt. "And if you don't get through?"

Dawes only laughed. But then he said, "Might you be nervous?"

"No."

"Didn't think so."

They were coming in sight of the guardhouse, which was about thirty yards before the large gate that blocked the road. Dawes began to whistle off-key, as he often did—it was a means of alerting the guards to their approach. There was no benefit to taking them by surprise, as it would only make them more suspicious. When they were close, a soldier stepped out of the gatehouse, holding a lantern.

"That you there, Corporal Fredericks?"

"Billy? Billy Dawes? Ain't seen you come through 'ere in, oh, must be a week."

Ben stopped the horse as Dawes said, "At least. I must be getting over to Roxbury, where my aunt is taken ill."

"Sorry to 'ear that," Fredericks said. He was stout and spoke with a heavy wheeze, the kind of soldier who would not be selected for a march into the countryside to seize weaponry and apprehend provincial leaders. As though such a mission were beneath his dignity, he sniffed loudly as he stepped up close to the horse. "Might we be well perfumed tonight, Billy?"

"I am much distressed over my aunt's condition." Dawes leaned sideways, nearly falling off the horse. "It be a grave condition, is my understanding."

"Aye, a pity, that."

"She's been good to me, my aunt." Dawes searched his vest until he located the pocket, and then came the click of coins. He leaned over unsteadily and extended his arm toward Benjamin. "That's a good lad, for your assistance. Now you get on back home."

Ben handed the reins up to Dawes, and then looking at the coin in his palm, he said, "Thank you, sir."

He turned to start back across the Neck, but Fredericks stepped in his way. "A shilling, Billy," he wheezed. "Rather steep, for a lad."

"Perhaps, but I have been feeling sorely, because of my aunt and all." Dawes reached inside his vest now, and for a moment he

seemed unable to find what he was searching for, until he produced a small glass bottle. He removed the cork and took a pull,
the sharp smell of rum spicing the salty air.

"Well, I'll tell you, Billy. We've got our orders tonight."

"How's that?"

"Can't exactly say, but we're supposed to keep a tight fist
on who comes and goes from Boston tonight. You understand.
Maybe you could visit your aunt tomorrow."

Dawes took another drink of rum. "Most likely I'll be visiting
her grave tomorrow." He offered the corporal the bottle. "This
is my last chance, you understand. I don't see her tonight and—"
He began to sob. Very convincing: just the slight intake of air,
and hint of a quiver in his shoulders.

"Come now, Billy," Fredericks said, his voice barely a
whisper.

Dawes leaned over and rested his head against the horse's neck.
Fredericks looked at the bottle in his hand, and then tipped it
up to his mouth. He winced as he swallowed, but then he took
another pull on the rum.

"Sir," Benjamin said. "If you won't let Mr. Dawes pass, perhaps
I could go to Roxbury and convey a message to his aunt."

Dawes raised his head from the horse's mane. "No, lad, that
won't do," he said sternly, yet helplessly awash in emotion. "It's
very kindly of you, but it wouldn't be the same."

Fredericks raised his lantern and gazed hard at Benjamin.
When he lowered his arm, the light cast deep shadows upwards
on his face. After further consideration, he took a last pull on the
rum and handed the bottle back to Dawes. "No, Billy," he said.
"The boy cannot go in your place. It wouldn't be right, for your
aunt, I mean." He looked out across the marsh toward Dorchester
Heights. "It's not right, is it? I had a sister died last fall. Her lungs,
you know. I didn't learn of it till January—near three months later,
an' all's I gets is a letter from me mum. Priscilla was her name, me
sister, that is. Had two little ones and a husband that's a cooper.

Don't much care for 'im, never did, and I worry about them kids, 'avin' no mum, an' all."

"I'm sorry, Fredericks." Dawes jammed the cork in the bottle and then held it out for the corporal. "At least keep this, to get you through the night. Fact is, I've had enough."

"I can see that, I can." Fredericks tucked the bottle inside his coat pocket. "Well now, Billy, you just be on your way before it's too late." He turned and raised his lantern as a signal to the two soldiers manning the gate. "Rider comin' through," he called out. "Open 'er up, boys."

"Are you sure?" Dawes asked.

"It's only right." Fredericks placed a hand on Benjamin's shoulder and giving him a firm squeeze. "And, like you said, this good lad should be on his way 'ome. In fact, it's well past me suppertime, so I may accompany 'im to that tavern there on down Orange Street so's I might take my evening repast."

"You are most kind, Fredericks," Dawes said. He straightened up in the saddle and walked the horse on as the gate was being swung open.

"Now, Ben," Fredericks said. "I will just inform me men that I'm going off-duty. It's a dark night and a lad such as you shouldn't be out alone."

"Much obliged, sir."

Frederick's hand remained on Benjamin's shoulder a moment longer, squeezing tighter, and then he went back into the gatehouse and spoke to another soldier, handing over the lantern.

Benjamin was tempted to turn and run. Fredericks would never catch him. But the young soldier standing in the gatehouse doorway looked barely sixteen, and if he couldn't run as fast as Benjamin, he might be a fair shot.

So Benjamin stayed put, waiting for the corporal to return.

As he looked toward the gate, Dawes and his sauntering horse disappeared into the night.

When Abigail let herself into the house, there were the two candles, which her mother always left on the table by the front door. Benjamin had not yet returned home—his tricorn was not hanging from its peg. She climbed the stairs, but at the landing she sat in the window seat, blowing out the candle and placing the holder on the sill. The darkness was scented with melted wax and the house was silent, except for the sound of her father's snoring in the room at the end of the hall. Suddenly, she was exhausted, so tired that it would take too much effort to climb the rest of the stairs to her bedroom. Since her youth, the window seat had been her favorite place in the house, and she could dwell there for hours, reading, dozing, or merely gazing out the window. Now, leaning her back against the paneling, she curled her legs up on the cushions. She wondered where Ezra was now. She had lived her entire life in Boston and had rarely ventured from the peninsula. She thought of the rest of the continent as being a vast, uncharted place, darker than the city. Yet there was promise out there, and she wished she knew whether he had run away from something here in Boston, or whether he had been drawn toward something out there. Her brother James, in his subtle way, would suggest that this was not the time for such thoughts, reminding her of the sacrifices soon to come. And she thought of Paul Revere, crossing the Charles to warn the countryside that British troops were coming out from Boston. Perhaps this was the beginning of what was to come, the hard times James said were drawing near. She was tired, exhausted really, and she knew she should go up to bed. But this was her window, her view, and the moon was on the rise over Boston, reason enough to linger a few minutes longer. From this angle, she looked across the rooftops toward the North End and Christ Church, the tallest steeple in Boston.

IV

Tea and Togas

THERE WAS A KNOCK AT THE DOOR AND ABIGAIL AWOKE, LYING on her bed, still fully clothed.

"You there, dear?"

"Why would you ask that, Mother?" Vaguely, she recalled getting up from the window seat in the middle of the night and making her way to her bedroom. "Where else would I be?"

"Coming down for breakfast, then?"

"I'll be just a few minutes."

The floorboards creaked in the hall as her mother moved toward the stairs, but then she returned, and this time her voice was barely a whisper. "Benjamin didn't come home last night."

Abigail was undoing buttons, but she paused and went to the door, saying, "He didn't?" Raising the latch, she opened the door—her mother looked startled and she shook her head. In the early morning light her pale eyes seemed to shine from within.

"I don't know what's happened to him," she said. "And there's word on the street—Jonas, the milkman, says that hundreds of soldiers crossed Back Bay last night."

"I know."

"The streets, they're quiet this morning. It's strange, and frightening." Her mother's voice had an unusual quiver to it. Over the winter she'd suffered from a long spell of the ague, and she still hadn't regained all her strength. Her step was slower now, her shoes often sliding along the floorboards, and, perhaps of greater concern, she seemed more forgetful. "Where would he be?"

"I don't know." Abigail took her mother's fidgeting hands. "He'll be all right." Her mother's hands, too, seemed reduced of late; thin, frail, and always cold, even though it was already quite a warm morning. "Let me just wash and change, Mother, and I'll be right down."

"Tea!" her father hollered from downstairs.

"He's—" her mother said, pulling her hands free. "Please hurry, dear."

Abigail watched her mother shuffle to the staircase and take hold of the banister as she eased herself down each step. At the landing, she paused to look back toward her daughter.

"I'll be right down," Abigail said.

She stepped back into her room, and as she shut the door she heard her father's voice again, louder. "Tea, woman! And biscuits."

After she finished getting dressed, Abigail quickly went down the hall and climbed the ladder to the attic. This was Benjamin's usual hiding place, in the house. Since he'd been small, she'd find him up here, sitting on some boards laid across the rafters. He would just sit, often after a row with Father, and he would refuse to speak, refuse to come down. But he was not in the attic this time. Still, this was not unusual. He had a tendency to wander, and sometimes days would pass without sight of him, and then he would walk through the kitchen door as though he hadn't been missing at all.

This morning, Father was wearing his toga. He sat at the head of the dining room table, taking his biscuits and tea as he leaned over several leather-bound tomes, muttering in Latin. When Abigail took her place at the table, always to his left, he did not look up from his reading, though she detected that the arch to one bushy white eyebrow was intended to convey disapproval. Pulling back the sleeve of his toga, he picked up his tea and sipped loudly.

Like many men of his station, John Lovell believed that he was a direct descendant of the learned Greeks and Romans. Boston was the new city, the new Athens, with its philosophers and senators. Daily newspapers such as the *Boston Observer* carried letters and broadsides that were signed with aliases: Archimedes, Euthymius, or Democritus. As schoolmaster of the Latin School, her father at times spoke English only as a last resort. But the toga at breakfast had become a recent development, as worrisome in its own way as was Abigail's mother's frailty in the wake of her extended winter illness. As the weather had warmed, he began wearing the loose, flowing toga around the house more and more frequently. Benjamin assured Abigail that their father wore nothing beneath the garment, and on more than one occasion she had noticed the front of his garment stained with urine. They simply never knew what to expect from their father. He was often pompous and distant, or relentlessly overbearing. Yet at times he would seem to possess the innocence of a savant. And there were also moments, perhaps most trying, when he would fawn lovingly over his children, taking satisfaction in simply watching them perform a task as mundane as tying a boot lace.

"Tea, dear?" her mother said.

Abigail only stared down at the biscuit on her plate.

While turning a page, her father cleared his throat.

As her mother took up the teapot, Abigail said, "No, thank you, Mother."

He removed his spectacles and laid them on top of an open book. "Why is it incumbent upon my children to begin each day with this mild form of gastronomic protest?"

"You know very well why," Abigail said. "We've been through this . . . for years."

"We have," her father said. Something about his voice seemed to rise up from the very depths of his lungs. It was a quality, a resonance that could fill a crowded Old South Meetinghouse, and could also strike fear into the hearts of the most recalcitrant pupil at the Latin School. "We have indeed for too long," he said, "and today, at last, it's going to stop." He leaned toward her. "And do you know why?"

Abigail ventured a look at her father, his eyes bulging beneath those brows. "Yes."

"Yes!" he shouted. "Because George the Third has finally taken matters in hand! Clearly, he's instructed General Gage that it's time to put a stop to this nonsense. You know he sent an expedition out into the country during the night?"

"Really?" Abigail said. "I trust they have a good map."

"They have a map, they have their Brown Bess firelocks, they have bayonets! They have orders to break this, this rebellious nonsense."

"Nonsense," Abigail said. "That's your favorite word. In English."

"It is," he said, now quietly, as though explaining a subtle philosophical point. "It means 'without sense,' the 'opposite of that which makes sense.' It perfectly defines what you and your brothers—and all those pathetic people out in the hills—think they're up to. Patriots, revolution: *non*sense. We are all subjects of the king. And as of today, he's directed his military to reassure each of us that he holds us all dear to his compassionate bosom." He glared down the table toward Abigail's mother, who was still holding the teapot. *"Pour,* my dear. Pour our daughter a cup of English tea—tea that was brought here so that we might partake of its beneficial properties and give thanks to that fair island from whence it came!"

"Taxed tea," Abigail said. "No thank you, Mother."

"Tea, like liberty," her father said, "does not come free."

"Taxed tea, taxed stamps," Abigail said.

"Mob rule," her father said. "That's what the likes of Samuel Adams are after."

"And you do understand," Abigail continued, "the issue is not the taxes—"

Imitating a whining child, her father said, "Tax*a*tion without represen*t*ation!"

"Next thing they'll tax the air we breathe, or perhaps the salt in the ocean?"

Her father raised his hand and slapped the table loudly, causing the china to clatter.

There was silence. This was the moment, usually, when Abigail could look across the table at her younger brother; on some occasions he would diffuse the moment with some remark that was so inappropriate that even his father would, if only momentarily, be drawn back from the brink of his rage. Recently, during such a pause in the argument, Benjamin had leaned sideways, crossed his eyes as he stared at Abigail, and then he broke wind—a long, resonant fart, which caused their father to get up from the table and storm off to his study.

But now Benjamin wasn't at the table, and there was only the silence, a deep, treacherous silence, which for years had made the days in this house often intolerable. Silence, until Abigail's mother put the teapot back on the coaster and said, "Well, my arm is growing weary." She spread butter on her biscuit, but soon put her knife down with a clatter, and stared at Abigail with round, moist eyes. "Tell me, is he in the attic?"

"No, Mother."

"He'll return," Father said, chewing. "Always does. Just like a dog that wanders off, sniffing about, only to return when he gets hungry enough."

"Benjamin is not like a dog," Abigail said.

"I suppose you're right." He pushed the last of his biscuit into his mouth. "More like the water rat, always going down to the wharves, or rowing out into the harbor, returning with sacks of fish or clams. The tides, that's about all he knows. Once we get this port in operation again, I should inquire about a position for him aboard some merchant vessel. See the world, a different sort of education, that."

"It would pain Benjamin greatly," Abigail said, "to leave Boston."

"You and I, as well," her mother murmured, without looking up from her plate.

"Well," Father said, "he can't learn anything. Lord knows I've tried to educate him."

"With your ferule," Abigail said. "He's not someone you can beat into submission."

"Can't hardly read or write—Latin *or* English." Father suddenly laughed, which he often did as an announcement that he was about to make a joke. "He's only well schooled in haddock, flounder, and cod." He slapped the table and howled. "Why, when the boy was three he could tell a fluke from a flounder! And he lacks patience to learn a trade. So send him to sea, where it's difficult to wander far from the deck of a boat."

"I do not want our youngest shipping out," Mother said firmly, though her voice quavered slightly. "It's no place for a boy who's—"

"Don't," Abigail said. "You think you can control our futures, dictate our lives."

"You need direction," her father said. "You both require direction."

Mother said, "And besides—"

Abigail pushed her chair back and sprang to her feet. "I can't listen to any more."

She rushed out of the dining room, veering down the hall to the kitchen. For a moment she was at a loss for what to do, and she considered simply going back up to bed. But she recalled that her mother had mentioned that they would need eggs for dinner, so dutifully, even thankfully, Abigail went out the kitchen door and crossed the small yard to the chicken coop.

It was warm inside, and dark. If Benjamin had his hiding places all about Boston, Abigail had the coop. Since she'd been a girl, she had often sought refuge here among the chattering hens, perched in straw bins. She had come in anger, sometimes in fear. And at times simply to be alone. She used to talk to the hens—as a child, she'd had names for all of them—and they seemed to respond with a nervous intensity that led her to imagine that when she was not there, they would talk about her amongst themselves. Mother insisted that chickens had no brains, but Abigail was convinced that they were actually quite perceptive, that they knew when it was she who reached into their straw nests to retrieve eggs. As she pulled the door shut behind her, they greeted her with a flurry of cackling and feather-ruffling.

Behind her, there were footsteps out in the yard, and then the door opened behind her. This time the hens went into a panic as her toga-clad father bent forward as he entered the coop. He yanked the door closed behind him and sat on the small crate in the corner.

"That door," he said shortly. "With the coming of warm weather it sticks—I have asked Benjamin to plane it down." He busied himself with tamping and lighting his clay pipe. "You really have no idea where he is?" He exhaled smoke, his voice soft now, almost pleading.

"No." Abigail extended her arm into the top bin and felt around in the straw. It was like being blind. The hens moved aside at her gentle insistence, reluctantly yielding their secret, their treasure.

"This hiding," he said. "It used to be a game when he was small, but now, now it's dangerous. The world is a dangerous place, Abigail. Boston is—we have been on the brink for so long now." He drew loudly on his pipe a moment. "You think I don't worry, we don't worry?"

She picked up an egg, warm in her palm.

"Loyalty is not a terrible thing," he said. "You know that. There is no greater loyalty than ours."

Abigail found another, and then another. "I know that, Father."

She went to her father then and carefully released the eggs in his lap—he spread his legs, allowing them to sink into the folds of his toga. Often, when she'd been younger, when she was upset (often after they had argued), he would know that he could find her here, in the coop. She would sit on his lap. He would pat her back, stroke her hair, his large hands warm, loving. Still, there was the scent of his tobacco, which she had always loved.

Now he merely took her hand in his (which no longer seemed so large, but frail, and disconcertingly so) and pressed her palm to his lips, before gently holding it on his shoulder. Perched, she thought, like a small bird.

"I—your mother and I—we believe in order, in learning. It's all we have to give to you. Without these things, I don't understand how one can thrive. We have always been loyal to the king. It's a source of pride, of honor."

"I understand that, Father. But we—we Bostonians—are not treated fairly."

He didn't answer for a moment, but with his other hand placed the long stem of his pipe in his mouth and inhaled, slowly releasing a blue plume of smoke which curled languidly in the dim light. "Suppose, for the sake of argument," he said. "Suppose I abandoned my allegiance to the king. What influence do you imagine that would have?"

"I imagine that James would think you'd come to your senses."

"And you? What influence do you think it would have, on us?"

"Us." Abigail felted tricked: the terms were changing. "The school would suffer."

"Indeed. We pride ourselves on accepting only the boys from Boston's best families, but what if they did not seek admittance? What if they elected to attend another school?"

"I imagine—" She paused. "I imagine that you could admit girls."

She expected him to laugh, but he only drew deeply on his pipe. "Perhaps," he said. "One day, perhaps. You have learned well. You are as bright as any of the boys that matriculate at the Latin School. It gives you a power, I see it in the way others address you. Some admire you, but others fear you. It is something a father can take pride in, that." He glanced up at her. "Is that the only result?"

"General Gage would no longer invite you to dinners at Province House."

He nodded his head. "True. I enjoy his company."

"He is a fair man," Abigail said.

"Most of our English brethren are."

"Some, indeed, Father. But if it were a majority, we would not be at such odds."

He considered this a moment and, surprisingly, seemed to accept the logic of it. "If I were no longer loyal to the crown, it would be met with great disappointment. It would be seen as giving up something precious, some might say sacred."

"You might find that you are free."

"Ah, yes. Freedom." He smiled as he gazed straight ahead. "Free to do what? I'm doing it now, don't you see? All that I do is for this, for us. How else could I provide for you, properly provide? I suspect you think I keep my nose close to the pages of my Latin texts and read my pupils' lessons, but I know how short the walk is from here on School Street down to Long Wharf. I do see this, Abigail." He pressed her palm into his shoulder. "Sometimes I feel I've lost James. Years ago, he drifted away, despite the fact that we work side by side in the school. And Benjamin, I've never been able to reach him, not the way I would like. Only you have—you and he have this bond, for which your mother and I are grateful. So I must confess that my fear of losing you is compounded by the fear of losing Benjamin as well."

Abigail turned slightly, causing him to hold her hand more tightly. "You would never *lose* me, Father," she said. "This is not possible, no matter what our differences."

"I thank God for that." He released her hand then. Carefully, he gathered up the eggs from his lap and placed them in her joined palms.

There came the sound of the kitchen door opening, and Mother called across the yard. "John, Abigail—you must come, quickly!"

He pushed himself up out of the chair and opened the coop door, admitting a blinding light. "What is it?"

He ducked out through the door and Abigail followed, and then they both sensed it, standing in the yard: at first, it was felt more than heard, a faint shudder, a rumble, which seemed to come up from the ground. Then there was sound, coming from the street out in front of the house—a rhythmic pounding—and there was dust, rising up above the shingled roof and chimney, obscuring the sun. Abigail rushed across the yard and into the house, placing the eggs in a bowl on the kitchen table, and then she continued down the hall, her parents following after her. She opened the front door and went out onto the stoop. Hundreds of soldiers were marching in formation down School Street, their officers shouting commands.

Behind her, Father shouted, "They're headed for the Common!"

"More soldiers?" Mother asked. "What does it mean?"

"Reinforcements," her father said.

"But why?" Abigail asked.

Her father held the sleeve of his toga over his face, as protection against the dust. "Perhaps General Gage is sending them in another direction."

Her mother turned to go back into the house, saying, "I just don't understand."

"It means . . ." Father said. "Well, we don't know for certain what it means."

Abigail stepped back inside the front door and took her shawl off the peg. "It means that something terrible is about to happen." She threw the shawl about her shoulders and leaped off the stoop.

"And where do you think you're going?" he shouted.

"I must find Benjamin."

Abigail walked away from the house, her father's voice quickly lost in the cadence of marching feet. She broke into a run alongside the column of redcoats, until she reached Tremont Street, where she turned the corner and headed for the North End.

Rachel Revere sat across the kitchen table from Abigail, her infant son Joshua in her arms, and at the end of the table, her mother-in-law, Mrs. Deborah Revere, was pouring the tea. Some of the older children could be heard laughing out in the yard.

"Contraband," Mrs. Revere said as she placed the teacup before Abigail. "No tax on these tea leaves. Landed at Newburyport and brought down the turnpike. But we don't have any sugar either." She struggled to pronounce each word because of the false teeth her son had affixed in her mouth by a series of wires.

"It's fine, thank you." Abigail took a sip of the tea, which was bitter but hot.

"Why are you so upset?" Rachel said. "You've been having the same argument with your father for years."

"I know," Abigail said. "But walking over here, I realized that it's not that we differ so. It's this: Father is convinced I only hold such opinions because James does. I'm not capable of truly comprehending an idea, so how can I form my own opinion? He believes it must be all James's doing, polluting the impressionable minds of his younger brother and sister."

"It's just what they do all day in the Latin School," Mrs. Revere said. "I've known your father a long time, and he has a reputation as a harsh disciplinarian."

"Yet he's revered for it." Rachel was a somewhat harried woman, mindful, and known to be outspoken. Her moods tossed easily between melancholy and a gleeful, desperate humor.

"Most every man of position and influence in Boston passes through the Latin School," Mrs. Revere said. Very slowly, using both hands, she picked up her cup of tea and took a sip. She was a Hitchbourn, a respected family that had long built boats and operated a wharf in the harbor. "Your father, and men like him, they represent order. He *has* to be a Tory. To be otherwise would be to deny everything he has ever known or stood for all these years."

"You speak of him with such sympathy," Abigail said.

"Yes," Rachel said, unbuttoning the top of her dress. "As though trying to explain why one breast gives more milk than another." She guided Joshua's mouth to her left nipple. "Why some women give out, bear children and die early, while others—"

"It's not sympathy, really," Mrs. Revere said. She pushed herself up from her seat. "It's observation, which leads to a form of curiosity. For instance, your brother James. For years now he's been the usher at the Latin School. Everyone knows that he and your father are opposites, the Tory and the Whig, the loyalist and the patriot. But your brother has a reputation for being the stricter disciplinarian of the two. He not only wields his ferule often, I understand that he seems to take pleasure in giving his pupils welts."

Abigail said nothing.

"And what do you make of that?" Mrs. Revere asked as she shuffled to the back door. Abigail turned, expecting that the old woman would offer an answer, but she merely opened the door and stood on the threshold. In the yard, the Revere children were sprinkling corn for the chickens, but now they were no longer laughing.

"It's true, I'm afraid," Abigail said.

"The children are about to argue and fight," Mrs. Revere said, looking over her shoulder a moment. "You can hear it in their voices, the complaint. They're restless. The little ones don't fully understand, but they sense that something is happening, and they don't sleep well, they suddenly argue and cry. It's like animals growing agitated before a thunderstorm." She walked out into the yard, clapping her hands to get the children's attention.

"And you don't know where Benjamin is?" Rachel asked.

"No, no word since last night."

The back of the baby's head was as smooth and round as Rachel's breast. She was Paul Revere's second wife. His first, Sarah, died two years earlier, only in her mid-thirties yet worn out from bearing eight children, each in an even-numbered year. Joshua was Rachel's first-born. "So many of the men have already fled Boston," Rachel said. "The countryside is safer for patriots now. After the flood of recoats today, you wonder how many will return. I don't know when I'll see Paul again."

"You're certain he got across the Charles safely last night?"

"All I know is that two friends rowed him across the harbor, passing close by the guns of the *Somerset,* which is at anchor in the mouth of the river. And that once he was across, he was given a good horse by the deacon in Charlestown. Then he rode off into the night." She smiled, seemingly in defiance of impending despair. "He's so careful in his arrangements—last weekend, when there were the first signs that the British were planning something, he had established that a signal would be sent from the Christ Church belfry. One lantern if Gage's expedition was leaving by land, two if by sea—in case he failed to get across the water. But last night, when he and his friends are on their way down to his skiff, they tell me it becomes a comedy of confusion."

"How so?" Abigail asked.

"First, it was his spurs. Paul left the house without them," Rachel said, nodding toward the old brown dog that was curled up in front of the hearth. "So he sends him home with a note—and I attached the spurs to the dog's collar, and he sprints down to the waterfront. And then, when they're about to shove off, they fear that the oars will make a frightful lot of noise creaking and groaning in their locks and alert the watch on board the *Somerset*." Now Rachel laughed, until the baby's head lolled away from her breast and began to cry. She eased him back to her nipple and looked at Abigail, a strange glee in her eyes. "So they need something to muffle the oars, and one of Paul's young associates goes down the lane to the house of the girl he's been courting, calls up to her window, and in a moment she throws down a pair of pantaloons—still warm." Both women laughed, though this time Rachel gently held the back of her son's head. And then they were silent for a moment, until she said, "Paul got across, that's all I know. I pray Benjamin's all right."

"But this isn't uncommon, Benjamin disappearing. He's always wandered the city, like a stray, he is. But with all the activity among the soldiers—he was supposed to accompany Billy Dawes to the Neck, and then report back to Dr. Warren, letting him know whether Dawes got out through the sentries all right."

"I've seen how Benjamin runs through the streets. He will not be easy to catch."

"He is quick," Abigail said. "But they often use him to convey letters, important letters, and I worry that if he gets caught . . ." She ran her finger around the rim of her teacup, causing a faint, sweet ringing. "He can't read, you know, hardly a word. And our brother, James, he won't say it outright, but I know he believes really important letters are safer with Benjamin."

"This be a hard business," Rachel said. "The men, they just disappear."

"They do."

"Suddenly, out into the countryside," Rachel said.

"First Ezra," Abigail said, "and now Benjamin."

"It's safer than here on the peninsula." She gazed at Abigail. "You've not mentioned Ezra before—I've been waiting. How long has it been . . . since January?"

"Yes."

"We were sorry to see him go. We were fond of him, too." She leaned forward, smiling. "Though it be a fondness of a different nature."

Embarrassed, Abigail looked down at her cup of tea.

"Every time Paul leaves Boston," Rachel said, "I wonder when I'll see him next. This time I fear he'll be in the countryside a good while."

Abigail finished her tea. "I should go to Dr. Warren's. At least they should be able to tell me if Benjamin came back from the Neck."

"They," Rachel said. She was smiling now, though her eyes seemed doubtful. "You mean both doctors, Warren and Church?"

"Yes. They were both at his surgery last night. Why?"

Rachel only smiled as she stroked her son's back, saying nothing.

Through the open door Abigail could see into the yard: old Mrs. Revere, with the children standing about her, and with the chickens circling around them. For the moment, the children appeared content.

Abigail left the North End, taking Fish Street, passing ships that were tied up along the wharves; dozens more rode anchor in the harbor. Since General Gage had closed the port, there was little activity along the waterfront, but today, a Wednesday, seemed quieter than usual—so quiet, you might think it was the Sabbath. Fish Street turned into Ann Street, and then she took the footbridge across Mill Creek, which divided the North End from the rest of Boston. Many stores were shuttered and vendors' stalls were closed. On Cornhill Street she saw the old man Elisha Bowen leaning against the bricks of Faneuil Hall. He was an octogenarian who spent his days in the streets. Half mad and with clipped ears—from an offense long forgotten—he was deemed harmless.

"Elisha, the shops, why are so many not opened?" Abigail asked.

He was nearly blind and he stared straight ahead as he began to laugh.

"Has something happened?"

He continued to laugh, until it churned up phlegm in his lungs and he began to wheeze and cough. But still he laughed, even after Abigail gave up and moved on down toward Marlborough Street.

At Dr. Warren's surgery, a chaise was stopped by the front door and Dr. Church climbed out. As the carriage continued on down the street, Abigail could see a woman's white-gloved hand resting idly on the windowsill.

When Dr. Church saw Abigail approaching, he at first seemed surprised, perhaps even embarrassed, but then he walked toward her with a sense of urgency. "You've heard, Abigail?"

"No," she said. "What—"

"Fighting, it broke out on Lexington Green early this morning. Please, come inside."

She felt confused, and realized he had a hand on her upper arm, as though he were trying to keep her from falling. "No, I—fighting?"

"We've just begun to receive word," he said, "but the information is contradictory."

"Where's—" she looked down the road at the chaise. "Where's Dr. Warren?"

Benjamin Church tried to guide her toward the front door, but Abigail resisted until he let go of her arm. "He's left already."

"Left?" She could not read his eyes.

"Left for Lexington," he said. "Reports have come in that the militia there engaged the British expedition at dawn. There are wounded and some dead, that seems quite certain. Then I understand they moved on to Concord. I'm preparing to go there now, though getting out of Boston will be even harder at this point. I'm arranging to be ferried across by a fisherman."

"That explains it," she said. "The markets, the shops—they're closed. And columns of soldiers are on the march."

"Reinforcements. They were sent for by the expedition's command."

"This can't bode well for the militia."

"It's difficult to say what it means, Abigail. You sure you can't come in for a moment? Before long, it's going to prove to be a warm day."

"No, thank you, Doctor." Now Abigail took hold of his sleeve. The oncoming heat of the day was the least of her worries. "My brother, my younger brother Benjamin. He was sent to the Neck with Mr. Dawes last night." She let go of his sleeve. "Benjamin was supposed to tell you if Dawes got through."

"Oh, Dawes got through, of that we're certain. But the boy—" He shrugged.

"Do you suppose he went through the gates with Mr. Dawes?"

"I don't know." Once again, he touched her sleeve, but this time it was a means of farewell. "Listen, I have to meet this boat—"

"Yes, of course."

"I'm sure Benjamin is all right." He leaned close, too close. "It's finally begun, Abigail. It could be over already. It could be over by nightfall."

"Doctor, I don't know how to ask, but Ezra, do you know what's become of him?"

He looked away, down the street for a long moment, and he seemed to be considering his answer carefully. "I haven't seen Ezra for months now." He appeared disappointed, hurt even, at the mere mention of his apprentice. "I realize that you and he would walk out, as young people do, but I don't—" He looked at her again, and now he spoke with a sense of urgency. "Listen, a great many people right now don't know where their loved ones are, and, yes, people are shutting themselves indoors—perhaps you should consider doing so yourself. Go home, Abigail. Go home to your mother and father." He had been holding his hat, a broad-brimmed leather hat, at his side, but now he pulled it down on his head. "I only wish for your safety."

"I see," she said. "Thank you, Doctor."

He touched the brim of his hat, and then turned and walked back toward the front door to Dr. Warren's surgery.

Abigail stood in the street, which was empty. Then in the distance—from the mainland—she heard the faint peal of church bells. In the house directly across from Dr. Warren's, the shutters on a third-story window swung open. An elderly woman leaned out, resting a plump arm on the sill. Shading her eyes, she gazed toward the west, and after a moment she looked down at Abigail in the street.

"Them's the bells over to Cambridge." Extending her arm and pointing more to the south, she said, "And them's the Roxbury bells. Whole countryside's in alarm, it is." She seemed delighted. "It's the alarm!" she said, and then she reached out and pulled the shutters closed.

V

The High Ground

SEVERAL HUNDRED PROVINCIALS STOOD ON THE RIDGE overlooking the Concord River. Graybeards and a good number of boys barely in their teens. Most were bearing firearms, though some had only a stick or a farm implement. In the distance, church bells could be heard sounding the alarm.

Benjamin stood apart, as he often did around strangers.

But then a voice behind him said, "And how'd you get free of Boston?"

He turned and saw Ezra Hammond striding toward him through the tall grass, a haversack slung over one shoulder and a musket and powder horn over the other. Ezra was perhaps seven or eight years older than Benjamin, and taller—something Benjamin was unaccustomed to—and he grinned broadly.

But when he reached Benjamin, he waved a hand in front of his nose. "*Phew.* You must have swum off that Boston peninsula. We're well inland for such a powerful low-tide stink."

Benjamin looked down at his britches, which were dry now and caked in hard black clay. "Marsh muck. I waded, mostly." He slapped at his legs, and clods of dirt fell to the ground. "To get past the guards at the Neck, I had to walk out into Dorchester Flats, and the tide was rising. There was this corporal—Fredericks—and after I give him Mr. Dawes's shilling, he heads off to a tavern, so I went out on the clam beds to get around the sentries at the gates."

"I see," Ezra said. "And overnight you walked all the way out here to Concord? Twenty miles at least, I'd say."

"I—" Benjamin hesitated, and realized that he was reluctant to mention his sister. "We haven't seen you about for some time."

"Months," Ezra said. He seemed chagrined, disappointed.

Benjamin cleared his throat and, surprising himself, spoke louder. "My sister—"

"Deserved an explanation," Ezra said, anticipating him.

"You used to come calling." He began walking away through the tall grass.

"It wasn't right, I know," Ezra said. "It wasn't proper."

Benjamin stopped and turned around. Something about Ezra's voice.

"She deserves better." There was such remorse in Ezra's eyes that Benjamin couldn't continue to walk away. "I came out to the countryside in January." Ezra began walking toward him. "My mother, she removed to Watertown to take employment there in an ordinary."

"You don't know how Abigail—she holds a thing inside."

"It's right that you're mad," Ezra stopped in front of Benjamin. "I wish it had been otherwise." He seemed not to know what else to say, and then he swung the haversack down off his shoulder and rummaged inside. "My mother, she prepared for me a wallet of victuals. I reckon after a walk like that, you might be some famished." He pulled out a wad of brown paper and began to unwrap it. "Don't suppose you'd mind a piece of salt cod?"

Benjamin hesitated, and then finally broke off a chunk of the dried fish and stuffed it in his mouth. He couldn't eat fast enough.

Beneath Ezra's wide-brimmed felt hat, his long brown hair was tied in a pigtail with a strand of leather. He gazed down the hill toward the river. "I can only hope she doesn't think ill of me."

"She has said nothing." Ezra's eyes slid toward Benjamin now, curious. "But she would not say anything to me, her little brother."

"I see." Ezra cleared his throat, as though it would be best that they move on from such embarrassing matters. "It couldn't be helped," he said—as though trying to convince himself. "I had no choice, really."

In an effort, it seemed, to distract himself from his discomfort, Ezra reached into the haversack again, producing a spyglass. He raised the long metal tube to his eye and scanned the lowlands beyond the river. Pointing, he said, "Look: redcoats, mostly grenadiers—those tall fellows with the high fur hats, very imposing. They're searching every house and barn in Concord, looking for armaments, ammunition, provisions, anything the militia might use. And a detail of light infantry is marching this way, toward the bridge." He turned and pointed farther upriver toward a farm. "I'll bet they're headed there, to Colonel Barrett's place, several miles upriver."

"I've been there," Benjamin said.

"Have you now?" Ezra looked at him, impressed.

"He's the commanding officer of the Concord militia—that's him on the bay, higher up the ridge."

"And I hear there is a cache of arms hidden on his property," Ezra said, peering through the spyglass. "Including cannon." Benjamin wanted to say that this was so, that he had helped smuggle and assemble the field pieces, but before he could Ezra said, "Our weaponry—that's why the British have come to Concord. Have a look."

Benjamin took the spyglass, raised it to his eye, and miraculously he could see the column of soldiers marching out from the village, passing beneath trees that were just beginning to leaf out.

"Now, this raises the question," Ezra said and then paused. Benjamin's father and older brother were forever posing questions. "How is it they know that cannon are hidden at Barrett's farm?"

Benjamin lowered the spyglass. "Somebody told them?"

"I suppose so."

"But who?"

"That, Benjamin, is a very good question." He took the spyglass raised it to his eye once more. "It's one thing for you and I to know about the cannon at Barrett's farm, but how do you suppose word of it got to General Gage in Boston?"

The name of the hill was Punkatasset, and the men gathered on its slopes watched as the column of soldiers advanced slowly toward the river and crossed the narrow footbridge, and there they halted as their commanders engaged in consultation. Finally, there was a decision to divide—one detail remained at the bridge, while the other continued on toward Colonel Barrett's farm, and about a half mile up the road a portion of that detail was also left to stand guard, facing the provincials on the hill above them.

It was mid-morning and the heat of the day seemed to increase by the minute. More and more provincials arrived from nearby villages, Acton, Carlisle, Chelmsford, and Sudbury—fathers, sons, grandfathers; cousins, uncles. Church bells continued to sound in the distance. Ezra estimated that at least four hundred men were gathered along the ridge, while there might be half as many lobsterbacks between North Bridge and Barrett's farm.

"I heard there was shooting this morning," Benjamin said.

"On Lexington Green, at dawn," Ezra said.

"Who started it?"

"Don't know. Don't matter now. Been waiting a long time for this day."

"We going to just stand here?"

"We'll see." Ezra looked Benjamin up and down with a critical eye. "I see you didn't bring a fowling piece, but then I understand you're better at killing fish."

"I wasn't exactly planning on coming out here . . ."

"I reckon. A gun would get wet in them clam flats anyway." He picked up his haversack and slung it over his shoulder. "Stick by me, will you? If things get hot, I do the shooting and you reload."

Benjamin was relieved but didn't want to show it. He nodded once.

At one point, a man from Lincoln named Nichols walked down the hill unarmed, intending to negotiate. When he reached the bridge, he spoke calmly with a captain for a good while. They might have been discussing crops or the price of a cow. Word went around on the hill that Nichols was English-born, a fact which seemed to suggest that a settlement might be achieved so everyone could go home. There were jokes about fields needing to be tended and children waiting to be conceived. It was getting very hot, standing in the sun. Finally, Nichols climbed back up the hill, took his gun, and said he was going back to Lincoln. A few others left as well, but most continued to wait on the hill.

When smoke rose above the trees in Concord, the provincials became agitated. Sitting on his horse, Colonel Barrett hollered, *"Will you let them burn the town down?"* And the men, shouted, *"No!"* The colonel gathered the elders together and, after a brief confab, word was passed along the hill that no one was to fire unless the redcoats fired first.

Ezra gave his powder horn and cartridge pouch to Benjamin, which he slung from his shoulders, the straps making an X across his chest and back. "Use your teeth to tear open the paper roll containing ball and powder," Ezra said. "Put a little of the powder into the pan of the firing mechanism, once I have it half-cocked, and then pour the rest of the powder down the barrel of the musket. Then the lead ball goes down the barrel, followed by the wadded-up paper, which keeps the ball from rolling out as I raise the gun up to my shoulder. Finally, you ram everything down snug, using the wide end of this iron rod, which slides out of this tube on the underside of the barrel. See?" He looked at Benjamin, who nodded his head. "We work together," Ezra continued, "we should be able to get off two or three shots in a minute." He watched Benjamin slide the rod back down the tube, and added, "It might get to the point where it's better not to bother doing that each time. Just stick the rod in the ground, but don't lose the damn thing."

Benjamin felt the cartridge pouch hanging at his side. "How many?"

"Twenty-three balls." He looked away. "We'll find more, off dead and wounded."

Smoke now billowed into the sky above the village. Orders were shouted and the provincials were organized in a column and a company from Acton led them down the hill. Colonel Barrett remained on horseback on the ridge, hollering that they should not be the first to fire. Benjamin walked beside Ezra through the tall grass. The air was filled with bugs and the sound of the men's equipment rattling with each step.

"I wish I had a gun," Benjamin said.

"So do I."

When they were about halfway down the hill, shots were fired. Benjamin couldn't tell where they came from—the reports seemed to roll up and down the hillside. Immediately, the line of provincials broke apart and firing commenced. The redcoats fired as well and quickly the air was filled with smoke, making it difficult to see. The sound of gunfire was constant, and again the echo off the hill made the barrage of noise seem to be near and far, as though there were fighting off in the distance as well. Clumps of earth leapt into the whistling air. Men were sprawled on the ground, bleeding into the grass. Amid the shouting, Benjamin heard Ezra's voice below him, and he ran down the hill. He took a cartridge from the pouch, tore it open, the taste of gunpowder filling his mouth, and together they reloaded the musket.

The redcoats on the near side of the river were falling back, and a few attempted to tear up planks in the bridge. But some were felled in the effort, and soon all the soldiers abandoned the bridge. The provincials continued to descend the hill—no order now, and men fired at will. Ezra took aim and fired, but there was too much smoke to see what he hit. He and Benjamin ran down the hill to level ground. Across the river, the redcoats were trying to organize themselves in lines, but they seemed to be having difficulty. Their shots, indicated by white bursts of smoke from the muzzles of their guns, did not slow the provincials' advance. As they started across the bridge, the redcoats began running back toward the village, leaving their own dead and wounded behind.

The smoke stung Benjamin's eyes and he hated the taste of gunpowder. He wanted nothing more than to lie down on the grassy riverbank and take a long drink of water.

Abigail was walking home from Dr. Warren's when a boy rode a swaybacked gray mare into Dock Square, shouting about fighting in Lexington. A great jostling crowd gathered about him. Shots had been exchanged on Lexington Green at dawn. Dozens of provincials had been killed and wounded. The redcoats then marched on to Concord, burning everything in their path. People in the crowd contributed what they had heard. Last night's expedition that had gathered on the Common was led by Lieutenant Colonel Smith, who was fat and incompetent, but his second in command was Major John Pitcairn, and that one there, Pitcairn, a man in a bloodied butcher's apron shouted, he be a strong advocate for just such a smart action: burn a few villages and the entire rebellious sentiment would itself go up in smoke. An old woman leaning on a walking stick surmised that the reinforcements that had left Boston this morning—perhaps a thousand soldiers—had been sent for so that the expedition might cut a wide swath of destruction through the countryside.

She asked the boy, "How'd you come by all this?"

"'Twas a fisherman," the boy said, his voice cracking with excitement. "He heard it from a girl who had come running down to the marshes by Lechmere Point, and he rowed for Boston, shouting the news across the Charles. I was on the shore, there near the Mill Pond, helping my uncle caulk his boat."

Abigail gathered up her skirts and rushed home. People were running everywhere, like ants, going in every direction. There was yelling from windows above the streets. When she reached School Street, pupils were fleeing the small building that housed the Latin School. Father, dressed in his wig and black robe, stood in the doorway, shouting in Latin.

She met him as he came out the gate. He seemed unsteady on his feet and didn't resist when she took his arm as they walked up the street toward home. He continued to mutter, in Latin.

When they reached the house, Mother came out on the front stoop. "I just heard—"

"I know," Father said. "Perhaps this nonsense will finally be over."

"Mother, has Benjamin—"

"No," she said. "He's not come home."

"I must find him," Abigail said.

"You shouldn't be out on these streets," her father said.

Her father looked at the frightened, angry Bostonians that had filled School Street, and said, "War's begun—school's done." He pushed his way by his wife and went into the house.

Remaining out on the stoop, Mother said, "We should all lock ourselves indoors and pray for deliverance. But where can Benjamin be?"

"I'll keep looking for him," Abigail said as she started down School Street.

"Look at James's house," Mother said.

"I doubt he'll be there, not now."

"Find him, please. But be careful." Mother turned and went inside, closing the door as though to keep a pestilence out.

Abigail worked her way through the crowd, heading down toward the waterfront. Benjamin's secret places—he was frequently drawn to the water. She went to Long Wharf, looking in doorways of taverns, sail lofts, and chandlers. She went by the ropewalk, but the men there hadn't seen Benjamin. Finally, she went to Anse Cole's clam shack and found his daughter alone there, sitting with her back against the shingles, mending baskets.

"Mariah, have you seen Benjamin?"

"No, I ain't, Miss," Mariah said, getting to her feet. She had a shucking knife in one hand, a ball of hemp in the other. "Ain't seen him in days." She was perhaps sixteen, thin and rather plain, but she had kind gray eyes and she took to Benjamin. Once last summer Abigail had come upon them in an alley off Salt Lane, kissing. He was frightfully embarrassed, but Mariah kept her arms about his neck a moment longer, possessively. "You look concerned," she said now. "Has he not been home?"

"Not last night, no," Abigail gazed out at the harbor. The water was glass, pastel blue. Ships at anchor seemed to rise up out of their reflections. "Tide's in, so he can't be clamming. Do you think he's out there fishing?"

"Could be," Mariah said. She nodded toward a row of skiffs pulled up on the shore, tilted over on their keels, leaning this way and that, looking like sleeping animals. "But if he'd a gone out, he'd a taken one of my father's boats, and they're all here."

"The sail loft." Abigail looked toward the longer building at the end of the row of clam shacks. "Might he be there?"

Mariah raised a finger to her mouth and bit on a nail. She had strong hands from shucking, the fingers scarred from the sharp edges of seashells. "He wouldn't be up there, alone." Again, the gray eyes, guarded now. She stood up and began to pick up a stack of baskets she'd been working on.

"Here, let me help you." Abigail took up several more baskets, and followed Mariah into the clam shack, where they set them down. It was damp inside, smelling deeply of the sea, and Mariah led Abigail back outside.

"Thank you, Miss. It wasn't necessary for you to—"

"So you have no idea where he might be?" Abigail's tone was doubtful.

Mariah's eyes suddenly grew large with trepidation. "I wish I knowed. I been worried about him, all his running for your older brother and the Sons of Liberty. And now there's word of this fighting out Lincoln way." Her eyes were pleading, for understanding, sympathy. "You know there will be more executions. Hangings from the Great Elm on the Common."

Abigail took a step closer, and for a moment she almost thought the girl was going to fall into her arms, weeping. But she began gnawing on another fingernail, broken and cracked. "If you see him, Mariah, you tell him to get home."

"I sure will, Miss. As I said, I been hoping he'd come by."

"Good." Abigail began to turn away, but then said, "Trimount. Did he go up there?"

Now the girl glanced toward the three hills that loomed above the waterfront and she seemed embarrassed as a blotchy flush came to her cheeks. "I don't venture up there with him, no." She was so frightened now, earnestly so, as though confessing. "No, I don't go up the Trimount, not to the top anyway. Maybe the lower pastures a couple of times, but never all the way up, no."

"I see," Abigail said softly.

She began walking down along the beach, thinking of heading toward the Charlestown ferry landing, and then on to Mill Pond. When she was a ways down the beach, she looked back toward the row of clam shacks. Mariah was sitting on her stool again, back against the weathered shingles, gazing out at the harbor. Abigail began to turn and continue on, but then, farther down the beach, she saw someone, a man, peering out from the corner of the sail loft.

A redcoat.

After the engagement at North Bridge, nothing happened. No more shots were fired. The redcoats had retreated to the village. The smoke rising from the village had stopped—so the urgency of saving Concord from burning seemed to have passed. Some men went looking for food and beverage at nearby houses and taverns. For the time being, the provincials just seemed to evaporate in the heat of the day.

Ezra and Benjamin, sitting in the shade of a tree on Punkatasset Hill, shared the wallet of victuals: more salt cod, and bread. Below, they watched as the redcoat detail that had gone to Barrett's farm returned, meeting no resistance as they crossed North Bridge. They collected their wounded and took them into Concord. The dead, however, were left behind, lying in the sun. Benjamin's eye kept wandering back to one body, lying near the bridge. A boy with an axe had approached the soldier, who was already mortally injured and crawling on all fours. The boy took the axe to the soldier's head, and for a long time after the man lay in his own blood, moaning, but now he was quiet and still.

It was difficult to determine what the British were doing in the village. The soldiers would form a column, parade in one direction, stop, and then after a considerable wait, they would be ordered to march in the opposite direction.

Both sides seemed to be in shock, stunned by their encounter, regretful that it had occurred, and now neither could decide what to do next.

At least two hours passed, and then around noon the soldiers began to march out of Concord, taking the road back toward Lexington.

There were no fife and drums, which in itself was a significant victory. The provincials began to follow the British column, at a distance, keeping to the woods. Ezra and Benjamin walked swiftly, sometimes jogging, through stands of trees. When they crossed pasture land, which locals called the Great Fields, it suddenly became apparent how many had responded to the alarm. Hundreds of men streamed across the field, creating rivulets in the long grass, which reminded Benjamin of the wind on the salt marsh.

They kept to the high ground. There was no order to it. Yet word was passed: about a mile from Concord there was a stream ahead, at Miriam's Corner. Get there before the British. And wait.

From the Great Fields they climbed up a wooded hill until they could see down to a fork in the road, one branch running north to Bedford, the other continuing east toward Lincoln and Lexington. Militia had gathered behind the Miriam farmhouse, barns, and outbuildings. Coming out from Concord, the British light infantry had been flanking both sides of the road, but here they would have to rejoin the column of grenadiers to take the narrow bridge across the stream.

The British column could be heard before it was seen, the sound of boots on the hard-packed dirt road. There was not the cadence of a march, but the shuffling sound of men who were tired. A cloud of dust rose above the trees. When they came into sight, the wounded could be seen walking between the columns. There were also a number of chaises, which carried other wounded.

"Officers," Ezra whispered. "They wear those silver plates hung about their necks."

As the column neared the bridge, the flanking infantrymen could be seen pinching in until they too were walking along the road. The men in the woods waited in silence. Benjamin thought that perhaps they were going to let the soldiers pass, allowing them to return to Boston without further harm. He was about to say as much to Ezra, when the first shot was fired, and then the shooting began, puffs of smoke drifting up through the trees until the hill was in a cloud. Soldiers fell, and the column broke into confusion. Some returned fire, but it was futile. Many ran for the bridge, and there they were soon shot. So many men piled up on the bridge that it became difficult for other soldiers to get across the stream.

Benjamin continued to reload the musket, his actions becoming swift and economical—the ramrod, he stabbed into the ground. His face and hands were coated with sweat, greasy and blackened with gun powder. Ezra was careful in his aim, and with almost every shot another soldier went down. *Officers,* he shouted. The barrage was so loud, Benjamin thought he would go deaf.

Abigail had gone to all of Benjamin's secret places—the ones she knew about—and found nothing. It was mid-afternoon and the heat and the sun shimmered off the water. The air didn't move and Boston was oddly quiet.

She had seen the redcoat several times. He kept his distance, often looking out from the corner of a house, once slipping behind a fishing smack on a cradle. It was then that she recognized him: the corporal. Lumley. The way the smell of liquor came off of him that dark night. The way he pinned her shoulders to the clapboard wall. The way Sergeant Munroe handled her breasts, until he found the letter. Angered, she began to walk back toward him. Scare him off, she hoped (he was, after all, hiding from her). She strode down the street, as though to flush him out there in that doorway, or there in the darkness of the barn door left ajar. But she didn't see him, and was startled when she heard footsteps to her left, running up an alley.

"I found you!"

It was Mariah Cole.

"What is it?" Abigail said. "Benjamin?"

Mariah emerged from the shade of the alley. "No, but I couldn't just sit mending baskets no longer, and I began to thinking." She raised a hand to shield her eyes from the sun, and gazed up toward Trimount. "I was afraid you'd climb up there—alone."

"Well—"

"Benjamin does go up there, you know. And as I said, I've been only as far as the lower pastures with him, but he . . ." She took her hand away and gazed at Abigail, her gray eyes large with regret. "I should have told you before, I suppose, but he has mentioned that he goes up there."

"Why?"

Mariah shrugged, but then she smiled, now complicit. "So he can see. He once said there was a great view. He said you can see everything from there: Lechmere Point, the Mill Pond, Charlestown, the Mystic River, Noddle's Island, the open ocean. He's wanted to show me, but I wouldn't go up."

"I will go up," Abigail said. "Thank you, Mariah."

"May I go, too?" Abigail looked at the girl, her face turned slightly toward the sun as she looked up at the Trimount. "I mean, you shouldn't venture there alone."

"No," Abigail said, glancing down the street. There was no sign of Lumley, though she doubted that he had fled. "I believe you're right. Please come, if you wish."

There were three hills: Cotton Hill, named after the Reverend John Cotton, who used to have a house there; Beacon; and Mount Vernon, which was to the west, overlooking the Charles River. It was often referred to as Mount Whoredom, and it was a place where respectable women should not go. Everyone knew of the stories about men going up the hill where there were women of leisure waiting in caves and copses. Stories of all-night revelry, dance, drinking, and fornication. There were few diversions in the city, not a single theater was allowed, a lingering consequence of Boston's Puritanical heritage, and yet prostitutes abounded, obliging the needs and fancy of the king's men. Bostonians saw this as the result of their confinement with the soldiers on this small peninsula. And one need not look far to see that it was not just the behavior of the redcoats that encouraged wanton behavior. Many a young Bostonian woman was already well along on her wedding day.

As they climbed up through the lower pastures, Abigail continued to look downhill for any signs that they were being followed, but Corporal Lumley was nowhere in sight.

Finally, she said to Mariah, "You care for him, don't you?"

"Benjamin has a good heart." Mariah swept strands of hair from her face. "I know your mother and father won't fancy me, being the daughter of a waterman."

"They don't know you."

"Are you afraid?"

Such a bold question—it took Abigail by surprise. "Why?"

"The way you look about, behind you, in front of you—"

"I'm looking for my brother and—and, yes, I'm afraid."

Abigail felt better for having said it.

"I am, too," Mariah said. "So many soldiers marched out into the country last night. I'm afeared people are dying out there."

"I know. For too long, we've all known it would come to this."

"When it comes, I just hope we fight back, whether we die or not."

Abigail stopped walking and waited for Mariah to pause and turn toward her. They were both a little out of breath from the climb. "My parents should meet you, one day." She smiled as she continued on up the path. "Not now, but one day, perhaps."

Grazing cows paused to look at the two women as they strode by. They crossed Beacon Hill to Mount Vernon, where they passed a few caves, mere holes in the ground, or occasional gaps in the rocks. They saw no one. Abigail frequently looked behind them, but did not see Lumley. Finally, they reached the steep bluff which afforded a view, all of Boston spread beneath them, surrounded by water and islands. They could see how the currents and tides shaped the harbor and the Charles. Shoals were pale green, while the deeper channels ran ink-blue; vast green planes of salt marsh knotted with inlets and pools.

"My God," Mariah whispered. "Will you look at this? It's worth fighting for, no?"

"Yes," Abigail said. "Yes, it is."

VI

Out of the Country

THEY CHASED THE REDCOATS ALL THE WAY BACK TO LEXINGTON. The provincials swarmed ahead, racing through the woods, taking up positions behind trees, stone walls, and barns. The British were in complete confusion, leaving dead and wounded behind, firing at random into the woods. Their fat commander, Lieutenant Colonel Smith, was wounded while on horseback, so he dismounted and walked with the soldiers, hiding among them. Major Pitcairn took command, but his horse was shot out from beneath him. Outside of Lexington, his officers drew their sabers and stood at the front of the panicked soldiers, swearing to cut down any man who did not form up in a column. As they fell in and marched, bedraggled and exhausted, the provincials continued to pick them off.

In Lexington there was an explosion. Word came up through the woods that a cannonball had struck the meetinghouse, and a mass of reinforcements had ventured out from Boston. Still more provincials arrived, and when the large formation of redcoats marched east toward Cambridge, the shooting continued. There was more of a threat to the provincials now, as packs of light infantrymen were seen running up into the woods.

When Ezra and Benjamin came to a farm in Menotomy, they sought food and water. The back door was open, and when they stepped into the kitchen they found a woman lying on the floor in a pool of blood. The saber slash had nearly severed her head. At the table an elderly man sat upright in his chair, a gaping bullet wound in his chest. Ezra picked up the pistol that lay on the table and handed it to Benjamin.

"Loaded, not even fired."

Benjamin had never held a pistol before and he liked its weight.

"No food," Ezra said, opening a tin on the sideboard, which was smeared with grease and breadcrumbs. "They're looking for the same thing."

He paused in the door, scanning the yard. "Careful, now."

They left the farm, crossed a plowed field, and entered the woods. By a stone wall, they found two men and a boy not ten years old, all shot in the back.

"We should have done more," Ezra said. "We should have left nothing—not one saber, not one firearm—for the reinforcements to bring back to Boston. They came out to destroy us, and we're losing our chance to destroy them. We might have ended it today. But this is only the beginning."

They kept to the stone wall in the woods. Up ahead they could hear shooting.

In Cambridge, the British were approaching another fork in the road, Ezra explained, but this time they knew enough not to take the bridge south across the Charles River that would lead them down to the Neck. Their only choice was to take the road east, which led to Charlestown; from there they could be ferried to Boston.

The provincials pursued the British column through Cambridge, though at a greater distance because here the land was more open. Ezra and Benjamin encountered the work of the light infantry: provincials lying dead and wounded among trees and in barnyards. By late afternoon, Ezra had only one cartridge left. Many provincials had gone home once they were out of ammunition, but Ezra said he wanted to stay, wanted to fire his last shot just as the redcoats crossed the spit of land that connected to the Charlestown peninsula. As they moved through the countryside, they could seldom see the column, though they could hear their boots and see the dust rising in the sky above them.

"We're chasing them all the way back to Boston," Ezra said.

"And then what?" Benjamin asked.

Ezra didn't answer at first, but then said, "I don't know, but Boston is not a place *I'd* want to be."

Not far outside Charlestown there was a wooden cage hanging from a tree next to the road. It had been there for years and contained the remains of a slave who had tried to escape his owner. There was nothing now but bones tangled in a heap of rags. Benjamin and Ezra lay in a stand of trees about a hundred yards away, watching the British soldiers pass beneath the tree. Many paused to look up at the cage, though some appeared too spent to even notice.

"Everywhere, signs of reprimand and punishment," Ezra said. "Someday they'll cut that cage down, I suppose, even though owning a slave is your right. Seems odd, though, all this business about liberty, yet we still keep slaves."

"I know a black man, from Haiti," Benjamin said. "Works at the granary. Often see him out in the harbor, fishing or digging clams. I lost an oar once and a storm was coming up, and he towed me in against the outgoing tide. Name's Obadiah."

"Someone own Obadiah?"

"Reginald Fiske, a merchant. But Obadiah, he acts like a freeman."

Ezra nodded toward the cage. "But he stays put because of such warnings."

"Wasn't for him, that tide would have taken me out to sea."

Ezra turned and looked back into the woods. "We're out of water. There's a spring down there a ways."

They got up and walked down to an outcropping of granite, where they could hear the gurgle of running water. The spring ran below the rocks and wound farther down through a glen. The stream ran clear, and moved fast enough that there was white water curling over stones. Something about the movement of water fascinated Benjamin. A stream, a pond, the harbor stretching toward the sea, he could stare at the movement of water endlessly. They knelt on the mossy bank and drank from their cupped hands, and then Ezra began to fill his canteen.

The shot came from above them, to their right. Ezra groaned as he seemed to be pushed into the stream. Blood-stained water ran downstream.

Benjamin looked back up at the granite outcropping and saw two redcoats. One was reloading his Brown Bess, while the other held his rifle across the top of the rock, taking aim. He fired, and Benjamin was sprayed by moss and clumps of dirt. Turning, he looked at Ezra, who was still lying on his side in the stream, holding his shoulder. His musket lay on the embankment and Benjamin picked it up, got to his feet, and ran toward the rocks. He could only see one of the soldiers, perhaps thirty yards away, ramming ball and powder down the barrel of his gun. Benjamin kept running toward him, dodging in and out behind tree trunks. When he had closed half the distance, the soldier raised his gun to his shoulder. Benjamin fell to the ground as the soldier fired. The ball hit the nearest tree, raining bark and splinters down on Benjamin, who remained on the ground. He took aim at the soldier, who was beginning to move to his right along the angled granite faces—his boots slipped on the stone, so that he fell, losing his rifle. He had acne on his face and neck, and he stared at Benjamin helplessly.

Benjamin got to his feet and moved until he was behind a wide tree trunk. It was quiet for a moment; there was only the sound of the stream behind him. When he peered around the trunk, he saw the other soldier running downhill. Benjamin shouldered Ezra's rifle and drew a bead and, just before the soldier reached a stand of bushes, he fired. The soldier's hands went up into the air, his gun clattered against the ground, and then he tumbled down the hill until he lay motionless, gazing at the sky.

There was a terrible ringing in Benjamin's right ear and it made him feel dazed. He leaned the musket against the tree and looked back toward the other soldier. He was on his feet and reloading his gun. Benjamin pressed his back against the trunk. He could see Ezra, who was now sitting up in the stream, his jacket slick with blood.

Turning, Benjamin stepped out from behind the tree and began walking quickly toward the soldier. He drew the old man's pistol from his belt. The soldier was pouring powder down his barrel, when he paused and looked up. Benjamin stopped a few feet away and extended his pistol toward the soldier. "Put it down."

The soldier seemed about the same age as Benjamin, perhaps even younger. He looked down toward the other soldier, and then back at Benjamin.

"Put it down or I'll fire."

"*Shoot!*" Ezra yelled from the stream. "*Shoot him!*"

Benjamin didn't take his eyes off the soldier. "You heard me."

"What will you do?"

"Put it down and I will let you walk out of here."

"*Shoot!*"

The soldier stared at the pistol, and then at Benjamin. The front of his red coat was covered with grass stains and sweat ran down his dirty face. He let go of the muzzle of his rifle and it fell to the ground. Slowly, he turned and began walking away through the woods. His hat was on crooked and when it fell off he didn't stop to pick it up. His hair was black, short, and cut unevenly. He was already developing a bald spot on the crown of his head. Once, he glanced over his shoulder, and then began to trot, with difficulty because he was encumbered with so much equipment. He disappeared into the trees in the direction of the Charlestown road.

They were walking down the hill when Mariah hesitated and said, "What's that?"

Abigail looked back out across the Charles. The land, in its new spring green, stretched toward the horizon beneath an afternoon sky crowded with towering clouds. She looked down the path, thinking that Mariah had caught sight of Lumley.

She heard it then, a faint clap, coming from miles away. The only other sound was the lowing of a cow, grazing well below them on the hill.

There came a succession of claps, more like the crackling of logs in a fire.

"Guns," she said.

They moved quickly, back along the ridge. The gunfire was constant now, coming from different quarters to the west.

"That's closer than Cambridge," Mariah said.

"Yes."

"It must be a slaughter, my God, it must be."

Minutes passed. The shooting became constant, moving closer to the vast salt marsh on the far side of the river. There was movement, a line of red, crossing to the Charlestown peninsula, advancing slowly, resembling a snake the way it moved sideways through and around the trees. It was redcoats, but something was wrong with the column, the way it was disorderly and bedraggled. Finally they stopped in the pastures above the Charlestown village, spreading out like a stain along the hillside.

"I don't understand," Mariah said. "Who's shooting?"

"We are."

"Can it be?"

"Must be. They must be in the woods." Abigail suddenly needed to sit down. She settled in the grass, and Mariah did the same, leaning toward her as if for protection. Abigail placed her arm around the girl, and could feel the faintest quiver in her shoulders. "They've run them out of the countryside." She stretched out her other arm and pointed. "See that cluster of soldiers at the head of the spit. They're holding us back. There must be thousands of men. They're safe on Charlestown peninsula, but trapped. They'll have to be ferried across the river. By nightfall, they'll be back here."

"And then what?" Mariah asked.

"Once in Boston, they've no place to go. I don't know what happens then."

VII

Bostoneers

THE FOLLOWING DAY BOSTONIANS' SHOCK AND AWE WERE AS great as the redcoats' exhaustion. Throughout the city there seemed to be no order. Drunken soldiers were everywhere; but there was also a peculiar stillness. It was eerie, this quiet, more threatening than the rattle of drums and the stamp of soldiers' feet during a parade drill. Commerce was sporadic and there was a reluctance to gather in the streets, yet rumors abounded: dozens of British soldiers were said to have been killed and several hundred wounded. There were stories of their anguished cries during the night as they were ferried over from Charlestown. The provincials suffered losses as well, though it was generally believed that they had fared better than the redcoats. And there were outlandish stories about provincials being slaughtered in their beds; houses and entire villages put to the torch. Repeatedly, there were descriptions of women being seen running naked from the redcoats. But there was also word of how, though greatly outnumbered, the militia stood at

Lexington and then at Concord, how they fought like Indians, shooting from behind trees and fences and barns, never confronting the British in the open as they pursued the redcoats all the way back to Charlestown. Perhaps, most horrifying, were the tales of soldiers being scalped.

The Latin School was closed, and would remain so for an undetermined period of time. Father shut himself up in his study, and a succession of his Tory friends came calling. Mother served them, but she was often on the verge of tears, worried about what had become of Benjamin.

"He may still be somewhere in hiding," Abigail said as she helped prepare another tray of tea and biscuits for Father's guests. "I've looked in all his usual places, but—"

"I went to James's house first thing this morning, thinking he knew something, but he assures me he doesn't know where Benjamin is either," her mother said. "The boy has gone and joined them—I know it. He's got himself out into the countryside and can't come back."

Abigail couldn't deny the possibility. But then she said, "If anybody can slip back into Boston, it's Benjamin."

Her mother took the tray down the hall to Father's study. Abigail went into the parlor, where she stopped at one of the windows. Corporal Lumley was walking down School Street and when he reached the house, he paused at the front stoop.

Abigail quickly went into the hall, opened the door, and said, "What is it you want?"

"I'm billeted just there." He said, pointed down the street. "And—"

Abigail came out on the threshold. "You were following me yesterday."

He appeared uncertain, embarrassed. "I meant you no harm, Miss."

"You've done enough already. Now go, go away from my house."

She stepped back and began to close the door, but hesitated when he reached inside his red tunic and produced an envelope.

"This is for you, Miss." Now he nodded in the direction of the house where he was staying. "He sent a messenger this morning, saying I was to deliver this to you personally."

"Why you?"

"I cannot say. It's all a muddle now."

"Who's it from?"

He only held the envelope out to her. "I meant no harm, I assure you. The other night, it was most inappropriate."

"Corporal Lumley, you search my brother's hat, you have the temerity to assist in the search of my person in the most improper fashion, and then you follow me up the Trimount."

He only lowered his head as though to acknowledge that this was abject behavior. "I wished only to speak to you, Miss. And now this messenger comes from the colonel, requesting that I—"

"The colonel?"

"Colonel Cleaveland. Seems he made inquiries and learned that I—" Once again, he nodded toward the house he was staying in farther down School Street. "The messenger he says, 'The colonel has learned that you knows the schoolmaster's daughter and he expects that you'll make delivery of this.'" Lumley gazed down at the envelope, which he still extended toward her. With a shrug, he added, "So says I, 'Yes, I know where Master Lovell lives,' and here I am, as instructed."

"Didn't Colonel Cleaveland go with the expedition to Lexington and Concord?"

"I believe so, yes."

"It's about my brother."

"That I cannot say. I have no knowledge of the contents of this letter."

"Are you sober, Corporal?"

"Indeed I am."

He seemed in earnest; different in some way that she couldn't fathom. Also, his extended arm appeared to be growing tired, which gave her a little satisfaction.

"You are pathetic, sir."

"I offer no rebuttal, mistress."

Abigail snatched the envelope from his hand, stepped back, and shut the door hard.

The demands of her parents' guests were immediate. She tucked the envelope inside Alexander Pope's translation of Homer's *The Odyssey,* which was on the shelf in the parlor, and then went about the business of assisting her mother. The afternoon wore on, and it wasn't until early evening that her duties were concluded. Her father was still locked away in his study, and her mother, exhausted in her rocking chair, had dozed off with her needles and yarn in her lap.

Abigail took the copy of *The Odyssey* upstairs and sat on the window seat on the landing. The late afternoon clouds had grown dark and a thunderstorm was approaching. The air was close, and rain would be a relief. She removed the envelope from the book, broke the seal of white wax, and removed a single folded sheet of parchment.

> *April 20, 1775*
>
> *My Dear Miss Lovell,*
>
> *I apologize for the forward and rather impersonal Nature of this communication as we have not been formally intro-duced, but I suspect that you will agree that the Events of the past few days have dramatically altered how you and I—to be sure, all of us—view even the most ordinary occur-rences. I find everything has changed Now and I cannot see where this will all lead. If you would do me the kindness of meeting me this Evening, I would be most Grateful. Of course, should you find it necessary to Decline, for whatever reason, I will fully understand and not trouble you further.*

However, I believe You and I have much to discuss and pray that you will do me the honor of your company at the Two Salutations at seven o'clock.

Your Humble Servant,
Colonel Samuel Cleaveland

Abigail looked out the window as the first raindrops streaked the whorled glass.

A soldier was waiting in the pouring rain outside the Two Salutations, and he escorted Abigail inside to the private room Colonel Cleaveland had secured. He was alone and the table was laden with poultry, fruit, and wine. Abigail took the seat when offered, but declined to eat. She kept her cloak on, only pushing the hood back onto her shoulders.

He poured her a glass of wine, which she did not touch. There was much different about him, and it was difficult to believe he was the same officer she had encountered in Dock Square two days earlier. Scratches ran down his face and the side of his neck, and there was a purplish bruise at his temple. His left hand was bandaged. And his eyes, though still a pale blue, seemed now to linger in a way that suggested newfound doubt. He stared at the wine glass in his hand as though he'd never seen one before, and once he picked up a knife and appeared to be looking at himself in the reflection of its blade. Beyond that, he was somehow diminished. Though his uniform was crisp, he seemed not quite able to fill it as he might have only days ago. He had, though, taken considerable pains with his hair, which, as before, was smoothed back from his forehead and tied in a neat queue.

"I appreciate your coming," he said, "particularly in such weather." When she didn't answer, he picked up his wine and drank down half the glass. "When I sent my letter, I was certain you wouldn't come. I got the impression—"

"What impression?"

"The private I sent, he only said you accepted the letter and made no commitment."

"The private?"

Cleaveland put his glass on the table. "Yes, the soldier who led you in here."

"That private, standing out in the rain? He didn't deliver the letter."

"I don't understand. I must ask him for clarification." Cleaveland began to get up.

"Colonel, please sit." When he did so, she decided to take a sip of wine. It was a full-bodied red and immediately she could feel it warm her cheeks. "For now, it's of little importance. The fact is that I received your letter. I assume you have something to tell me."

"I have."

"About my brother."

"Your brother?"

"Benjamin?"

He stared across the table at her. "I have learned that your father, the schoolmaster, is indeed very much the loyalist, and that you have an older brother, James, who is—" He glanced down in an attempt to be circumspect. "But your younger brother, that boy in Dock Square, I don't—"

"You didn't ask me here to tell me about my younger brother Benjamin?"

He shook his head, genuinely bewildered. "Why would I?"

Abigail took a breath. "He's, he's gone missing."

The colonel seemed relieved. "I'm afraid this is true of many men, on both sides."

"You have no news of his whereabouts?"

"No, I'm sorry to say."

"This is my own fault. I've been so concerned about him that I've been grasping at straws. Of course, why would you know about him?" Disgusted with herself, she began to get up from her chair, but then paused. "Why *did* you invite me here?"

He took another sip of his wine and seemed much preoccupied. "Circumstances," he said, leaning toward her and barely whispering. "It's the circumstances, I believe."

"What circumstances, Colonel?"

He straightened up in his chair and shook his head wearily. "I must apologize, Miss Lovell. I've gone about this all wrong. These past few days, everything has changed. No one could have foreseen these events."

"You mean the expedition, Lexington and Concord."

"I was correct," he said adamantly. "In retrospect, I was right, though you'll be hard pressed to find an officer who will admit that this is so. I told them, I argued that we needed to take artillery with us on this expedition. That is my responsibility, you see. I'm in charge of artillery, and I said it was foolhardy to venture into the countryside without cannon. They not only refused, as though such a proposition were preposterous, they found the very idea that we would require such armaments insulting. You must understand that this army is—well, it's organized in a fashion and imbued with traditions that often prove to be its own worst enemy. In this case, my expressed concerns were not just ignored but ridiculed, by some. They anticipated no real resistance once outside of Boston and claimed we wouldn't need to burden ourselves with such heavy equipment, that we could move swiftly without it. Of course, they also believed that our expedition could actually march out into the countryside without anyone even taking notice. Good God. Furthermore, they said, essential to our purpose was to locate the provincials' artillery—confiscate it and bring it back to Boston, and if that proved too unwieldy a task then we would spike the cannons where we found them. That would be my responsibility. That was why I had to accompany the march. Not to oversee the transport and deployment of *our* artillery, but to see to it that, if necessary, we would properly render *their* guns ineffective." He finished his wine, and then refilled his glass from the decanter. "Those were the 'circumstances' at the outset, and from there things only seemed to spiral further and further out of control. Do you understand what I'm saying?"

"I understand, Colonel," Abigail said. "But I don't see why I'm here, why you're telling me all this."

Colonel Cleaveland put his elbows on the table and for a moment massaged his forehead with the fingers of his bandaged hand. "I'm sorry. Still, I'm going about this all wrong."

"How did you do that?" she asked. "Your hand."

He looked at his bandage. "You know, I don't remember."

"The stories we've heard . . . horrible."

His expression changed, his eyes becoming distant, but then he looked at her in a way that took Abigail by surprise. He almost appeared to be pleading, his eyes seeking some kind of acceptance, some recognition. "None of this should ever have happened, but now it has."

"What will this mean, do you suppose?" she asked. "What will become of us?" He seemed delighted by the questions. "Colonel, my brother is missing. All of Boston is traumatized. Can you tell me, what *are* the circumstances?"

"Yes." He took a moment, gazing about the room. "This is the question. I would say that it does not bode well, for any of us. We—General Gage's army—are now trapped here on this crowded little peninsula. Our intelligence sources tell us that the provincial army is establishing camps on Dorchester Heights to the south, in Charlestown to the north, that there are thousands of men from all over New England pouring into the camp in Cambridge, and that many of the rebel leaders have taken up residence upriver in Watertown. We are surrounded, confined." He studied her a moment, his expression turning sympathetic. "You. You Bostoneers are in a worse plight than your country people. You are here on this peninsula with us, your enemy—we

101

are enemies now, to be sure. Life here will become very difficult. Today the word 'siege' was used by my superiors. They said Boston is in a state of siege. And there's no knowing how long that will last." He surveyed the table a moment, and then said, "Sure you wouldn't like something to eat?"

"No, really. But please, do not refrain on my account."

Something had eased in him. He took up a chicken leg and bit into it, and then as he ate he continued to explain the circumstances. It was all rumor and speculation at this point, but there had already been communication between sides. Evidently, Dr. Warren, who, despite his views, was held in the highest regard by the command, had already been in communication with General Gage regarding the situation. There was another doctor, a Dr. Benjamin Church, who had managed to return to Boston, and apparently he had brought a letter from Warren which expressed concern for the citizens of Boston who were in support of the provincials. Likewise, Gage was concerned that there would be further repercussions regarding the loyalists who lived out in the country. Certainly there had already been ample evidence that rebels could not respect the property of those who were loyal to the king. It was true, perhaps, that there had been instances where British soldiers had taken certain liberties with some Boston residents, but one had to admit that General Gage had been very consistent in his response to such provocations, so much so that he had sown both fear and anger among the ranks. Many of his officers complained that he had gone too far in his restrictions on the men and, when necessary, he had ordered unduly harsh reprimand upon the Regulars. What was clear was that there was now even greater potential for further untoward behavior.

"It appears that Gage and Warren are negotiating a swap." The colonel was now eating grapes. "Tory sympathizers living in the country would be allowed to remove to Boston, while those who supported the rebel cause in Boston would be allowed to evacuate the city. It seems an equitable solution."

"You said Dr. Church has returned to Boston?" Abigail said.

"Quite extraordinary. He arrived at the gates on the Neck and was apprehended. They took him straightaway to Province House, where he met with General Gage. I understand that his stockings were bloodied from the fighting."

"And Dr. Warren sent him?"

The colonel shrugged as he leaned back from the table. "Warren's taken up residence in Watertown. There's word that a musket ball passed so close to his head that it cut off a lock of his hair. There are those among us, of course, who believe that killing the likes of Church and Hancock and that little monster Sam Adams would bring a swift end to this rebellion. Cut the chicken's head off."

"But you?"

"Oh. One must acknowledge and admire Dr. Warren for his many attributes: persistence, ardor, and his damned eloquence. But at the bottom of it he's a reasonable man who bears true dignity. Take that away and you're left with Adams and his mob. If it were left to him, they would scalp every Tory in the countryside, rape their women, burn their houses, and to hell with whatever repercussions rebel sympathizers in Boston would face in retaliation." Cleaveland looked out the window. The rain had stopped. "If you read history," he said, "you know that cities under siege can lead to long and protracted suffering." Looking at Abigail, he said, "I appreciated your coming, Miss Lovell. Your company is a much needed antidote. I wonder if we might possibly meet again?"

Abigail drew the hood up over her head. The colonel looked down at the table, the bones on his plate. She began to get to her feet, but then said, "Colonel, would you know a soldier named Lumley, a corporal?"

"Lumley?" He shook his head. "No. Why?"

"It's not important." She got up from her chair, and the captain did so as well. "He's billeted near our house, is all."

"I see." Colonel Cleaveland seemed to struggle now, and Abigail was afraid of what she was certain he wanted to say. Finally, he managed: "Might I escort you home?"

"Thank you, no."

"Then my private, waiting outside, he could at least accompany you?"

"Colonel, you've been very cordial. I accepted your invitation thinking that I might learn something of my brother's whereabouts." She thought of Ezra, too, who most likely was out there somewhere, among the country people. "I fear for people very dear to me, people who would be here, here in Boston, if it weren't for your . . . *presence.*"

"I understand," he said, and for the moment he seemed sincerely distraught. "My intentions were—they were purely honorable, I assure you. Forgive me, but my purpose was not to ask you here under false pretenses." He studied the chicken bones remaining on his plate as though he might read his fortune in them. "I'm just a soldier who is a long way from home, and that evening when I encountered you and your brother in Dock Square, engaged in that unfortunate business with the street patrol, I found you to be remarkably forthright."

"'Unfortunate,' indeed. The sergeant had his saber point held to my brother's neck."

"You were calm and brave, and—"

"And I could tell you a few more things about that sergeant."

"I'm only offering to escort you home."

Abigail pulled on her gloves in haste. "I'm a Bostonian, not a Bostoneer—as you and General Gage like to put it—and I assure you, Colonel, I know my way home."

The next few days confirmed what Colonel Cleaveland had said: There was much congestion in the streets as carts and wagons, loaded with the belongings of patriots, streamed out of the city. The only stipulation was that all evacuees had to surrender any weapons—firearms, pistols, bayonets, and blunderbusses—to the British.

At breakfast Saturday, Abigail's father and mother discussed this possibility of evacuation, though it was clear from the outset that Father had no intention of leaving their home on School Street. It was bad enough that the Latin School was closed indefinitely, leaving some hundred boys to their own mischief, but Father refused to entertain the thought of abandoning their home.

"You should go, though," he said, looking down the table and gesturing with his butter knife.

"John, please," Mother said.

"It might be best," he said, "if both you and Abigail quit the city."

"And leave you here alone?" Mother asked.

"You think I can't manage?" Father laughed suddenly. This was not uncommon; though he was often brooding and serious, he would also find the humor at the most unlikely times. "My dear, James is right down the street. He's certainly not going anywhere. I'm sure they would set another place at their table for me. I'll not starve, though his wife is perhaps too fond of pepper."

Abigail's mother had a tendency to gnaw on her lower lip when she was upset, and she did so for quite some time now.

"Where would you go?" Father said, though she had said nothing. "There are any number of my former students living outside the city who I'm sure would be happy to accommodate you. Considering your health this past winter, it might be best if you were away from this city. If fact, it might be wise to leave Massachusetts entirely. Perhaps someplace sensible—like New York."

Mother didn't seem to hear.

"It's Benjamin," Abigail said, turning to her father.

Father's eyes appeared to soften with uncertainty. "The boy's like a stray dog," he said quietly. "I spoke to James about him last night. He's convinced that Benjamin has left the city. He's out there, among *them*. James would be, too, if his health weren't so . . ."

Mother pushed her chair back from the table, but she didn't seem to possess the strength to get up. She sat there, as though waiting for divine intervention.

That afternoon, when Father's guests had finally departed, Abigail went up to her room. She lay down on her bed with the copy of Pope's translation of Homer, but she found herself only able to stare out the window. They were a family divided, in so many ways. When Mother and Father had finally discovered that Abigail had a beau—a friend had seen her and Ezra walking by the Mill Pond— they of course insisted upon knowing about him, about his family. It was what Abigail feared; it was why she was willing to maintain her affections in secret. Ezra was an apprentice to a physician, but he didn't come from *family,* none at least that would be recognizable, and therefore acceptable, to her parents. Ezra lived with his mother, a tall, still quite handsome woman, and there was never any mention of his father. This was enough to cast doubt upon Ezra, whom Abigail defended to her parents relentlessly.

He was invited to tea once, upon Mother's insistence. It didn't go well. Father thought he was a merely a young man intent upon bettering himself by association with the daughter of a schoolmaster (*association* being his word—he couldn't even bring himself to mention the prospect of marriage). Mother proved more understanding; she found Ezra polite and well-mannered, and she admitted that he was indeed handsome, though his broad shoulders seemed the result of strenuous physical labor. After the occasion, Abigail kept to her room for days, barely speaking to her parents, and in the months that followed there had developed a smoldering tension within the house. Every time she went out, she felt their suspicions stalking after her. She didn't want to lie or deceive, but the more she felt their wish to deny her this *association,* the more she desired to be with him. Their meetings were often swift, furtive encounters, increasingly more reckless. Only Rachel understood and made every effort to help them arrange their trysts.

Slowly, a sense of futility caused the egg, their egg, to crack and break open. They had begun to discuss marriage, but Ezra was still only an apprentice physician, in no position to assume such responsibilities; and if they did marry, he was certain they would not receive her parents' benediction. Abigail claimed that it only mattered that they loved each other—she knew that in time her parents would come to realize that, and accept it. But he could see how torn she was over this notion of defying her parents, whom she loved dearly. Here was where they began to argue. Ezra was certain that to marry under such circumstances would eventually lead to disaster; soon enough she would regret such an impulsive decision and come to resent him. Yet his saying this only convinced her more of his love for her.

The last time she had seen him, in January, it was a raw, damp evening. It had been an unusually warm winter, but this only made the east wind off of the Atlantic all the more brutal. She had spent the afternoon at Rachel's house—it was the first time she'd seen their new baby boy—and on the walk home she paused at the canal which ran from the Mill Pond down to the harbor, separating the North End from the rest of the city. As was her habit, she stopped soon after crossing the footbridge to Ann Street. There was a stable, sided with weathered clapboards: tucked in an open knothole near the corner-board was a pebble. They called it the Egg.

It had been approaching five o'clock; nearly dark. Abigail looked up and down Ann Street, which was quiet, and then slipped down the alley, and behind the stable she came to an outbuilding. The door was ajar; she stepped inside and into Ezra's arms.

She raised her face to his and they kissed, but after a moment she leaned away so she could see his face in the dim light coming through the door. "What is it?"

"Nothing—" and he pulled her to him. His kiss this time was unlike any other. At first it confused her, but then it brought up her own heat. They fell back against the wall, which was hung with harnesses and tack. If anything, the smell of leather and horsehide only made them more ardent, to the point where Abigail began to laugh.

"You've made a decision—I sense it," she whispered.

He pressed his cheek to her forehead. "I have." He was holding her tightly, so tightly that it occurred to her that he might be afraid.

"Well, tell me," said.

"I—I can't. Not yet."

"Something's happened."

"Yes, something has happened, Abigail. It changes everything."

But she couldn't get it out of him. The more they kissed, the more she realized that he was desperate and distracted, that he was fearful. She'd never seen him afraid; never imagined that he could be afraid. His eyes, even in the near dark, seemed to be seeking acceptance from her, or perhaps some form of absolution. Or understanding, yet he would not say what it was that he wanted her to comprehend.

Now, gazing out her bedroom window, she recalled how she finally became angry with him. It was very confusing, those last few minutes. She must have expected him to fight back, and in doing so divulge what was tormenting him. He did neither. Worse than afraid, he seemed defeated. His last words before he left the outbuilding were "I hope you can forgive me one day." Then he was gone, his footsteps echoing off the stable walls as he walked up the alley to Ann Street.

She stopped often at the stable, looking for the pebble in the knothole. But the Egg wasn't there.

The knock at the door woke her and she had no idea how long she'd been asleep.

"Abigail?" her mother said.

"Yes?"

"Are you all right?"

"Of course."

"May I come in?" Before Abigail could answer, the latch was lifted and the door opened. Her mother came into the room, closed the door behind her. "I—I'm sorry." She couldn't look directly at Abigail.

"Come," Abigail said, sitting and arranging the pillows. Moving with difficulty, her mother sat next to her on the bed. Abigail took her frail hand in hers. "Cold," she said, rubbing the fingers.

"I must ask you," her mother hesitated. "Benjamin, he's always been closest to you. Ever since you were small, he would cling to you."

"I know. James was so much older, he was like a third parent. But Benjamin, he would often come and climb in bed with me at night, because of the cold or a storm."

"I'm so—have you any . . ."

"What, Mother?"

"Is there anything you're not telling us?"

"About Benjamin?" For a moment Abigail wanted to chastise her mother for such a suggestion, but then she realized it would be neither fair nor true. "No," she said. "I don't know anything."

"He's been a courier, hasn't he?" Abigail said nothing but the answer was obvious, and her mother squeezed her hand. "I knew it, Abigail."

"How did you know?"

Pulling her hand free of Abigail's, she said, "I am your mother, after all." She carefully turned and slid her legs off the bed. Standing, she said, "I worry about you, the way you wander the streets. Boston's no longer a safe place for a young woman—"

"Would you have me locked away here in this house?"

Her mother didn't answer, but went to the door.

"I will find him," Abigail said. "I will."

Her mother paused, her hand on the door latch. "It's the not knowing that is so terrible. Please, do be careful." She let herself out of the room.

VIII

Brothers in Arms

EZRA DETERMINED THAT HIS WOUND, THOUGH BLOODY, WAS
not serious. The musket ball had grazed his upper arm. He had
removed the leather string from his hair and told Benjamin to tie
it tightly above the wound, to slow the loss of blood. They walked
back to Cambridge, arriving in the early evening. A camp was
being established on the common, and the first few nights there
was a great amount of revelry, followed by complete exhaustion.
Each morning, when Benjamin awoke, he found himself among
several thousand provincials, sleeping in the grass or makeshift
tents and lean-tos. Being a doctor's apprentice, with surgical
experience, Ezra was immediately put to work in the field hospital. There was little order in the camp, and food and water were
scarce. Though there were some attempts at sharing among the
men, there was more likely suspicion and not a little theft. Men
bartered and traded. From one quarter of Cambridge Common
there would be song and festivity, while from another it would
be likely that fisticuffs would break out.

On Saturday, Benjamin was waiting outside the hospital tent when a hand suddenly gripped his shoulders. He turned and Dr. Warren said, "Ezra told me you and he were sharing a lean-to on the Common."

"Yes, sir."

"There is much disease among the men. You are getting enough to eat?"

"Sometimes Ezra visits his mother in Concord and brings back victuals."

"Very well. You stay close to him."

There was something peculiar about Dr. Warren. One portion of his wavy blond hair stuck out from the side of his head as though it had been snipped away abruptly. He raised a hand and tried to smooth it back against his ear, but it only curled out again. "Something in the air yesterday," he said with a smile.

"Sir?"

"Bullets."

"You were . . ."

"Shorn. Not shot, shorn. Yet another reason why we must seek our liberty." The doctor took Benjamin by the arm and guided him toward the shade of a maple tree. "I was quite concerned about you, Benjamin. You were instructed to return to my surgery and let me know if Mr. Dawes got through the gates at the Neck. What happened?"

Benjamin lowered his head.

"Were you detained?"

"Not exactly, sir."

Dr. Warren didn't say anything, and when Benjamin raised his head the doctor was eyeing him with suspicion. "I think I should be quite upset with you," he said. "You disobeyed an order."

Benjamin nodded. "It seemed there'd be some fighting, and I wanted to make myself . . . useful, sir."

Warren studied him a moment, and said sternly, "Forgiven, this once. But from now on, you do as I tell you."

"Yes, sir."

The doctor clutched Benjamin's shoulder as he nodded toward the Common. "There is hardly any semblance of order as yet, I know, but that will come. At this point no one knows really who is in command, what the orders are, and if there *are* orders they're not followed. There is much to the organization of an army that remains to be done." The doctor's sleeves were rolled up and his pale forearms were spattered with blood. Suddenly, he sat on the ground, and gestured for Benjamin to do the same. He appeared weary, exhausted, but seemed relieved to take a moment in the shade of a tree. "I can remain only a moment, for I have duties to attend to. Now listen to me, Benjamin. There will be much confusion. If you need anything, you come to me—we are setting up offices in Hastings House."

"Thank you, sir," Benjamin said. "I was wondering . . . when I might go back."

The doctor seemed not to understand, and then he said, "To Boston?"

"I can get across. Often I swim the Charles when the tide is right."

"Listen to me." Dr. Warren's eyes now seemed determined to hold Benjamin's attention. "I do not want you to attempt to get back into the city." Then he seemed to reconsider. "At least not for now. You've been one of my most reliable runners, and there may be a time when I might need you to go into Boston—but not until I say so, understand?"

"Yes, sir."

"Right now isn't the time. Dr. Church, much to our surprise, announced that he was returning and I expect that he's now being held in captivity. If he can get out of Boston, we're hoping he might bring some medical supplies. We're suffering a shortage of everything. And there's a great deal of illness developing among the men—no surprise under these conditions. I fear that it may reach epidemic proportions. Still, at the moment, it's safer for you here in Cambridge."

"If I returned, the redcoats would not bother with me, I suspect," Benjamin said. "Why did Dr. Church go back, if he knew he'd be captured?"

Dr. Warren smiled. It was the kind of smile Benjamin seemed to receive from adults all his life, one which that said that there are reasons and explanations for everything, and there is no point in your knowing them—you're too young.

"I don't understand," Benjamin said.

Dr. Warren got to his feet. When Benjamin began to do so, the doctor halted him by placing a hand on his shoulder. "You ask a fair question, Benjamin. I'm not certain of the answer, really, though in Dr. Church's case it may have to do with a woman." Now he appeared serious. "Do you have a girl, pining away for you in Boston?"

Benjamin felt caught and embarrassed, which only seemed to make Dr. Warren's stare even more indulgent.

"Does she have a name?"

"Mariah, sir."

"I see." The doctor pulled down on his waistcoat and tried once more, unsuccessfully, to tame the hair that stuck out from the side of his head. "Well, I suggest you keep your desires for Mariah in check, for the time being. You're both still quite young and will savor such sacrifice later."

"Sir?"

"Never mind. You stay close at hand here in Cambridge. That's an order. I will need runners."

When Abigail entered North Square, she saw a carriage stopped before the Reveres' house. Two soldiers were standing guard outside the front door, and as she approached the stoop one of the redcoats, a boy still in his teens, held his bayoneted musket across the entryway.

"If you please, state your business."

"My business is my own," she said. "In this case, it's to visit the Reveres' house, obviously. What is the purpose of your visit, soldier?"

He seemed confused by her challenge, and after exchanging glances with the other young redcoat, he said, "You may knock."

"I'm much obliged to you, sir, but that is my intention."

Abigail tapped the brass knocker, forged by Paul Revere himself, against the weathered plank door. While she waited, she studied the boy's face, which was thin and pale and appeared malnourished. He remained at attention, staring straight ahead into the square, but she could tell that her inspection was making him uncomfortable.

"I'll wager that you miss your home," she said at last. His eyelids fluttered and his cheeks became blotchy with color, but he was steadfast in his refusal to look at her. And after a moment she felt a pang of guilt, and said, "I beg your pardon. I'm sure you really do."

The boy seemed about to look at her, but the door opened and Rachel stepped out on the threshold, her infant son cradled in one arm. "I'm glad you're here."

"What's happened?" Abigail asked. "Why these guards?"

With her free hand Rachel took Abigail by the arm and drew her inside, kicking the door shut behind them. "We have word from Paul," she said, guiding Abigail through the house.

"But those soldiers, why—"

They entered the kitchen, and Abigail stopped. Benjamin Church, who was seated at the table, pushed back his chair and got to his feet. Today he was wearing a wig, and he bowed, saying, "Abigail, it's good to see you again."

"You went out of Boston, and have returned?"

"I am in the 'care' of General Gage himself," the doctor said. "He has allowed me some freedom of movement, though with an escort, as you see."

They sat at the table and Rachel skillfully poured Abigail a cup of tea while she balanced her sleeping son on her shoulder. "Dr. Church has brought word from Paul," she said. "He is safe."

"Yes," Benjamin Church said. "He acquitted himself brilliantly the night before the redcoats engaged the militia in Lexington and Concord. He rode through the countryside sounding the alarm, and at one point he was captured by several British officers, only to elude them and outrun them on horseback. There were numerous riders alerting the towns, but at dawn Paul found himself in Lexington, where he warned John Hancock and Sam Adams that they needed to flee before the British expedition arrived. They got away from Lexington just in time, with his assistance, and I understand that as the militia faced off against the redcoats, Paul and another patriot were carrying Hancock's trunk out of the village."

Abigail glanced at Rachel, who was smiling proudly, and then she looked back at the doctor. "A trunk?"

"A trunk containing papers belonging to Adams and Hancock," Benjamin Church said. "If those documents had fallen into the hands of the British, there's no knowing what damage could have been done. By now, they should be on their way to the Continental Congress in Philadelphia."

"I see."

"John Hancock, a true patriot, though he tends to complicate matters." Benjamin Church ran a hand back over his wig, and for the briefest moment he seemed on the verge of a smile. "Hancock's one of the wealthiest men in Boston—inherited money, you know—and he can be . . . an irritant. Evidently, he's traveling not just with Sam Adams, but they're also accompanied by his fiancée *and* her mother. And in the midst of battle there was some business about a fish, a rather good-sized salmon, I understand, which in their haste to depart Lexington they had left behind. I'm not certain, but I believe Hancock sent Paul back in harm's way to retrieve their dinner."

"Which he did?" Abigail asked.

"Admirably so, I'm sure," the doctor said. "Really, it would be better if Hancock were on the other side. Of course, there have been times when he has exhibited a tendency to . . . sway. As for the fish—no one knows what became of that salmon."

Abigail hadn't touched her teacup. Her brother was missing and the doctor was telling a story about a fish. Benjamin Church seemed to avoid her eyes, which she found perplexing. And yet there was always this sense that he was watching her, waiting for some indication from her. Of what, she was not certain. "Doctor, please tell me. Have you any word about my younger brother? We've not heard from Benjamin since you and Dr. Warren sent him to the Neck with William Dawes. Do you have any idea what's become of him?"

Warily, it seemed, Church stared at her now and said, "None, I'm afraid. Under these circumstances, people go missing—first my apprentice, Ezra, and now your brother. You might say they are lost to a cause." He glanced at Rachel a moment. "But consider the alternative, remaining together under the yoke of tyranny."

"True," Rachel said, "there's no safety in that."

Church straightened up in his chair, as though he were attempting to show resolve by example. "I can tell you both that thousands of men have gathered and encamped outside the city. More are arriving every day. I trust the men you care about—Ezra, Benjamin, and Paul—are among them, and that they're in good company. Where this is headed and how long this will go on, it's impossible to say."

"Yes, we are now under siege," Abigail said. "It's quite remarkable that you reentered Boston."

"Someone had to," Church said.

"You might have been shot on sight," Rachel said. "Or hanged."

"We must all accept risks," he said. "I am in custody, though I'm afforded a certain cordiality and latitude. And I will be allowed to leave the city again in order to conduct General Gage's response to Dr. Warren regarding the evacuation that's about to begin. It will surely make for difficulties, but it's important that both sides maintain the ability to communicate."

"Of course." Rachel patted her son's back as she looked at Abigail. "Paul has requested that I send him socks and linen. But what he really needs is money, and I'm going to send it out to him, through Dr. Church. One hundred and twenty-five pounds."

"A hundred and twenty-five?" Abigail said. *"Pounds?"*

"I know," Rachel said. "It's a goodly sum, but there's no knowing how long he'll have to stay out in the country. Paul's mother has gone to relatives to seek their assistance."

Dr. Church got to his feet. "I shouldn't keep my escort waiting too long. They get suspicious, you understand. I would be happy to convey the money to your husband, but we must make the transaction quickly because I will have leave Boston soon—tomorrow."

"Paul's mother should return by evening," Rachel said. "I'll have it by tonight."

"Excellent," Church said, but then he hesitated. "But I'm not sure I will be allowed to return here again."

"I see . . ." Rachel said, exasperated.

Abigail said, "I suppose that I could deliver it for you."

"That would best," Rachel said.

Now Benjamin Church stared directly at Abigail. "And perhaps you might bring it to my surgery tomorrow morning?"

"Certainly," she said.

"I regret to make such a request of you on the Sabbath, but I expect I'll depart for the country by midday."

"I understand, Doctor," Abigail said.

He gave the slightest bow and then left the kitchen.

Rachel got up and said to the doctor, "I'll see you out." She brought the baby around the table and handed him to Abigail.

Swaddled in his blanket, the child conformed easily to Abigail's shoulder, and the top of his warm head rested against her cheek.

He had recently been bathed, for the fine hair that brushed lightly against her skin held the faintest smell of lye soap.

When Rachel returned to the kitchen, she cast an assessing eye upon Abigail. "That baby is fast asleep in your arms. Usually, he'd be wailing by now. You hold him for a spell—you need the practice."

"Stop."

Rachel grinned as she went to the kitchen door. "Come with me."

They went out into the dooryard, attracting a flock of chickens, and crossed the yard to Paul's workshop, next to the stable. Inside the workshop were a forge and a large stone chimney, and along one wall stood a workbench fitted with several anvils and blocks, above which hung the tools of a silversmith: clamps, hammers, pliers, saws, chisels, awls. Rachel took a small wooden box down from a shelf and placed it on the workbench; then she got a crock from another shelf. After removing the lid, she took out a wad of paper money. Slowly, she peeled off bills and smoothed them out on the bench.

"We will need more," she said. "Paul's mother believes she can raise at least fifty."

She opened the wooden box, which contained a quill, an inkpot, and a sheaf of foolscap. Finally, when she had every-thing laid out, she regarded Abigail for a long moment. "I see the way he—"

"What are you saying?"

"Dr. Church—I see the way he avoids looking at you, as though he's afraid to give himself away."

"What do you mean?"

"You were courted by his apprentice, and something went wrong there, am I right?" After a moment, Rachel smiled. "You're so tight-lipped. I'm now an old married woman, but I still have an eye for these things. What happened between you and Ezra—"

"Nothing."

"I see. All that trysting, and it comes to nothing. Things didn't go a bit too far?"

"Rachel—"

"*Ha!* Are you blushing because it's none of my business, or because I'm right?" Before Abigail could answer, Rachel said, "Doesn't matter whether I'm right or not, though, does it? What matters is what the good Doctor Benjamin Church thinks." She suddenly laughed. "These older men—I married one of them, remember? They get on the scent and then they circle."

"What do you take me for?"

"Quarry! Ah now, that cuts you to the quim, doesn't it!"

"You're despicable—"

"Indeed I am," Rachel said, delighted. Then she whispered, "You do understand that Dr. Church has a wife?"

"Yes, I've heard this is so."

"Yet she is a woman seldom seen, mind you." Rachel took up the quill and dipped its point into the inkpot. "But this *other,* she can be quite public and extravagant in her ways."

"What other?"

Rachel ignored the question and commenced to write on the foolscap. There was only the sound of the quill scratching across the page. She worked slowly, leaning to her task. When she paused to dip the quill again, she said, "I'm obliged to you for taking this money to his house, but I'm afeared, too."

"Rachel, be plain."

"Plainly, he keeps another woman. But then this is not so uncommon in Boston." Rachel glanced up from her work and light from the window cut across her face, illuminating her right eye. "Even your own brother, James—before he was married, he kept that woman, right? She was somewhat older, I understand, and she had a son, which she took with her to—where was it?"

Abigail sighed. "New York."

119

"New York, yes, a city full of Boston bastards, it is. But at least your brother's the well-bred kind and I'll bet he sends her a regular assistance."

"I wouldn't know," Abigail said. "It was years ago."

"I wouldn't know," Rachel mimicked. "It was years ago."

"It's not my business, anyway."

"*There* you go, love. Mind your own business." Rachel laughed again. "They're like a bad tooth, men. The ache never quite goes away."

She continued to compose her letter, and Abigail said nothing. The baby's arms and legs struggled within the blanket, and she softly patted his back. When Rachel was finished, she laid the quill back in the box and took out a small bottle; after removing the cork, she sprinkled sand on the ink.

Rachel picked up the piece of paper, bent it so that she could pour the sand back in the bottle, and then laid the sheet on the bench in front of Abigail. "Tell me, schoolmaster's daughter, does this suffice?"

> *My dear, by Doct'r Church I send a hundred & twenty-five pounds & beg you will take the best care of yourself & not attempt coming into this towne again & if I have an opportunity of coming or sending out any of the children I shall do it. Pray keep up your spirits & trust yourself & us in the Hands of a good God who will take care of us. Tis all my dependence, for vain is the help of man. Adieu my Love.*
>
> *From your Affectionate R. Revere*

"It's fine," Abigail said.

"Now," Rachel said, counting the wad of notes on the bench. "I hope Mother returns with the rest of the money. Please come by in the morning, the earlier the better, I think. You will do me a great kindness in conveying this to Dr. Church. I don't wish to put you in harm's way, but—"

"I'm glad to help, Rachel." The baby, nestled against Abigail's neck, began to stir and whimper.

"Seriously," Rachel said, putting a hand on Abigail's cheek. "I don't know what I'd do without you. I would miss you so." Her eyes suddenly grew large, brimming with tears.

"Rachel, if you could get the children out of Boston, would you go?"

Nodding, her tears ran down her cheeks. "It's *you* who are despicable. That's the question, all right. Their father is out there," Rachel said as she lifted the baby off Abigail's shoulder. "The thought of leaving Boston frightens me so. It is all I've ever known." Unbuttoning her dress, she eased her son's mouth to her breast. "But then if we stay here," she said, "what would happen to us?"

Abigail walked home, pausing several times in doorways to wait out an intermittent spring shower. When she entered School Street, there was a redcoat standing outside the door of her house, speaking to her mother; it wasn't Lumley, so Abigail approached as the young soldier walked off down the street.

"My dear, we are honored," her mother said when Abigail reached the stoop, "so many messages from the British command." Though she claimed to be a staunch supporter of her husband's political views, her comments to Abigail were at times rather sarcastic in tone, and she spoke them as though they shared a carefully guarded secret. "Now we have two—imagine, two in one afternoon! I look forward to the day when King George addresses us directly." She led Abigail into the house.

"Two?" Abigail said, removing her damp shawl and hanging it on a wall peg.

"Earlier, General Gage sent a request that your father attend a meeting at Province House tomorrow. He's sending round a coach!" In the vestibule she handed Abigail a folded letter, sealed in wax. "And this just arrived for you, my dear. Far be it for me to

inquire as to who is sending missives to my fair young daughter."
She walked down the hall toward the kitchen.

Abigail went into the parlor and, standing by the window, she
broke the seal and opened the letter.

April 22, 1775
My Dear Miss Lovell,

*I am most grateful for your company the other night and
only hope that I did not appear to be too much engrossed in
the current events that have beleaguered you Bostonians. If it
is not too Impertinent, nor too great an imposition, I wonder
if we might meet again, for it would be a great benefit for
this weary Soldier to bask for even a few minutes in Your
Gentile Presence. However, the purpose of this request is not
entirely selfish (though it is that, to be sure), in that I have,
after making some discreet Inquiries, obtained information
regarding the subjects we discussed, which I would very much
like to convey to you personally. If this Proposition is agree-
able to you, I would appreciate your meeting me this evening
at the same time and place as before.*

Your Humble Servant,
Colonel Samuel Cleaveland

Abigail folded up the letter and went into the kitchen.

"Let me guess," her mother said, standing before the fireplace, where she leaned over the large cauldron, wooden ladle
in hand. "You won't be staying for supper. And we're having
haddock, one of your favorites. You're off, God knows where,
and I do worry—"

"Mother, I am not about to lock myself away in this house, no
matter how many of the king's soldiers are sent to guard over us."

"The soldiers, I presume," her mother said, "are here to protect us."

"From what, ourselves?"

"Precisely." Her father, seated at the table by the window, did not look up from his book.

"I just worry about her safety," Mother said.

Father removed his clay pipe and said, "She's meeting a gentleman, an officer, I gather." When he looked up at Abigail, he smiled. "Who else would send a Regular with a letter?"

"If that is so, then it follows that you need not worry about my safety." Abigail turned and started back down the hall toward the stairs. "I must change before I go out."

"Precisely," her father called. "Tomorrow afternoon I'm away to Province House and I will expect you to accompany me."

"Why, John?" Mother asked.

"That's where she'll meet the finest British officers, and we want them to see her, what a gem she is." Raising his voice, he said, "Displaying her before such promising company is a loving father's obligation, you realize." He waited. Abigail began climbing the stairs. "Perhaps I must send my own daughter an invitation by courier?"

Abigail paused on the landing and thought of Margaret Kemble Gage, dressed in fine raiment as she stood in the window of Province House. "No, Father," she called down the stairs. "I would be honored to accompany you."

"Praise be to the Lord!" her father shouted. And then he laughed—too seldom, Abigail realized, did her father do so. "We'll make a respectable Tory out of our daughter yet!"

At dusk, Abigail arrived at the Two Salutations, only to find a soldier, standing by a chaise, who approached her eagerly.

"Miss Lovell?"

"Yes?"

"Colonel Cleaveland regrets that he has been detained." The boy gestured toward the chaise. "So he has asked that I drive you to a suitable meeting place."

"Where might that be?"

"The Common, Miss."

"I see," she said. "All right, then."

The soldier helped her into the chaise and then climbed onto the bench, where he took up the reins. He drove through the streets as the lamps were being lit for the evening. When they arrived at the Common, the chaise stopped at the north end of the Mall, a lane that was bordered by a row of budding maples. Colonel Cleaveland was standing beneath one of the first trees, a basket leaning against the base of the trunk. He stepped forward and offered his hand as Abigail climbed down from the chaise.

"I appreciate your coming." He saw Abigail glance toward the basket, and said, "The truth is I found our meeting in the tavern a bit confining. It's a beautiful evening after the rain, so I thought we might have something to eat here by the Mall, followed by a stroll. I've been in Boston long enough to understand that a constitutional is one of the great pleasures of this city."

"It is, Colonel," Abigail said, looking down the empty lane that ran between the rows of maples. "But, as you can see, the current circumstances are keeping most Bostonians from partaking of such pleasures."

"So we have it to ourselves," he said smiling. "And perhaps by example we might encourage others to venture out of doors." When she didn't respond, he asked, "Would you prefer to eat first? Or would you like to walk?"

She glanced back toward the chaise, where the young soldier was strapping a feedbag about the horse's head. "Walk," she said.

"I agree. Food tastes better after exercise." The colonel took her arm and they started down the gravel path. "Could I also make a small request?"

"What would that be, Colonel?"

"It's that exactly—'Colonel.' I realize much has changed in the past few days, and that in everything one must start anew. But I would appreciate it if you would at least call me Samuel."

After a moment, she said, "Yes. That would be all right."

"Thank you." He glanced at her as though to make sure he hadn't taken too great a liberty. "Thank you, Abigail. I walk here often, actually. It's the open field dotted with grazing cows, I think, as well as these splendid trees. All this space reminds me of my family's pastures in Surrey."

"Where exactly is Surrey?"

"South of London. We have a townhouse there, of course, but I prefer the farm, and I look forward to the day when I can return there. Raise cattle, breed horses, hunt and fish, that sort of thing. So I'm thankful for this Common, particularly on a night like this when the air is fresh after the rain."

"I've lived a short walk from this Common my entire life," Abigail said. "I've always loved to come here, but since I was a child there's always been something dark and dangerous about this open space."

"How so?"

"It's the history of Boston." She pointed toward a lone elm tree on a knoll. "That's the Great Elm," she said. "Witches were hanged there. Children still believe their spirits roam the Common. And after the witches came Quakers, and then Baptists. The Puritans held tight rein over this town for generations, showing little tolerance for deviance."

"And now we redcoats are here, new oppressors. In the eyes of Bostonians, we're the hangmen." She glanced at him, but he was looking up at the trees arching overhead. "I don't like this role," he said. "It doesn't suit me, but I am here to do my duty." When she didn't respond, he said, "Not always a pleasant task, duty."

"No, I'm sure it isn't."

"This siege, it will take its toll on all of us." With his free arm he gestured toward the trees ahead of them. "You know there's a committee of officers who are responsible for providing wood."

"Wood?"

"To burn," he said. "Now that General Gage finds his army trapped on this peninsula, unable to venture out into the countryside, there's great concern about these things—wood, to fire the ovens that provide meals for our men in the barracks."

"The Mall trees?"

"It's a possibility. They're drawing up a list."

"A list?"

"Historically, the state of siege is a long, drawn-out, withering affair. Essential practicalities have to be taken into account. If the siege of Boston continues, say, beyond the summer, then there will be the problem of providing sufficient heat through the winter."

"You think it will last that long?"

"No one knows. Cities under siege often languish for years. The trees will be exhausted in due course, so other sources of fuel have to be found."

Abigail freed her arm from his gentle grip and stopped walking. "What other sources are there? What has your committee put on this list?"

"It's not *my* committee, Abigail. These matters don't concern me directly. I'm in charge of artillery." Yet he faced her, his hands clasped behind his back, as though he was prepared for a reprimand. "It's not my decision, but you can understand that in time the necessity will arise."

She took a step back in the direction of the chaise, but then turned to him again. "I want to know what is on this list."

"I don't know all the particulars, and I don't believe anything has been determined with certainty yet—"

"Colonel Cleaveland."

He was clearly surprised at how sharply she had spoken, and whispered, "Churches."

Abigail couldn't look at his face, and for a moment studied the gold buttons on his uniform. *"Churches?"*

"I'm afraid so."

"Pews, perhaps," she said. "And I know that there have been instances where metal has been removed from churches for the purpose of making shot. The organ pipes in a church over to Charlestown, they were torn out and melted down. So is that it? General Gage would have the pews removed from our churches for firewood?"

"No." He waited until she raised her eyes to his. "Churches, Abigail. They will tear them down."

"Tear them *down?*"

"Board by board."

"Which ones?"

"As I said, that has not yet been determined with certainty."

She looked up at the budding branches overhead. The small pale green maple leaves were luminescent in the last light of day. "If you know anything about Bostonians, you will know that we consider these trees as sacred as our churches."

"I do know," he said. "I really do. God's wood."

She began walking quickly, back in the direction of the chaise, repulsed by his sincerity as much as by the idea that Boston could become so barren of wood. He strode alongside her, his hands still clasped behind his back. "I'm really sorry to upset you. That wasn't my intention. I was only, only being truthful."

"Truthful," she said, without looking at him. "You said you would inquire about my brother Benjamin. Have you learned anything?"

"Nothing, I'm afraid. I can only tell you that he is not in any of our prisons."

"Thank you! Thank you, Colonel, for putting my mind at rest."

But sarcasm couldn't suppress her sudden anger. "My brother has gone missing, and in an effort to be of assistance you make inquiries regarding prison inmates. Logical, perhaps, but you do see why such logic can be so disconcerting."

"I was merely trying to help, Abigail."

She walked even faster, leaving him behind, though she could hear his boots quickening. "I suggest, *Colonel,* that you get thee back to your farmhouse in . . . Surrey. You have no duty in Boston." She passed the tree with the basket of food, passed the chaise and the young soldier, who was stroking the horse's nose as he watched them with interest, and when she heard the colonel's boots finally drag in the gravel and come to a halt, she picked up her skirts and began to run for home.

IX
Fog

SUNDAY MORNING, ABIGAIL DRESSED FOR CHURCH BUT DECLINED to accompany her parents to the service at Old South, claiming that she would instead attend at Old North with Rachel and her children. This naturally brought objections from her father, but her mother saw the importance of giving succor to a woman with a houseful of children and suddenly no husband. Abigail promised to return home before one o'clock, in time to accompany her father to Province House.

She walked to Rachel's house, collected the letter and the hundred and twenty-five pounds, all wrapped in a small leather satchel, which she carried through the streets beneath her good Sunday cape. Overnight the wind had turned easterly and raw, bringing salty fog in off the harbor. When she arrived at Dr. Church's townhouse, an elderly maid admitted her to a drawing room, where she waited for several minutes. She could hear voices in the adjacent room, Dr. Church's and a woman's; he sounded harried, and the woman seemed more than a little put out. When he finally entered the drawing room he was wearing his vest, with his shirt collar open. He was clearly distracted.

"Forgive me, Abigail. I'm preparing to depart and there are so many preparations that I'm—but, please, can I have Mrs. McColl bring you tea?"

"No, thank you, Doctor." Abigail handed him the satchel. "I only came to deliver this from Rachel Revere, as we planned."

He appeared confused. "I didn't really expect her to find the money."

"You will see Mr. Revere?"

"I expect so. He may be off doing out-of-doors work for the Committee of Safety, but he'll return to Cambridge in a few days, I'm sure." When he saw that she was confused, he added, "These express rides he takes to the other provinces, we often refer to it as 'out-of-doors work.'" He attempted a smile, but it faded as they both could hear the woman's voice in the next room, where she was sharply reprimanding someone, most likely the maid, Mrs. McColl.

"I see," Abigail said. "Well, I understand that you're busy and I shouldn't keep you."

A door slammed somewhere in the back of the house.

Benjamin Church was now truly alarmed. "Please, will you give me a minute?"

"I should go and leave you to your preparations."

"No, please—I'll be right back." He went out into the hall and Abigail listened to his footsteps rush through the house.

She sat down and minutes passed. There was, she realized, something about the room that was lacking; there was no evidence of a wife's care, nor was there anything really personal, such as a framed portrait. Only a small painting hung above the mantelpiece, depicting cows grazing by a stream.

Suddenly, outside there was the clatter of horses' hooves. Abigail went to a window that looked out at a drive that ran along the side of the house to the street. A carriage entered the drive but halted at the back corner of the house. Abigail couldn't see well, as she was looking through glass at such an angle that the whorls and imperfections distorted her view. Clearly, the man who approached the carriage was Dr. Church—his arms were folded against the chill air. Abigail caught a glimpse of a woman in the carriage but only enough to assume that she was wearing an ample wig. They spoke for a minute, and then the carriage came down the drive, and as it passed the window Abigail saw a woman's hand, wearing a white glove, resting on the window.

Reluctantly, Abigail sat down again and waited. She wanted to leave, but to do so would be impolite. Finally, Dr. Church returned to the drawing room.

"Please forgive me," he said. "I'm so preoccupied."

"Not at all," she said, standing.

"You see it has been arranged that I may safely leave the city with a quantity of medication, with the understanding that it will be used to the benefit of captured soldiers who are injured, as well as provincials."

"That is most considerate."

"General Gage is that," the doctor said. "Quite so, for an adversary."

"Is he?" She stared at him a long moment. "That's—interesting to know. I'm to accompany my father to Province House this afternoon, in fact."

"Really?"

"Yes. There's a meeting between the general and representatives of the city."

"Well . . ." Dr. Church looked about the room as though he were trying to find something. Suddenly, he took a step toward her and said, "Abigail, I—you may have heard, or perhaps you will hear things about me, about the way I conduct my affairs, and I want you to know that I . . ." He seemed to give up, at a loss for words, until finally he said, "Just know I have always held the greatest affection for . . . for you."

Awkwardly, he extended his hand and she took it. There was something about the way he said *you*. He didn't seem to be referring to her—or to her alone. She wasn't sure to whom he was referring, and when he released her hand she turned away quickly and walked to the front door. He accompanied her, and they said goodbye, though she didn't look at him again as she stepped out into the fogbound street.

Exactly at one o'clock, a coach and four, accompanied by a small detail of soldiers, arrived in front of the house. It was a well-appointed vehicle, and while they traveled the short distance to Province House Abigail had the distinct impression that her father was solemn—they might have been on the way to a funeral.

"It should never have come to this," he said, gazing out his window. "There is a reason for authority and order, and by challenging it Bostonians could very likely destroy their own city."

"If that authority is unjust, Father, why not challenge it?"

He smiled and said, "Fog's in."

"Don't treat me as though I were some pet kitten that can't possibly understand."

She turned and stared out her window, refusing to gaze at him during the remainder of the trip.

When they arrived at Province House, they were assisted from the coach by footmen and entered the governor-general's mansion by the front door. The lobby was elegant, the furniture of fine polished wood and luxurious fabrics. At least two dozen Boston men were present, all Tories, and perhaps twice as many members of General Gage's staff, including Colonel Cleaveland, who made no attempt to acknowledge Abigail's presence. There were other women, most of them wives of some of Boston's representatives. After some initial mingling in the lobby, the men were sequestered in a room, the double doors closed behind them, while the women were ushered into a vast living room which had walls lined with enormous portraits and a grand piano at one end. Tea was served by a fleet of maids, and the Boston women gathered in small groups and talked quietly. Abigail took her tea and stood at a window where she could look across the courtyard at the stable.

When Mrs. Gage came into the room, all the women got to their feet and curtsied. She was famous for her wardrobe, and Abigail had never seen such satin gloss. Her hair was wrapped in a silk turban which today was the deepest blue imaginable. She spent time talking with various groups of women and finally came down to the end of the room where Abigail had remained, staring out the window.

"And you are Master Lovell's daughter, I understand."

"Yes, Ma'am." Abigail curtsied. "I'm not sure why I'm here."

"Of course you are," Mrs. Gage said. She had a direct gaze that was unsettling; it seemed to place added significance to every word she spoke. "Your father wants to display you before the officers under my husband's charge." She looked Abigail up and down. "My dear, when this meeting concludes, you should prepare yourself for a stampede of men in uniform, vying for your attention." She glanced out the window a moment, and then said quietly, "But this is not your first visit to Province House, I believe. Our groom Seth tells me you were here not long ago."

"Yes, Ma'am."

Mrs. Gage sighed. "I won't miss much of what Boston has offered. You must realize I seldom escape this house. Yet a pretty prison it has been, and I'm particularly fond of the orchard and the stables. I'm from Pennsylvania, and my father raised horses."

"Excuse me, Mrs. Gage, are you leaving Boston?"

Now she stared at Abigail so long, it seemed she was unable to answer, until she said, "I had hoped to return to Pennsylvania, but with the fear that hostilities may eventually engulf all the colonies—well, it's simply out of the question. American-born though I may be, my husband insists that I sail to England. I get out of prison, so to speak, though this may be a more severe form

of punishment, as my loyalties have of late been called into question." She smiled weakly. "American-born, as I said."

Abigail didn't know what to say. Most disarming was the fact
that Mrs. Gage continued to smile as she gazed out the window.
And then there was a commotion in the lobby as the men
adjourned their meeting.

Turning to Abigail, Mrs. Gage touched her hand for a moment.
"You will give my regards to your brother James?"

"Of course, Ma'am."

"Now I must see to the punch." Then Mrs. Gage moved
toward the dining room, where a buffet had been laid out. A boy,
not more than thirteen, dressed in a blue satin jacket and breeches,
sat at the piano and began playing.

The rooms became quite festive, as though they were gathered
to celebrate some momentous occasion, a wedding or a christening.
Abigail fixed her father a plate and when she brought it to him, he
was engaged in a conversation about the evacuation process that
was just beginning. It had been confirmed that Bostonians sympathetic to the rebel cause would be granted safe passage to the
country, and likewise Tories out in the villages would be allowed
to enter the city, where they would remain under the protection
of the British army. During the meeting, General Gage had apparently been very clear that the homes of those who departed the
city would be shuttered so as to not suffer any undue harm. Father
expressed support for this endeavor, arguing that no matter what
happened in the countryside, Boston would remain a bastion for
loyalists, who inevitably would be rewarded for remaining true
to the king. The men he was talking with were in full agreement, though one man, a Mr. Alsmire, said that from his house
on Copp's Hill he could see that British soldiers were beginning
to construct a redoubt facing northwest across the water. Some
officers, quite disrespectfully, he noted, were using gravestones
on the hill for target practice. Charlestown to the north, another
man said, and Dorchester to the south—that's where the damned

provincials are gathering their forces, and General Gage must do everything possible to protect Boston. Once the militia gains a foothold in those hills, they will be able to bombard portions of the city mercilessly. Another man, Joseph Towle, whose merchant ships had long been confined to port, said that supplies would become scarce—even if General Gage lifted the ban on commerce, vessels trying to leave the harbor could be bombed and sunk. To which another said in disgust that the provincials had neither the forces nor the armaments to threaten Boston. He had heard that the bonfires that could now be seen burning on the hills of Dorchester and Charlestown were just that, bonfires, tended by only small, ill-equipped bands of men who lacked both discipline and leadership.

Abigail politely excused herself and drifted into the dining room, where a maid was taking an empty glass punchbowl into the kitchen. When Abigail opened the swinging door for her, the woman said, "These meetings, you know, there's no end to their thirst."

Across the kitchen, Abigail could see out a window to the courtyard. Colonel Cleaveland was walking toward the stable; he was smoking a cigar and as he disappeared inside, he left a trail of smoke to mingle with the fog.

Abigail went through the kitchen, which was bustling with cooks, scullions, and servants, and found a door that opened onto the courtyard. She crossed to the stable, her arms folded against the cold, and upon entering the stable she was startled to find Cleaveland leaning against the first stall, one foot angled up so his boot heel rested on the gate. Her surprise was not that he was there, of course, but it had something to do with his attitude. He seemed overwrought and leaned against the wood gate as though he'd been pushed by some invisible force. For the first time she thought she could actually see him despite his uniform. He was a young man, far from home, serving in capacities not of his choosing and certainly not to his liking. When he had said yesterday that he was only trying to help, she realized he was being sincere. Prison *was* the first logical place to look for her brother. What he was telling her was that if Benjamin wasn't in a prison cell, then most likely he was free—free in a way that Samuel himself was not. His prison was the tight-fitting uniform, the red coat with gold lapel and epaulets, and buttons, so many brass buttons. She tried to imagine him out of uniform, dressed as though he were home in Surrey. There, he would be a man at ease, wearing the loose, drab attire of a country gentleman, and she imagined him wandering the fields, a walking stick in hand, accompanied by a good dog.

As she approached, he glanced up at her, and then gazed at the floor again.

"Samuel," she said.

He removed the cigar from his mouth, exhaling smoke. "So, we're still on a first-name basis?" He smiled as he continued to look at the dirt floor and then stuck the cigar back in his mouth.

"I feel I should apologize. I behaved—I was unfair last night." She waited but he didn't respond, didn't look up at her. "You were right, Samuel. You were only being truthful. It was what you said—about the trees on the Mall, about our churches—it was such a shock. I realize now that you were only informing me of—"

He raised his head, speaking around the cigar. "Running away is the smartest thing you can do. You're very smart, as bright as you are pretty, and you're wise to get as far away from me as possible." He took his foot off the gate and stood up straight, giving her the impression that he was preparing to make a statement that would be definitive and final. "One piece of advice, Miss Lovell." He dropped the cigar on the dirt floor and crushed it out with his boot, carefully, thoroughly, making sure that it had been shredded, its heat extinguished. "Leave Boston. Your father is a prominent loyalist but he should remove his entire family during this evacuation. Leave Massachusetts. New England will burn."

"He won't go."

"He said as much during our meeting. He may be master at the Latin School, well versed, but he's a damned fool, believe me. He thinks he's being . . . stalwart, brave even." Then he raised his voice, and said, "Your father should not remain in Boston."

"Leaving our home is out of the question," she said. "He won't—"

"Then *you* convince him."

"We are at odds most of the time. I can never convince him of anything."

"I doubt that." His voice was not just loud but angry, and a number of horses stirred in their stalls. Then, quietly, he said, "I doubt that very much." He looked as though he regretted speaking his mind at all.

To her own surprise, Abigail stepped toward him, throwing her arms up around his shoulders, and, bringing her face up to his, she kissed him hard on the mouth. He didn't move, didn't respond at first, but then suddenly he embraced her tightly and together they fell against the stall gate, as he covered her face and neck with kisses.

When they finally let go of each other, they were embarrassed. As she fixed her hair, she glanced at him and he appeared boyishly chagrined. They walked slowly down the length of the stable, passing stalls where horses hung their heads over the gates, some eying them with hope, others with suspicion. She stopped at the last stall. There was a gray, an old horse. As she stroked its soft nose, warm air pushing out of its nostrils, Samuel stood behind her, his arms around her waist.

"I'm afraid I spoiled a perfectly good picnic last night," she said.

At the far end of the stable there was the sound of footsteps. The light was so dim, Abigail couldn't see who it was—only that it was a man, striding toward the open door. Samuel quickly moved away from her, took her by the hand, and guided her out a door next to the stall. The chill fog was a startling antidote to the warm, horse-tinged air of the stable. They walked swiftly, arm in arm now, into an orchard, beneath rows of trees that seemed poised to lower their limbs, draw them in, and conceal them.

They sat on a bench deep in the orchard, surrounded by fog that smelled of the sea. She was chilled, and he removed his red jacket and draped it over her shoulders. They didn't talk for a while. Something had changed, something had opened up, and Abigail preferred the silence, broken occasionally by the caw of a seagull.

Finally, she said, "I appreciate your making inquiries regarding my brother. But I believe that last night you were going to tell me about Corporal Lumley, as well."

"I had planned to, yes. Why did you ask about him?" He leaned forward and rested his elbows on his knees. "I barely know him, but made some inquiries and it appears he's been in a spot of difficulty. The usual thing, I gather. We have too many Regulars who drink a great deal of your New England rum, and, of course, there's the matter of women. He's known to obtain the services of prostitutes. He hasn't made any advances toward you?"

"No."

"But there's something else, which I don't understand and must look into further—"

"What's that?"

"There's Munroe, the sergeant he was on patrol with when that incident occurred in Dock Square. I met with him yesterday and his responses weren't altogether satisfactory." He glanced at her. "There's something he was trying to tell me, about Lumley, but—the men, they usually keep mum about each other because it doesn't go down well if it becomes common knowledge that they've been spouting off to their superiors, that's not good. But it seems that Munroe and Lumley had some falling out. Munroe said, in effect, that Lumley wasn't to be trusted. That's the best I could make of it. But, you see, you can't trust most of them. By and large they're a miserable lot. Most of them don't want to be here. There's a reason why General Gage insists that we maintain stiff discipline. The first sign that men aren't following orders, we look for an example."

"But Lumley hasn't done anything—"

"Not that I know of. Is there something you're not telling me?"

"No," she said. "He just seems, I don't know, curious."

"I'd keep clear of his sort."

"That, Colonel, is hard to do. We are occupied, you know."

Cleaveland said no more, and after a moment he got to his feet. "I should get you back. Don't want your father to think you disappeared in the fog."

They began walking through the orchard, Province House looming faintly above the trees. Abigail removed his coat and handed it to him. When he took it, he stopped, pulled it on, but then gathered her in his arms and kissed her again, gently. "We might try another picnic?"

"All right," she said.

When they emerged from the orchard, they found that carriages and chaises had lined up in the courtyard as the general's guests were preparing to leave. Abigail squeezed Samuel's arm, smiled up at him, and then waded into the crowd to search for her father.

PART TWO

May: The Siege

There are but very few who are permitted to
come out in a day; they delay giving passes, make
them wait from hour to hour . . . One day, their
household furniture is to come out; the next,
only wearing apparel; the next, Pharaoh's heart
is hardened, and he refuseth to hearken to them,
and will not let the people go.

—Abigail Adams

From a plentiful town we were reduced to the
disagreeable necessity of living on salt provisions,
and fairly blocked up in Boston.

—Ensign de Berniere,
British Soldier

X

Tea and Sympathetic Ink

AS HE HAD IN BOSTON, DR. WARREN MADE USE OF BENJAMIN as a currier. Every day he came and went from Hastings House, which was becoming the seat of the provincial government. Often for Benjamin it was a matter of idling away hours, waiting for meetings behind closed doors to conclude, but there were also times when the doctor or one of his colleagues would summon him and give him a correspondence that had to be delivered quickly. He often ran, though occasionally he was given the use of a horse.

One rainy afternoon, Dr. Warren called Benjamin into his chambers in Hastings House. He found the doctor alone, lying on a daybed staring out a window. "This weather isn't helping the condition of our men," Dr. Warren said.

"I suppose not, sir."

"Still interested in slipping into Boston?"

"Yes, sir."

Dr. Warren turned from the window. He suffered from frequent and severe headaches. Though he was an unusually pale man with delicate features, his eyes appeared weary from enduring intense pain. He had a small writing board on his lap, his quill standing in the inkpot on the windowsill, and there were several sealed envelopes lying on the floor. With some effort, he gathered them up and held them out to Benjamin.

"You mentioned swimming across the Charles, but these must be kept dry."

"I will find a boat."

For a moment the doctor massaged his forehead. "You are to convey these to your brother James. He will give you instructions from there."

"Yes, Doctor. I'll leave immediately and should make Boston after dark."

Dr. Warren gazed up at Benjamin a moment, as his fingers continued to knead his brow. "If you are stopped by the British, they can't get those." He nodded toward the letters as Benjamin tucked them in the pocket of his coat. "Better you destroy them, if it comes to that. Understand?"

"Yes, sir." Dr. Warren did not appear fully convinced. "I will find two small flat stones on the shore," Benjamin said. "I will place the letters between them and tie the bundle together with a piece of leather. That way if a British boat approaches and I drop them in the water, they will sink to the bottom of the Charles."

"And if you are stopped on land?"

"I have been stopped and have never given up a missive yet."

Despite his migraine, the doctor managed the faintest smile as he dismissed Benjamin with a wave of the hand.

Benjamin went to the field hospital, where he found Ezra leaning over a barrel of rain water, washing his hands and arms. His surgeon's apron was smeared with blood. "I fear that my greatest service to this war," he said, "will be performed with a saw. Years from now there'll be plenty of fellows who'll see me coming down the street and they'll say 'There's the bloke that hacked off me hand—or me foot. Right quick about it, too. Like pruning a tree, it was.'" There was a towel hanging from a post, and Benjamin handed it to Ezra. As he toweled off, he said, "Long face."

"Dr. Warren's sending me into Boston with letters for my brother."

"If anybody can get in there, it's you. Good luck."

"I was wondering . . ." Benjamin hesitated.

As Ezra hung the towel on the post, a nurse came to the open flap that served as the entrance to the hospital tent and waved to him urgently. "Duty beckons." He took a deep draught of air. "It's the smell. The air in there is—" He suddenly regarded Benjamin with a cautious stare. "You were wondering, what?"

"My sister," Benjamin said. "It's just that, if I see her, I was wondering if you—is there some message you wish to convey?"

Ezra folded his arms and studied the ground. He might have been trying to determine whether a limb could be saved. Finally, he said, "No. No message. I would prefer it if you didn't mention me to her at all. Don't even tell her you've seen me." He began to walk toward the hospital tent, but then paused and looked back at Benjamin. "It's better that way. I don't exist."

Supply wagons were constantly moving in and out of Cambridge, and Benjamin had no difficulty getting a ride to Charlestown. Like Boston, Charlestown was a peninsula, a smaller fist of land that jutted into the harbor, which could only be accessed by a narrow spit of land that crossed a vast salt marsh. Most of the peninsula was open pasture, cattle grazing on Breed's Hill and Bunker Hill, with the village clustered at the water's edge, looking across the water to Boston's North End. There were several British naval ships at anchor, the *Somerset* being perched close to the river mouth, and farther down the harbor the prison ship, the *Preston,* her streaked and fouled sides giving some indication of the conditions below decks. Ordinarily there was a ferryboat that ran between Charlestown and the North End, but that service had been suspended since the siege began.

Early evening, Benjamin stood on a pier below the village, glad for the smell of low tide. The rain had passed but there was a heavy sky above the water. The only real activity was fishing smacks gathering their nets and clam diggers working the marshes upriver off Lechmere Point. Occasionally in the failing light he could make out a British longboat, patrolling the harbor.

He waited until after dark. There were plenty of dinghies tied up along the piers and he took one and sculled away from the shore, careful not to splash as he dipped the oars. He rowed well out into the harbor to avoid the lights of the *Somerset,* and then worked his way east toward the lights of the North End. The tide had turned, so it was heavy work pulling against the current. Even in the dark, he knew the Boston shoreline—the seawall across Mill Pond, the creeks and inlets, the marshes, all beneath the dark, looming presence of Trimount.

He heard the splash of oars between his boat and the shore, and finally he located it: a longboat, barely visible. An officer, a faint white cross on his chest, stood in the bow. Benjamin shipped his oars and slid off his thwart. Lying down in the bottom of the dinghy, he peered over the gunwale, watching as the longboat drew near, close enough that he could hear the officer's command to his tillerman. "Steady on with this current, Mr. Paltreen—two points to starboard." The oars were becoming louder, creaking in their locks. Benjamin considered slipping over the transom and swimming for shore, which was at least three hundred yards off, but the letters, the letters must be kept dry. Abruptly, with a sense of urgency, the officer hollered, "Port now. We're getting too far out to observe activity ashore." And the longboat began to turn, taking the waves broadside, creating a slapping sound that diminished with each stroke of the crew.

Benjamin began rowing again, working his way east, heading for Anse Cole's small pier, which ran out from the beach below a row of clam shacks. There were few lights along the shoreline there, only the occasional lantern in a window, its reflection dancing on the chop. He pulled well past Cole's pier, and then let the tide draw him in, only working the oars to keep his bow to the current, which allowed him to sit facing the shore. The beach emerged as a faint line of white, and Cole's pier was perhaps fifty yards off to the right. He turned the dinghy around and drove it up through the small beach break, until the bottom scraped sand and came to a stop. Climbing out, he dragged the boat a ways up the beach, and then began walking toward the pier.

Anse Cole's house was up a lane above the pier. It was dark— this part of Boston didn't have streetlamps. It was quiet except for the occasional caw of a seagull. The house was small, its shingles weathered and curled. Benjamin looked in a front window and saw Mariah sitting in the rocker by the fireplace, and her father was stretched out on the floor with a pillow under his head— something he often did for his sore back after a long day of fishing. Benjamin tapped on the isinglass, and just as Mariah looked up from her needlepoint, a voice said, "What do you think you're doing there?"

He turned and saw two redcoats coming down the lane. Without thinking, he began to run back toward the beach. He heard the soldiers' boots pounding behind him, but they were loaded down with rifles and gear and he was faster. When he reached the row of shacks he headed toward the dory, thinking he could pull out into the safety of the dark harbor. At the very least, he could get into water deep enough to drop the letters, still wrapped in stones, overboard. He raced along the firm, wet sand just above the shore break. He looked back and saw that the soldiers were well behind him, but then he tripped on some kelp and hit the sand hard.

His knee was painfully twisted, and when he struggled to his feet he could barely put weight on it. He hopped toward the dory but had difficulty pushing it down the beach. The pain in his leg was overwhelming, causing him to collapse in the sand, where he watched as the redcoats came toward him, one of them slinging his rifle down off his shoulder. Benjamin held his knee and he was out of breath—they were all out of breath—and there were voices, other voices now, coming up the beach toward them. Benjamin tried to get to his feet again, but then he was struck in the face with the rifle butt.

He may have passed out, because he realized he was now lying curled up on his side. He tasted blood, and sand coated his tongue and mouth. His head, as well as his leg, throbbed, and he wasn't sure what was happening, other than he was lying on a beach and there was some fierce argument going on about him. Then he realized it was Anse Cole who was yelling at the soldiers, while Mariah knelt in the sand and lifted Benjamin until his head was nestled in her arms. She was crying, saying "Benjamin, Benjamin," but then she screamed when the redcoats began to pummel her father. There was a great deal of shouting, until the old man lay motionless in the shore break. The soldiers, winded, cursing, pulled Mariah away from Benjamin, and the last thing he remembered was being hauled up off the sand by his arms.

Abigail gazed at the cup of tea. Her mother had poured it, as she did every morning, as though it were nothing, no more significant than the biscuits, the butter, and the blackberry jam—all of which they had made themselves—that also graced their breakfast table. And every morning Abigail ignored the cup of tea, while her father and mother drank theirs and talked, pretending to ignore their daughter's untouched cup of tea.

But this morning was different. She was not outnumbered; she had an ally: her brother, James, seated across the table from her, with a second untouched cup of tea in front of him.

"You're only wasting it on me, Mother," he said. "On me, and on Abigail."

Their mother put down the teapot, adjusting the cozy, which she had knitted while recuperating from her illness during the winter. "Jemmy, you sit at this table so seldom now, I wish you would—" She stopped abruptly, looking at her husband, who put his cup of tea in its saucer with a loud clatter.

"It is a question of honor, you think?" he said. "Abigail doesn't drink tea in our house, and yet I have no doubt that every time she runs off to visit with the *second* Mrs. Paul Revere she imbibes all the *contra*band tea that woman offers." He stared at James, his eyes protuberant beneath his bushy eyebrows—the same close inspection he'd bestowed upon his students for years. "You, on the other hand, don't visit the Revere house to drink tea, though I understand you often write letters to her husband, wherever he may be, out there riding through the country, stirring up revolution."

Before James could answer, his mother said, kindly, "Tea gives you strength, dear."

James smiled across the table at Abigail. His face was narrow and pallid, and there was no joy in his eyes. "The king's tea does not 'give strength.' Besides, I was strong enough to venture here this morning."

"I suspect you're going to leave Boston," his father said. "You're going to take your wife and children and flee to the hills with the rest of the . . . patriots." Father looked down the table at his wife, "You see what is happening in this city, my dear? Thousands of 'patriots' have packed up and left, granted safe passage by General Gage—something *we* negotiated as a matter of decency and honor—"

"And at the same time," James said, "Tories are being allowed to pass safely into Boston. But that is not, on the part of the provincial government, an act of decency and honor?"

Father smiled; he enjoyed a good debate at the dinner table, though there was weariness and perhaps even sorrow in his voice. "There most certainly is a difference," he said. "If these loyal subjects remained out in the country, they'd come to harm, no doubt. You've heard the stories—you can't deny them. It's a rabble out there. Mobs have destroyed property, burned houses, tarred and feathered innocent souls, have committed the most heinous acts of indecency."

James adjusted his wig, and then proceeded to butter his biscuit, as though he hadn't heard what his father had just said. This was, at times, their only, best weapon: silence.

"The behavior of some redcoats," Abigail said, "has not exactly been civil."

"True, on occasion," her father said. "And when there have been transgressions the generals have taken swift disciplinary action. This situation is too much for one man. Aided by generals Howe, Burgoyne, and Clinton, General Gage will soon have this situation under control. See, one of the many failures on the part of the patriots is that they all think that the king is lazy and daft, and that his advisors in London are all in favor of rebellion. *Hardly.* The British are by and large informed by the love of God and an appreciation of the virtues of common sense." He inserted the last of his biscuit into his mouth and chewed with obvious satisfaction.

Abigail kept her hands folded in her lap. She didn't want this to go any further. It was bad enough that she had to endure such conversations each morning (while she practically went hungry as a meager form of protest), but now, with James present at table, she feared this amiable discussion would turn into an argument that would only result in her mother retreating to her bedroom, feeling poorly for the remainder of the day.

But James placed both elbows on the table and leaned forward until his face nearly touched his joined hands. "Father," he said patiently, "can you not see what is happening to Boston? To all of New England? Thousands of patriotic Bostonians have fled the city, while at the same time thousands of Tories have entered it, many taking up residence in houses that have been abandoned." His father was about to speak, but James turned one palm toward him, begging to continue. "You know it's true. No matter what the generals' official policy is—and I grant you that in some ways Gage has acted as a true gentleman—some of these Tories are inhabiting houses left by their rightful owners. Others—and this is of greater concern—are being used by soldiers."

"The men require billeting," Father said. "And it is our responsibility to provide for them. After all, they do us a great service."

"I wouldn't call it a *service*," James said. "The fact is, between the redcoats and the Tories, we are now outnumbered about three to one, by some estimates."

Father smiled. "Which, I submit, is consistent with the sentiment throughout the colonies—easily three out of four are loyal to His Majesty."

"I would venture that a good number of colonists are hesitant to take sides," James said. "Some, I understand, in anticipation of hostilities, have begun to flee."

"Quite," his father said. "Even the general's lovely wife has fled."

"She was sent," Abigail said. "Sent to England by her husband, the gentleman."

"Yes, a wise precaution," Father said. "Perhaps she can write letters to you, James, informing you of the weather in London?"

"She's the victim of rumor and speculation, nothing more," James said.

"She couldn't hide her true sentiments," Father said, and then he laughed. "Not beneath those . . . Turkish *turbans.*"

When no one joined him, he stopped laughing abruptly. He leaned toward his son and said, "If *you* leave Boston, you might find the odds more to your liking out *there*—in Dorchester and Cambridge and Charlestown, where they have this city you claim to love so much surrounded."

"He's not going anywhere," Mother said. "Not in his condition, and not with another child on the way."

James considered her a moment, his eyes softening. "No, I'm not leaving for the country, Mother. Though I would if I could."

"Better to stay here," his father said, "and compose your secret missives."

James lowered his hands to the table.

"Sympathetic ink," his father muttered.

James only stared at Abigail.

"Informers, you realize," his father said, "commit acts of treason."

"Action not taken lightly," James said. "Taken after much careful consideration."

"Of what?"

"Years of injustice."

His father mumbled something in Latin. Abigail caught the word *officium*—duty.

"You know, for years—ever since I can remember—we've sat at this table and voiced our differences, with passion and well-churned butter." James smiled at Abigail. "But it wasn't until just now that I understood that when Father begins to spout in Latin he realizes that his argument is weak. When I was a boy, he could wield Latin—and Greek, and French—"

"Moi!" his father said. "No!"

"But it was always an act of desperation, a debater's ploy."

"I only heed the word of God," Father announced, "and seek the light of truth."

"School's out," James said. "We converse only in English now."

"I agree, James," Father said. "And, sadly, we can't understand each other at all."

For a moment, no one spoke, no one moved, and then James got up from the table, leaned toward his mother, kissed her on the forehead. As he walked out of the dining room, Father stared down at his tea cup. They listened to James close the front door behind him.

"You see how gingerly he walks?" Mother said. "Can't you see he's ill?"

"I know," Father said.

"We've one son missing and the other—"

"Lost," Father said. "Missing and lost. It aggrieves me terribly." He considered Abigail for a moment. "But you, dear, are still with us."

Abigail looked down at her untouched cup of tea.

"See, Mother?" he said with sudden delight. "See how our pretty girl *blushes?*"

Abigail got up from her chair. "Thank you, Mother, but if you'll excuse me."

"She has a *beau,*" her father said in a proud whisper.

As she left the room, Abigail hesitated, but then continued out into the hall.

Her father said, louder, "An officer and a gentleman, he is, too!"

She collected her shawl and bolted from the house.

At first she considered following James home. But to do what? Commiserate? Weep? Drink some contraband tea and rail against their mercurial father? As long as she could remember, there had been such encounters, often at table. Countless meals ruined. As children they fled, yelling, screaming, in tears, and in that there was some sweet release, whereas now her anger seemed to boil inside, and Abigail realized that the only comfort was walking.

So she walked, swiftly, gazing at the ground before her. Packed earth and cobblestones. When she did look up, what she saw, despite the fact that it was a sunny morning, with the faintest sea breeze cooling the air, was truly a different city—much changed from just a few weeks ago. Bostonians didn't look at each other in the street the way they used to; there was something furtive and distrustful about how they regarded each other in passing. Tories tended not to look directly at anyone, their haughty gaze averted (Abigail was certain she could tell which ones were newly arrived from the country), and those who sympathized with the patriots now looked beleaguered, fearful.

The military presence had changed as well. For years the sight of redcoats was all too common, but now that Boston was in a state of siege there were more patrols, more marching drills (the beat of the drum so frequent, beckoning from different neighborhoods, that she only took notice when the distant rattle ceased). There was a greater exercise of British authority. They now treated the peninsula not so much a city as a fortress. Indeed, they were building a massive redoubt on Copp's Hill, its earthen walls facing Charlestown, and at the Neck the gate was being substantially fortified. There was among the soldiers an alertness that had not existed before, which resulted in encounters with the natives that were often formal and stern.

Natives: this was the word Samuel used in his last letter, as though he were reporting from some remote, exotic island in the South Pacific. He had written to Abigail often over the past few weeks. Days would pass when he was too occupied and could not see her. Happily, he said, the command once again, after the disastrous expedition to Lexington and Concord, fully appreciated the role of artillery, thus he had been deeply involved in the fortifications at both the Neck and Copp's Hill. But the letters (always delivered by a young Regular) sometimes lamented the dullness and routine of his days, as well as the fact that he was unable to see her more frequently; other letters tended to reminisce about home, particularly his family's country estate in Surrey. *What I would give to walk those fields now, to show you the gentle contour of the land.* And there were moments recently when Abigail dwelt on such a possibility, and this was an occupation of another sort: an invasion of the mind by daydreams, stupid daydreams. Life in Boston, never easy, was getting harder by the day. By contrast Surrey, where Abigail imagined green hillocks dotted with grazing sheep, and a house maintained by a fleet of servants, offered images that were too rich for a colonial schoolmaster's daughter. But then there was Margaret Kemble, Pennsylvania-born, who became Mrs. Thomas Gage, and who, for whatever reasons, whatever transgressions, had been put on board ship, bound for the safe, distant shores of England.

And when Samuel did get away from his duties for an evening there was now something different about how they talked. There was restraint, and there was tenderness, of course; but there was also a sense of urgency, and before parting they would find some place to be absolutely alone, invisible except to each other. She welcomed his hands, how they seemed to shape her, remake her, while they kissed and burrowed into each other. It was always swift, febrile, and then it was over and she was alone again. The last time she had seen him, they had strolled at dusk beneath the trees along the Mall, before she was driven home in a closed carriage. They clung to each other as the vehicle jounced through the streets, and just as they arrived in front of her house he talked frantically about a room, how he could acquire a room. She said nothing, but alighted and rushed inside.

Now Abigail found herself climbing the slope of Trimount. Alone. Soon the city began to spread out beneath her, punctuated by church spires, with an apron of blue water extending from her jagged shores. The harbor was speckled with patrol ships, with patrol boats, the sails of fishing smacks.

She paused to sit on a rock at a turn in the path and looked down at the deep, angular trench that had been dug into the side of Copp's Hill. The sounds of labor—hammers, saws, the clap of boards—came up to her, and almost seemed to soothe the anger she had brought away from the house. More walking, more climbing was required, she thought, but as she stood up she looked back down the path, and there she saw red.

Corporal Lumley. Again.

Looking up the path, she realized that in her fury she had failed to take into account that here on Trimount she would be very much alone. Turning, she watched him climb the path. He made no attempt to hide this time.

And she started back down the hill, long, determined strides that caused him to stop and watch her approach with a combination of fear and relief. He appeared winded, his face flushed, his damp hair plastered to his high forehead.

"What do you think you're doing?" she demanded.

"I've been—" He took a deep breath. "Following you."

"I *know* that."

"You, you set a good pace."

"Not good enough."

"I wanted to hail you down in the streets, but you moved so fast—and I thought it best that we not be seen talking as it might, it might be misconstrued."

"Corporal Lumley. You have followed me before, though never this boldly."

"I apologize," he said. "I have only wished the proper opportunity to speak with you . . . about matters . . . about my . . . situation."

"Your situation?"

"Yes, but at the moment there's something more pressing that I must convey to you." He was standing downhill from her, which made him seem small and frail. "It's about your brother."

"James?"

"No, Benjamin."

She grabbed him by the shoulders, and then, realizing what she had done, pushed him away. "What of Benjamin?"

Lumley took a deep breath. "He was captured last night."

"Where?"

"Here."

"In Boston?"

"Yes." Lumley looked up at the sun and said, "It's getting warm. Might we—" He took a few steps off the path until he was in the shade of a tree. He waited for Abigail to join him, and then continued, seeming relieved to be in the cooler air. "We were on patrol last night, me and Munroe, and we came upon a fellow who seemed to be up to something, he be gazing in the window of a house on the shore in the North End there, and so we call out to inquire about his business and he immediately sets to running off, and I tell you he is swift, runs like you walk, if I might say so, Miss, so I conclude it be in the family blood." He offered a thin smile to indicate he was attempting humor, but it disappeared almost immediately.

"You chased after him."

Lumley nodded.

"But you said he was captured."

"It be some chase, I tell you, yes, and we did collect him after he took a spill on the beach, being tripped up by the kelp and such."

Abigail looked back down the path. "Where have you got him? I must go—"

As she began to move out of the shade, Lumley placed one hand on her shoulder, held her in place, and then, rather politely, removed his hand. "We don't have him, Miss."

"What do you mean? Where is he?"

"Don't quite know. He skipped off."

"Escaped?"

"He did, yes." Lumley seemed pleased with himself. "Had a little assistance there."

"What are you saying, Corporal?"

"Well, there wasn't much to it, really. We brought him to the jailhouse on Court Street, where he was thoroughly examined. This went on for hours, quite through the night, I tell you, until the captain he tires of it."

"Tires of what?"

"The interrogation. Exhausting work, it can be."

"My brother, was he hurt?"

Lumley looked away. "Some, indeed he was, but he'll be right soon enough. He's young and—and you see it was Munroe who, on the beach, he was a bit rough with the lad. But the important thing is they didn't get anything out of him. Your brother, he's strong-willed, which I suspect also runs in your family. Very frustrating for the captain, who's skilled at getting a man to talk."

Now Lumley faced Abigail. "But you see, the lad had an ally, and there was nothing for him to give up, and it helped him endure the interrogation."

"What ally?"

Lumley stood up straighter.

"You?"

He nodded.

"I don't believe it."

"When the captain was through with him, I took the lad to his cell, and there I allowed him to escape. Look, Miss, I'm going to catch hell for it, I can tell you, but they've been in for me a long time now, so I figure I got nothing to lose anymore."

"*You* let him escape—please, Corporal."

Abigail began to turn away, but paused when Lumley began to fidget with the buttons on his uniform, saying, "Miss, I can prove it." He undid the top buttons and reached inside his tunic. "Your brother couldn't be made to talk because he didn't know anything, you see. Because he was carrying letters."

"Letters?"

Lumley removed several envelopes from inside his tunic and held them out to her. Reluctantly, Abigail accepted them, three envelopes, tied between two flat stones, their wax seals unbroken. She looked at the corporal as he fastened up his tunic.

"I got them off your brother shortly after we apprehended him on the beach. We were walking through the streets to the courthouse and Munroe takes a moment in an alley for the call of nature, and I found the letters on the boy. You see, at that point I near had to carry him."

"Because he was injured."

"Indeed."

"The result of Munroe—"

"The butt of his Brown Bess. Gave him a good crack in the face, he did. And the lad hurt his knee when he took the fall in the sand."

Abigail turned and walked away from the corporal, looking at the envelopes in her hand. "There's no way of knowing if these are genuine."

"That be true, Miss. But perhaps you might let your brother James examine them? I suspect the lad intended to deliver them to him."

"But he didn't tell you this."

"No, not exactly."

She gazed down toward the North End, where the noise from the construction of the redoubt on Copp's Hill continued to fill the warm spring air. "You say they have it in for you. What do you mean?"

"It be a long story, Miss. But I tell you they want to make an example of me."

Abigail turned to Lumley. "Why did you do this?" she said, holding out the letters. "What is it you want?"

He took a few steps toward her, though he hesitated from getting too close. "Out," he said. "I want out of Boston, out of this army."

"You want to desert?"

He nodded. "We hear of the offers from the provincials. Land, in New Hampshire, in Vermont, if we come over." His eyes brightened, a child conjuring a dream, a daydream. "They say there are valleys in Vermont with swift running streams full of trout, and good soil." Then he took a few steps closer. "What I want, what I ask, Miss, is that you help me. You ascertain that these letters be genuine, and then you give me assistance in getting free of Boston. I will fight, I will fight for your provincials, I tell you. I will earn my land."

"You want to be smuggled out."

He took one last step toward her. "I need someone I can trust."

Abigail tucked the letters away beneath her shawl. "Well, I need to find Benjamin."

"I wish I knew where he be."

"You said you and Munroe came upon him looking in a window?"

"North End. Down by the shoreline."

"A fisherman's house?"

"From the looks of it, yes, Miss." Now Lumley averted his eyes.

"What?"

"On the beach, there were others—an old man and a girl. The girl, she showed affection for your brother after he was struck, but Munroe, I fear he did worse by the old man."

"Cole," Abigail said. "Anse Cole."

"Munroe, you understand, he believes only in force. You've seen it yourself, Miss."

"That, Corporal, is the truth." Abigail began walking down the path. Lumley followed behind. "No, Mr. Lumley," she said over her shoulder. "We shall not be seen together descending this hill."

"But will you help me?"

She walked faster down the path.

XI

Services, of a Certain Nature

FROM THE LOFT OF THE GRANARY, BENJAMIN COULD LOOK OUT A
window and see across the graveyard to School Street. The granary
was a large building where corn was stored, and since he'd been a
boy he'd gone there often, drawn by the noise, the bustle; it fascinated him as much as watching a ship's crew as it made ready for the
sea. There were dozens of men who drove wagons and worked with
shovels mostly, strong men who were very kindly toward Benjamin.
Obadiah was a Haitian, owned by the granary manager Reginald
Fiske, and he had worked there so long that he was often referred
as the Turnkey, because he had been entrusted with the keys to all
the granary doors, large keys that hung from his belt and jangled
when he walked. When he arrived at dawn to open the building,
he found Benjamin lying in a hay pile half unconscious, and he carried the boy inside, all the way to a vacant storage room on the top
floor. During the course of the day, he tended to Benjamin's wounds
as best he could, washing the laceration that ran across his purple,
swollen left cheek, and in the evening he brought some bread and

soup, prepared by his wife. He also provided a crutch, fashioned out of a maple branch, which he said he'd used after taking a fall on some ice the previous winter.

"You know, there be talk about you," he said, watching Benjamin carefully insert the spoon between his swollen lips—the teeth on the left side ached terribly from the blow from the soldier's rifle, coupled with the beating he'd taken while being questioned in the jailhouse. "You help Billy Dawes get through the Neck that night before Lexington and Concord. You must be hiding from the Brits."

Even a simple nod caused pain that ran down his neck to his shoulders.

"You kin stay up here. We've cleared all the corn from this floor, so nobody'll be takin' the lift all the way up here." Obadiah had enormous shoulders and his clothing was powdered with corn dust. He nodded toward the small window that looked out on School Street. "You don't want to be going home just now."

Benjamin just managed to shake his head slowly.

"It's your father. Respected, educated man that he is, but he be a Tory. Well, you must rest now." He glanced toward the pile of straw he'd sent up on the lift. "Not much of a bed, I know."

"It's fine," Benjamin said through his aching teeth. He put the empty bowl on the floor. "I'll be fine here. Thank you."

"And I brung this horse blanket, 'cause it kin still get cold nights." Obadiah started to duck out through the low door, but then paused. "No knowing how long this will go on. There be no shipments of corn coming into the city. And every day they been carting more away from here, to feed the troops. Their horses, they're eating better'n some Bostonians now. At this rate the granary will be empty before the weather turns. This continues into winter, people'll starve." And then he was gone, his keys echoing in the vast open space beneath the rafters of the great building as he slowly descended the stairs.

Benjamin moved the stool in front of the window and sat down: a seagull's view of Boston, gazing down on shingled roofs clustered between winding streets. He could see the Province House, backed by its stable and vast orchard. Looking down School Street, his house looked small, but there was smoke curling from the chimney, which meant that his mother and sister were preparing dinner. One night, when they were all seated at table, Abigail had asked *Why is there Latin? Why Greek?* And their father glanced up from the books that he often read right through the meal. He didn't seem to understand the question. Benjamin must have been about nine, which would make Abigail fourteen, and she was often asking questions that baffled or angered their parents. *Why so many tongues, Father? Why don't people all over the world just speak one language?*

"I said I'd meet him tomorrow," Abigail said.

James raised his head. First there was reluctance clouding his eyes, but then they grew wide with alarm. "Where?"

"Trimount."

Her brother took a moment to fold up the letters she had given him, and she knew he was deliberately taking his time. In this he and his father were quite the opposite: where father would react immediately in an outburst of emotion, James often gave himself time to consider his response. Abigail had always hated these moments, the waiting, the anticipation. James was like a third parent to her and to Benjamin, and he could be every bit the disciplinarian that their father was—but it was usually harder to accept, because he *was* their older brother.

"Not alone," James said.

"I must. Lumley was insistent. He's very—he's frightened."

"You shouldn't go up Trimount at all, Abigail. And certainly not to meet a British soldier." He glanced down at the letters on his desk. "But maintaining communication with this corporal seems, under the circumstances, prudent."

"So. Under the circumstances, I do as I had promised and meet him there."

James said nothing.

"They're genuine, aren't they?"

He nodded slowly, without looking up from the letters. "They appear to be, but—"

"I believe Benjamin bore them across the water." Abigail picked up the smooth, flat stones which lay on the desk. "Because of these. This is his doing—you know it is, James."

Her brother nodded. "I believe so. Our younger brother, he's something of a beach stone, isn't he?"

"Shaped by the tides and currents and tides." She put one stone back on the desk, and kept the other, which fit comfortably in her palm. "The letters, what do they say?"

She watched as James's hand drifted down his jacket and settled on his stomach. He was pale, his face as white as the wig he wore, despite the heat from the fire in the hearth. "What they say, I shouldn't reveal to you," he said. "What if you are taken into custody—what if you are questioned as Benjamin was? It's better that you not know."

"They're important?"

"Matters regarding our troop strength and deployment in the hills surrounding Boston."

"So it's best I not know," she said. "Though they'd be more likely to question you."

He didn't deny this, but pressed on. "We have to consider this in full light. These are letters that were written by Joseph Warren, in Cambridge. Or so it appears. I would swear that this is his hand, which I know as well as my own. But I also know that General Gage is remarkably adept at matters of espionage, and who knows what he's capable of? I could be wrong. They *could* be very clever forgeries." He paused to drink from the glass of water that he kept on the desk. "And look how we've obtained these letters. Purportedly, our younger brother Benjamin, whom we haven't seen or heard from since before the engagements at Lexington and Concord, received these letters from Dr. Warren, with the express instructions to slip into Boston—a difficult enough feat, though I think we both agree that if anyone is capable of such action it is our Benjamin—and deliver them to me. *But.* But he is captured. He is beaten. He is interrogated. And there's this British corporal, who took the letters from him in an effort to keep them from the hands of his own commanders, and then he aids Benjamin in his escape from the jail. And *then* he, this Corporal Lumley, follows you up Trimount and gives you the letters—be*cause* he wants us to help him desert and fight for our side, his reward being farmland in Vermont."

"I believe him," Abigail said.

James smiled wearily. "I gather that you do."

"I will meet him as planned."

"You know what happens to most Boston women who meet soldiers up there?"

"They sell their services."

"Or they're simply taken." James stared at her. "It's not safe. You can't go."

"I can."

"We don't need him, Abigail."

"We owe him," she said. "I believe he helped our brother, and we owe him."

James turned toward the fireplace and for a moment his hand touched his wig. Then he sighed. "I was afraid that Benjamin had been killed during the engagement. I have heard that there are a number of provincials who still are not accounted for."

"I feared this, too. I've thought of little else."

"You and he," James said, looking at her, his eyes surprisingly fond. "You and Benjamin, you've always been so close." His smile was weak. "There were times when I envied you that, both of you."

"We always looked up to you."

"Yes, the older brother, but it's not the same thing. Yours is a most genuine love, and believe me, all of us, Mother, Father, and I, basked in it."

Abigail's legs suddenly felt unsteady. There was a chair next to the desk and she sat down. "It was not intended to exclude you."

"No need to explain." He picked up the stone that Abigail had placed back on the desk; the way he held it, rubbing it with his fingertips, it might have been the rarest of gems. "Now if we could just find Benjamin."

Benjamin slept fitfully on the straw bed, awakening periodically, chilled, feverish, and his foul-smelling clothing drenched in sweat. In the morning Obadiah's son came up to the loft with a jar of milk, some bread and cheese.

"Father says you must remain here. British come and go downstairs all day long."

"What's your name?" Benjamin soaked a piece of bread in the milk and then eased it into his mouth.

"Ezekiel." He stole a glance at Benjamin's bruised face.

"Your father likes to fish, dig clams. I see him out on the harbor or in the flats. You a good fisherman, too?"

The boy nodded uncertainly.

"How old, Ezekiel?"

"Twelve, this summer." He was a lean boy who looked like he had swift feet.

"I need a courier. Will you do that for me?"

"Yes."

It started with this, running through the streets of Boston, bearing a message.

"Good. I want you to go to the waterfront for me. You must ask your father's permission. If it's granted, go to the house of Anse Cole, a fisherman who lives not far from the Mill Pond. Can you find that?" The boy nodded. "Then I want you to talk to Miss

Cole, Mariah Cole, nobody else. Ask after her father. Tell her I am safe and will see her as soon as I can. Ask her to get word to my sister. But don't say where I am. Understand?"

Ezekiel nodded.

"Now go."

The boy turned and ran across the loft and his boots clattered loudly as he descended the stairs.

Benjamin slept through the morning, until he was awakened by the rattle of drums, accompanied by an officer's shouted commands. He looked out the window, shielding his eyes from the midday sun, and watched a detail of redcoats as they marched past King's Chapel, on the way to the Common. Farther down School Street he saw a chaise, stopped before the front door of his house. Several well-dressed men were being welcomed by his father. Tories. It was a city full of loyalists now.

There would be no returning home. This had started years ago, when he was about Ezekiel's age. The lessons in his father's classroom had never sat well with Benjamin. Greek and Latin: Abigail was right to ask why there wasn't just one language. His father singled him out for punishment, as an example for the other boys: frequent verbal reprimands, and the ferule—lashings on the palms, the backs of the legs. Until one day, it was a cold morning in February, just as his father was about to strike again, Benjamin reached out and grabbed his wrist. The boys at their desks gasped: it was forbidden to touch the schoolmaster. But Benjamin didn't let go and he was strong enough to stay his father's hand.

He was expelled, and never readmitted to the Latin School, despite the protests from his mother and sister; even James, who was perhaps a harsher disciplinarian than their father, advocated for Benjamin's return to school. Father refused, citing that principles must be enforced if they were to instill their pupils with the character and integrity necessary to become civic leaders. In lieu of a formal education, James made certain he could do his sums and he read with Abigail, though he never had the patience for a book. They provided surreptitious instruction, which he valued far more than anything he'd ever been taught in a classroom. And he spent his days learning the water from fishermen, clam diggers, sailors, cordwainers, and shipwrights. One day, when the port was reopened, he wanted to go to sea.

Again, there were duties of hospitality while Father entertained a succession of prominent Tories. Mother worked in the kitchen, while Abigail served tea and cake in Father's study. When she returned for more cream, she saw one of the Revere girls, Frances, standing outside in the kitchen dooryard.

"Rachel has sent for you," Mother said. "She says it's urgent."

"But I must help here."

"I can manage." Mother refilled her glass creamer. "Besides, I dislike the way some of these men leer at you. So go."

Abigail went out the kitchen door. Frances Revere was firmly built, like her father. "They are in the granary burying ground." She was only about ten and she took Abigail's hand as they walked down the alley that would come out near King's Chapel. "We go there often, to pray at Mother's stone."

From the Common there was the sound of drums and marching. Daily, the redcoats conducted exercises, and the constant noise seemed to charge the air in Boston. Mother claimed it affected her nerves and made her blood hot, disturbing her sleep. There was also in the distance the sound of hammering and boards falling—deconstruction: the British were tearing down certain houses which had been abandoned by rebel sympathizers. It was claimed that they needed the wood for fuel, but also the materials were used to build the redoubt on Copp's Hill.

"The church in North Square," Frances said. "It is rumored they will take it down. And the steeple in the West End church also, because they believe it was used to signal Charlestown. Nobody dares correct them, for fear that they will tear down Christ's Church instead. Grandmother says they mean to level Boston."

They entered the burying ground. All the Revere children were there, placing wildflowers at the gravestone of Sarah Orne, the first Mrs. Revere, who had been laid to rest not two years earlier. Rachel sat on a nearby bench, her baby in her arms.

"Thank you," she said to Frances. "Now you go and join the others."

The girl ran off through the shaggy grass.

"Have you heard?" Rachel said, shifting her infant son to her other shoulder.

"About North Church? Frances just told me."

"Yes, but something else is causing a great stir in the North End." She looked toward the granary, looming above the burying ground. "The fisherman Anse Cole, he was assaulted by redcoats."

"I heard, yes."

"He died last night."

Upon hearing this, Abigail needed to sit down on the bench.

"You know about Mariah," Rachel asked. "About her and your brother?"

"Yes, yes, I know. I saw her just yesterday." She sat still, without speaking. Rachel gently patted her son's back, while in the distance the Revere children prayed at their mother's grave.

"These damned street patrols," Rachel said, her eyes welling up. "But why Anse Cole?"

Abigail couldn't stop fidgeting with her cap, and finally she took it off, allowing her hair to swirl about her face in the breeze. And tears blurred her vision as well, the children, the rows of stones, the granary in the distance all appearing to slide together. "It's because he's was one of us," she said.

"That is not a reason," Rachel said. "But for them it's reason enough."

Benjamin wanted to shout.

He wanted to lean out the window and call down to his sister in the burying ground. But he didn't. He couldn't. So he watched her and Rachel Revere, and even from this distance, this seagull's height, he could tell that something had happened. Rachel said something that caused Abigail to sit next to her on the bench, and then she kept touching her cap until she pulled it off. He loved Abigail's fine dark hair, the way the wind tossed it about her face. She and Rachel never looked at each other. They barely spoke. He realized that they were crying. He was certain of it, two women, sitting in a graveyard crying.

That evening, Abigail climbed Trimount and found Corporal Lumley standing beneath the tree where they had met the day before. He looked up and down the path nervously as she approached. "We should not remain here," he said.

"You are afraid to be seen on this hill with me?"

"No, it's just—"

"All too common, I understand, trysts with a Boston woman."

"Certainly, you could not be mistaken for, for *that*, Miss."

"Such high compliment. I should be flattered."

"Please." He took a step closer. "There is a rock only a little farther up the path where we might be better concealed."

"To what purpose?" Abigail started up the path, with Lumley close behind.

"I did not come up here alone, you see."

She looked over her shoulder. His face was drawn, even haggard. "Who else?"

"Munroe," he said. "He insisted we go together."

"But what is his purpose? And where is he?"

"His purpose—it be the usual thing, and he continued higher up. After mess we found our way to the tavern, as we often do— tonight we are off-duty. He told me he had received a note from a woman . . . and they agreed to meet up here."

"One of *those* Boston women."

"Yes. They can be bold. They send letters to us, offering of various—"

"Services, of a certain nature. And Munroe finds it flattering."

"In a word, yes."

"He engages in this sort of thing often."

"Yes."

"You, of course, are of a different disposition."

Lumley cleared his throat. "Please, Miss. Here are the rocks."

There was a large crevice which formed a cave between the rocks. "You want me to go in there, with you?" He looked up the path and then back at Abigail. "Very well," she said.

She had to stoop to get into the cave, but found that inside it was open to the sky and quite spacious, illuminated by the last light of day. Overhead there were birds twittering in nests they'd built in the rocks. Lumley ducked until he too was inside the cave and, as if to confirm that he was of honorable intentions, he walked to the far end of the cave, keeping his back to her.

"I must leave Boston soon." His voice reverberated off the rock walls. "Increasingly, there is great suspicion within our ranks. If I stay longer, I will be found out." He turned around and faced her. "Those letters. Did you deliver them to your brother James?"

"I did."

"And he found them to be genuine?"

Abigail merely tipped her head to one side.

"You will assist me?"

"Perhaps," she said. "You have no idea what has happened to Benjamin?"

"No. If I knew, I'd tell you."

"I heard news today, terrible news."

Even in the failing light she could see Lumley's eyes grow large with fear. "You've heard, then?" She waited. "It wasn't me. It be Munroe that struck them. Your brother and that old man. Our patrols in the North End today—they were greeted with much anger and hostility."

"If what you say is true—"

"It is."

"And if you want to serve the patriotic cause, then perhaps you should identify Munroe as Anse Cole's murderer."

He stared at her now, horrified. "I couldn't do that. I—I wouldn't survive." Again, she waited. "You see, some officers suspect me already, because I have said things and shown a certain sympathy for the provincials. You're either with them, or you're not—there be no middle ground, not since Lexington and Concord." He took a step toward her, but stopped as though he was afraid to get too close. "If I accused Munroe, they would only see that as confirmation. He is much liked. They would wrap me in a white shroud and hang me from the Great Elm on the Common—that's what they do when they want to make an example for the troops. It's being inside the white shroud that is so frightening, the anonymity of it. . . ."

Lumley had a long, sleek nose and Abigail watched a bead of sweat run down the bridge, dwell at the tip for a moment, and then fall to the ground. "And you wish to fight for the provincials?" she said. "We need sterner stuff, Mr. Lumley."

"I can provide information," he said hastily, "tactical information. And plans."

"Plans? Such as?"

It was so dark now that she could not see his eyes. "Noddle's Island."

"What about it?"

"I would first require assurances that you will help me get out of Boston."

"It's getting too dark in here," she said, turning toward the opening in the rocks. "I need to think about this. I need to talk with—"

"But I haven't much time!"

She ducked through the opening in the rock and came out into the path, where cooler air came up the hill, smelling of low tide. Lumley passed through the opening as well, and then he grabbed her upper arm he said, "You must needs understand my predicament, Mistress, that I'm—"

There was a scream from higher up the hill. Abigail heard running footsteps coming toward her. Lumley let go of her arm and disappeared downhill. The footsteps from above were coming closer and she moved toward the tree by the side of the path, but just as she placed a hand on the trunk, her forehead struck a branch and she fell down in the grass.

Benjamin was awakened by footsteps on the stairs. He sat up on the straw bedding, a sense of alarm coursing through his veins. There were two pairs of boots coming across the loft toward the room, one heavy and slow, the other lighter, swifter. He looked at the open window, the night sky above the harbor. If he was found out, if they were redcoats come to arrest him, he would not endure such an interrogation again.

Jump.

He would: a swift fall into a graveyard, where they would not be able to beat information out of him. Names. Troop strength. Plans for deployment. Things he heard while acting as courier in Cambridge. The dead don't tell secrets.

He moved toward the window, the pain in his knee such that he rested a haunch on the windowsill, and then he faced the door.

The door swung open. Obadiah stepped into the room. He was not wearing his key ring and he was followed by his son Ezekiel. "My boy has been to the North End," Obadiah said. "We have much news."

Benjamin inhaled deeply, surprised by the smell of fish. The boy walked toward him, carrying a pail covered with a white cloth. "Haddock?"

"And bread and potatoes," Ezekiel said, handing him the pail.

Benjamin removed the cloth and heat rose up, warming his face. "Thank you, Ezekiel, and thank your mother for me." Then, looking at Obadiah, he said, "What news?"

"Eat." Obadiah leaned against the door jamb and slid down the wall until he was resting on his heels. As he draped his arms over his knees, he said, "There's been a murder—two, actually: one Bostonian and one redcoat. And I'm not sure it's safe for you to stay here any longer."

XII

The Seventh Psalm

LIGHT, PIERCING LIGHT, AND BRIEF SPIKES OF CONSCIOUSNESS parted her dream: *a dory in the harbor beneath a mackerel sky, with Benjamin laughing as he hauls in one mackerel after another, and the countryside—Surrey, England?—smells of sweet grass, moist air, grazing sheep, where Mrs. Margaret Kemble Gage carefully wraps her hair in a red silk turban saying One day we must travel to Constantinople together, leave our husbands and children behind, just you and I, and in the distance there is a hunting party, red coats, black helmets, the horses snorting with the effort of the chase, while in the woods beyond the yelping of the hounds, as Mother feeds her fish chowder and Father sits by the window in her room, his book open, mumbling in Latin, until Samuel dismounts his horse, his white jodhpurs and polished riding boots spattered with fox blood.*

Whose blood?

When Dr. Phelan unwound the bandage, she saw the red-soaked linen just before he dropped it into the pan on the floor. "This is a terrible gash," he said. "I suspect you have quite the

175

headache." Turning to Mother and Father, he said, "But it appears her fever's passed."

Her head felt as though it had been split open just above the left eye. She laid back into the pillows and closed her eyes.

Ezra's hand cupped the side of her face briefly, and then he went to the doorway, where he paused a moment before leaving the outbuilding . . . She watched him walk up the alley and disappear around the corner of the stable. His footsteps grew faint, moving down Ann Street to the footbridge, and when he reached the other side of the canal there was only silence.

It was Dr. Phelan, his fingers touching her cheek, smelling of tobacco, and he whispered, "More rest and you'll be fine, though I hope you won't go knocking this pretty skull against any more trees."

The redcoats want to cut down the trees.

He didn't seem to hear that, and he said, "Hard as wood, her noggin is."

They plan to clear-cut the Mall, leaving only the Great Elm in the Common for hangings.

And all the churches, too. For fuel.

Paul Revere's mother says they will level Boston.

But none of them seemed to hear her, and Mother opened the bedroom door for Dr. Phelan, while Father sat again in the chair by window, his eyes large with worry before he resumed reading his Latin.

Samuel's coat was red. He too looked worried, though he smiled down at her.

"Finally," he whispered, "I have you alone in bed."

She looked toward the window, expecting to see her father there, his face flushed at such impertinence, but the chair was empty.

"I believe I ran into a tree," she said weakly.

"Yes, and you have given everyone a fright," Samuel said.

"It was dark. There was a scream."

His smile could not hold. Concern flooded his eyes. "There was, I'm sure."

"Do you know what happened?"

He seemed to consider how to respond for too long. "Don't you know?"

She moved her head from side to side, gently. Something behind her forehead drifted, dislodged, a yoke inside an egg. She touched the bandage above her ear. "It's too tight."

His hand caught hers. "Best to leave it. Doctor's orders. Besides . . . in time it will grow back."

"What will?"

"Your hair. I'm afraid that in order to clean the wound, the doctor had to cut away a portion of your lovely hair, here in front, above your left eye. I must say you had us worried there."

"How long?"

"Two days." He held her hand on the counterpane. "Listen to me now. There are going to be inquiries, of course. And the rumors—what were you doing up there?"

"On Trimount?"

"Yes. It's no place for you to go."

"I was walking. Am I not allowed to go for a walk?"

"But you do understand what goes on up there."

"Your soldiers go there, seeking . . . services. Perhaps you should place restrictions."

"We have, for now." He straightened up, his eyes averted; he was thinking of something else. "It's strictly off limits until we determine what happened to Munroe."

"Munroe? Sergeant Munroe?" Samuel nodded. "What hap-pened to him?"

"We don't know for certain who killed him."

"On Trimount—that was his scream?"

"I imagine so. I suppose one might scream as his throat is being cut."

177

"But who? What rumors?"

He turned and glanced toward the closed door. "It was kind of your parents to let me visit with you, though we'll be alone only a few minutes." Looking back down at her he said urgently, "You remember nothing?"

Again, she shook her head slowly. The pain was dull, heavy, left side, then right.

"You were found up there, beneath a tree, covered with blood. Yours, certainly, though there is speculation—but there was no weapon, no knife, or whatever was used to kill Munroe. You didn't see him up there?"

She remembered then: Lumley and the cave. Talking about his defection. "No, I didn't see Munroe."

He stared at her.

"Who found me?"

"Two soldiers. They carried you down the hill."

"What were their names?"

"I'm not sure—"

"It wasn't Corporal Lumley? He often patrolled the streets with Munroe."

"Lumley? No . . . but he's been reported missing, which is curious." There was the sound of footsteps on the stairs and he turned toward the door again. "Listen, I must be off."

"What happens now?"

"You rest."

"But you mentioned inquiries."

"Yes," he said. "They will be necessary for you to be cleared."

"Cleared?"

"A soldier has been murdered, so there must be an inquiry, and . . . and you were found close by, covered in blood. They wanted you to appear at Province House, but I said I'd heard you weren't well enough."

"When?"

"Soon. They offered to come here."

"Who did?"

"The officers conducting the inquiry."

"You are one of them?"

"Yes."

She sat up in bed. "Not here. I will go there. The sooner the better. Today."

"Today? Are you sure you're capable?" She nodded. There were footsteps outside the door and Samuel got to his feet hastily. "Then you must rest. That's what's important now—that you get well."

The door opened, and her mother entered with a tray. "I thought a little chicken broth. You've hardly eaten a thing in two days."

Obadiah arranged it. Though Benjamin still had great difficulty walking, even with his crutch, he was taken down on the lift and placed in a tool crate in the back of a wagon. The ride was jarring, the air inside the crate stifling, smelling of corn. But then he was let out and in the North End, and he worked his way through the lanes and alleys down to the waterside, until he came to Anse Cole's house.

The front door was draped with black ribbon. He knocked with his crutch, and after a moment he heard footsteps on the pine floorboards. When the door opened, Mariah looked out, squinting against the light. Sorrowful, weary eyes, red from crying, but then she flung her arms about his neck and pressed herself against him, pulling him back into the house. She wept as she clung to him, deep convulsions of grief surging up from her chest.

And then they separated, embarrassed. She rubbed her long, thin hands on the front of her skirt. "Thank God you're all right," she said.

"Your father, what happened? That soldier with the rifle killed him?"

She nodded. "Come, look."

It was a small house, built around a central chimney. Benjamin's crutch knocked loudly on the pine floorboards. Anse Cole's body, wrapped in old sailcloth, which was stitched with heavy thread, lay on a pallet before the stone fireplace.

"The Brits won't let us take him out into the harbor," she said, "and I'll not have him buried in the ground. He was insistent that he be buried at sea, like we did when my mother died."

The air was close; there was a smell. "He can't stay here much longer, Mariah."

"They've restricted all boats on the harbor now. Permits are required, and of course you have to pay dearly for them. There are patrols along the beaches. They shot at Myles Lapham when they saw him rowing out to the marshes, and they've put holes in a good many of the boats down in the cove there."

She left the room and he followed her through the kitchen and out the back door, where they sat on the steps. "I heard you were interrogated, but then you escaped. They hurt you bad, did they not?"

"I'll be all right."

"Your face, Benjamin." She touched his cheek, gently. "Are you hiding?"

He looked across the dooryard toward the alley. "I am."

"Then we shouldn't remain outside, not in the daylight." She got to her feet and helped him up, and they entered the house, with her arm about his waist.

"But . . . the air in here, Mariah. We must do something soon."

"Tonight," she said as she eased him into a chair at the kitchen table. "Relatives, neighbors, they're all coming and we will get him in the water tonight, while the tide's falling. In the meantime, you can rest. You look like you haven't eaten in—I'll make some chowder." She began to move away from him, toward the fireplace, but she came back and began to sit in his lap, which made him wince. "Oh, your poor knee, I'm sorry." Standing, she gathered his head in her arms as she wept uncontrollably.

Abigail's father accompanied her to Province House, and they were admitted to the room at the end of the lobby. It was a chamber where official business was conducted, a place where a woman was seldom allowed. Seated behind a long table were three British officers, the youngest of them Samuel Cleaveland. The other two were of her father's generation, and they greeted him warmly. They were extremely cordial toward Abigail, asking her to sit in a fine polished chair in front of them. The two older officers, General Smythe and General Armbruster, maintained the blank, noncommittal expression of judges. Samuel, leaning back, with one arm draped over the back of his chair, appeared disinterested. Then the door behind Abigail was opened by the guard and everyone stood up as General Gage entered, taking a seat to Abigail's left; he was tall and elegant, and he crossed his legs.

"Carry on, please," he said. "I'm merely here as an observer."

"Then we will begin," General Smythe said. He had a long face and thin, loose jowls. "Miss Lovell, if you please, why did you climb up Trimount two nights ago?"

"For the exercise, General."

"The exercise? Were you accompanied by anyone?"

"No."

"A woman, alone on Trimount, at night? Were you not afraid to go up there?"

"I am Boston born and bred, General. I have never felt any reluctance or hesitation to walk anywhere in this city."

General Armbruster's plump cheeks were shiny as a russet apple, and he kept working his tongue into the left side of his mouth as though trying to dislodge something from between his teeth. "A woman of your breeding—" he glanced deferentially toward Abigail's father—"should know that walking up Trimount is simply not the proper thing to do."

Abigail's father stirred in his chair, preparing to speak, but she turned to him and said quietly, "That does not deserve a response, Father." At first he looked as though he were determined to argue the point—with her, she imagined—but then he sat back, folding his hands over the silver knob of his cane, looking discontented.

Samuel leaned forward in his chair, placing both elbows on the table. "You acknowledge that you were there on the Trimount, Miss Lovell, so please tell us what you observed."

"It wasn't much, Colonel," she said. "I was starting my descent as it was nearly dark, when I heard a scream. Then there were running footsteps coming down the path toward me, and as I attempted to get out of the way I struck a tree branch with my head."

"The blow was sufficient to knock you unconscious," Samuel said. "And there was much blood."

"I gather this is so," Abigail said. "I was unconscious for most of the next two days."

General Smythe leaned to his right and conferred with General Armbruster for a moment, while Samuel tried not to appear insulted. Finally, General Smythe looked past Abigail, toward the guard at the door. "Bring the two soldiers in."

Abigail turned in her seat and watched as two Regulars marched in to the room. They were both younger than she, perhaps still in their teens. They approached the side of the table, and General Smythe said, "Miss Lovell, have you ever seen either of these soldiers before?"

"Not that I recall, General."

"Well," General Armbruster said. "This is Private Lodge and Private Dayton, and they have seen you. Private Lodge, tell us what happened up there on Trimount."

He appeared to be the older of the two, had good military bearing, and he looked straight ahead as he spoke. "Sir, we was taking our constitutional on the Trimount when we comes across this woman. She was knocked out of her wits and quite bloodied, so me and Dayton carries her down the hill and soon enough some hag by the King's Chapel recognizes her and points to the house she lives at and we delivers her to the gentleman there, who we understand to be the master at the Latin School."

General Smythe was about to speak, but Samuel placed a hand on his forearm, and then turned to Lodge. "Private, you took a constitutional on the Trimount?"

"Yes, sir," Lodge said.

"Just you and Dayton."

"Yes, sir."

"You didn't meet anyone?"

"No, sir."

"No assignation?"

"Sir?"

"You didn't arrange to meet anyone?" Samuel waited a moment, and then asked, "Do you and Dayton know a Molly Collins?" Lodge didn't answer. "Didn't you arrange to meet Molly Collins and another girl, named Eliza, on the Trimount?" Samuel waited again, but then spoke quite severely. "Private Lodge, I can have Molly Collins brought here to testify that you and Dayton have made such arrangements in the past, and that they were going to meet you that night on the Trimount, after dark. Am I correct, Private? You and Dayton went up there early with a flask and had a few nips in anticipation of your assignation with these two women, who, it is my understanding, have considerable reputations on the street." Samuel leaned back in his chair, which creaked loudly, echoing off the high ceiling. "Well, Lodge?"

The private continued to stare straight ahead, but he did blink before he said, "Yes, sir. We know these women, they being familiar with a lot of the Regulars, you know? And we went up there . . . like you says."

General Armbruster raised a hand off the table, but Samuel said, "All right, Private Lodge. Now, tell us what you heard up there."

"Heard, sir?"

"Did you hear anything? A scream perhaps?"

"No," Lodge said. "We didn't hear no scream."

"Dayton," Samuel said. "You hear any scream?"

"N–no, sir," Dayton said.

"Miss Lovell here," Samuel said. "She testified that she heard a scream. You were in the vicinity—how could you not hear it?"

"With all due respect," General Smythe said. "We have two soldiers who claim they heard no scream, while this young woman—who was found covered in blood and was knocked unconscious—claims that she did."

Samuel folded his hands in front of him, studying his knuckles with care. "Their word against hers, the daughter of Boston's most respected schoolmaster."

"No slight intended," Smythe said, glancing toward Abigail's father. "Miss Lovell claims she was knocked unconscious for two days. Perhaps she imagined—or even dreamed—that she heard a scream."

"Miss Lovell's statement was clear enough, I think," Samuel said, looking up from his hands. "Private Lodge, and Private Dayton, you both know Corporal Lumley?"

Lodge began to turn his head toward the table, but then looked straight ahead again.

"Yes, sir," Dayton said. "We knows him."

"Have you seen him lately?" Samuel asked.

"No, sir," Dayton said. "He's . . ."

"Gone missing," Samuel said. "Correct?"

"Yes, sir," Dayton said. "He's not been at parade drills and such."

"Missing since the night all of you were on Trimount, the night that Sergeant Munroe was killed. Isn't it true that both men, Munroe and Lumley, walked street patrol together regularly? Isn't it true that on the night Munroe died, both men set out for Trimount not long before sunset? I have talked with other soldiers who claim that Munroe and Lumley were seen together in a tavern, and then they left together, heading in the direction of those hills, and no one has seen Lumley since. Isn't that so?"

Lodge cleared his throat. "Yes, sir. I have heard that among the men."

"Soldiers do talk," Samuel said, "and there has been talk about a row between Munroe and Lumley—are you aware of that?" Samuel didn't wait for a reply from Lodge or Dayton. "They argued over an incident which occurred recently in the North End. While on patrol, they came upon some suspicious behavior on the beach, and the result was that a fisherman was killed—by Munroe, is my understanding—and a boy was taken into custody for questioning."

General Gage shifted in his chair so he could look over his shoulder and out the windows. Clearly, he was reluctant to be a direct participant in the proceedings.

"What boy was this?" General Armbruster asked.

"We don't know, sir," Samuel said. "He wouldn't volunteer his name, and . . ."

"And?" Armbruster said.

"My understanding," Samuel said, "is that the boy escaped custody."

General Gage turned away from the windows and faced the officers, none of whom dared look at him.

Samuel said, "Thank you, Lodge and Dayton."

After a moment, General Armbruster said, "That is all, men. Dismissed."

The two privates left the room, and once the door was closed behind them Samuel said, "I would like to find Lumley . . . I would like to find that boy."

Well," General Smythe said finally, and he began to get out of his chair.

But then he paused when General Gage beckoned toward the soldier at the door. He conferred with the soldier a moment, and then sat back, crossing his legs the other way. The soldier went around the table and whispered to General Smythe. When he was through, he returned to his position by the door.

General Smythe looked at Abigail and raised a hand toward his scalp. "That cloth, it's a fine red satin—"

"It's a turban," Abigail said.

"Yes, a turban." Smythe seemed embarrassed, but then he looked toward General Gage a moment, and said, "Would you be so kind as to remove it for us?"

Abigail's father shifted in his chair, but she said, "Not at all, General."

She was keenly aware of the men watching her as she raised her arms and untied the knot at the back of her head. When she unwound the turban, her hair fell down to her shoulders and over her face. With one hand, she drew the veil of hair aside, and turned toward General Gage so that he could see the gash that ran at an angle from her forehead up into her scalp. There was something unnerving and even intimate in the way General Gage looked at her wound. But then he seemed to have come to a decision and he got to his feet, causing the three officers to also rise. He bowed slightly toward Abigail, almost as a gesture of apology, and then he went to the door, which the guard opened for him.

No one moved as they listened to the general's boots in the lobby. Neither Smythe or Armbruster would look at Abigail, and Samuel only ventured a brief glance, which seemed difficult to decipher—he appeared disappointed, even concerned.

Father got to his feet then, rapping his cane on the floor to get the officers' attention. "I would like to know what conclusion you draw from this inquiry."

All three officers stared at him, though after a moment Samuel lowered his eyes. Smythe, who seemed perturbed that the question had been asked, said, "This inquiry is ended, for the time being. And we have not come to a conclusion." Louder, he said, "There is as yet no conclusion."

They began to arrive shortly after sunset, when the western sky was still light. Mariah was at first confused, but by the time it was dark, there were hundreds of people crowded into the narrow lane in front of the house. There were fishermen and their families who knew Anse Cole, but word had worked its way through the neighborhoods of Boston and by ten o'clock a crowd extended all the way down to the beach at the end of the lane. Six relatives, lobstermen and clam-diggers all, hoisted Anse Cole's shrouded body on to their shoulders and made their way down the lane behind the Reverend Whitman, while Mariah and the womenfolk in the family, children in hand, followed behind. As they proceeded, the crowd parted silently, faces glistening in the light from lanterns. As the procession moved down to the beach, Benjamin fell in toward the rear, his hat pulled low over his eyes, relying heavily on his crutch.

At the cove they were met by a patrol, two Regulars, who after an extended discussion with the Reverend Whitman, stood aside as Anse Cole's body was placed inside his dory and rowed out into the harbor, accompanied by several other boats, bearing Mariah and her immediate relatives. Hymns were sung, prayers recited.

More soldiers soon appeared on the beach, led by an officer on horseback. Despite his warnings, the crowd would not disperse. Eventually, he ordered his men to form a line and take aim, but when the Reverend Whitman stepped to the front of the crowd and by lantern light recited the seventh Pslam—*"Let the enemy persecute my soul, and take it!"*—the officer elected to withdraw his men farther down the beach.

XIII

Coiled Rope

THIS TIME IT WAS YOUNG PAUL REVERE WHO APPEARED IN THE dooryard, requesting that Abigail accompany him to North Square. Rachel sat knitting on the front step, watching the children as they played in the square. Paul was a solidly built adolescent who favored his father and said he had to get back to work and went inside the house.

"He will take over the shop," Rachel said, gazing out at the square.

"You're going to leave Boston."

Rachel sighed. "We have obtained an evacuation pass, yes."

"Perhaps it's best."

"It's getting worse by the day. Food is very scarce—it's even difficult to get fish, now that there are restrictions on boats venturing into the harbor." Rachel pointed to the North Church, which was across the square. "They're going to tear it down. Fuel. It's May, and the weather has finally turned warm, but they're already planning for the winter. But it's not just fuel, it's a form of retribution, this tearing-down business. There's talk that they're going to cut down the trees in the Mall."

"I had heard that, but it just seems unbelievable."

"And Old South."

"Rachel, Old South? They can't tear *that* down."

"They're not. But they've cleared out the pews and covered the floor with dirt so that officers can exercise their horses, regardless of the weather. Old South—there's not a church, nay, a building that has greater importance to Bostonians." She glanced at Abigail, the red silk turban about her head. "Very stylish, really, most exotic." She smiled, if only briefly. "How are you getting on?"

"Better. Every day I walk more. But I will have to wear turbans for months until my hair grows back—caps and bonnets don't conceal the awful space in my scalp."

A carriage entered the square and stopped at a house a few doors down from the Revere's. A footman opened the door and an officer stepped out; he looked about briefly and then entered the house.

"Major Pitcairn is billeted there," Rachel said. "Some evenings he has sweets sent out to the street. Can't catch their fathers, so he kills the children with kindness." She had been knitting, but her needles lay in her lap, idle.

"Rachel, what? You're worried about leaving, I know, but—"

"I've been thinking about Dr. Church lately." She stared at Abigail for a long moment. "You delivered the money I intended for Paul to him?"

"Of course."

Rachel nodded.

"Why? Have you heard from Paul?"

"One letter has been smuggled in, encouraging me to bring his mother and the children out, and his sisters too, though I think they plan to remain here." Rachel looked out at the children, who were crouched about a frog, prodding it with a stick and cheering each time it leaped forward in the dirt. "But there's so much talk, and, believe me, I hear it, rumor and speculation, and then . . . there's what you don't hear." A fly bobbed in front of her face, which she shooed away with her hand. "Mary Burke lives just down Moon Lane there, and I heard that that her husband Matthew got word to her. He was in Cambridge, but now he's encamped with the troops in Charlestown. He got word across the harbor by the ferry boat, and it sounds like they're marching constantly and burning those bonfires we see on the hills at night—it's all an effort to make their force seem more impressive. So I go by Mary's yesterday and ask if Matthew had any word about Paul—they being good friends and all. And she says yes, Matthew has seen Paul several times, and she even said that Paul told Matthew that he wanted to get word across that he wanted me to be informed that he was well."

"That is good news," Abigail said. Rachel stared at her again. "But there's been no mention of the money you sent out—either in Paul's letter or from Mary?"

"Exactly."

"There must be an explanation."

"Yes, I suppose there is."

"I delivered your letter and the money to Dr. Church."

"I know you did."

They both looked out into the square again.

"Do you suppose something's happened to Dr. Church?" Abigail asked.

"It's possible."

They didn't speak for a minute, and then Abigail got up off the step, smoothing her skirt. "I should walk, because later I must get back home to help Mother. We are frequently entertaining Tories, and I am . . . I'm so fed up with being pleasant to them."

Rachel got to her feet. She put her arms about Abigail and hugged her. "We shall be away soon, and I may not see you . . .

for a good while." They began to let go of each other, but then Rachel clutched at her more tightly, and said in her ear. "I suggest you walk by and visit Mariah Cole."

"I've been meaning to, to pay my respects."

Rachel released her, and, smiling, she said with some urgency, "Go—go see her."

Abigail leaned back so she could study Rachel, look in her eyes. "I will, once I've regained my strength—the walk this far from the house has about exhausted me."

"Yes, but visit her, soon." Rachel pulled herself free and turned to open the door. "Soon as you are well enough."

"You're usually so blunt. Why are you being so cryptic?"

"Consider it a symptom," Rachel said, and then she laughed. "It has been too long since I've lain with my husband."

"Boston won't be the same without you."

"I leave our city in your capable hands." Rachel entered the house, shutting the weathered oak door behind her.

Benjamin had spent several days recuperating in the shed behind Mariah's house. He lay on a bed of old sailcloth, surrounded by nets, buoys, anchors, block pulleys, clam rakes, shucking knives, coiled rope, and more rope. There were chipmunks, and the occasional rat. Seagulls' claws scratched on the roof shingles, and the few chickens in the yard behind the house squabbled as they pecked relentlessly at the dirt. Mariah insisted that he not venture into the yard until nightfall, as a matter of safety and propriety. She would not admit him to the house, but brought his meals out to him. Too often there were unexpected visits from people who wished to pay their respects, and it would not do to find that Anse Cole's daughter was not as she seemed, alone.

By mid afternoon it was very hot in the shed, the heat and humidity bringing out the smell of salt and fish, so that, sweating in his damp shirtsleeves, Benjamin thought of himself as a quahog, moist and formless, encased in its hard shell. He was dozing when he was startled by the sound of familiar voices. He peeked out through a wide crack in the door and saw that Mariah and his sister had come out the kitchen door to sit in two wooden chairs she had set by the chopping block. They sat there in the shade, facing the shed, a plate of gingerbread and two glasses of water on the block.

Mariah seemed to be attempting to stare right through the shed door, while Abigail paid her condolences. She was wearing her white linen dress, which she reserved for the warmest days of the year, and her hair was concealed beneath a yellow turban; the fabric had a gloss even in the shade. It gave her a foreign appearance, and her face, browned by the sun, seemed fuller for not having her dark curls draped around it.

Benjamin wanted to shout her name.

He wanted to pull open the door and hobble out into the yard, scattering chickens, giving his sister a fright and then an enormous hug. He wanted to tell her all about the fighting, about driving the British back to Boston, about working for Dr. Warren, about living among the men encamped on Cambridge Common. He wanted to tell her about Ezra, that he was safe and that they had become like brothers, brothers in arms. But then Benjamin realized that he could not tell her: he had promised not to say anything about Ezra to Abigail. Why would Ezra make such a request? What was being concealed? Or revealed? Benjamin retreated to his bed of sailcloth, lay down, and gazed up at the rafters, where spiders had woven elaborate webs, cluttered with the remains of dead bugs.

It was understandable, Abigail supposed, that Mariah seemed distracted as they sat in her yard. She looked like she'd gotten little sleep, and her posture suggested that she was thoroughly spent and weary. And nervous: her hands fidgeted in her lap (she wouldn't touch the cornbread and only occasionally sipped water), and her eyes stared hard about the small yard. She seemed afraid to look at any one thing for very long, and when she did look at Abigail it was a momentary, furtive glance. Baffling, but what did Abigail know about mourning, how it affected different people?

"I heard how there was a large gathering on the beach for your father," she said, "and that they proved defiant when the redcoats ordered them to disperse." Mariah only nodded, as though she didn't quite remember. "Your father gives us strength, you must know that, Mariah."

The girl turned to her then, as if just discovering that she was not alone. "Everyone has been so kind." She then shook her head. "No, I mean it, Abigail. I've been saying that to people who come by, but truly, I thank you." Then she looked down at her hands, worrying in her lap.

"I must ask—" Abigail waited, hoping she would look up again, but she didn't. "You saw my brother? I hear that he landed here by boat and this was what brought on the incident with your father." Mariah still didn't look up, though her shoulders seemed to lift and tighten, as if there was a need to fend off the next question. "Have you seen Benjamin since?"

Mariah looked up and stared at her, but did not answer.

"I know he was taken into custody," Abigail said. "But he escaped and no one's seen him since." She paused; Mariah's eyes were large with fear. "I hear he was not well treated, and fear that he might be injured."

Mariah was on the verge of tears. She turned her head away, staring toward the back of the yard. Abigail picked up her water and finished it. Putting her glass down on the chopping block, she leaned forward. "Mariah, what is it?"

Tears welled up in the girl's eyes and ran down her cheeks. She shook her head.

"There's something . . . I know you're grieving, but there's something else—I can feel it." Abigail waited, and then got up from her chair. "Well, I should be going."

Mariah walked her to the fence gate at the side of the house, where they could see a woman and two little girls coming down the lane, both carrying baskets. "My cousin Anne," Mariah said. "They've all been so good to me, bringing food and whatnot." She waved, trying to smile, but when she looked at Abigail she seemed to come to a decision. "Listen, could you come back tonight?"

"Of course—"

"After dark," she said, opening the gate for Abigail.

Family and friends visited Mariah throughout the afternoon and on into the evening. Children played in the yard, chasing each other, pestering chickens, while the adults sat in the shade of the house. On one occasion, Benjamin heard footsteps approach the shed, and he saw an eye—a child's eye—gazing through the crack in the door. It was dark inside, and Benjamin remained absolutely still, and quickly the child was warned by her mother not to go in the shed.

Then Mariah said, "It's full of dangerous things."

"What things?" the girl asked, still standing in front of the shed door.

"Well, sometimes when a fisherman dies," Mariah said. "His ghost comes back for his nets, so we don't want to disturb those things, just in case."

The other woman laughed as her daughter ran from the shed, yelling, "You mean it's haunted? The shed is haunted?"

"Perhaps a little," Mariah said. "I avoid going in there. It's so hot—won't you have some more water?"

And the little girl said, "Thank you."

That evening Samuel came around to the house on horseback and, after paying his respects to Mr. and Mrs. Lovell, he and Abigail walked over to the Mall. He let his horse wander out on to the Common to graze while they watched the sunset beyond the trees. On the far side of the Common, soldiers had erected rows of tents near the banks of the Charles, and smoke billowed from their campfires.

"You didn't tell the truth, did you?" he asked.

"Pardon?"

"At the inquiry."

"What do you mean?"

"Did you really go up Trimount alone?"

"That's what I said. Why won't you believe me?"

He stared out across the Common. The warm air was golden and there were moths and butterflies everywhere, flecks of sunlight. "This business about Munroe and Lumley. Believe me, if General Gage bothers to sit in on such a thing, then they mean to get to the bottom of it."

"Why would you think I had—"

"There was something about the way you responded to certain questions."

"You actually think I murdered Munroe?"

"No. No, I don't." He began to walk down the Mall beneath the trees. "But I don't think they're convinced."

"Smyth and Armbruster?"

"And Gage," he said. "They were being very . . . deferential."

"Because of my father."

"Well, yes, because he's a loyalist and Gage is particularly fond of him. The general appreciates culture and learning. He envisions himself as possessing such traits."

"Yet he ships his wife overseas."

Samuel didn't answer. He walked with his hands clasped behind his back, and as a couple of soldiers passed by in the other direction he acknowledged their salutes with a curt nod.

"He may be cultured and learned," she said, "but he's also highly suspicious."

"He has good reason to be. We are surrounded here in Boston—you only have to look out at the hills of Dorchester and Charlestown. Things are bad and they're going to get worse.

There's a distinct tightening of discipline, and when soldiers go missing—or end up dead—it's something that can't simply be overlooked." He stopped walking and turned to her. "I don't believe you had anything to do with Munroe's death, but I think you know more than you're letting on. I feel it. I felt it during the inquiry."

Abigail began to walk away, back in the direction of her house.

"They will find out," Samuel said. "Smythe and Armbruster, they will find out, and if they aren't satisfied, they're not above arranging things to their liking." She stopped walking. "They're not above it, Abigail," he said. "Schoolmaster's daughter or not. They need to show results." He came to her then and waited until she looked up at him. "Lumley's the key. They're searching hard for Lumley, and when they find him they'll determine how they want to play it." He took her by the arm. "Listen, they're suspicious of me as well. I had to work things to get on that inquiry, and they know I'm your . . . advocate."

"How do they know that?" she asked. "How, Samuel?"

"They just do. We've been seen together enough, like this, and, well, I'm no better at dissembling than you are."

He took her hand then, and she didn't pull away. "I do—I did appreciate how you handled the questioning, you know," she said. "Almost as much as how you came to visit me when I was confined to bed."

"I would like to think that you injured your head simply so that I could visit your bedchamber. That it was all a ploy."

She smiled, but then she said, "You do realize how difficult this is for me?"

"Consorting with a British officer? Yes, I understand."

"You have been kind and generous to me, but—"

"But whatever good qualities I possess, they're obscured by this uniform."

"It's difficult to see who you really are." He glanced at her, and she realized he was hesitant to say something. "What?"

"There's something else," he said. "Someone else." When she turned toward at him this time, he continued to walk with his head lowered, his hands clasped behind his back. She realized he was afraid to look at her. "Someone who has broken your heart."

"How—"

"I just know. I can sense these things. On one hand, I'm very sorry for you, but on the other I'm rather grateful. This—whatever it was, whoever it was—has driven you toward me, and for that I'm grateful." He looked at her now, quickly, his eyes earnest but wary of surrendering too much.

"You're right, Samuel. This is not easy, none of it. And now this inquiry. Sometimes I felt they were looking at me as though I were guilty simply because I am a woman, or because I am a Bostonian. Or both."

"I know it's very hard on you—though they'll never mistake you for, what was her name? Molly Collins."

"It's not like that."

"No. It would be easier if it were. A simple transaction, which soldiers understand, and nothing more. This . . . *this* is no simple transaction for you?"

She shook her head. "Far too complicated. I see it—when I go to market, it's in the eyes of vendors. The butcher used to give us a choice cut, but now . . . And Bostonians can be more effective in what they don't say and do. Too often now, as I walk the streets, they will just look away and pass in silence."

He touched her elbow gently, and then let go. They went out on the Common, where he gathered up the reins and led his horse back toward School Street. It was nearly dark when they passed the granary, which loomed above the burying ground. When they reached the brick wall which enclosed the granary yard, Samuel tied the reins to a hitching post and led Abigail behind a lilac bush.

Benjamin was awakened by footsteps, coming across the yard. It was dark and he sat up. He couldn't tell how much time had passed since Mariah had brought out some supper, and then a pan of water, lye soap, a towel, and one of her father's shirts. It felt good to be clean, to wear a shirt that had been laundered and ironed—so much so that he had been reluctant to lie down in it. But now the shed door latch clicked and he got to his feet, reaching for his cane and raising it as his only means of defense.

The door swung open and Mariah whispered, "It's all right, Benjamin. Someone here to see you."

He lowered his cane and stepped out into the cool night air. Though it was a moonless night, he could see that it was Abigail standing in the middle of the yard. She rushed to him and threw her arms about his neck, pressing her face into his shoulder.

They had spent perhaps an hour sitting in the dark in the yard, whispering. To light a lantern would only draw the curiosity of neighbors, and attract still more mosquitoes and flies. As she walked home, Abigail wanted to find some way to tell her parents—her mother, at least—that Benjamin was safe. But they had all agreed before she'd left that they shouldn't tell anyone, except James, who was most adept at keeping secrets. It was too late to go to her older brother; the children would be bedded down; she would visit in the morning. Once Benjamin's knee was fully recovered—he said he was much better, though even in the dark she could see the damage done to his face—they would have to arrange to get him out of the city again.

Her elation over seeing her younger brother was tempered by the other thing: her moment with Samuel behind the lilac bush. Her sudden desire rose unexectedly. She didn't know whether it was because she was broken-hearted, as Samuel had suggested, or whether it was because of Samuel. Perhaps she was falling in love with him, despite what his uniform represented. Or perhaps she was just deluding herself with some notion that she could actually escape everything and find herself in a country manor in Surrey. A silly, ridiculous dream, certainly. But there was something about Samuel that made it real, possible. *If you could see me as I really am,* he'd whispered when they were behind the lilac bush, *without this blasted uniform.* But teasing, too—meaning unclothed, naked. *If I could only see you, and, admit it, I know you want to reveal yourself.*

It was true. She could only admit it to herself. *It is true.*

So many girls she knew got married while they were still in their teens, and more often than not they were quite pregnant by the time the wedding took place. Many of them by now, in their early twenties, had a brood of children. Some chided Abigail about the danger of becoming a spinster, though they also expressed some jealousy because men had always paid such attention to her. Playfully (usually) they accused her of harboring herself, trying to preserve her looks against the inevitable. But such childhood friends were now mostly preoccupied with their families, and they were at times dismissive of her when they met in the street. Once during the winter, at the market in Dock Square, a fishmonger's wife named Tilda Poole, while weighing a cod, said *Y'know, some women is just not strongly inclined.* And at the next booth Chastity, who was fond of making a joke of her name after she married William Dunne, looked up from shucking clams and said *That be true! Some just don't take to it at first, not until they meets up with a right good bowsprit.* They cackled knowingly, and as Abigail walked away, a hefty cod in her sack knocking against her thigh, she heard Tilda say *That's what the refinements will do for you—Latin and Greek, they won't help you see them stars at night!* And they howled as she slipped away through the crowded market.

There was no truth to it, not at all. She had unbuttoned her dress, allowing Samuel's hand inside, while his other hand clutched the small of her back so that his hardness pressed against her until they both shuddered. Afterwards, he talked about acquiring a room (he knew a woman who had a house overlooking an alley off Union Street; she was widowed and she was blind, reducing any danger of their being identified) and though Abigail had intended to say no, her only response was to kiss him again. Once they had abandoned the privacy of the lilac bush, he walked her down School Street toward home, again talking of the farm in Surrey, where he longed to live after this dreadful tour in Massachusetts was over. When he left her in front of King's Chapel, she watched him mount his horse, which he eased up into a trot as he headed toward Cornhill Street, and she recalled a fragment of her dream, where he rode toward her, his white jodhpurs spattered with blood. Fox blood, from the green fields of Surrey.

When Abigail turned to walk home, she heard a noise and looked into the shadows of the chapel. Someone was standing there behind a column. She hesitated, and, looking down School Street, which was empty—where were the ubiquitous patrols now?—she considered running for home.

"Miss Lovell?" A woman's voice, young and timid.

"Who is it? Who's there?"

The woman stepped away from the column's shadow. She was barely five feet tall and her clothes were filthy. "My name is Molly Collins."

XIV

Hunger and Other Carnal Afflictions

AFTER ABIGAIL LEFT, BENJAMIN AND MARIAH REMAINED sitting in the dooryard.

"Thank you for arranging that," he whispered.

"You know what this means?"

He did, but he didn't say anything.

"You'll be away, again. She'll talk to your brother—they'll get you out of Boston."

"Perhaps," he said.

"I will be alone here. I fear that more than anything."

"I'll return, Mariah."

"This will go on and on. You get out, no knowing when you return."

"You could leave Boston, too."

"I could. Maybe I should. But this is my father's house." He could barely see her in the dark. "I cannot just leave it." Her voice was quivering. "It is not so easy for me, what with my father just dying."

"There's something else," he said. "Isn't there?"

She turned her head away, and then said, "How's your knee?"

"Better, much better."

She got up and came to him, gently sitting on his lap. "How's that?"

"It's fine."

She hugged him tightly, her cheek pressed against the side of his head, and he could feel the warmth coming off her skin, which always smelled faintly of salt from the harbor.

As they walked beneath a streetlamp, Abigail got a look at Molly Collins's face. She wasn't yet twenty, boyishly slender in the hips, but with a powdered bosom that was pushed up so that it seemed on the verge of spilling out of her bodice. Black kohl was smeared around the eyes, which made the whites seem large and protuberant, as though she were in a state of high expectation. Her mouth was painted, full, beckoning, and there was a tiny scar running at an angle down from the corner of her lower lip. She'd already lost some teeth and when she spoke there was a slight whistle about the S's.

Boston was full of prostitutes and since her youth Abigail had been fascinated by them. She was warned, of course, to avoid them, but often she and her friends used to follow such women through the streets, dispersing only after they had been treated to a barrage of foul language, accompanied by hurled stones and dirt. Her friends liked to taunt them, but Abigail always found them as sad as they were interesting.

"There's a soldier wants to talk to you," Molly said. "Name's Lumley."

"You know him, and you knew Munroe."

"I know me lots of men. Soldiers, sailors, and not a few that parade about in a coach-'n'-four with fine liveried footmen."

They were heading toward the waterfront, until Molly took Abigail's sleeve and led her down an alley. "These patrols, you know. In my profession you learn that they move like clockwork. This way we'll avoid one that come up from Long Wharf this time of night." She walked quickly but with a slight limp, and there was the sound of her toe dragging along the cobblestones.

"'Ere we ahh," she said cheerfully.

She led Abigail up a narrow set of stairs that groaned under their weight, until they came to a door, which she opened with a key. Inside, the room was lit by one dim lantern and the air reeked of perfume and unwashed clothes. Lumley sat at a table by the window, looking out on the harbor, and through a door that had been left ajar Abigail could see a plump girl lying on a cot, snoring gently.

Lumley got up and held the other chair for Abigail, and then sat down across from her. Molly went to a cabinet and brought a bottle of rum and three tumblers, which she filled without spilling a drop.

Lumley looked exhausted. "You are dressed in small-clothes," Abigail said.

"No more uniform for me," he said.

As she returned the bottle to the cabinet, Molly sang softly:

> *Fifty lashes I got for selling me coat*
> *Fifty for selling me blanket*
> *If ever I 'list for a soldier again*
> *The devil shall be me sergeant.*

"In the taverns we often sing 'The Rogues' March,'" Lumley said, attempting a smile. "And now the boys are singing it for me. I've hardly ventured out since that night we were on Trimount. Molly here tells me they're all searching for me."

Abigail turned to Molly. "The soldiers, none have been here?"

"Oh, sure they 'ave, Love. We've got to eat, y'know." She rolled her eyes toward the low, beamed ceiling. "We pack him up to the attic while we're entertainin'. In an hour's time some Regulars will be comin' over from the Two Palavers, if they can still walk a straight line. So it's best you conduct your business and be on your way." Molly went into the other room, and as she closed the door she said, "A girl's got to make herself presentable, now, don't she?"

Lumley picked up his tumbler of rum and tossed it back.

"You ran off, Corporal Lumley," Abigail said.

"I know I did. Had to, and please don't call me corporal no more."

"Did you know I was brought before an inquiry into Munroe's death?"

"I heard. Molly and Eliza acquire all sorts of information."

"They suspect I killed him," Abigail said, "and it has been suggested that even if they can't prove it, they may make it seem to be so."

"Believe me, Miss, I'd speak on your behalf if it would do any good, but that's not likely. They'd rather put a noose about me neck and swing me from the Great Elm on the Common."

"I suppose." Abigail rarely drank rum, and then only on the coldest of winter nights, but now she took a sip and waited as its heat spread down through her. "You knew Munroe was up on Trimount, too. There was testimony that beforehand, you and he were in a tavern, and that you left together."

"We started out from the tavern, yes, but we argued, which was to your benefit. It allowed me to stay behind and come up later to meet you."

"And who did Munroe meet?" She nodded toward the now-closed door. "Molly and Eliza, they were mentioned at the inquiry."

"*They* killed him?" Lumley said. "Lord, no, not them. They can take a man's money without doing him in. I don't know who it was, but I can say that Munroe was eager to get up there. He was glad to leave me behind and climbed the hill with great urgency. He did fancy the ladies."

"What did you argue about?"

Lumley gazed out the window momentarily. "My loyalty. Munroe was beginning to suspect my intentions." He looked her squarely now. "I've got to get out of Boston. They'll catch me eventually. You can help, I know you can. Your brother James, I know he's thick with all of them. He can arrange it." He waited, and then said, "It's not some trap. I'm not spying for General Gage, if that's what you think."

"These things are difficult to determine. Everyone must be cautious." Abigail finished her rum and began to get up. "I'm sorry but I can't help you—"

Lumley reached across the table and took hold of her wrist, forcing her to settle back in her chair. She tried to pull free but his grip tightened as he leaned toward her. "I have information, which your brother might use." He nodded, and then let go of her wrist, looking apologetic. "When we met on Trimount, I mentioned something that I'd only heard in rumor, but since then I've heard more."

Abigail rubbed her wrist. "Noddle's Island."

"Yes," Lumley said. "You know how food is scarce in Boston. Dogs, cats disappearing. Chickens fewer by the day. It's mostly all salt fish. The troops are hungry. There's plenty of smuggling going on, but it's not enough to feed an army, and our good friend Tommy Gage understands that there's nothing worse than a hungry soldier."

The following morning, Abigail persuaded James to venture out for some air. Since the Latin School had closed, he rarely left his house. She took his arm—his gait was erratic, unstable—and they walked down to the granary burying ground.

"Shall we rest?" she said, when they reached the bench where she had sat with Rachel a few days earlier.

"I think so."

She helped James ease down onto the bench; his face was white, as though he'd never before been in the sun. Despite the heat, he'd insisted on wearing a wig.

"How does it go at home?" he asked.

"Mother is emptying the larder, feeding all of their Tory friends."

"I heard about the inquiry. Father actually came to talk with me about it. This hearing, and that gash on your head—he's worried about you. He conceals his affections often, but that's not to say they're not there."

"I know," Abigail said. "When I was confined to bed, he sat for hours in my room, his books open in his lap, muttering in Greek and Latin."

"You have some news?" he said. Surprised, she glanced at him and he smiled weakly, squinting into the morning sun. "Somehow I don't think this stroll is purely for my constitutional wellbeing."

"I do have news, yes. I saw Benjamin. He's well. You know he was captured and interrogated, but he's all right. Healing."

James exhaled slowly. "He's young, strong."

"Yes. He's still in Boston—"

"Don't tell me where, Abigail. The British have been watching my house regularly—I could be arrested at any time. I can't tell them what I don't know."

"All right."

"But he is well. That's good."

Abigail looked about the cemetery; there was an old man on his knees, clipping the grass about a grave with shears. "There's a soldier," she said, "a corporal named Lumley, who wants to escape Boston and join the provincials."

"No doubt there are plenty who would like to get off this peninsula. He wants assistance, I gather. I hope you told him no—it's too risky."

"He's genuine, I really think so. He has information."

"They all have information."

She decided not to respond. James had to come around of his own accord; he could not be pushed in a direction he did not want to go. They sat for a minute, listening to the sounds of the old man's shears snipping grass and a cluster of chickadees that hid in the lilac bush over by the granary wall. Finally, she said, "I love this spot. Better because it's a graveyard."

"I know," James said. "I think of it as the hub of Boston. Everything radiates out from it. It's the center of our universe."

"Last time I sat here was with Rachel Revere. They're packing up and evacuating. I shall miss her terribly."

"It's better for them. Have you considered going?"

"Me?"

"I could make arrangements for you to stay in—"

"No. I'll not leave Boston."

James shielded his eyes with a frail hand. "That man trimming the grass. Name's Boit, a rather good tailor. From my window I see him come in here every day to tend to his wife's grave. That's devotion." He lowered his hand and placed it over his stomach. "I shouldn't stay much longer, I'm afraid. Shall we head back?"

She helped him get up and they walked out to the street.

As they passed King's Chapel he said, "All right, what information?"

"It's about food."

"Yes, Boston is on the brink of starvation."

"Lumley says that Gage is planning on raiding some of the islands in the harbor."

"Which ones?"

"Noddle, and possibly Grape and Hog."

"Of course. There are plenty of cattle, sheep, and horses grazing out there, and they're in desperate need of hay for their horses." They walked down to James's front door, where he placed his free hand on the iron railing for support. "Such an expedition

will require a fair number of men, and ships—not just longboats—
to transport the animals. Did Lumley say when?"

"Not exactly, but soon."

James looked beyond Abigail, and smiled. "We have an
observer, as usual. I don't recognize him—must be new on the
job. All right, kiss me on the cheek for our friend's sake. Perhaps
he'll report that I've taken up with a beautiful young mistress
adorned with a turban."

He leaned forward, and Abigail put her arms about his neck
and kissed his cheek.

"And this Colonel Cleaveland," he said. "I'd be cautious there,
Abigail."

She began to let go of her brother, but then clung to him more
tightly.

"Remember, I speak from some experience in such matters.
Ask yourself what you want, what you really want."

"At the moment, what I want is to send Lumley and Benjamin
out of Boston together."

"I see."

She let go of him, and when he straightened up he didn't even
look at her before turning to open the door. "Yes, that might do.
They are watching me too closely, so you'll have to arrange it. I
will provide you with the necessary contacts." He paused after he
stepped up on to the threshold, quite exhausted. "Give my love
to Mother, and keep Father and his guests content, as distasteful
a task as that may be."

Benjamin awoke in the shed, and for a moment he was confused,
baffled as to how he had got there, but then he recalled that while
it was still dark Mariah had shaken him awake, kissed him once
more, saying he must get out of the house before daylight for fear
that someone might see him, so he got up from the bed, pulled
on his clothes, and walked out the kitchen door, and it was there
on the back steps that he heard the sound of alarmed chickens

coming from the coop, and then saw a boy crawl out from the small cage, a chicken, its neck already wrung, dangling from his fist, and the boy got to his feet and froze when he saw Benjamin staring down at him from the kitchen steps.

Or maybe Benjamin had only dreamed it. Maybe Mariah didn't take him to her bed with such urgency. Maybe the boy didn't stare for a long moment and then ask *You be a ghost?* And maybe Benjamin didn't answer *Yes, the ghost of Anse Cole,* causing the boy to drop the chicken and run to the back fence and leap over it, falling heavily and groaning in pain, before his footsteps beat down the alley.

Benjamin got up off his bed of sailcloth and peered through the crack in the shed door, to see a dead chicken lying in the dooryard. And then Mariah opened the kitchen door and stepped out into the early morning sunlight. She crossed the yard and picked the chicken up by its neck and said, "Already had three stolen since father died. No respect for the dead."

"The ghost of Anse Cole saved that chicken for you," Benjamin whispered through the crack in the door.

For the first time since he'd returned, she smiled, "Thank you, Father. And I best not waste thy gift. I'll make a fine chicken dinner, and with the carcass, a good stock."

He whistled gently. "But first, come into the shed."

Mariah gazed so long at the shed that he wondered if she could see right through the door. "First? First," she countered, "I must attend to my chores. I will keep this gift of a fine chicken in a cool, shaded place and tend to you later. Not first. Last—at last."

"Would it do any good to beg?" he whispered.

"It would not." She laughed as she walked away from the shed, the pendulous chicken swinging at her side in time to the sway of her hips.

XV

Departures

ABIGAIL'S DAYS AND NIGHTS HAD BEEN FRANTIC. SHE VISITED Mariah each day and informed Benjamin of their progress in arranging his escape from Boston, and she often went straight to Molly Collins's rooms near Dock Square to confer with Lumley. Then, representing James, she met with men in water-front taverns and chandleries, and made plans to smuggle both Benjamin and a British deserter off the peninsula. Bostonians were terrified of being captured by the British patrols; there were numerous incidents where people were incarcerated for the slightest infraction. Several fishermen initially refused to help Abigail, but finally it was settled that Benjamin and Lumley would be taken across the water to Charlestown in an oyster boat.

Donning a completely different guise, she also walked out frequently with Samuel. It was difficult to be in public with him, but she had learned to ignore the gaze of passing Bostonians (Samuel pretended not to notice). He had told her that he loved her with a straightforward sincerity that seemed determined to overcome any perceived obstacle—occupied and occupier. He talked frequently about the future, about his family's property in Surrey, and she listened intently. But as they grew closer, more familiar, more passionate, she became aware of something within him that was restrained, withheld. It seemed to be a matter of preparation, but for what she did not know. He seldom discussed military matters, other than offhand remarks which suggested that things were only getting worse.

One evening, walking her home from a stroll down to Windmill Point, he said, "This is a delicate situation, the two of us."

"Yes, I suppose it is."

"I just hope you're able to see beyond this uniform."

"I believe I can. We're both in rather contradictory situations."

"Sometimes I feel you're watching me, for some sign."

"Of what?" she asked.

"I don't know. And I must admit that at times I . . ."

"What, Samuel?"

"I'm almost spying on you. Do you know that there are regular reports regarding your brother James? There is great activity, comings and goings from his house. Some under General Gage's command would have done something, taken James into custody—there's no question where his sympathies lie—but there's great reluctance because your father and the general are so close."

"James is not well, you must know that."

"I do."

Suddenly, Abigail stopped walking and waited until Samuel did so as well. His hair was tied back in a queue and his face tanned from conducting drills with his men in the afternoon sun. "What are you really saying?" He shook his head and began walking again, but she caught his arm. "No, tell me, Samuel. Are you saying we are safe because of you?" He wouldn't look her in the eye. "You're protecting us?"

"I try. I do try." Then he almost seemed to plead. "You don't make it easy, Abigail. It is difficult, and dangerous. For us both."

Her hand was still on his arm. She kept it there as they looked at each other, and then they continued walking.

Benjamin was unaware of the circumstances surrounding his departure from Boston until the night before he was to leave, when Abigail arranged for him to meet her in a back room at the Green Dragon Tavern. She said James would join them briefly. And then she introduced Benjamin to a man named Lumley, a British corporal who wanted to desert and fight for the patriots. Benjamin was wary and he wanted to object, but then his older brother arrived. James's handshake was soft, the fingers chilled and stiff. His physical frailty had advanced greatly in the weeks since they'd last seen each other.

"It's best I were away quickly," James said. "But I did want to see you for just a moment before you go." He gave Benjamin a packet of letters. "Take these and Lumley to Dr. Warren—he needs to know about Gage's designs on the harbor islands. I hear you were badly treated when captured, but you look like you are recovering well." He glanced at Abigail. "I understand you are being well cared for. You might be cautious there, little brother. You know the trouble I got into when I was young."

Benjamin only smiled at his brother.

"Now, I must not stay." James looked at Lumley. "It might be understood if I were found in the company of my renegade brother, but assisting a British soldier who wishes to desert—that would be a very different circumstance."

Then he placed a hand on Benjamin's shoulder before leaving the room.

Lumley was drinking flip from a bowl so large, it required two handles. The beverage was comprised of strong beer, sweetened with molasses and a gill of rum—all stirred with a red-hot loggerhead, an iron poker, which churned the beverage into a bubbling, frothing concoction.

Benjamin leaned toward Abigail and said, "I need to talk to you. Alone."

They went out the back door to the alley behind the tavern. "You have to take Lumley," his sister said, anticipating his objections. "He wants to join the provincials, I'm certain of it, and he's desperate."

"I don't like it."

"The alternative is to leave him be and eventually the redcoats will pick him up and make a great show of executing him."

"Seems the likely end for a deserter, no matter which side he's on."

"Perhaps," she said. "But if we get him out of Boston safely, it might encourage other soldiers to defect. There are plenty who want to."

Benjamin leaned against the clapboard wall. "Ever since I was small I've been crushed by the logic of your arguments," he said. "I just don't like this one, no matter what you tell me."

"I'm telling you that it's been arranged, and it wasn't easy, Benjamin. We'll meet tomorrow night, as planned." Angrily, she yanked open the door, but then she put her arm about his neck and hugged him quickly before disappearing inside the tavern.

Abigail spent the following morning at the Reveres' house, helping Rachel and her mother prepare to evacuate. There had been talk of crossing on the Charlestown ferry, but the necessary permit (which naturally would require a bribe) hadn't been secured. So a pass had been obtained to get them through the gates at the Neck. There were trunks to be packed in the wagon, enough linen and bedding and clothing for all the children. Though food was not allowed to be taken out of the city, a basket of wine was loaded, in anticipation that meager forms of bribery would be required along the way, and a neighbor's gift of a shank of lamb was covered with burlap and sewn inside one of the mattresses. A letter from Paul had gotten through to Rachel, saying they could be put up in Watertown at the home of a Mr. Van Ee. Paul requested that she bring him clean socks and undergarments. Oddly, his letter made no mention of the money she had sent out with Dr. Church.

"That one hundred and twenty-five pounds, disappeared," Rachel said. And then laughing giddily, she added, "His copper plates have already been smuggled out. Since no one has any money, we'll just have to print some!"

Young Paul Revere was going to remain behind to manage his father's shop, with the assistance of an English engraver, Isaac Clemens, whose shop was next door on Clark's Wharf. When the wagon was packed with children and belongings, Rachel took up the reins and rode from North Square to King's Chapel, where Abigail kissed her and climbed down.

Rachel stared toward the granary burying ground a moment. "I'm trying to think of a joke, something that'll leave us laughing."

"You could save it for when next we meet."

"All right. I promise to think of something quite randy before I get to Watertown."

She drove on and as the wagon turned down Cornhill Road she laughed without looking back, raising one hand in the air.

That night, Benjamin and Lumley departed as well. It happened very fast. No time for lingering goodbyes, for hugs and kisses. Abigail and Mariah huddled together at the end of the pier, watching as Benjamin and Lumley boarded the oyster boat. Molly Collins stood a ways behind them, reeking of perfume and liquor. Quickly, the boat moved out into the harbor as the oysterman and his son pulled on their oars, while Benjamin and Lumley lay down out of sight. It was a night where the overcast sky appeared to be smoke rising up off the black water, and the boat soon vanished in the dark.

"So, did you give your boy a fondling farewell?" Molly said.

Mariah glared at her but said nothing.

"Most likely that's the last you'll see of 'im, so I hopes you did. We gave old Lum a fine sendoff, me and Eliza did. A good rogering, that's what they needs with this fighting that's a-coming. Takes their mind off of the dying."

Mariah turned around again, but Abigail put a hand on her arm.

"That's what they wants, don't matter which side they're on, ye know? A right hard fuck. Them British chaps, they like a good mouth on a girl, too. Lum couldn't get enough of that, no. He tells me it's on account of their red coats, and they don't want to get nothin' on 'em." Molly laughed loudly.

Abigail and Mariah looked once more toward where the boat had disappeared into the night, and then started back along the pier.

Molly clutched her shawl about her shoulders. "Ain't it so, Mistress Lovell?"

They walked past her.

"Ain't *your* officer careful of his fine red coat?"

Abigail stopped and resisted Mariah's hand, which now clutched her arm, urging her to continue on and ignore Molly's indecent taunts.

"Well, then maybe you don't know what he likes." Molly snorted. "I kin tell ye, if you want. Save ye lots of trouble, it will. See, ye know a man's wants, and you kin own 'im."

Abigail turned around and faced her.

"I see ye," Molly said, delighted. "The colonel walking out of an evening with his schoolmaster's daughter, all fine and lovely she is, but where do ye think he goes when he wants to get himself done right and proper, like? Huh? Eliza and me, we do him good, but I think, ye know, he always kind of fancies me more. Something about Eliza being a bit too plump for his taste. And, ye know, I have the mouth."

Abigail felt weak suddenly, and she realized Mariah's hand was holding her upper arm, helping her keep her balance. She began to turn away, to walk off the pier, but then Molly laughed.

"That's what he says, ye know, I give the best suck in Boston."

Abigail pulled her arm free from Mariah's grip, went back to Molly, and pushed her, so hard that she staggered backwards and then fell off the pier, landing in the harbor with a great splash.

Molly struggled to get up—she was standing in about four feet of water—and, looking at Abigail through matted hair, she began to laugh again. "I know about the both of ye! You was up on Trimount that night." She peeled the shawl off of her neck. "I *seen* you! And I know what you was up'tah. *I seen you!*"

Mariah took Abigail by the arm again, and together they hurried off the pier.

The following afternoon, Benjamin and Lumley were shown in to Dr. Warren's office in Hastings House.

"I'm glad you're safe." Dr. Warren shook Benjamin's hand and gripped his shoulder—an unusual show of affection. "I'm told that you've had quite an ordeal."

During their journey from Charlestown to Cambridge, both Benjamin and Lumley had been required to repeat their stories to various officers, most skeptical at best, though eventually they would be sent on with an escort.

"My brother asked me to deliver these to you." Ben took the packet of letters from his coat pocket and handed them to Warren.

Dr. Church, who had been sitting on the broad windowsill, now crossed the room, staring at Lumley. "And you're the deserter."

Lumley only stared at Church, dumbfounded. Odd, Benjamin thought, because during their trip out of Boston the man rarely shut up. "I am here to assist in your cause, however I can," Lumley said finally.

Warren placed the letters on his desk. "Yes. Well, we've been getting a fair number of redcoats coming across, and we certainly can use more help. But I understand you have information that might be particularly useful."

Lumley still seemed reluctant to speak.

"So?" Dr. Church said.

"The food shortage in Boston is becoming dire," Lumley said, looking at Warren. "General Gage is planning raids on the islands in the harbor, to procure livestock and hay."

Church said, "It would help if—"

"I don't know exactly when," Lumley said, "but soon. They are awaiting reinforcements from England. When they arrive, Gage will begin plans to penetrate the countryside."

Church went to the desk and picked up the letters. "Coming from James Lovell, these will no doubt be difficult to decipher. I should take them downstairs and have our men begin work on them immediately."

Warren nodded without looking away from Lumley. When Church reached the door, he said, "I'll see if they can find something for these two to eat. They looked rather famished."

"Of course."

Lumley watched Dr. Church open the door and leave the room, and then he turned to Dr. Warren. "I've seen him, sir, many times, at Province House."

"Dr. Church?" Warren asked.

"While on guard duty there, yes."

"He has been back to Boston since Lexington and Concord," Warren said. "We know he was picked up and questioned."

"Sir, he would arrive in a fine carriage." Lumley was speaking rapidly now. "More like an honored guest of the general."

Warren clasped his hands behind his back and walked over to the desk. "I'd like to speak with Benjamin a moment. You go on downstairs, and after you've had something to eat you'll be assigned to a company."

"Yes, sir," Lumley said. He walked to the door, opened it, but then looked back at Benjamin. "Thanks to you—and your brother and sister—for getting me out of that wretched city."

Benjamin nodded, and then Lumley went out of the room, closing the door behind him. Warren sat at his desk and seemed preoccupied with the papers before him. "How was he?"

"Nipping at a bottle as we crossed the harbor in an oyster boat. He prefers dry land."

Warren looked up from papers. "You think he's genuine?"

"Well." Benjamin had to look away from Warren's gaze. "I suspect he is. What he says about Dr. Church is rather odd. I mean, he just got here and all. Why would he make up something like that? Wouldn't he just try and fit in?"

Dr. Warren was a man famous for his manners and his eloquence, yet now he maintained a silence that made Benjamin nervous. When he ventured to look at the doctor again, Warren merely nodded. "Go get yourself something to eat." As Benjamin went and opened the door, Warren said, "And rest. I notice that you're walking with a limp. I want you to remain close at hand— you stay here in Hastings House—because I will want you to run messages for me."

"Sir, if I may say so . . ." Warren suddenly looked impatient. "I'd like to fight."

"I understand, and no doubt that will all come in time. But for the moment I need a good runner, so you should rest. Besides, I may have to send you back."

"To Boston?"

"Eventually." He smiled. "You still possess a talent for slipping in and out of the city. And even when captured, they don't have a prison that can hold you."

XVI

Bold Suggestions

FOR DAYS, ABIGAIL REFUSED TO SEE SAMUEL WHEN HE CALLED at the house. Her mother and father were baffled and eventually overwrought from making up excuses to the colonel. Finally, he stopped coming.

She spent much of her time in her room, which was becoming increasingly uncomfortable as May proved to be a warm month. Rachel was gone, Benjamin was gone. Occasionally she visited James, and regularly she would go to Mariah's house, usually after supper, when the day's heat was diminishing. Mariah was herself often distracted, but she seemed to welcome Abigail's visits.

"You've heard nothing from Benjamin?" she said one night as they walked the beach below her house.

"Nothing." It was dusk. They had their shoes off and held their skirts up so that the hems wouldn't trail in the wet sand. "I look forward to this all day," Abigail said.

"I know. This heat." Mariah stared down at her bare feet and avoided broken shells in her path. "My cousins, they have

suggested that I evacuate, but I'm not going to. They want me
to go up to an aunt's in New Hampshire—Concord, which is so
far inland. At least we get some relief from the heat down here at
waterside." She stopped and picked up a shell, and then another;
wading out into the water, she rinsed them off and deposited
them in the sack she always carried over her shoulder during their
walks. "I don't know how I'm to live, nor do they. There's little
food. Right after father died, they brought food around, but now
it's so scarce. I comb the beaches and sometimes find something,
usually a bunch of mussels clinging to a rock. Yesterday I found
a bracelet and sold it in Dock Square." She walked on, coming
back up to the sand. "I think some relatives really want to get the
house—they have families and . . . and I suppose it's selfish of me
to live there all alone. But it is my house."

"Of course." Abigail picked up a conch; it wasn't broken and
had a dark purple streak emerging from its smooth interior. "This
one?"

"Yes, I think so." Mariah took the shell and placed it in her
sack. "There's something I should tell you. It's about that woman,
Molly Collins." She looked out at the harbor, where high pink
clouds were gathered over Noddle's Island. "What she said that
night on the pier."

"I've not seen Samuel Cleaveland since then."

Mariah nodded. "Not surprised, though eventually you will."
She glanced at Abigail, and for a moment her eyes seemed as old
and wise as they were sad. "You know that, don't you?"

Abigail inhaled a deep draft of salt air and released it slowly.

"It's the other thing she said, about Trimount," Mariah said.
Now she sounded slightly winded, as though she were confessing
something long repressed. "Do you remember what Molly
said?"

"About being up on Trimount the night Sergeant Munroe was
killed, yes." Abigail's hair had come loose in the sea breeze and she
gathered it at the side of her neck as she turned to Mariah. "She

said she saw both of us—it didn't occur to me until now—she saw both of us up there. You were on Trimount?"

Mariah stooped over and picked up another shell.

"You saw Munroe?" Abigail said. "Why? How?"

After a brief inspection, Mariah dropped the shell in the sand. "I sent him a note, asking him to meet me up there. I lured him there. He didn't know who I was, but I made bold suggestions."

"Because . . ." Abigail hesitated, gazing out at the water. "Because of your father."

"Yes."

"No. Mariah—"

"I cut his throat."

"Oh, please Lord, no."

"I used a shucking knife, the one my father had so long that the handle was worn down to smooth ridges by the grip of his fingers." The wind swirled hair about her face, but she didn't seem to notice. "I was much surprised," she said, her slow voice now filled with wonder, "at how easy 'twas—easy as carving a quahog out of its shell."

They stood for a moment longer, and then Mariah began walking again, back toward her house. It was nearly dark now.

When Abigail caught up, Mariah said, "I shouldn't have told you. It's not your burden. It's mine, and I'll bear it the rest of me days. And I might as well tell you the other."

"What other?"

"Colonel Cleaveland, he sent a messenger to my house this afternoon. I'm to meet him tomorrow, at the Two Salutations Tavern."

"We first met there," Abigail said.

"Now that you've refused him, do you suppose the colonel harbors amorous intentions toward me?" Mariah's laugh surprised Abigail—it was sly, even devious. "Or do you suppose Molly has been using that fine mouth of hers again?"

Benjamin spent his days going to and from Hastings House, delivering messages for Dr. Warren. He slept in a storage bin in the cellar, which was cool if damp. It was better—and dryer—than lying in a tent on Cambridge Common, where several thousand men, the bulk of the American army, now lived in their own filth.

One evening he was sent to Medford, to deliver a message to General John Stark, leader of the militia that had come down from New Hampshire. Benjamin spent that night in Charlestown, where several hundred men were encamped in the hills above the village, with a view across the Charles River to Boston. Marching exercises were conducted and bonfires were burned, in an effort to give the impression that the troops were disciplined and great in number. In fact, provincials came and went from home at will; there was little order, and a great deal of illness.

Benjamin discovered that Ezra was living in a tent on the north pasture on Bunker Hill. He offered Benjamin a bit of ham, which he'd brought from a recent visit to his mother in Concord. Afterwards they walked down to Morton's Point, a small hill overlooking the mouth of the Mystic River. They sat in the tall grass, lightning bugs weaving about their heads.

"When you were in Boston there," Ezra said, "you saw your family?"

"My parents, no. James and Abigail, yes, but briefly."

"Did you mention that you saw me, to your sister?"

"No," Benjamin said. "You asked me not to."

Ezra handed him the spyglass. "I did. So Abigail asked after me?"

"No."

"How does she fare?"

Benjamin held the glass up to his eye and scanned the harbor, seeing nothing unusual, just a few fishing boats beating for Boston, their lanterns swinging gently, their light reflected on the chop. "She's well."

"Good," Ezra said. "I'm glad to hear of it."

Benjamin continued to gaze out at the harbor. He knew Ezra was staring at him in the near dark. Finally, he said, "This siege in Boston—they are in hard times. Food is becoming scarce." Benjamin returned the spyglass. "But she is well, Ezra."

Evenings, Abigail often walked to the Mall alone. There was growing consternation in the city that the British were going to cut down the trees lining the path. So much damage had been done—houses and churches dismantled in a matter of days—that nothing seemed safe any longer. Rumor had it that John Andrews had begun a vigorous campaign, writing letters to General Gage, protesting the possibility that the Mall trees might be felled for firewood. She had heard her father in conversation with some of his Tory friends, and even they expressed dismay at the ravaging of the city, fearing that by winter the town would be barren as the moon.

There was little news from the countryside—a great deal of conjecture, but little news. There were constant rumors that the provincials were about to launch an attack on the city, which caused the British to labor tirelessly at their fortifications. And there were reports—verifiable and often accompanied by the most outlandish details regarding the redcoats' behavior—of occasional skirmishes, often the result of a boatload of British soldiers stealing ashore to take a few pigs or set fire to a barn. There was news of a raid on Grape Island, south of Boston, which led to watches being set up along the coast.

Abigail was so deep in thought during her stroll that she didn't notice the sound of a horse's hooves approaching from behind, until suddenly the white head of Samuel's stallion was nearly breathing on her shoulder. When she looked up, Samuel touched the brim of his hat in a rather formal manner.

"Might I walk with you a spell?"

Abigail looked straight ahead. "I prefer not, thank you."

"It'll be dark soon, and do you think it wise to be out unaccompanied?"

"I am long accustomed to walking Boston by myself."

"Yes, I know. But things have changed."

"And who is responsible for that?"

"A fair question," he said. "Which requires a complicated answer."

"You may withdraw, and the question will no longer be pertinent."

"Withdraw?"

"To England. All of you."

Samuel didn't reply, and Abigail listened to his mount's easy tread upon the path. She glanced toward the horse's head, his large brown eye suggesting that he was content to keep pace. His coat gave off a fine scented heat.

Finally, Samuel said, "That would present difficulties, I'm afraid."

"It shouldn't, really. Simply pack your men aboard the ships in the harbor and depart."

"Back to England?" Samuel laughed. "That is . . . impossible. Imagine the reception we'd receive, an army sent to quell dissention in the colonies coming home without having accomplished its mission."

"If it would help troop morale, we would gladly provide you with a rousing sendoff."

"I am sure," Samuel said. "No, I believe we have no choice but to stay."

He pulled up on the reins and the horse stopped, but Abigail continued on, listening to the creak of the leather saddle as he dismounted. When he said her name, she paused and turned around. The sun had just set and the buttons on his coat seemed to absorb the last light of day. The horse nudged his shoulder and with one hand he pushed its snout away.

"Why are you doing this?" he asked. He walked toward her and she took a step backwards, which caused him to hesitate. "How many times have I called at your house and you've refused to see me?"

"Tell me, Colonel. What is your interest in Mariah Cole?"

"Mariah Cole."

"You wish to question her, I understand, regarding Sergeant Munroe?"

"Oh, yes. It's possible that she was on Trimount the night he was murdered."

"What is your source of information?"

He stood up a little straighter. "I'm afraid I can't divulge—"

"It's Molly Collins." Abigail began walking toward him. "She provided you with the information, didn't she?" As she passed him, she said, "And that's not all she's provided."

"I do not take your meaning, Abigail."

"I believe you do, Colonel." She continued down the Mall, the last moments of sunlight streaming through the canopy of leaves overhead.

XVII

The Livestock Skirmish

LUMLEY WAS INTERVIEWED REPEATEDLY AT HASTINGS HOUSE, and he seemed to relish the attention. "Nobody in Tommy Gage's army ever heeded my words so," he told Benjamin after emerging from yet another session with the American command. "That was a right good interrogation. Your Dr. Warren's a bit of a fop with his fine clothes—a real gentleman he is—but I've never seen a man so devoted to a cause. This General Artemas Ward, though, he'll have to go. Too old, and can't make up his mind. His subordinates are walking all over him. All these questions make me hungry, and thirsty." They went out the front door, past two guards sleeping on the steps. Lumley nudged one, rousing him. "You could be whipped for that in Boston." He smiled at Benjamin as they walked down into the street, which was littered with piles of manure, strong in the warm air. "And this Dr. Church," Lumley said. "He's the smooth one."

"What do you mean?"

"Every time they haul me in for one of these confabs, he makes himself scarce. I haven't seen him since that first time you and I met Dr. Warren." Lumley tapped a finger to his forehead. "Church, he knows."

"Knows what?"

"That *I* know."

They wended through the roiling tent camp that was now Cambridge Commons, and went down Garden Street to a small tavern they'd taken a liking to, The Sign of the Dancing Crane. Ezra was awaiting them at a table, his shirtsleeves encrusted with dried blood from the day's operations. The ale here was good and cool, the meat charred black. As they hovered over their trenchers, Lumley reviewed what he had told the officers at Hastings House. "It all comes down to this," he concluded, nodding toward the shank of lamb in his hands. "General Gage is running out of fresh meat and his horses are in desperate need of hay."

"Cut off an army's food supply," Ezra said, "and it grows weak."

"Exactly." Lumley raised his empty tankard, seeking a barmaid's attention. "I'm so pleased to be quit of that army and taken in by you provincials, I thought it only just that I offer my assistance."

"To do what?" Benjamin asked.

"Preemptive military action," Lumley said. "And, needless to say, I did both of you the honor of volunteering your services as well." He stripped another chunk of meat off his shank and chewed vigorously.

Ezra leaned across the table. *"What* exactly did you volunteer us for?"

"Why, shepherding, of course." Lumley's eyes were still intent upon his ample bone. "I grew up on a sheep farm and I'll tell you, gentlemen, the trick is to keep the animals in front of you, and to watch your step."

Truer words were never spoken, and the following Saturday they marched with a small detachment to Charlestown, where in the early morning hours they ferried across the Mystic River to Hog Island. At low water they forded the tidal inlet between Hog and Noddle's islands and began herding livestock back toward the mainland—hundreds of sheep and lambs, and a lesser number of cattle and horses. It was one thing to step in it, another to slip and fall in it. Piles of it. This, Lumley informed Benjamin as he helped him up off the ground, was how his own grandfather had died, losing his purchase in mud and dung and cracking his skull open on a rock. Lumley employed a staff, and he implored Benjamin and Ezra to do the same.

By midday, they could see a British schooner and a sloop beating across the harbor from Boston. The Americans continued to herd animals as the ships approached, until the schooner cruised up the inlet at flood tide in an attempt to cut off any provincial retreat. A landing party of redcoats fanned out into the marshes, and their steady fire forced the provincials to take refuge in a shallow ravine. They exchanged sporadic fire into the afternoon, and portions of the hayfields were torched, consuming the island with smoke.

Benjamin lay on the slope of the ravine alongside Ezra and Lumley. They had limited ammunition, so would shoot only occasionally. Late afternoon Lumley's ball caught a soldier in the thigh. As the man hobbled back to the schooner, which was out of firing range, Lumley handed his gun to Ezra and slid down to the bottom of the ravine. He sat, his arms embracing his knees, staring back toward the burning hayfield.

Ezra and Benjamin began to reload the musket. "He's got a good eye, a steady hand."

"That he does," Benjamin said.

They glanced down at Lumley but he took no heed.

When the musket was reloaded, Ezra and Benjamin crawled up to the lip of the ravine. The redcoats were retreating to the schooner.

"The tide," Benjamin said finally. "It's turning."

For the next hour they watched as the British tried to move the vessel down the creek toward the deep water of the harbor. They kedged with anchors, they put men out in tow boats, while others pulled lines from the shore, yet the hull made little progress downstream. Meanwhile, from the left, perhaps a hundred yards across the hayfield, there was steady report of British firearms, enough to keep the provincials from leaving the ravine and descending upon the ship.

Eventually, Benjamin slid down in the dirt until he was crouching in front of Lumley. Since coming over from Boston, Lumley had been in high spirits, delighted in his newfound freedom. But now the tracks of his tears ran down through the soot and ash that were caked on his cheeks.

"Tide's falling," Benjamin offered.

Lumley didn't seem to hear.

From above, Ezra said, "By nightfall she'll be grounded, then we'll take her."

Abigail had been hanging linens in the dooryard, when boys ran down School Street crying out about a skirmish on Noddle's Island. She went in haste to the North End, and all along her route Bostonians were crowded in upper-story windows; boys perched on roofs, clinging to chimneys and weather vanes as they gazed toward the harbor. When she found Mariah in her kitchen, oblivious to events, they rushed down to her uncle's waterside sail loft.

"The Brits have sent acrost the schooner *Diana*," Joshua Tigge said. Mariah's uncle held a spyglass to his eye with a gnarled hand. "She's gone up Chelsea Creek, meaning to keep our boys from getting back to the mainland. And a sloop has landed a small party of soldiers on the beach at Noddle's."

He offered Abigail the glass, and what it bore was quite remarkable. She could make out redcoats, hunkered down in the dune grass. Occasionally there was a burst of white smoke from their guns, and a few heartbeats later she could hear the faint report come across the water, sounding like the crackle from a distant fire. Beyond, the hayfields were in flames, the breeze pushing a column of smoke out over the harbor. "I cannot see our men," she said as she gave the spyglass to Mariah.

Joshua raked his fingers through the vast gray beard that fanned out on his chest. "Them fools will run aground if they don't get that schooner back down the creek."

"I see a puff of smoke—two," Mariah said. "It must be the Americans returning fire."

Joshua's eyes were bright with joy. "The bastards have been raiding the islands for livestock. Our best chance is to drive the flock inland. Deer Island, Pettick's Island—all grazing pastures. We best remove them all. I've been talking with other fishermen. After dark, our smacks will help take sheep off the outer islands."

Mariah returned the spyglass to him and said, "I wish to assist you, Uncle." He collapsed the spyglass and thrust it down into a small leather pouch, seemingly an act of refusal. Hotly, she added, "You know how often I put out with my father and helped him haul in his nets. And I know every island shore in this harbor."

"Mariah, your father will back come to haunt me for putting you in harm's way."

"Father, I'm sure, will see to it that we come to no harm."

Joshua shook his head. "So, I be cursed."

"Not if we accompany you," Abigail said, and then Mariah touched her sleeve. "With our help, we can gather sheep faster."

"We?" Joshua's rheumy eyes were the palest blue, and they bore in on Abigail with undivided attention. "You have been abroad on the harbor? The currents and the wind, they can be most unpredictable."

"I have fished and worked the clam beds with my brother oftentimes," Abigail said.

Only in half jest, Mariah said, "Uncle, think you not this lady too delicate."

As he lifted his eyes skyward, as if asking forgiveness, the graybeard muttered, "I pray my brother Anse is so preoccupied in heaven that he does not cast an eye upon me this day." He started for the loft stairs. "I will go down the beach and talk to others. We will make our preparations and push off after sunset."

The exchange of fire continued through the afternoon, but provincial reinforcements streamed on to the island—hundreds of men, including Dr. Warren and General Israel Putnam, from Connecticut. In the early evening, Old Put climbed up over the lip of the ravine and stood in full view of the British schooner, which was now hopelessly aground in the tidal mud. He was a stout man with an enormous deep voice and he bellowed out that if the crew surrendered, he promised them safe passage off the island. He walked slowly back to the ravine, defiantly, almost taunting the British to fire. None did. Several minutes passed and then the British responded by setting off two of their deck carronades. The balls whistled through the smoky air and fell well short of the ravine, landing in the sand with a dull thud.

Word soon passed down the ravine that they would attack at sunset. The men gathered in small groups. There were cooking fires, the smell of meat roasting on a spit. Some slept, while others preoccupied themselves with betting on caterpillar races in the sand. The heat built through the afternoon, and by early evening the lengthening shadows in the ravine were welcome.

Ezra shared some salt pork with Benjamin and Lumley. "You appear less distracted now."

Lumley had been working at his flask of rum since shooting the soldier. "I have much considered my actions, but drawing the blood of one of my own—strange, isn't it?—this I did not foresee." He attempted a smile, revealing stained, crooked teeth. "What I truly desire is to live this soldier's life no more, but it is not time yet."

"What do you desire, then?" Benjamin asked.

"Land—it's all you provincials have to offer," Lumley said. "Land has been promised. I want to farm. Maybe even have a few sheep, eh?"

"You shall, one day when this is finished," Ezra said. "I hear there is good soil in New Hampshire and Vermont."

"Do you wish to farm?" Lumley asked him.

"I have considered it," Ezra said. "What is the future but a dream?"

Lumley nodded. "To good Vermont soil then." He took another pull from his flask.

"A mite far inland for me," Benjamin said.

"When the port is reopened, you will go to sea?" Ezra asked.

"I have considered it." Benjamin smiled. "But there's ample cod and shellfish right here in the harbor. That would be my harvest. You would go to Vermont, Ezra, rather than remain in Concord?"

Ezra appeared reluctant to answer, but finally said, "It is getting crowded in Concord." To Lumley, he added, "My mother has removed there from Boston, to be with relatives."

Benjamin said, "I look to the day when there is not one red-coat in Boston." When both Ezra and Lumley regarded him with skepticism, he asked "You do not think this can be?"

Lumley regarded him a moment. "He has much youthful hope."

"Aye," Ezra said.

"It be no different," Lumley said, "this soldiering on the one side or the other. Before battle, we would talk of the time when we will soldier no more." There was some humor in Lumley's eyes. "And, of course, women."

Benjamin flushed at the reference.

"You have a girl?" Lumley did not wait for a reply. "Most certainly you do. And does she not treat you well? Does she pull you to her in hot desperation?"

Benjamin turned to Ezra, who also seemed embarrassed, though curious.

"What is her name?" Lumley coaxed.

Benjamin felt his face heat up. "Mariah."

"Ah. Mariah." Lumley took another pull. He planted the flask in the sand, an offering the other two had yet to accept. "Would I have a lass named Mariah, I'd think on the lightness of her long tresses, the way it sweeps across my face, gently swinging as she rises and falls on top of me." His look was of genuine curiosity. "She does come down on top of you? Some women much prefer this, though there is too the way of animals—hands and knees, down on all fours, this serves to good purpose," he said with delight, reveling in watching Benjamin squirm with embarassment. "It gives your haunch the freedom of full thrust, no? So powerful it seems like you are both about to burst upon each other." He leaned close, and Benjamin could smell the reek of whiskey. "Do you not think on how she cries out when she reaches her due?" Laughing, he sat back. "But you are young! You will hear many a maiden's song, Benjamin, and you will find that each bears her own sweet tune. No two songs alike." And then turning, he said, "That right, Ezra?"

As he unfolded his legs, Ezra said, "I do not speak of these matters." He got to his feet and walked off a ways, to a small bush where he unlaced his trousers. They were silent, listening to his water drive into the sand.

"Must be descended from these strict Puritans," Lumley said. "Though I understand that despite their righteous ways, they are wont to procreate a multitude."

Finished, Ezra climbed up the slope of the ravine, lay down, and peered over the lip toward the tidal creek.

Lumley whispered conspiratorially, "I fear I have insulted him, Benjamin. It is because he has something to conceal, no?"

Benjamin said, "Maybe this is so."

It seemed Lumley had caught a scent in the air now, and he looked from Benjamin to Ezra as though to identify its nature and source. "Whores?" he said, as though he had come to a great insight. "I know something of your Boston whores—is that what keeps Ezra so silent?'

Slowly, Benjamin said, "I don't think so."

But Lumley wasn't listening. Flask in hand, poised to take another drink, he said, "True, they take your coin, but what they cede in return—now there's something to think on before a battle. A whore's fine mouth and obliging tongue—"

A small stone struck him on the neck.

"Enough," Ezra said, weighing a larger rock in his palm. "Enough of your blather."

"Before we go into battle, we can—" Lumley began, but he stopped when Benjamin got to his feet. He took another pull on his flask and would not look up.

"Ezra's right. Speaking of this does not help."

Lumley continued to study them both with satisfaction, as though he had made some great discovery that he could use to his own purpose. "You two are thick," he said. And then he lay back in the sand. "Thick."

Joshua's smack was piled with nets, so that if they were stopped by a patrol boat they would give the impression of tending to a weir. At sunset, the wind fell off as it turned southerly and warm, but they made good speed on the outbound tide. As the sky darkened, the burning hayfields cast a flickering scarlet glow on the chop. The sound of gunfire from Noddle's Island was constant, but standing on the deck of Joshua's boat, Abigail could not determine how the Americans fared. She could see other boats making boldly for the islands, and there was no sight of British patrols on the water. This alone, Bostonian vessels once again abroad on the harbor, seemed a great victory.

Upon reaching Pettick's Island, Joshua coasted around to the leeward side, and when they neared the shore, Mariah, standing in the bow, suddenly moved with great agility. She removed her petticoat and skirt and stowed them in a locker. "Skirts were not made for boats," she said. "Since my childhood, Father allowed me to work on the water in my pantaloons."

Without hesitation, Abigail unfastened her skirt.

"Is that not a welcome relief?" Mariah asked.

"It is indeed."

They both laughed while, at the tiller, old Joshua rolled his eyes and sighed an oath.

He steered dangerously close to the beach—clearly he knew these depths—and then came up into the wind and eased the mainsheet. Mariah and Abigail slipped over the gunwale, yelping as they entered the cold water that was waist-deep. They waded ashore and climbed a dune, from which they could see across the small island, faintly illuminated by the distant fires on Noddle's Island. Everywhere in the darkness was the tremulous puling of sheep as men and women herded them toward the beach.

Mariah broke into a sprint, moving in a wide arc, and Abigail lost sight of her, until she suddenly reappeared, a good dozen sheep thundering before her in a panic. When they reached the dune, some lambs tumbled down its face to the beach, and Mariah let out a scream of delight. Then Abigail joined in the chase, her legs, shed of the weight and inhibition of skirts, carrying her swiftly over the sand.

On Noddle's Island, the exchange of gunfire extended through the night. The British set off their carronades from the decks of the schooner, and the Americans returned the favor with small cannon brought from the mainland. Old Put's voice could be heard bellowing constantly, telling the men to keep up their barrage. Dr. Warren walked along the ravine, encouraging the men. Such was his reputation that when he drew near a group of men, they often paused to doff their hats and address him respectfully. It was difficult to see in the dark. Still, from the left, British soldiers maintained a regular fire. Yet, because they were hunkered down in the ravine, not one provincial was felled.

By first light, they could see that the schooner was nearly aban-doned, despite the fact that she was again afloat on the high tide. Only a few men remained to provide cover while the rest of her crew made their way down the inlet to the harbor, where they were taken aboard a British sloop and several longboats. Old Put shouted for a ceasefire. Dr. Warren came down the ravine again, saying that about a dozen volunteers were needed to storm the schooner. Most of the men spoke up, crowding about the doctor. He demanded that they quiet themselves and then began to make his selection.

When he picked Ezra, Benjamin stepped forward, "Doctor, I wish to accompany him."

"You are my runner, Benjamin." Dr. Warren seemed both perplexed and amused. "I cannot bear to forfeit your speed."

"Sir, I will be first to the ship."

"That I do not doubt," Dr. Warren said. He turned away and considered other men, pausing in front of Lumley, who was clearly overtaken with drink. "We should send you first," he said. "Your brethren would concentrate their lead on thee."

The men laughed.

"I offer my services, sir," Lumley said. "I will be your decoy."

Dr. Warren leaned toward him and inhaled, and then waved a hand before his nose. "I think not today, Mr. Lumley. When we require a sacrificial lamb, he must not volunteer under any potent influences. But I thank you."

"Then I will go," Benjamin said.

Disappointed, Dr. Warren again regarded him with cold blue eyes. "To what purpose?"

"To see to Ezra's safety," Benjamin said. This brought laughter from the men: Ezra was not only older but taller and stronger than Benjamin. Flustered, Benjamin blurted out, "I have promised."

The men quieted and Dr. Warren appeared curious. "Promised what? To whom?"

"To protect him," Benjamin said. Laughter, again. "For his beloved."

This brought a gasp of surprise. One man called out, "That be his beautiful sister, the schoolmaster's daughter. Doctor, you must not deny the lad such an obligation."

Dr. Warren put his fists on his hips and looked about at the men.

"This is . . ." Ezra said, ill at ease. "This is unjustified."

He was about to press further, but Dr. Warren raised a hand. "Loyalty," he said. "Is that what we're fighting for?" He gazed around at the men. "Right, then," the doctor said to Benjamin. "You take Ezra with you on this mission. He is your responsibility. You look after him as though he were your own brother."

"I will," Benjamin said. "I will, Doctor."

Ezra appeared furious.

There were a dozen men chosen. As they readied their arms, General Putnam selected Isaac Baldwin to lead them. They gathered at the lip of the ravine and upon Baldwin's signal began the descent down to the tidal creek. It was perhaps a hundred yards across salt hay that mostly lay flat. Benjamin ran between Baldwin and Ezra. There was much shouting and whooping, while a fife urged them on from the ravine. The percussive thud of cannon rolled in from the British sloop standing off Noddle's Island. The balls whistled through the smoky air, one burrowing into the mud not ten yards before Benjamin. From the schooner several gunshots were fired, but as the men reached the marsh flats the last of the British were seen rowing away from the vessel, hastily pulling downstream for open water.

The provincials waded into the inlet. Benjamin swam the last twenty yards, holding his pistol in the air above his head. He followed Baldwin up over the taffrail of the schooner's stern. The deck was in great disarray with the lines from the spars and masts that had been severed by the American barrage. When all the men were on board, they let out a cheer, despite the fact that British cannons were still being fired from the distant sloop. They set to work quickly. Swivel guns were dismounted. Powder kegs and provisions were sent ashore. In an hour, the schooner was stripped of ammunition and weaponry.

Benjamin discovered a cutlass in the officers' quarters and he strapped it about his waist. Ezra and several others found jugs of kerosene, which they splashed over the deck. Baldwin ordered the men ashore, and then remained behind to set the fire. As he swam away, the flames consumed the deck and raced up the masts as though driven by a gust of wind. The British bombardment continued from the harbor, but Benjamin stood with the others on the mudflats, soaking wet, mesmerized by the pressing heat that came off the burning vessel. Behind them, a series of huzzahs swelled from the ravine.

For several days, it seemed that Bostonians had reclaimed their harbor. The British continued a fitful engagement with the provincials on Noddle's Island, but they dared not send out their usual fleet of patrol boats. Increasing numbers of fishing smacks ventured out to the islands to assist in removing the livestock. Abigail, Mariah, and Joshua spent long, exhausting days herding and ferrying sheep. Entire families had sailed out to assist and there was an air of festivity, the sound of children's laughter as they chased sheep about the pastures. The days were hot and humid, the evenings warm, the air gentle and still. Abigail and Mariah slept on the deck of Joshua's smack one night, in the dunes another. Their unbound hair became encrusted with salt, their faces taut from the sun. They went about the islands barefoot, the soles of their feet toughened from running in the sand, their pantaloons torn on brambles. Joshua calculated that several thousand sheep were removed to the mainland, out of reach of the British. Animals that could not be taken off the islands were slaughtered. At night there were great feasts, song, and dancing about bonfires.

The British finally quit Noddle's Island and quietly retreated to Boston. The last night of May, Joshua said they also must return to the city and they set out in the evening. He cruised by Noddle's Island, where they could see the carcass of the schooner, burned to the waterline in the tidal creek. Everything on the island had been destroyed. The hayfields were blackened, and the house and barn, owned by a man named Williams, were in charred ruins. As the smack ran close to shore, groups of men came down to the beach, calling out and beckoning to Abigail and Mariah.

As Joshua brought the smack about for the city, Mariah screamed. Abigail looked toward the shore. There, on the spit of sand at the mouth of the tidal inlet, stood Benjamin, Ezra, and Lumley. The sun was setting and their shadows were long on the wet sand. Mariah jumped up and down on the deck as she waved both of her arms, calling out to Benjamin. And then Abigail joined in, shouting as she had never done before. Benjamin and Lumley raised their arms in greeting. Ezra only stared, bewildered.

"Joshua, take us closer," Mariah pleaded.

"Too shallow," the graybeard said. "And the current here's tricky."

They slid past the spit of sand. Abigail and Mariah continued to wave, to call out. Benjamin waded into the water to get closer. "I will return to Boston," he yelled. "Soon, I promise."

Lumley was drinking from a flask. "I won't," he said with a derisive laugh. "But you Boston lasses will always be in my heart!"

Abigail watched Ezra, who continued to stare at her—she suddenly realized that she was still in her pantaloons, which were pressed against her legs as the boat made headway in the breeze. He seemed perturbed, dejected. She continued to wave, hoping that he would raise an arm and return the gesture. But he suddenly began walking along the spit, and only once glanced back just before he disappeared over a sand dune. He looked ashamed, Abigail thought, ashamed and guilty.

Joshua steered for open water, where the wind freshened.

Ahead, darkness was falling on the city, save for the last moments of sunlight which cast the Christ Church steeple in a rose hue.

PART THREE

June: The Battle

These fellows say we won't fight! By Heaven, I
hope I shall die up to my knees in blood!
                                    —Dr. Joseph Warren

A dear bought victory, another such would have
ruined us.
                            —General Thomas Gage

XVIII

Love and Loyalty

WHEN BENJAMIN RETURNED TO CAMBRIDGE, HE FOUND THE
provincial army, such as it was, invigorated by the reports of
Noddle's Island. What had been a skirmish lasting several days
had, in the eyes of the Americans, become a major military victory. Lumley was quick to correct anyone who would listen,
telling them that the British army, pent up on Boston peninsula,
was now faced with starvation and capable of behaving like a
ravenous animal. To assuage his gloom, he went off in search of
a house of ill repute, of which there were several servicing the
camp on Cambridge Common. Benjamin sought and was granted
permission from Dr. Warren to accompany Ezra, who wished
to visit his mother in Concord for a night. Before they left, Dr.
Warren too expressed concern about how General Gage would
respond to Noddle's Island, and he told Benjamin that he would
soon be needed to return to Boston.

They walked to Concord, Ezra and Benjamin. Everyone
they encountered on the road was impressed with the American

victory. At a tavern in Menotomy, the boys were well fed and all attempts at compensation were refused. Though great concern was expressed regarding the British and what they might do next, there was perhaps more anxiety over the weather, for the warmth and fecundity of an early spring had given way to extreme heat—the kind that New England usually experiences in July or August. Further, there was no sign of substantial rain, and farmers feared what effect a severe drought would have on the crops.

During the course of their day's journey, the countryside baked and sizzled, the humid air thick with bugs and mosquitoes, and the trees filled with the loud sawing of cicadas. Ezra harbored a reluctance which baffled Benjamin. He seemed gloomier as they neared Concord village, and the one time that Benjamin made mention of Abigail—how wonderful it had been to see her and Mariah, if even at a distance across water—Ezra studied the heat rising off a cornfield and said nothing.

"When we were on the beach, why did you walk away?"

They were passing beneath the shade of a maple; Ezra paused to sit on the stone wall separating the road from a pasture. From his haversack he produced his jug of water, which they shared.

"When Dr. Warren sends me back into Boston," Benjamin added, "I'll see Abigail." He waited, but Ezra only continued to stare out the field, baking in the sun. "She will ask about you, Ezra. You know she will."

"I asked you to say nothing to her."

"She waved and called out." Benjamin drank warm water from the jug. "Clearly she was happy to see you. Has she offended you in some way?" He handed the jug back to Ezra.

"No, no offense on her part." Ezra corked the jug and stuffed it in his haversack.

"Then what? Perhaps you are offended . . . by her attitude?"

"I said she has committed no offense."

"My sister can be outspoken and bold. This does not appeal to everyone."

"Her nature is one of her finest traits."

"As long as I can remember, it has driven my father and mother to distraction."

Impatiently, Ezra got up off the stone wall. "Best mind *your* attitude."

"The pantaloons," Benjamin said suddenly.

"Benjamin, you must stop this—"

"You are not put off by the sight of her in pantaloons?"

"Let's go," Ezra demanded.

"I could look at Mariah in pantaloons all day. It's all I've been thinking about—"

With one hand, Ezra grabbed the front of Benjamin's vest and lifted him off the stone wall. He was about to speak, leaning down so that his face was only inches from Benjamin's—but then he appeared to have a change of mind and, releasing his grip, turned and started down the road.

They walked on, Benjamin keeping a few strides behind Ezra, who maintained a good pace. They passed through Lexington without exchanging a word. Finally, when the village of Concord was in sight, Ezra slowed and Benjamin ventured to walk at his side.

"There is something I must explain." Ezra's blond hair was matted against his forehead and his muslin shirt clung to his chest. They continued to walk and he didn't say anything.

"About Abigail," Benjamin offered.

Ezra seemed pained just to hear her name. But then he said, "No, about my mother."

"Your mother?"

"Yes. You never met her, before she removed from Boston?"

"No. But I remember seeing her, in the markets."

"Did you notice anything about her?" Ezra continued to stare ahead at the dirt road.

"No, she seemed . . ."

"Young," Ezra said. "Did she not strike you as young?"

"I'm—Ezra, I'm afraid I'm not skilled at judging such things about women."

"She is quite young, for a woman who has a son who is twenty-six." For the first time since they'd left the stone wall in the shade, he looked at Benjamin. His expression was fiercely earnest, causing Benjamin to step to his right to keep a distance between them. "My mother was but fifteen when she had me, and my father—I know nothing of him. She has only said that he had gone to sea and never returned. For years I thought he had died, but then occasionally she would receive a small sum, delivered by a sailor, and though she would never say so directly I took it to mean that it had been sent by my father. My mother is—she is very secretive about certain things."

"I see."

"No, you don't," Ezra wiped his face with his hand. "You see, when we stay with my mother, there'll be another—there will my brother, my half-brother."

Benjamin began to slow down. Ezra continued on, and when Benjamin caught up, he said, "I'll be glad to meet him."

Ezra laughed, but there was no joy to it and he merely stared ahead at the village, which appeared to shimmer in the late afternoon sun.

After Noddle's Island, Bostonians (not Tories) were emboldened and more openly defiant, which resulted in even stricter patrolling of the streets. British soldiers continued their demolition of houses for fuel; the destruction of churches inspired particular outrage. There was great concern regarding food. There seemed more nourishment in rumors, which were constant: the provincial army would attack the city any day, and the British were planning to march another substantial detail out into the countryside. What was indisputable was the fact that the rebels were building up their forces on the high ground that commanded the Boston peninsula. Everyone could observe the increased activity on the hills of Charlestown to the north and Dorchester Heights to the south. The heat and humidity of the first days of June only made the town seem more confining, and there was not even a breath of a sea breeze to bring relief.

Abigail's parents were exceedingly upset that she had gone missing for several days, only to learn that she had participated in the evacuation of livestock from the harbor islands. Mother had spent much of her time upstairs weeping, while Father had locked himself away in his study. James came for tea that day after Abigail returned, on the condition that they would all sit together at the dining room table.

"And no Greek or Latin," he said to Father.

Father pushed back the sleeve of his toga and, as he began the serious work of preparing his biscuit with butter and jam, he whispered something in French.

"English," James said. "The King's English, Father."

Abigail stole a glance at Mother, who had stopped pouring the tea to see what her husband would do. He bit into his biscuit, allowing crumbs to fall on the tablecloth. Since closing the school on April 19, he seemed to have withered, his energy depleted, his commands diminished to pleas and complaints. Satisfied that there would be no outburst, Mother continued to pour the tea.

"Look at her," Father said, pointing his butter knife at Abigail. "Her face all sunburnt, and her hair—a tangled mass smelling of the tides."

James gazed fondly across the table. "Reminds me of when we were children, after walks on the beach collecting shells. I'm glad to see that you've dispensed with that turban. With your hair in such profusion you can't see the scar. And the sun makes it quite radiant."

"And her arms, too," Mother said, passing teacups around the table. "It's indecent."

Smiling, James took his cup and saucer. "I would like to have been out there on the islands."

"I suppose you would, an educated man reduced to herding sheep," Father said. "That's what all of you want, right? A country that honors no king, where everyone is a shepherd."

"I was thinking more about all those young women running about the pastures, barefoot. I hear girls had dispensed with their skirts and herded in their pantaloons."

Father choked on his biscuit. "Please, not at the dinner table."

"It's been so hot," Abigail said, "I think Mother and I ought to be allowed to remove our skirts." Father looked at her, aghast. "Just in the house, of course, Father."

He was about to speak, when James said, "That would only be sensible, and fair."

"Fair?" Father asked.

James leaned toward his father, eyeing him conspiratorially. "Be honest now. What garments do you wear beneath your Roman toga?"

Father sat up straight, the blood rising in his cheeks.

Then Mother burst out laughing. "Oh, John, you never wear anything under there."

He settled back in his chair, quite defeated.

Mother said to Abigail, "Here in the house, while this infernal heat persists, I think it would be healthy if we shed some of our outer garments."

"Thank you, Mother," Abigail said, raising her cup to her mouth.

"*Look,*" Father whispered, incredulous. "Tea—she's drinking *tea.*"

"It must be the heat," James said, raising his cup to his lips.

"Well, it is only sensible," Mother said. "There's little else to eat. No chicken, no meat. Our preserves are running low. Fortunately there's fish and oysters, but they are getting so expensive—and now that school is closed. This summer there will be vegetables in the garden, provided we get some rain, but by fall I fear things will become very hard, very hard for all of us."

No one spoke. They ate in a somber, methodical fashion, gazing at their plates.

Slowly, Abigail looked up. "I must tell you something." They all stared at her, expectantly. "I didn't want to do this, because I was afraid it would be too upsetting, but I just realized that to keep it to myself would be . . . unfair." She looked from her mother to her father to James, and then back at her mother. "When I was on the islands," slowly, as though making an admission, "I saw Benjamin."

As she feared, her mother dropped her teaspoon and put her hands over her mouth, her eyes wide with shock. Abigail reached down the table and took one of her hands. "He's fine, Mother. Really, he looks well."

"Where?" Father said.

She turned to him. "It was on the islands, as I said."

"Was it Noddle's?"

Abigail took a breath. "It was."

Her father appeared crushed. "He's joined them. He's fighting the king's own."

"What did he say?" Mother asked, tugging on Abigail's hand.

Turning, Abigail said, "I only saw him from a distance—I was on a boat and he and some . . . some others were on the beach. He waved, that's all."

"He waved." Her mother squeezed Abigail's hand.

"And you say he is well?" Father asked.

"Yes. He appeared to be fine."

Father's eyes misted over as he stared down the table toward Mother. "Our youngest has come to no harm." He took up his napkin and buried his face in it, sobbing uncontrollably.

Abigail began to well up, and across the table she saw that James's mouth was quivering. Then, crying and sniffling, and even laughing at themselves for doing so, they all commenced to eat what little they had before them, glancing at each other, embarrassed, shy, but oddly content.

"So Benjamin," Mrs. Hammond said, "I trust you are taking good care of my Ezra."

"I think, Ma'am, it's the other way around."

Her eyes were gentle but weary. She was attended to by two girls, cousins named Bartlett—it seemed most everyone in Concord was named Bartlett—and the house was filled with women; in the kitchen there had been several older women and more children, all busy cleaning up after dinner. Mrs. Hammond had not joined them for the meal. She required much rest, they had said, but now she was up, sitting in a rocker, the baby in her arms. He remembered her, in the streets of Boston, a tall, slender woman who had what his mother often referred to as good bearing. But now the lines about her mouth suggested great frailty and exhaustion.

"We do worry about you so," she said, parting the blanket to better reveal the child's face.

Babies made Benjamin nervous. This one had a pink, wrinkled face, and its fat arms and legs struggled as it opened its mouth, its chest heaving.

But it was silent.

She looked up, and there was something direct and imploring about her stare.

"He's . . . quiet," Benjamin said.

She glanced at Ezra, who was leaning on a windowsill.

Benjamin felt as though he'd said the wrong thing, so he asked, "What's his name?"

"Jonah." Ezra gazed at Benjamin a moment, and then looked out the window.

"Jonah," Benjamin repeated. You were supposed to say something nice about a child's name, he believed, but all he could think of was Jonah in the belly of a whale, and somehow the idea of a baby being swallowed up at sea didn't seem appropriate. "Jonah," he said once again, as if the name spoke for itself.

"He is quiet," Mrs. Hammond said. "You're very observant, Benjamin."

Confused, he turned to Ezra, who was now gazing out the window at the last light on the hills outside Concord. "You see, he's mute," Ezra said patiently. "He's not made a sound."

"And we fear he's deaf," Mrs. Hammond added.

Benjamin looked at the baby again, and suddenly he thought of this tiny child as a person. Jonah. Deaf Jonah. "How do you know?" He immediately regretted asking, but she seemed pleased.

"His birth—" she glanced toward the cousins, who were sitting patiently on the sofa across the room—"it was hard, very hard. There were complications. But we soon realized that when he appeared to cry, he made no sound. And while he slept, the midwife clapped her hands, and he wasn't disturbed."

Ezra shifted on the windowsill. "So I took up a Bible and dropped it on the floor. He stirred but did not wake up."

"That's how he got his name," Mrs. Hammond said. "The book fell open to the passage about Jonah." She gazed down at the baby a moment, and then said to the cousins, "I think it's time I lie down, I'm afraid." One of the girls came across the room and took Jonah, placing him in his wooden crib by the fireplace. The other cousin and Ezra helped Mrs. Hammond out of the rocking chair, and, holding on to their arms, she made her way slowly to the parlor door, where she paused. Gazing back at Benjamin, she smiled weakly. "We all worry about what is to come. This is the beginning of a terrible thing, and I don't see how we can stop the British. It's just impossible. I wish it had never started."

"None of us does," Benjamin said. "But it has."

"I'm sorry that you have to return to Cambridge tomorrow," she said. "You will look after Ezra, Benjamin."

"I'll try, Ma'am."

In the evening, not long after James left, a chaise arrived, accompanied by two soldiers. They were tight-lipped, only saying that they had been instructed to deliver Abigail to Old South Church. Father stood in the doorway in his toga as Abigail climbed into the carriage. "I have not heard from Colonel Cleaveland since Noddle's Island," she said, "and no doubt this is his doing."

When delivered to Old South Church, Abigail was appalled: the pews and the pulpit had been removed and dirt spread on the floor so the British officers could exercise their horses. Abigail was escorted to the balcony, where Samuel sat at a table with a bottle of wine. He stood and bowed, offering her a seat.

"A house of God should not smell of manure, Colonel."

"I agree," he said. "But this way, the command is unlikely to tear this venerable old building down for firewood. Please, be seated."

After a moment, Abigail sat down. He returned to his chair and poured her a glass of wine, which she ignored. Below, there were two horsemen posting on their steeds about the ring. The sound of their hooves echoed off the rafters, where an audience of pigeons cooed.

"Likewise," Samuel said, his eyes following the riders, "a well-exercised horse is less likely to become dinner for the troops encamped on the Common."

"If you had me brought here to complain about the conditions in Boston, there really was no need, Colonel," she said.

He picked up his glass of Madeira and took a drink. His face was flushed, from the heat—it was stifling in the church—as well as from the wine. "I wish that we could discuss other matters, Abigail, believe me. Though I doubt you will believe me, I asked you here to convey a warning."

"I was not *asked*."

He put his wine glass down on the table. There was something disturbingly patient about him; clearly he anticipated her wrath and was resolved to weather it.

"Just tell me what you have to say," she said.

"Thank you, I will." He stared at her a moment, for the first time showing a hint of sympathy. "I must tell you that your situation is not improved by your recent actions." He waited and when she didn't respond, he said, "Did you think that spending days out on the islands herding sheep would go unappreciated?"

"Unappreciated? It never occurred to me."

"I gather that. Even in pantaloons. I'm sorry I missed that. You see, the fact that your father is much in favor of General Gage has allowed you considerable liberties, but I have to tell you that said liberties are coming to an end." When she did not respond, he took up his glass once again and drained it. "You will soon be informed that the tribunal will reconvene. Their deliberations have become reinvigorated of late, since the disappearance of a particular soldier. That would be Corporal Lumley."

"What about him?"

"You know where he is?"

"No."

"It is believed that you do."

"By whom?"

"Members of the tribunal."

"Including you?"

He merely stared at her.

"Samuel, why would you think I know where he is?"

"It is believed that you may have had a direct hand in helping him escape from Boston."

Abigail watched the riders. The horses were working hard in such heat, breathing and snorting as they circled the ring. "Do you know for a fact that he's left Boston?" she asked.

"It is assumed that he has defected. This is happening with too great a frequency."

"Are you surprised? Perhaps he was hungry."

"Perhaps."

"If you're hungry, you might consider defecting." When he didn't respond, she turned to him. "Would you like me to arrange it?"

He leaned sideways in his chair, propping his elbow on the armrest so that he could cradle his chin in his palm. "Could you?"

"You seem to think so. You give me great credit."

"Not enough, is more like it. I appreciate your offer, but at the moment I must decline. I do not envy Lumley and men like him."

"Are you sure?"

"He has lost all sense of loyalty."

"Or perhaps he has discovered where his true loyalties reside."

"This is possible," he said. "But loyalty or love—is it not common to confuse the two?"

"That is a good question."

"It may be *the* question, especially where the tribunal is concerned." He suddenly got to his feet and took a few steps toward the balcony railing.

Abigail understood that their interview was over, and she rose from her chair. Samuel continued to stare down at the two officers, who were now dismounted; their assistants were vigorously toweling the lather from the horses' coats. She went downstairs and a young soldier opened the front door for her. The carriage stood waiting in the road. But she walked past the chaise, causing the coachman to say, "Ride, Miss?"

It was hot, so very hot, and the traffic in the road filled the air with dust, which took on a yellow haze in the sunlight. "No, thank you," Abigail said. "I prefer to walk."

XIX

Nocturnal Affairs

DR. WARREN KEPT A SMALL BOOK OF POETRY IN HIS POCKET AT all times, which he used to hold letters and papers. He was forever pulling from it sheets of foolscap and making notations. Benjamin stood, hands clasped behind his back, in the Hastings House office when the doctor laid the book on his desk and said, "My little volume of diversion and dreams, my receptacle for revolutionary documents. What I need is a personal amanuensis." He saw that Benjamin did not know the word—there was no concealing *that*. "If this war ever ends, Benjamin, you must needs return to your father's school for a proper education."

Benjamin looked out the window; the constant passage of soldiers, horses, and wagons maintained a cloud of dust above Brattle Street.

"What?" the doctor asked.

"That is unlikely, sir. I was expelled some time ago by my father, and it is a point of honor that he not make an exception for me, his own son."

"I see." Warren seemed impressed. "And how do we feel about that?" At times he referred to *we,* often meaning the provincials who sought to divest themselves of British tyranny. But now he employed a more personal *we,* as though he and Benjamin were one and the same.

Benjamin did not answer immediately; the doctor was addressing something he had long ago tried to put behind him. "I believe, sir, that I admire him for it. My father is a much principled man—despite his attitude regarding current events."

Dr. Warren revealed a hint of a smile. "You are capable of fair assessment, judgment unspoiled by personal bias, Benjamin, and this too is an admirable trait, which, I gather, runs in your family."

He leafed through his poetry book, fat and misshapen with paper, until he withdrew a sheet. This was customary; it meant that Benjamin would make another delivery. The doctor took up his quill and began writing, furiously, and as he did so—this being another aspect of the doctor that fascinated Benjamin—he spoke, as well. It was as though the man were capable of entertaining two distinct trains of thought at the same time, though sometimes, such as at the moment, it seemed that what the doctor said—muttered, really, half to himself and half to Benjamin— was almost in response to whatever it was he was scribbling. It had occurred to Benjamin that Dr. Warren had two brains (he often said he was "of two minds" regarding a particular subject), capable of conversation and debate with each other. And as he dipped his quill and scratched away on the sheet, he talked about everything all at once.

"We are blessed with so many talents," he uttered. "Look at Billy Dawes, who has smuggled gold and artillery out of Boston, and who has recently brought Paul Revere's plates out, metal plates which are now being used for printing money. Because, you understand, all revolutions require money, and since Massachusetts has no money, the only solution is to make our own.

Money that is not worth the paper it's printed on, to be sure, but still it gives a good impression, with the image of a sword in hand on one side, while on the other there's Mr. Revere's finely etched view of Boston. Worthless these notes might be, but they are an absolute necessity when it comes to procuring essentials for this burgeoning army." The doctor hesitated a moment, and then dipped his quill and continued writing. "Our powers of deception and illusion are, perhaps, our greatest gifts. You no doubt have heard about Ticonderoga, where Ethan Allen and his Green Mountain Boys have captured British artillery. The question is, of course, what good are such armaments doing us out there, when we have the British army hemmed in here in Boston? So it appears we hope to send a detail out to Ticonderoga to bring those guns to Boston. Neck by concealing it in her skirts?" The doctor laughed, without missing a stroke in composition. "And, yes, I know, Benjamin of your great affection for artillery, but it could be some time before an expedition to New York is organized and I need you here, for the time being. I would like you to take this missive to Watertown, where the Reveres are staying. Unless—" and here the doctor took a moment to look up at Benjamin—"unless you'd like to accept the offer of amnesty that General Gage has just issued to all provincials. I learned of this just today. New generals, Howe, Clinton, and Burgoyne, have recently arrived from London, and they have inspired Gage to issue a proclamation that offers amnesty to any provincial who lays down his arms, *except*—with tyranny, there are always the exceptions—except for two individuals. And do you know who they are? Well, you can guess, right? Samuel Adams, of course, and John Hancock. Even Paul Revere and I could easily slip back into the good graces of George the Third as easily as we could slip beneath the warm sheets of our dear mothers on a winter's night, to once more nestle against their warm, nourishing bosom." Dr. Warren stopped writing and gazed up, his bright blue eyes wide with inquiry. "Would you like that, Benjamin? Would you like to accept such a generous offer of amnesty so you can return to your loving mother?"

"No, sir."

"Thus our fates are sealed, as the poets would have it." He sanded the sheet he had been writing on, and then folded the paper so that he could pour the excess back into the jar. "So instead you will risk your neck by taking this to Watertown." He folded the letter up, sealed it with candle wax, and handed it to Benjamin. "Go. You'll find them residing in the house of Mr. Van Ee. Procure a horse from the stable and be back here tonight, for tomorrow I will have another errand for you, provided you think you can get back into Boston once more."

Then Dr. Warren curled over his book again and began reading, not just reading but consuming the lines on the page as though they—and only they—could provide rare spiritual and intellectual sustenance. And this too Benjamin found a remarkable habit, how the doctor could immediately disengage himself, only to immediately reinvest himself in some other enterprise.

Once more, Abigail appeared before three British officers at Province House. Her father sat in the chair next to her, his stout fingers worrying in his lap, to the point where she finally reached over and placed a hand over his, calming them. Startled, he turned his head, but then his eyes seemed to melt into a grateful if febrile stare. "I'm sorry," he whispered, leaning toward her, smelling of his pipe tobacco, "I expected General Gage to be present."

"He has been most kind to you and mother," she said. When this did not seem to satisfy him, she added, "The last time, he did not join the proceedings until well after they began." She attempted a smile. "His army is besieged on this peninsula and I image that keeps him occupied."

Father was about to respond, but one of the generals cleared his throat, indicating that they were ready to commence. Father and

Abigail looked toward the polished mahogany table, where three officers sat, as before; but now, instead of Armbruster, General John Burgoyne sat on the left and Samuel Cleaveland on the right, while, between them, not General Smythe, but General Henry Clinton was poring over a stack of documents.

They waited. More than the absence of General Gage, the presence of these two new officers concerned Abigail. They had arrived, along with a third general, William Howe, from England in the last days of May. Supposition immediately ricocheted about Boston: Gage's days as governor-general were numbered; the new generals came with direct orders to launch a major assault on the provincials; and, most often repeated, all of Massachusetts would be burned and razed as a warning to the other colonies. No matter what the rumor, the arrival of these new generals did not bode well for Boston, where in the streets one could not help but notice how the patrols seemed invigorated, stricter and unwilling to ignore the slightest taunts and accusations. But what worried Abigail at this moment was Samuel, who sat up very erect in his chair with his hands folded on the table, an acquiescent schoolboy on his best behavior. He seemed determined not to stare directly at Abigail.

Finally, looking up from the documents, General Clinton said, "Abigail Lovell, you are the daughter of John Lovell, headmaster at the Latin School." She was about to confirm that this was so, but he continued: "And you have been under investigation by this tribunal in regards to the murder of a British sergeant, named—" he glanced down at the documents in his hands—"Munroe." She felt her father stir next to her, but the general regarded him with nothing short of scorn. "You, sir, are this woman's father, I take it, but I do not see the purpose of your presence during these proceedings."

"But, General, if I may—" Father began.

Clinton looked toward one of the soldiers standing guard by the door. "Mr. Lovell shall be escorted from the room at once."

The soldier stepped forward, his boot heels hard and brisk on the wood floor, and reluctantly Father clambered out of his chair. Abigail knew he was leaning down toward her, but she did not turn to him; instead she kept her eyes on General Clinton. He seemed quite young for a general, perhaps not even forty. He had a deep dimple in his chin and his periwig was flawlessly groomed and curled. His protuberant eyes gazed back at her, seeming to possess neither curiosity nor feeling. They might have been marbles, smooth, polished stones. She had heard—rumor, again—that of the three new generals, he was the one to be most feared, that he was querulous and assertive, that he suffered no lack of self-confidence. She listened to her father's shuffling footsteps as he left, and the door closed behind him with an ominous echo.

"Now, Miss Lovell, on the night in question, you were at the place locally referred to as Trimount." She was prepared to speak, but then realized that it wouldn't stop him. "And it was there that Sergeant Munroe met his death."

"Yes, General, it is so, but I was not—"

"You are said to have been covered in blood." There was something about his voice, how it seemed to tear through each syllable with dauntless precision. "Is this not true?"

"It was—"

"No weapon was found, but a knife, it is presumed, or some sharp implement was employed to cut the sergeant's throat," Clinton announced, not really to her, but to the entire room as though he were addressing a vast audience. "He was covered in blood—"

"But it was not—"

"—and you were covered in blood."

"I never saw Sergeant Munroe on Trimount, General."

"How then did you come to have this blood on you?"

"It was not his blood, sir. It was my own blood. I explained the last time I was here—"

"Come now, Miss Lovell, do you expect this inquiry to believe that you both were bloodied at the same time, in the same place, but that there is no connection between these incidents?"

"Yes, I struck my head on a tree, in the dark."

"A tree, in the dark." General Clinton. "Really, Miss Lovell, we have—"

"General," John Burgoyne said. "If I may."

General Burgoyne was a much more substantial man, and significantly older, certainly over fifty; yet Clinton was clearly the superior officer and, seeming to take this request as a personal insult, settled back in his chair.

Burgoyne placed his forearms on the table (no clutter of documents there) and squared his shoulders. Despite his age, his ruddy face was nothing short of dashingly handsome. No wig, he possessed a full head of dark wavy hair, with hints of gray descending into his meticulously trimmed sideburns. "Tell me, Abigail," he said. "How did you come to bloody yourself?"

"As I said, it was dark and I struck a tree."

"This claim is preposterous," Clinton snapped: "It's all in the record from the previous session of this inquiry."

"I wasn't at the previous session," Burgoyne replied, without looking at Clinton. "Now, Abigail, where exactly did you suffer your injury?"

Burgoyne's eyes were large and kind, and not without the suggestion of humor. There was something else about them which Abigail had seen all too often: they were greedy. He used this question to allow his eyes to inspect her person—her neck, her shoulders, and finally clearly settling on her bosom.

Samuel, seated on the other side of Clinton, stirred in his chair. "She received a laceration to her scalp, as was demonstrated at the last session of this inquiry."

Clinton swung his head toward Samuel, and Abigail would not have been surprised if he'd taken a bite out of the shoulder of his red jacket. "*Colonel*," he said.

"Sir," Samuel said politely, "I was at the first session of the inquiry, and I have seen the wound to her scalp."

Such impertinence forced Clinton to consider the documents in his hands, but then, quickly, he looked up at her and said, "Yes, I read here that you wore a turban during the last session."

"I did, sir. Perhaps——" she hesitated. Clinton appeared nearly apoplectic, while Samuel looked resigned—to his fate, as well as hers—and Burgoyne's gaze continued to be transfixed upon her breasts. "Perhaps I could show you?" Uncertainly, Abigail raised an arm so that she could push the curls aside from her forehead.

Samuel lowered his eyes as though out of decency, while Burgoyne's mouth fell open.

"That will *not* be necessary," Clinton nearly shouted.

"But it has significant bearing on this matter," Burgoyne said, almost pleading.

"Such a laceration," Clinton said, "could have been inflicted at any time."

Slowly, Abigail took her fingers out of her hair and lowered her arm, much to Burgoyne's disappointment.

"Miss Lovell," Clinton continued. "Would you tell us why you ventured up to this place called Trimount?"

"I was taking a walk," she said

"In the dark of night."

"I—yes, it was night."

"You make a practice of walking about Boston, at night?" Clinton asked.

"I took offense at the implication the last time I was here, General, and I do so now."

"Do you indeed?" Clinton asked.

If possible, Burgoyne's face seemed to become more crimson as he gazed at her. With great concentration, Samuel kept running his thumb back and forth along the edge of the table, while his somber upside-down image was reflected in its vast, glossy surface.

"Indeed," Clinton repeated, and then he looked toward the guards at the door. "In that case, it would be appropriate to seek testimony from a new witness who might shed light on the nocturnal affairs of Boston."

It was ever so slight, but Samuel's shoulders collapsed and his chest seemed to deflate.

Abigail heard the door behind her open and quickly turned in her chair. Molly Collins strode in from the vestibule, wearing a yellow dress that was fairly clean, though the hem was powdered with road dust. She appeared taller, more robust; her cheeks were artfully rouged and her wide blue eyes nothing short of triumphant. A guardsman led her to the chair next to Abigail, where she sat down and demurely arranged her skirt. Her hair was piled up on top of her head, revealing a remarkably slender neck, which had a poorly stitched scar just above the collarbone. She made no attempt to acknowledge Abigail and gave her full attention to the officers at the table.

"You are Molly Collins," General Clinton said, "a resident of Boston."

"I'yam."

Burgoyne's eyes shifted back and forth between the two women, and he appeared to be in a genuine quandary.

"And you were on Trimount the night that Sergeant Munroe was murdered," Clinton said.

"'Tis true."

"General." Samuel's voice was exasperated, weary. "The testimony of this woman—"

"Had it been sought at the first session," Clinton said, "we might not need to be here now."

"But General," Samuel said. "This woman is—"

"Is what?" Clinton demanded. "Are you going to tell me she walks the streets at night? It seems that this is the occupation of virtually every provincial woman in the city of Boston."

"Sir, her testimony cannot be considered valid in this matter," Samuel said, though now he clearly realized he was engaged in a futile exercise.

Burgoyne, without taking his eyes off Molly, said, "If she was present at the incident, I would like to hear what she has to say. Then we can judge how best to view her sentiments."

"How magnanimous of you," Clinton said, smiling, quite wickedly, for the first time. Unlike Burgoyne, he seemed resistant to the idea of looking directly at Molly, so he shuffled through his papers and took up his quill. "So, if you please, Miss Collins, would you confirm a few things for us?" Before she could answer, he continued: "That night on Trimount, you went up there to meet two soldiers, I believe their names were Lodge and Dayton."

"Don't recall their names exactly," Molly said sweetly, "but, yes, I met two soldiers up the hill there."

Burgoyne's mouth hung open in alarm. "You met *two* soldiers?"

"Well, there was me and Eliza," Molly said. "Me cousin, she is."

Clinton had dipped his quill and was writing, but paused to ask, "And what did you do with these two soldiers up the hill *there?*" His voice was also sweet, but mockingly so.

Abigail stole a glance at Molly. Though she had full, overly puckered lips, her profile was rather flat and her jaw slung forward enough that she suffered from a mild degree of underbite. Her mouth faintly resembled that of a cod. She had boasted that she was the best suck in Boston, and Abigail wondered if this had resulted in her slight deformity. Molly's eyes moved over the three officers, gauging the situation, until she suddenly brightened and said, "Yes, well, we was invited up the hill there to share a picnic with these two blokes." Then, proudly, and with a smirk, she added, "Members of the King's Own Foot, so they claimed."

"A picnic," Clinton asked. "At night."

"Yes, it was evening," she said. "All very on the up and up, you know. Proper, like."

"No doubt, no doubt," Clinton intoned, scratching away rapidly. He paused to dip his quill. "And then?"

"And I hear this scream," Molly said, "this *'orrible* scream from up the path."

Samuel cleared his throat. "I distinctly recall that Lodge and Dayton testified that they heard no scream." He looked toward Clinton. "It would be in your records, sir."

Clinton laid down his quill. Reluctantly he considered Molly.

"Well, they was preoccupied," Molly said. "With their food and beverage, you see. And there was a great deal of laughter, and to tell you the truth I think they'd both imbibed a bit much by then."

"What did you *see?*" Clinton asked.

"See?" Molly asked.

Clinton merely gazed back at her.

"Well," she said, sighing. "I seen this other soldier running down the path by us—some scared out of his wits, he was. And that's what alerted Lodge and Dayton, and they goes up the hill and discovers Miss Lovell there, and your other soldier, this Sergeant Munroe. In quite a state they was."

"Who?" Clinton asked.

"Everyone. But Lodge and Dayton, they sobered up right quick, I tell you." Molly smiled, but only Burgoyne complied.

"Who was this other soldier, running down the hill?" Clinton asked.

"That would be Corporal Lumley, I believe," Molly said. "Yes, it was definitely he."

"So you didn't see—" Samuel began, but paused when Clinton placed a hand on his arm.

"What happened then?" Clinton asked.

"We was told to go down the hill, Eliza and me. That's what Lodge told us to do. And glad to go, I was. So we rushed down the path after Lumley."

"You're sure it was Lumley?" Clinton asked. "It was dark."

"It was Lumley." Molly hesitated a moment. "Gone missing, ain't he?"

"That is true," Clinton said. "Do you know anything about that?"

"Indeed I do." She took a moment to fuss with her sleeve, the lace there frequently mended.

"What can you tell us about Corporal Lumley?" Clinton said impatiently.

Molly continued to fidget with her garment as she said, "He was right jealous, if you ask me." And looking up at the officers, she said, as though it were obvious: "Lumley, he and Munroe they was mates, you know, on patrol together and such. But then they both became enamored of—" she tilted her head in Abigail's direction—"of this schoolmaster's fine daughter."

"Lumley and Munroe?" Clinton asked.

"The bot' of them, yes," Molly said, surprised at such lack of understanding. "Lumley, you know he was billeted there in School Street, but a few houses from where she resides. And Munroe, he was the mouthy kind, you understand, and in the taverns and such he was bragging about her, her attributes. Oh, he had it bad. She gave him a taste and he was besotted. Mind you, what I don't know for certain is which of 'em got to her first, or perhaps she was playing them bot' at the same time. But they was bound to find out eventually, being mates, and when they did they had this grand argument—on that very night—and not long after dark they're all up there on Trimount and it's Munroe that ends up with his throat cut. It's kind of prophetic, in'it? Trimount, meaning three hills, and here you have your love triangle all played out on its slopes there. Like a bard's tragedy, it is."

"There is no truth to this," Abigail said. "None at all." Though Clinton held his hand up to stop her, she continued. "The fact that Lumley billeted on my street doesn't prove anything, and as for Munroe—" She gazed down at her hands in her lap and saw that they were shaking. Looking at Clinton, she said, "One night I encountered them while I was on my way to my brother's house. It was April eighteen, a Tuesday, the night that the British troops ferried across the Charles and marched out into the countryside. Munroe and Lumley remained here on street patrol. You must have records of that—you could check. They were on patrol and they were both quite drunk and they stopped me and by force they fondled me in the rudest way."

"Both men?" Burgoyne asked.

Abigail nearly stood up, but she only came to the edge of her seat. "Lumley held me by the shoulders, pressing me against the wall of the house, while Munroe put his hands on me. They both reeked of rum." She glanced at Molly, who was looking at her as though she were a child spawning an outrageous fib. "They took from me what they pay to get from the likes of Molly Collins. Ask her how many of your soldiers have had their hands on her." She looked at Samuel. "How many, Colonel? You've been in Boston for some time. How many of you have bought her paltry favors?" Again, Clinton raised his hand, but Abigail said loudly, "You can't possibly take her word for any of this. If you do so, it is only because it suits your own purposes. This is not a court. This has nothing to do with justice. Why are you here, in this room? Why are you all here, in Boston?"

Clinton slapped the tabletop repeatedly, the sound reverberating throughout the room. "That will be enough, do you hear?"

Abigail sat back and folded her arms. She took long slow breaths.

None of the officers seemed to know what to do, and for a moment Burgoyne leaned over and whispered in Clinton's ear. Samuel gazed at the tabletop, shaking his head slowly.

"If you please," Molly said with remarkable poise. "Sirs, you wish to know about Lumley. Let me tell you about your corporal that is gone missing." She turned away from Abigail ever so slightly and glared at the officers.

267

Clinton said, "Go on."

"I'll tell you," Molly said, her voice now hurt, deeply insulted. "I'll tell you about this fine daughter of a schoolmaster. Lumley and Munroe they took her younger brother Benjamin into custody on suspicion of espionage, and, lo, the boy manages to break free. How? Lumley, that's how. And then they both escape Boston together. That's the truth." Now she extended her arm, pointing at Abigail. "This woman—*this* woman arranged for them to be ferried across the harbor in a working boat. I was *there!* I tried to stop it, and what does she *do?* She throws me into the water, she does. With one great shove, just as the boat is pulling away from the dock."

Abigail slapped Molly's hand away from her face and got to her feet. "It wasn't like that at all," she shouted. "You know that!"

Folding her arms and turning her back on Abigail, Molly said, "I speak the truth."

"All lies," Abigail shouted. "This *isn't* justice!"

And then she was grabbed from behind as one of the guards took her by the shoulders and forced her to sit down in the chair. She shrugged until he released her, shouting, "Take your hands off me!"

All the while, Clinton was again slapping his hand on the table. Finally, when he stopped, the room was quiet for a moment and no one, it seemed, dared to move. Then Clinton gathered up his documents and got to his feet. He was not a tall man, and quite stout, less imposing without a fine table in front of him. Burgoyne and Samuel also got to their feet, all seeming eager to leave, but then Clinton had a change of mind and put his papers down. "You are right about one thing, Abigail Lovell," he said, placing his fists on the tabletop and leaning forward as though making ready to pounce. "It is my understanding that, sadly, the legal system in this colony has by and large ceased to function. And the reason that is so has to do with numerous provincials' threats against judges and lawyers, against any person who would participate in a court of law in any way. Death threats—death threats have been posted on lawyers' doors. Damning letters have been published in local broadsides and journals. There is no court in Boston, at the moment. But there *is* justice. Here in this room, there will be justice. Now I will confer with my fellow officers and you will be summoned shortly—in a matter of days—and then you will hear our determination." Looking toward the guards, he said, "Take her out to her father and see that they are away from this house promptly." Then, looking at Molly Collins, who was still seated, he added, "And see to it that this young woman is provided with a coach and four to convey her home."

XX

Bête Noire

"IT'S HARD TO LOOK AT HIM," RACHEL REVERE SAID. "BUT after a while you don't notice it so much. What comes through is the kindness in his eyes, and his gestures—I don't know where we'd be if it weren't for Mr. Van Ee taking us in."

Benjamin looked down toward the riverbank, where the man was sitting, smoking his pipe, minding Rachel's little ones. It was a long, sloping plane of grass, between two fields of vegetables above the Charles. Now, approaching sunset, the river mirrored pink clouds and a lambent hatch of flies drifted in the angled light.

"What happened to him?" Benjamin asked.

"He's Dutch," she said, as though that explained everything. "Didn't have a farthing when he came over some thirty years ago. Now, this." She nodded toward the house that lay at the top of the slope, a three-story manse with chimneys and ells as testimony to decades of accumulation. "When he first arrived he worked as a farmhand, and he promptly fell headfirst into a wagonload of manure." Rachel's eyes sparkled with the delight of telling. She found lustful humor in the lurid and grotesque; Abigail said that no one could make her laugh like Rachel. "He was stuck, up to his waist, and about to suffocate when they grabbed him by the heels and yanked him out. Potent stuff, that fertilizer. Burned and deformed his head and hands. But he likes to say it had no effect on his better half." Her grin was sly, conspiratorial. "Sired fourteen children—all in the dark of night, I presume—which accounts for so many additions on the house. A fireplace in each bedroom. Can you imagine?"

"So now he's here alone?"

"Wife long dead, children grown and dispersed," she said. "Alone, save for this fleet of maids." She looked down the table at two of the girls who were clearing away the dinner plates. "I was cooped up in that little house in the North End with Paul's brood, his mother, plus our own little one, and now—" she leaned back in her chair, clasped her hands behind her head and gazed at the sky. "I could get used to this life of ease. Paul wants still more children, and I would be happy to oblige him under these circumstances. But, alas, our time for making babies will have to wait." She sat up and eyed Benjamin closely. "Revolution tends to make for hasty lovemaking, don't you think?"

Embarrassed, he turned toward the river. Rachel laughed.

"Abigail tells me you're sweet on the fisherman Anse Cole's daughter."

He watched the sun's slow descent behind trees on the far bank of the Charles. The hatch, now aglow like embers, danced a reel above the water's sheen.

"You're becoming such a pretty young man," she said, taking his hand. "You don't notice how the younger maids watch you?" Alarmed, he looked down the table, where one of the girls hastily lowered her head, shielding her eyes with the brim of her bonnet as she scraped fish bones from a plate into a slop bucket.

"What's her name?" Rachel coaxed.

"Her name?"

"Your girl's." Rachel released his hand, and her fingers crawled up his forearm.

With reluctance he volunteered, "Mariah."

"Mariah!"

Rachel's hand jumped from his arm down to his knee, which she squeezed, making him sit up. Her laugh now was akin to a cat's purr. And down by the riverbank the children screamed with delight, chasing bubbles, which Mr. Van Ee was blowing through a ring.

"Rachel, can you tell me something—something that a younger brother isn't supposed to know about?"

"You need a lesson in love, for the benefit of your darling Mariah?" She then leaned forward in her chair, her hand still on his knee. "What do you want to know, dear?" Her voice was frighteningly coy and playful. "Is there something your school-master father, fine, educated man that he is, has not explained to your satisfaction?"

"No . . . um, it's about my sister. Abigail and Ezra. Do you know what happened?"

Rachel's hand fell from his knee. "Dear Lord," she sighed. "That. I don't know for certain. Abigail is like a sister to me, you know that, but she does hold her feelings tight within her bodice. If anyone can prod and pry it out of someone, it's me, but with her it's like scratching at a stone. I only know that there's the blackest heartbreak. After Ezra left Boston, she was clearly distraught. In a strange way, I think this war benefits someone like your sister. It distracts her, preoccupies her."

"With Ezra, too," Benjamin said.

"You mentioned him earlier. You've seen much of him since Lexington and Concord."

"He and I are mates. He's asked that I promise not to tell Abigail that I've seen him."

Now it was Rachel who stared down toward the darkening river in need of solace. "It's like he wishes to be dead to her. When Paul began courting me, not long after his first wife Sarah died, he refused to speak of her. It was my hardest work, truly, to convince him that she could live on in his thoughts." Her eyes sought Benjamin's. "When he understood that, when he began telling me about her, it was then that I knew that he loved me. The heart, such a dark, strange chamber."

"Soon Dr. Warren is sending me back into Boston, and I feel I should tell her something. Especially since she saw us together on shore at Noddle's Island, plus the fact that Ezra acted so queerly. He would not even wave back to her."

Again Rachel took his hand, but this time it wasn't playful. "No, you must honor your friend's request," she said, barely a whisper. "These things cannot be manipulated, as much as one would love to try."

He nodded. "It's for them to sort out."

She held his hand tightly. "But you can tell your sister that I miss her greatly."

"Yes, of course."

"There's also something I'd like you to tell her—" Rachel said, but she then turned as her children screamed. They were running barefoot up the grassy slope, shouting out, "Mother! Mother, we have found a *bullfrog!* And Mr. Van Ee says we must ask you if we can keep it in a *jar!*"

The dooryard was silent. It had been coming for weeks, Abigail realized, this loss of sound. All the neighbors' yards, boxed off by fences, were silent. No cackle of chickens, no grunting and squealing of pigs. They'd all been eaten. Or stolen. Too much of that lately. Too little food; too much theft.

Samuel didn't notice any of this. He had arrived at the front door, polite, as always, but with a sense of urgency that none of them had ever seen before; after paying cursory respects to Father and Mother, he insisted that he and Abigail talk somewhere privately. So here they came, out to the dooryard, with the last light of day cutting across the rooftops.

His voice pushed relentlessly against the heavy night air. After a while she stopped trying to follow him, but just listened to the sound of him—angular, inexorable phrases spilling forth. She'd become accustomed to his accent, which she gathered was unique to Surrey, but now she paid close attention to the lengthened *a's,* the open *r's.* Not that different from a Boston accent, but richer, deeper, each syllable more involved. He would probably insist that the Boston accent was a descendant, weak and diluted. Had he said that once? She couldn't be sure. And he was whispering, as though someone might be on the other side of the fence listening. She was tempted to tell him that Old Mrs. Symmons was, as she liked to say (shout) herself, deaf as a haddock.

Finally, she put a hand on his arm to stop him. "It's clear that you're concerned for my well-being, but I don't understand what you want me to do."

It had been a good while since she had touched him, and it seemed to calm him. "Abigail, you need to understand what happened at that inquiry today. With these new generals arrived in Boston, everything has changed."

"I understand that they intend to make an example out of me, regardless of the facts."

"I'm afraid this is so."

"So there really isn't anything I can do. I've been thinking that I might be more useful."

"Like a martyr."

"Yes." She had been thinking something else, as well: fleeing Boston.

"It's too dramatic a term—burning at the stake with eyes lifted toward the heavens—that's for papists, and Frenchmen," he said. "No, you'll be an example, a form of reprimand. They mean to show you—show all of you colonists—what you're in for. Push back against the king and you will have met your bête noire." He took hold of her hand, which she rather welcomed. She had to admit she was frightened. "You're perfectly suited, you see. You're not part of Sam Adams's mob, his rabble. You're the daughter of a schoolmaster loyal to the crown."

"Samuel, I did not kill Sergeant Munroe."

"I know that. But Clinton believes that the mere possibility that you murdered him is sufficient for his needs. There's enough evidence, enough blood. In Clinton's mind, it doesn't really matter which of you cut Munroe's throat."

"They actually believe Molly Collins?"

"It doesn't matter, Abigail. What matters is that she has served her purpose."

"That is her one skill. A well-honed skill it is."

He gasped, but then in exasperation said, "Don't you *see?* What's equally important is that you helped Lumley get out of Boston. The corporal's defection is an act of treason."

Her legs suddenly felt as though they would give way. "I need—can we please sit down?"

There was a bench by the gate that opened to the alley, its maple slats warped by the seasons. It was dark now, and as they sat, he put his arm around her shoulders.

"I realized something after the inquiry," she said. "In your own way, you were trying to protect me. It's a strange logic, just like Old South Church."

"How so?"

"You had something to do with turning Old South Church into an exercise course."

"Well, I may have, but—"

"I understand. Houses and buildings are being demolished all over Boston," she said. "The way you 'save' Old South is to denigrate it. The only way to preserve our place of worship is with dirt, sawdust, and horse manure."

"I hadn't thought of it that way, but—listen to me. I have no real influence, less so now with the new generals. I'm surprised I wasn't relieved of duty on this inquiry, along with Smythe and

Armbruster, but, see, that's how Clinton operates: everything for the appearance of impartiality and fairness, when the real design is to achieve the necessary outcome."

"I was guilty before I walked into Province House today."

"I'm afraid so."

"What will they do to me?" He didn't answer, and, placing her hand on his chest, she could feel that his breathing was shallow. She put her head on his shoulder. "You can tell me."

"I don't know. Yet. Nothing has been determined. This isn't just about you. It's about the balance of power. Gage has it. Clinton wants it, and William Howe nearly has it."

"He wasn't even there today."

"A sign of his strength. Howe won't become directly involved until it's absolutely necessary. And then the question will be who will win. Clinton will want to make an example of you. Burgoyne, he took one look and the old dog was won over by your beauty. He will plead for mercy, as I will. So finally it all comes down to Clinton."

"Gage, he doesn't—"

"Forget about Gage. He won't last long here. They're questioning his tactics, why he hasn't taken a firmer hand, why he didn't long ago establish outposts in the countryside so that there was little chance of the provincials even thinking of challenging the army—let alone managing to coop us up here in Boston. It's really up to General Howe. He's a gambler and a drunkard, but has a reputation for courage on the battlefield— all the attributes of a fine British commander. If Howe sides with Clinton, he will demonstrate that he has the stuff to lay down the law in Massachusetts. That's why they were sent here, after all."

"If I am to be found guilty," she said, "if they decide against being merciful . . ." She couldn't go on. She lifted her head off his chest and looked up at him, but he continued to stare straight ahead into the night.

His arm tightened about her shoulders. "For this, you can hang."

The next hour, until dark, was devoted to the bullfrog. Rachel had struck a bargain with the children: the frog could be their guest for the night, but they must agree to release it down by the river in the morning. They agreed, and their excitement proved contagious. Everyone got involved: Mr. Van Ee asked that Mrs. Burke find an appropriate jar in the pantry, and then he sent her daughters out into the yard to pull grass, which the children then used to create a bed for the bullfrog. Once ensconced in his glass abode, the children all leaned in close, attracted and repulsed. They commented on the frog's lumpy, spotted, slick skin, his bulging eyes, his swelling, pulsating throat. They debated names and finally settled on Mr. Van Ee's suggestion of John, short for John Bull. But then there was the question of the frog's sex, which no one knew how to determine, a question which Mrs. Burke settled (a role she apparently played often in the Van Ee household) by flatly claiming that it had to be male because such an ugly creature couldn't possibly be female. All the while, Rachel dropped hints that the inevitable was approaching: bedtime. The children were resistant. There were some tears, there was pleading, but eventually, after much cajoling and horseplay, they were all tucked away for the night.

When it was time for Benjamin to leave, Rachel walked him out to the stable.

"The days here are good for the children, but exhausting for me," she said. "The air, the river, it increases their appetites, their energy, and then they collapse in bed. And I must get to sleep soon, because in a few hours the baby will be awake for his feeding."

There was something in Rachel's voice that Benjamin didn't understand, and he concentrated on tightening the cinch under the horse's belly.

"When you return to Boston," she said, "you will be careful?"

"I will not announce my arrival with fife and drum."

She laughed, but nervously. "If you see Abigail, you will tell her how I miss her."

"Of course."

"And I wonder if you could ask her something for me." He tucked the leather strap through the buckle and turned to her. The lantern that she held illuminated one side of her face. Though she was only about ten years older, the light revealed lines caused by worry, and her eye was hard and direct. "Soon after Lexington and Concord, I received a letter from Paul saying he was in desperate need of clothing and money. I gave these to Abigail, and it was arranged that she would convey them to Dr. Church, who had managed to get into Boston and was taking medical supplies out, for the aid of both American and British wounded. Would you—I hope she doesn't take this in the wrong way, because I mentioned this to her before I left Boston—but would you ask her if she delivered everything to Dr. Church?"

"Of course," Benjamin said. "Mr. Revere did not receive it?"

She shook her head. "It has us baffled. Dr. Church is, he is such an honorable man, a member of the Committee of Safety, and—there must be some explanation."

"Have you seen him since you've left Boston?"

"I haven't. Paul has, when in consultation with Dr. Warren and others. He has not asked Dr. Church directly. . . ."

Benjamin understood. Paul Revere was an artisan, a mechanic, while Benjamin Church, he was quite the other thing, a doctor and a gentleman. For all the talk of freedom and equality, there were still distinctions to be made.

"It was a substantial sum," Rachel said. He took hold of the reins, hoping that he wasn't revealing his desire to know the amount. "One hundred and twenty-five pounds, Benjamin."

In an attempt to conceal his surprise, Benjamin placed his boot in the stirrup and hoisted himself up into the saddle. "Of course, I will ask her."

Rachel touched his knee and smiled. "And you will see your Mariah. Perhaps the revolution can stop for one night. I hope so." She squeezed his knee, let go, and then stepped back.

He pressed his heels into the horse's sides and touched the brim of his hat in farewell.

XXI

Heat

On a warm, still night in the second week of June, Benjamin rowed across the Charles, avoiding the watch on the *Somerset,* as well as the British patrol boats that plied the harbor. At first light, he entered the city, working his way through the maze of alleys that ran behind the main streets, until he came to James's house. All the windows were dark. He placed Dr. Warren's letter, tied between two flat stones again, on the left corner of the kitchen stoop, and then went off to the granary. From the top floor, he watched the sun rise above Long Wharf, which ran a half mile into the harbor, and beyond that the outer islands and Nantasket Roads. Exhausted, but thankful for the smell of salt water, he curled up on the straw ticking and fell asleep to the belligerent cawing of seagulls.

Abigail was exhausted. She had hardly slept during the night, after the message had been delivered the previous evening that she was to appear before the inquiry the following afternoon. While preparing for the appointment, James came up to Abigail's room. "I wonder if I should pack some belongings," she said. "If they sentence me, then will I be taken straight away to prison?"

"I will come with you," he said.

"Absolutely not. You of all people shouldn't go near Province House. It's bad enough that both Father and Mother insist on coming this time. Father won't forgive himself for not protesting his removal from the room the last time. If you should show up, these generals are likely to find a reason to haul you in with me."

"Kill two birds with one stone." James sat heavily in the chair in the corner and looked out the window a moment. "I believe," he began, "I believe we have been granted certain latitude, because of Father's association with General Gage, but that, that is over now." Something was on his mind.

"What?" she said. "What is it?"

"Benjamin is back." He turned to her and before she could speak, he said, "He arrived the night before last. I can't tell you where he's staying for fear that they might somehow get it out of you." James sat forward on the chair; it almost looked as though he were preparing to drop down on the floor and pray. "Listen. He has brought information from Dr. Warren that Gage and the new generals are finalizing plans to make a foray out of the city." Again, she was about to speak, when he said, "Soon. Very soon. I believe they have devised a plan where they will attack us on Dorchester Heights." James touched his fingers to his lips a moment. "Benjamin is going to try to return to Cambridge tonight. You must go with him."

It was so warm. Abigail pressed her sleeve against her forehead. "How? Father has arranged for the carriage to come around immediately."

"We go downstairs right now," he said, getting to his feet. "We go out the kitchen to the dooryard gate."

She could barely breathe. "I can't, I can't—think."

He took her by the elbow. "Now, Abigail. Benjamin, he's very close. Believe me, I can take you to him—in a matter of minutes. We hide both of you until it's dark, and then he rows you across the harbor. By morning you'll be safe. You can stay with Rachel."

"Rachel? He has seen Rachel?"

"Yes, he says she and her family are staying in a house in Watertown. He'll take you there and you'll be fine."

"But—"

With his other hand, James opened her bedroom door. "Now. We must go right now."

"I have nothing." She looked toward her bureau. "I would need—"

"You take nothing. You just go."

He drew her out into the hall and then down the stairs. She hesitated at the landing, but his hand was still holding her elbow and he urged her on, down to the narrow hallway, where sunlight streamed in through the open front door, reflecting off the floorboards. Her father was standing on the front stoop. The carriage had arrived, the smell of horse coming down the hall. Her mother came out of the parlor and took her shawl down off the peg by the front door. Without looking back down the hallway, she went out the door, and Father helped her climb up into the carriage.

"Now," James whispered. "We must do it *now*, Abigail."

Father stepped up into the doorway, a silhouette against the glaring light. "Your mother," he said, "is impossible. She insists on going, too. Come now, we don't want to be late."

James looked at their father, and then back at Abigail. He was still holding her arm.

"Today we will see justice done," Father said. "You'll see, Abigail. We'll be there with you." It was in his voice: he was trying to be brave, his confidence a thin veneer, barely concealing his worry. "And James," he added, hopefully, "perhaps you should come today, as well. It may be instructive for you to see how the

King's men conduct themselves. And—and at the very least we should be together."

James continued to look at Abigail. "I know how the King's men conduct themselves, thank you, Father." He let go of her arm. *Make up your own mind.*

Abigail offered her brother a smile. "I think it is a matter of curiosity."

Disappointed, he nodded, and she walked up the hallway toward the light that streamed in behind her father.

As before, Obadiah and his son Ezekiel found Benjamin, asleep in the granary loft.

"This will not do," Obadiah said. "Soldiers come here every day now. Like everything else, grain is scarce, and the redcoats insist on knowing exactly what we have in storage, and where every wagonload goes out of here." He looked at his son. "Go down and fetch my satchel. Your mother has packed us some bread and cheese. Bring it up here."

The boy ran from the room. Obadiah took a moment to settle his girth onto the stool in the corner. "You cannot stay here, not in this room."

"Just for one more night? There's no grain up here."

"Not safe." Obadiah glanced out the door, apparently to make sure his son had begun his descent down the stairs. "This room, it serves a purpose that has nothing to do with . . . grain." He eyed the straw ticking beneath Benjamin. "There is a captain who marches the detail here most every day. He is one very arrogant man. He has the usual weaknesses. It is not uncommon for him to meet with women up here in the afternoon. Lately it is a young wife who works in one of the vendors' shambles in Dock Square." Obadiah shook his head. "He brings sausages, meats. She does this for her children—this is how desperate we have become."

Benjamin got up off the ticking and brushed straw from his shirt and trousers.

"We'll give you something to eat," Obadiah said, "but then we must get you out of here before noon. Is there nowhere else you can hide?"

"I'll find some place."

Ezekiel's boots could be heard on the stairs. He came into the room, and his father took the leather satchel from his shoulder. Obadiah removed a loaf of bread and a wedge of cheese, and with his knife he cut a good portion of each, which he gave to Benjamin. Obadiah looked at his son, tilted his head, and the boy understood that he was expected to leave the room.

"Thank you for sharing your noonday meal, Ezekiel," Benjamin said.

The boy smiled and then ran out of the room and back down the stairs.

"It was weeks ago that we ate our last chicken," Obadiah said. "Most of them had already been pilfered. Sometimes this captain's woman, she will leave a bit of sausage here, by way of payment for the room, and for my silence."

Benjamin nodded and then he began to eat quickly.

"There is something else you should know." Obadiah got up off the stool. "There is news about your sister. There has been an inquiry into the death of a sergeant, and the disappearance of a corporal. This afternoon your sister is to appear at Province House again—the third time. Word comes out of the stable there, and it does not look well for her."

"Today?"

Obadiah nodded.

This time Abigail was shown into a different room in Province House; larger, with a railing that separated a gallery of pews, filled with officers—so much red; red jackets and white waistcoats, and buttons of bronze or pewter. The men were well fed; some grossly fat. As they spoke, their jowls quivered above their high, tight collars. Many wore wigs, or some had their hair greased into a tight stick, which was powdered. The deep murmur of their voices swelled as a guard led Abigail to a small table in the center of the room. He held the chair for her, but instead she turned to face the gallery. Among the officers were some of Father's Tory associates and friends, all dressed as if for Sunday meeting. Aside from Mother, who sat near the door with Father, there were only two other women, Molly Collins and Mariah Cole. They sat quite apart from each other. Mariah's cheeks were flushed and her breathing seemed labored. Molly waved a fan beneath her chin and her blue eyes gazed back at Abigail as though she were a delicious morsel. The chamber was extremely hot, yet all of the windows were closed.

Suddenly the officers all clambered to their feet. Abigail turned around and watched as General Clinton led Burgoyne and Samuel into the chamber. They seated themselves behind the long table of well-polished mahogany. A fourth officer followed and sat in an armchair off to the side. She suspected that this was General William Howe. Thomas Gage was not present.

Abigail sat down and folded her hands on the table, while behind her the audience settled into the gallery pews. Samuel gazed at her, his eyes somber, even remorseful.

General Clinton, again sitting between Burgoyne and Samuel, cleared his throat, bringing silence to the room. He took his time, sorting through the papers before him. He appeared to be looking for something in particular, which Abigail found humorous—it was as though he had forgotten why they were all here. When he looked up from his papers, he seemed surprised by her expression.

He cleared his throat again and said, "Abigail Lovell, after much deliberation and review of the evidence, this inquiry has reached a conclusion regarding the murder of Sergeant Edmund Munroe, who was found with his throat cut on the Trimount in April of this year. It is our determination that you—"

A pew creaked loudly behind Abigail; turning, she saw that her father had gotten to his feet.

"General," he said. "I implore you—"

"Mr. Lovell," Clinton said. "Your testimony is not required at these proceedings."

"Sir," Father said, louder. "I must protest—my daughter has been provided no legal counsel, and no real opportunity to defend herself against these charges."

Clinton slapped his palm on the tabletop. "Mr. Lovell, you were removed before, and I—"

The officer sitting to Abigail's left—General Howe—shifted in his armchair, and after a moment Clinton said in a more conciliatory manner, "If you please, Mr. Lovell, be seated."

"I would like to know why General Gage is not present," Father said, remaining on his feet. "Thomas Gage knows my daughter, he knows my family. He has been a guest in our home. He knows very well that Abigail is not capable of such a crime. You have no—"

Clinton said, "Sir, we acknowledge your objections but we must proceed."

"You have *no* witnesses. You have provided no one who actually *saw* what you claim happened on Trimount. *You have no—*"

Clinton nodded toward the door and one of the guards went over and stood next to Father's pew. *"Sir.* Please be seated."

Father stood his ground, staring back at Clinton, until Mother placed her hand on his forearm, and slowly he sat down. A deep murmur ran through the chamber, until Clinton again cleared his throat.

"Now," he said. "As I as saying, we have made a determination, based on the information presented before this inquiry." He paused, staring at Abigail. She didn't understand what it was he wanted from her, but then Samuel raised his head slightly.

"You want me to stand?" she said.

General Burgoyne said, "If you please."

Abigail got to her feet, and the effort made her lightheaded for a moment. Burgoyne was looking at her—not at her face but at her, all of her. She stared at him hard, until he looked away.

"Now," Clinton said. Again, he was studying his documents, and he began to read, "As it is hereby determined that you are guilty of taking the life of a British—"

"No." This from the other side of the gallery—Mariah's voice. Abigail turned and watched her get up from her pew. *"No,"* Mariah nearly shouted over the voices of the officers. She moved sideways quickly and then came to the railing, where she opened the gate, but there she was intercepted by a guard. "Abigail didn't do this," she said. The guard took her by the arm, and she resisted. "She didn't kill the sergeant."

There was a slight struggle, and then the guard began to push her back toward the door.

"Let her speak." Abigail turned again. It was General Howe who had spoken. Softly, but it silenced the room. "Bring her forward," he said.

"Sir?" Clinton said.

"Let's hear what she has to say." Howe had large eyes, heavy lids. He appeared to have just awakened from a heavy sleep, and there was something quite startled about him.

The guard escorted Mariah to the table, where she stood next to Abigail. She would only look at the three officers seated at the front of the chamber.

"Well," Clinton said, annoyed, "what is it you have to say?"

"Abigail didn't kill Sergeant Munroe," Mariah said.

"You are?"

"My name is Mariah Cole."

"You have proof, Mariah Cole?" Clinton said. "You can provide evidence?"

"I tell you she didn't do it," Mariah said. "She didn't do it. I did."

The officers' voices echoed through the room and only subsided after Clinton slapped the table repeatedly. When it was finally quiet again, he said, "You—you claim that you killed the sergeant? How?"

"With a shucking knife." Her voice trembled and she still wouldn't look at Abigail. "I still have it. It was one of my father's, and it's at my house, covered with the sergeant's blood."

Clinton's mouth moved but he uttered no sound, until he managed to say, "A shucking knife?"

"Yes," Mariah said. "You know, with the short, stiff blade, for opening oysters and clams. My father had many, but I used his favorite. He must have opened thousands of shells with it. I gave it some thought and decided that that knife would be most appropriate, you understand?"

"But why?" General Burgoyne said. "Why did you murder the sergeant?"

"Because he killed my father," Mariah said. At first she appeared to think this explained everything, but then she realized it wasn't enough. This made her slightly impatient, having to explain everything to the men who were supposed to be so learned. "Your sergeant killed my father, you see, on the beach below our house, using the butt of his rifle. My father was a fisherman—he set his nets, he dug in the beds at low tide. His whole life, he worked Boston harbor. He was unarmed and your sergeant struck him in the chest—I was there, I saw it," she said. "Nothing was done. You did nothing about it, did you? Why would you? You demand our loyalty to the king and you kill an old waterman. So. So, I sent the sergeant a note. I enticed him to Trimount, allowing him to think I was offering him—what women frequently offer up there. So he came up the hill that night and I killed him with the shucking knife that belonged to my father."

"Mariah," Abigail said. Her voice was barely audible. Mariah didn't seem to hear her, or perhaps she didn't want to hear. *"Mariah,"* she said again, and then she had to place her hands on the table before her.

Still looking at the officers, Mariah said, "And Corporal Lumley? There was no love affair, no cause for jealousy between him and the sergeant. The sergeant, he came up Trimount because he thought I was a prostitute. There's only one reason why your men go up there. And Lumley? For days before he escaped from Boston, he stayed with a *real* prostitute." She turned toward the gallery, extended her arm, and pointed at Molly Collins. "That one there."

"No!" Molly shouted, struggling to her feet.

"She hid him from you. She harbored him until he could get out of Boston."

There was pandemonium then.

Officers were standing, many of them shouting.

Their voices drowned out Clinton's fist as it pounded the tabletop, reverberating through the chamber, which began to tilt, causing Abigail to lean to her right, trying to halt the movement, but it only got worse, and she looked toward the windows, thinking that if someone only opened them there might be a breeze off the harbor, and there was a sweet sensation that allowed her to look at the plaster medallion in the center of the ceiling, which reminded her of cake, a cake with white frosting, like the one that had been prepared for James's wedding, made by a baker whose shop was near the Mill Pond, and whose name she couldn't now remember, but she had once promised herself that if she and Ezra ever did marry, they would request the very same cake with white frosting, so that when Ezra had abruptly left Boston her first thought was *There will be no need for the cake now.*

Which she may have said now, she wasn't sure, as she realized that she was gazing up at Samuel who was leaning over her, his head backed by the ceiling medallion, as though it were a halo.

Benjamin didn't dare get too close. There was a crowd gathered in front of Province House, facing a line of British sentries. He watched from down the street, leaning against a brick wall at the entrance to an alley. He recognized people in the crowd, shopkeeps from Dock Square, the Teele's Irish maid, a fishmonger's wife, a cooper and his son. The crowd was silent, as though they might be able to overhear the proceedings inside the house. The sun and heat were fierce.

When the front door of Province House opened, the crowd pressed forward, but the sentries held them back. There was a moment of tense jostling, but then all at once the crowd seemed to freeze as Abigail appeared in the doorway. Father and Mother were at her side, supporting her by the arms, and they helped her down the steps and into the waiting carriage. There was absolute silence in the street, until slowly, as the carriage pulled away from the house, the crowd began to stir. Benjamin didn't know exactly what it meant, but the people began to wave and clap their hands. A few cheered and laughed, while others shouted at the sentries.

A man emerged from the crowd, heading toward Benjamin. Thin, frail, wearing a long coat despite the heat, he walked with a cane and kept his head lowered so that his broad-brimmed leather hat shielded his face. Benjamin was about to slip back into the alley, when he realized it was James. He couldn't remember the last time he'd seen his brother outside—it was always in his house, or at their parents'. James turned in to the alley, saying quietly, "Don't follow me. Long Wharf, tonight at ten," and he continued on.

Benjamin looked back toward the crowd and saw that another man was walking toward him. He was trying to appear casual, but his stride was too energetic. Benjamin turned and walked down the street in the opposite direction. When he looked around, he saw the man enter the alley.

Abigail slept well into the evening. The curtain on the west window was a bright rose color in the sunset. She had been vaguely aware that her mother had come into her room at least once, to bring tea (which went untouched). Eventually, she was awakened by footsteps coming up the stairs. Boots: heavy and familiar. She rolled on her back, drawing the bed sheet up to her shoulders. If anything, the air was closer now than it had been at noon.

Before he knocked, she said, "Come in, Samuel."

He opened the door. "You're awake. You parents said you were exhausted all afternoon." He left the door slightly ajar and looked at her uncertainly, once glancing at the chair in the corner.

"This intolerable heat." But she gazed directly at him, and he came to the bed. She moved her hand on the coverlet. "It isn't just any man that my parents allow to visit their daughter's bedroom."

He sat on the edge of the bed, where her hand had been.

"Tell me," she said.

Samuel studied the glowing curtain a moment, and he took a deep breath, as though he needed to prepare himself for the news he bore. "They've both been taken into custody." She began to sit up, but he put his other hand on her shoulder. "There's nothing to be done," he said. "They've been remanded to prison. I don't know what will happen. The process will be slow. The command, it is quite preoccupied now."

"Was Mariah sentenced?"

"No, not yet. But after today it's merely a formality. Unlike you, she doesn't come from a respected family, or have anyone—"

"She's just a waterman's daughter."

"Who freely admitted to murdering a British soldier," he said. "I'm sorry, Abigail, I really am. She did a brave thing today."

"There's something else," she said, studying his face. He did not conceal worry or concern well, and now made a weak attempt at smiling. "There's going to be an assault, isn't there? You're going on maneuvers."

He only stared at her, helpless. "Your mother says you haven't eaten a thing."

"You're going to march out into the countryside."

"You need to eat, and to rest," he said. "That's what's important at the moment."

The light was changing very quickly in the room. Everything had remarkable clarity, the buttons on his uniform, his blue eyes. "What's going to happen?"

"No one can say." He leaned toward her slightly. "Whatever happens, it won't change the way I feel about you. Do you understand that, Abigail?"

She nodded. "You aren't like the other officers. You have tried to be fair by me."

He bent down and kissed her, gently, briefly, and as he began to straighten up, she withdrew her arm from beneath the sheet, put it about his neck, and pulled him down to her.

Long Wharf ran nearly a half mile out into the harbor. A year ago, it was the heart of Boston commerce; but after General Gage closed the port, the wharf had become desolate. Grass and weeds sprouted where carts and wagons had passed, laden with ships' cargo. Many of the grog shops and chandleries were closed, and idle vessels quickly had fallen into disrepair. Benjamin walked out along the darkened wharf, which was nearly silent, save the lament of groaning dock lines.

Browne's Sail Loft had belonged to his mother's brother, Leander. It used to be one of Benjamin's favorite places to go when he was small. While his father tried to get him to conjugate Greek and Latin verbs, he preferred lessons he could learn at Uncle Leander's loft. The door was locked and the windows boarded up, but Benjamin stepped into the dark shadows and leaned against the shingle wall and waited. He could hear the current work around the pilings beneath him.

On the dock boards, James's arrival was announced by the triple knock of his uneven gait—*step, cane, step*—and when he reached the front of the sail loft, Benjamin said quietly, "Here."

James entered the shadows. His shoulders were crooked; he was carrying a satchel. "My wife sends you dinner. It's not much, but these days that's more than nothing."

"You weren't followed?"

"It took me about an hour to lose my friend, but no."

They went to the back of the small building and sat on pulley blocks. There was salt cod, black bread, a cooked potato, still warm. "I always thought no one baked a better loaf," Benjamin said with his mouth full.

"Soon even the ingredients for bread will be hard to come by," James said. In the distance they could see the lights of North Battery. "I gather you eat better on the mainland."

"Aye. There's plenty to be had. Next time I return to Boston, perhaps I should bring a shank with me? I'd bring chickens, but their clucking would certainly alert the harbor patrols."

"We are so hungry," James said, "a chicken would likely alert the entire city."

"I remember," Benjamin said, biting into the potato, "that when Father would get too upset with me—which was often—I'd come down here. I had dreams of shipping out as a cabin boy, and Uncle Leander would humor me, keeping me preoccupied until you came and retrieved me."

"You've always been good at hiding out," James said. "But your love of salt water was a dead giveaway. Perhaps someday this harbor will be reopened and you'll get to ship out." After a moment, he added, "It's too bad that Uncle Leander won't be here to see it. He'd be proud." He was leading up to something. Long ago, Benjamin had learned that you had to give James time—room, he really thought of it as room—to say what he was going to say. "Mother received a letter from Leander not long ago, and it sounds as though they are fairly well established now in New York. The harbor there is thriving, and his talents at sailmaking are in much demand."

"Why is it that Boston's misery always seems to benefit New York?"

"That is a question for the ages," James said.

Benjamin finished the potato and the last of the salt cod.

"I have learned," James said deliberately, "much of what transpired at Province House today. At first I thought that the way Abigail looked when she was being helped down the steps, I was sure it was because the decision had gone against her."

"That is not the case?"

James shook his head. "She looked so weak because she collapsed during the proceedings. The heat, that had something to do with it, I'm sure, but there was something else." He paused but continued to stare out at the lights reflected on the still water. "It has to do with Mariah."

"Mariah?"

"I'm afraid so," James said. "She confessed to killing that sergeant in revenge for her father's death. She has been imprisoned." He turned his head now, and though it was dark, Benjamin could see his right eye, which was steady and direct. "She's in prison, Benjamin, and I don't think there's anything anyone can do."

Benjamin wiped his hands on his trousers. "Nothing?"

"No. She will likely languish there for a good while, and then . . ."

"She will hang?"

They did not speak for a good while, but only stared out at the lights on the water. Finally, James picked up his satchel. "Have you a place to stay tonight?"

Benjamin, lost in thought, didn't answer at first. "I'll manage." He then looked at James. "What do you want me to do? Am I to return to Cambridge with a message for Dr. Warren?"

"No, not now." James got to his feet and hung the satchel from his shoulder. "I will need you here. Things are going to heat up. Soon, in a few days. I will know more tomorrow, I hope. Meet me after dark. But not here. Abigail will want to see you, so somewhere close to the house." He hesitated a moment. "I will need both of you to help me in the next few days."

"All right," Benjamin said. "I'll be in the granary graveyard after dark."

James placed a hand on Benjamin's shoulder, and then moved off toward the city, disappearing in the shadows.

XXII

Dark Maneuvers

ABIGAIL COULD FEEL IT. THEY ALL COULD. THE CONGREGATION at Sunday meeting seemed inattentive, distracted. Frequent glances toward the windows.

It wasn't that the heavy air was filled with the sound of drums and officers' commands, or that all day soldiers paraded through the streets—these were daily occurrences in Boston. But it was different now. The noise, the dust, the way a column of regulars marching down School Street would rattle the teacups in their saucers and make the pictures hanging in the hallway clatter against the wall.

After meeting, James stopped by the house briefly. He seemed more animated with Mother and Father than he'd been in some time. They were celebrating Abigail's freedom. But she recognized that he was acting with purpose, and was not surprised that when they were alone in the dining room—Mother had gone to the kitchen, Father to his study to consult a dictionary after a minor dispute over a Latin term for *justice*—James leaned over the table and whispered, "Benjamin's back. Tonight in the granary grave-yard, after dark." And before he took his leave, he made innocent arrangements with Abigail to come to his house that evening to help them rearrange the furniture in the parlor.

When Samuel came for afternoon tea, she could see that he felt it too. He ate little and barely touched his tea, claiming that the heat had put his appetite off. But there were moments when he gazed across the table at Abigail with a longing that made her cheeks flush. Could not her parents see it? Yesterday, in her room, when she had pulled him down to her, they had embraced as never before. It may have been the heat; it may have been the fact that she was lying in bed. Her nightgown was damp with perspiration, and there was a relief when his hand slid the fabric down off her shoulders. It only lasted a minute—the door, for discretion's sake, had been left ajar—but when Samuel kissed her breasts, his mouth hot and moist as it sucked on her nipples, she arched her back, as though he might consume all of her. But then, as quickly as it happened, there was a creak of a floorboard at the bottom of the stairs, and Samuel was standing up next to the bed, saying *Yes, Mrs. Lovell, I believe your patient could use some refreshment.* And as quickly, while Mother's slow steps climbed the stairs, Abigail pulled her nightgown about her shoulders and drew the sheet up to her chin.

But her parents weren't aware of any of this. Or perhaps they were, but they didn't let on. The veneer of formality was so thin, his gaze so indiscreet, and yet both Father and Mother seemed overjoyed by his presence. Abigail knew they had expectations. After the inquiry, they viewed Samuel as her savior, her protector. Perhaps they were willing to look the other way, hoping that all would soon be justified with a proposal of marriage.

And then, at the front door, after they said goodbye, Mother and Father skillfully made a retreat to the kitchen. Samuel held Abigail's hand. He had something to say, something awkward and difficult—she could always tell by the way his eyes would drift away. Finally, when she asked what it was, he said that he wouldn't be able to see her for a while.

"It's this," he said, "it's like time is tightening upon us, and that soon events will—"

"I know," she urged. "Everything is on the brink of changing. And you—"

"I can't say any more, but I'm sure you've surmised."

"Your maneuvers."

He merely cleared his throat, as though she had come close enough.

"How long?"

"Who knows." He looked at her then. "I really don't know."

"You'll be out of Boston."

His silence was confirmation.

"We are at war, aren't we?" she said.

"It is about to begin, Abigail. There will be great uncertainty. I have my orders." He stepped out onto the stoop. "You will always be in my thoughts." He looked at her as he had the previous afternoon, but now, here in the street, in public view, as it were, he gave her a polite bow, and then he was gone.

Benjamin waited in the graveyard, back by the granary wall. He could see across the field of headstones to the corner of Beacon and School streets. It was night and he felt invisible. The dark had always been safe, always harbored him. It was the dark that had saved him during the previous night, when, after meeting James at Long Wharf, he had made his way to Mariah's house. He planned to spend the night in the shed in her dooryard tonight, sleeping again amid her father's fishing gear. It tortured him, knowing that she wasn't there in that house, knowing there was no way he could get to her. But her house, particularly the shed, was probably his only safe haven in Boston now.

Though exhausted, he had difficulty falling asleep, wondering where they were keeping her—there were numerous jails and garrisons throughout the city, and there was the *Preston,* the much-detested prison ship moored in the harbor. Once he did manage to close his eyes, he was soon startled awake by the sound of breaking glass. He got up and looked through the crack in the door. Lanterns had been lit inside the house, and after a moment he saw soldiers moving about, pulling out drawers, emptying crocks and jars on the floor. The kitchen door was thrown open and one of the men said, "I'll have a look in that shed."

"Anythin' of value, Sergeant," another joked, "we get to split amongst ourselves?"

"Something of value? In this fisherman's 'ovel?" The sergeant snorted and then he crossed the dooryard. By his gait and the way the lantern swung erratically from his hand, it was clear he'd been drinking. Over his shoulder, he said, "You find that girl's undergarments, be careful not to tear them!"

The others laughed as they continued to ransack the house. The sergeant approached the shed, and Benjamin moved back into a corner, standing next to a roll of netting that smelled of fish and brine. His shoulder pressed against something sharp, something protruding from the wall—a blade, with a finely honed edge. It was a shipwright's adze, hanging from a nail, used to trim boards in the repair of a skiff. Benjamin had seen Anse Cole use it several times, always marveling at his skill at shaping a board that might replace a cracked plank in the lapstrake hull. Benjamin groped in the dark, finding the adze handle, and then with both hands raised it above his head, his only chance to deliver one swift blow.

The shed door was yanked open and the sergeant stepped inside.

"Found it!" one of the soldiers hollered from the house. *"Sergeant, I 'ave found the shucking knife!"*

Turning in the doorway, the sergeant called, "It be the right one?"

"Covered with blood, it is! It's got to be the right fucking knife. It's the fucking shucking knife, sir!"

All the soldiers in the house laughed.

The sergeant laughed too, but then he leaned a shoulder against the doorframe. For a moment it looked as though he was so besotted that he might simply fall back into the shed and pass out. The rum stench coming off him overwhelmed the smell of the sea in the shed.

One of the soldiers came to the open kitchen door. "Might we torch 'er, sir?"

"Whot?" the sergeant said.

"The 'ouse. Burn 'er to the ground."

The sergeant straightened up, becoming more alert. "No, you idiot. In this heat the entire neighborhood is like to go up in flames. But what I can do is make a recommendation that this place be put on the list for demolition. Make for good kindling, this, and it'll be like it was never 'ere." He stepped out into the dooryard, leaving the shed door open, and made his way back toward the house.

Left in the dark, Benjamin lowered the adze to the dirt floor.

Now, it was well after dark in the granary burying ground, but still no sign of James or Abigail. Benjamin waited so long, he began to fear something had gone amiss. He began feeling watched. He moved among the headstones, until he saw a woman walking up the street. Despite the heat, she wore a full cape, with the hood up. At the entrance, she paused and then came into the graveyard. It was Abigail—her stride was as balanced and graceful as James's was not—and she continued toward the brick wall of the granary.

Benjamin followed her, and when she suddenly stopped, he whispered, "It's only me." She came toward him and threw her arms around him, holding him tightly. Then she kissed him on both cheeks and then on the mouth. Her skin was hot, and she wouldn't let go, until he finally said, "James, where's James?"

She stepped back from him. "He isn't here?"

"I've been waiting over an hour, since before nine bells."

"He must be having difficulty getting away. Mother and Father, they kept delaying me. I said I was to go to James's to help move furniture, and Mother wanted to accompany me, but eventually she realized how tired she was from all this heat."

"James, they're constantly watching him," Benjamin said.

"I know. He won't come unless he's certain he's not being followed."

Benjamin took his sister by the arm and walked her toward the granary, where they stood amid some bushes. He could feel the heat come off the brick wall.

"Have you been well?" Abigail whispered, touching his face with her hand.

"Yes, yes."

"How long will you be in Boston?"

"I don't know. I thought James would send me back out with information for Dr. Warren, but last night he said he needed me to remain here. Something's up—the redcoats are preparing for something."

"Yes, and James is, too." She looked toward the street. "We must wait as long as we can." Then, turning to him, she said, "But where are you staying?"

"I shouldn't say."

She took hold of his forearm. "Have you eaten? I should have thought to bring—"

"Stop, please stop. I'm fine."

"Well, tell me, where have you been? The last time I saw you was on the beach on Noddle's Island. Mariah and I waved—oh, do you know about—"

"I was outside Province House when you left. James told me everything last night."

"There must be something we can do for Mariah."

Benjamin didn't answer. He didn't know how to, and for a moment they stared at each other in the dark. "Rachel," he said suddenly. "I saw Rachel. They're all in Watertown, where the

Provincial Congress has been established. Rachel, the children, they're all well cared for, staying at a fine house owned by a Mr. Van Ee."

"You saw her?"

"Just a few nights ago. She wanted me to ask you about her money, the hundred and twenty-five pounds she sent out for Mr. Revere."

"Yes?"

"He never got it."

Abigail didn't seem to comprehend what he had said, until she finally said, "But I gave it to Dr. Church. I told her so before I left Boston. The clothing and the money—"

"She said so, Abigail. She's not doubting you, but now she's seen Mr. Revere and the money's just disappeared. Mr. Revere never received it."

They both leaned against the wall, lost in thought for several minutes. Once Abigail said, "How—" but she couldn't continue.

Benjamin saw someone out in the street and, taking Abigail's arm, he pulled her in behind a bush. It was a woman, bent over with a sack on one shoulder. She came into the graveyard and began to wander haltingly among the headstones, until she paused by a bench. Slowly, she eased her burden down to the bench, and then straightened up, revealing her overlarge belly.

Abigail suddenly whispered, *"Mary."*

She stepped out from behind the bush and approached James's wife.

"Abigail?" Mary said, slowly getting to her feet. "Benjamin?"

They rushed to her and helped her sit on the bench.

"Where's James?" Abigail sat next to her. "Is he all right?"

Mary tried to catch her breath.

"Are *you* all right?" Benjamin asked.

"Benjamin," she sighed, relieved. "It's good to see you. We worry about you so. I'm fine, really—though you might say my condition is greater than when you last saw me." She placed her hand over her mouth to suppress a nervous laugh. "I have not walked such a distance in a good while, and I cannot stay but a minute. General Gage's men watch our house all the time. James went out earlier but he was unable to lose them, so he returned and then went out a second time, to lead them from the house so I could bring you this." She stuffed her hand inside a pocket of her cloak and produced several envelopes. She gave one to Abigail. "He has learned that the British will march out the day after tomorrow and we must do what we can. I don't know the contents of the letter, but he said you—" she looked at Abigail— "will understand that something might be possible because of your association with Colonel Cleaveland."

After a moment, Abigail nodded once.

Mary gave another envelope to Benjamin. "This one is for you." She then handed him a second envelope. "And these James wants you to deliver to Dr. Warren when you get out of Boston. We all know that much will happen soon. James said that in a few days many Americans will die, and we must do what we can."

Mary struggled to stand, and both Benjamin and Abigail took her by the arm and helped her up off the bench.

"Let us walk you home, at least part way," he said.

"That won't be necessary." Mary looked down at the sack on the bench. "This is for you, Benjamin. I hope it fits. My journey home will go much easier without it." She raised her face to him, kissing him on the cheek. He could see that her eyes, often so playful, were quite exhausted, but she attempted a smile. "If I have more children after this, please God allow them to be born in winter." She hugged Abigail, and then started back toward the entrance to the street, one hand on her hip.

XXIII

The Armory

THE FOLLOWING EVENING, ABIGAIL SET OUT FOR THE GARRISON AT North Battery, a basket on her arm. It had been another hot day, the air humid and still. While she prepared the food for Samuel—bread, cheese, pickled cabbage, and quahog pie—her mother had asked when the colonel would be arriving. Abigail said that she was taking the meal to North Battery, where Samuel was on duty. When her father suggested a carriage take her, she insisted on walking. *In this heat?* While the pie cooked slowly in the oven, she ushered her parents out of the kitchen, filled the tin bathtub and bathed, and then donned her finest summer linens. Now, as she walked through the North End, the basket became quite heavy and she shifted it from one arm to the other. A few minutes after eight bells, she passed Mariah's house, and when she heard the footsteps approaching behind her she did not turn around, did not slow her pace.

The uniform wasn't a bad fit. A bit short in the waistcoat, but the red jacket with brass buttons was ample in the shoulders. The white breeches were tight, as they were supposed to be, and the gaiters were so snug that they practically made his feet go numb. Which might have been for the best, because the shoes were terribly painful. He'd always heard how bad the British soldiers' footgear was, how there was no left or right shoe. If anything made him look convincing, he figured it was his walk, which was tender and careful, as though slogging through salt-marsh muck at low tide.

Abigail passed Mariah's house right on schedule. Benjamin, who had spent the day cooped up in the sweltering shed behind the house, came out of the dooryard and followed her as she continued on toward North Battery. She did not slow down for him, did not look around. Ordinarily, he would have easily caught up with her, but in these infernal shoes he could not walk fast. But eventually, he caught up to her, and without looking at him she handed him the basket.

"I'm supposed to be your escort," he muttered, "not your manservant."

"I'm supposed to be a proper Bostonian, who would insist. Besides, it may distract attention away from the fact that you bear no arms. In the past, Samuel often sent an escort who has carried the basket for me. Your mission is to deliver the colonel his supper."

"Samuel. It's Samuel?"

"And you'll be best to keep your mouth shut, unless you can put on some kind of a Cockney accent as easily as you put on that uniform."

"How or where did James get this outfit?"

"Our brother has his sources."

"I think it comes from several, actually."

She glanced at him. "What's the matter with you?"

"These shoes, they're killing me."

"The stiff queue is quite appropriate, though. I've never seen your hair dressed up so."

"Found a candle in the shed and waxed it."

"A little tallow works wonders for you."

Benjamin smiled, if only for a moment. "These getups are impressive," he said, "but I don't know how they fight in them. And yet they're the best army in the world."

"When we get there," she said, "don't change anything about that walk. Most of the regulars are boys, and they all look obedient, ready for a reprimand. They all look a long ways away from home."

"That smell," Benjamin said, gazing down at the towel that covered the basket. "Quahog pie?" When she didn't answer, he added, "At least you're well armed. Nothing could be more distracting. I've tasted none better."

"I only hope it's sufficient."

"And if it's not?"

Abigail didn't answer him at first, but then said, "I just don't know. But I know what James said about American lives in the coming days. No matter what happens, Benjamin, we have to do what we can. We've no choice." They walked on in silence, until she added, "And I know what sweet Rachel would say if she were here: 'It's either the quahog pie or your virtue.'"

He knew she hoped he would smile or even laugh, but he didn't.

Abigail had been Samuel's guest at North Battery several times. The sight of a woman was not uncommon around the garrisons, but they were usually wives, maids, charwomen. Abigail was another matter, and the guards at the outer gate hardly took note of Benjamin. The soldier in charge studied her carefully, and after he let them through she heard laughter among the men.

The battery jutted into the harbor and in places it had stone walls, while the British had recently added earthen parapets and fortifications. As they walked to Samuel's quarters in the armory, soldiers on guard, soldiers passing by paused to look at Abigail, at her white linen dress. It was getting dark and she could see the harbor, the water black as ink. The piers below the battery walls were cluttered with dozens of longboats and barges.

They came in sight of the armory, a long building of stone with only a few small windows. "This is his domain," she said. "Commander of artillery. He has his office, and down the hall his private quarters," she said. "You should wait outside the office door—that's what my escort has done in the past. I will try to get him to go to his private quarters. Then you can go through the office into the storeroom."

"And if you don't?"

"He eats his quahog pie in his office and then I leave, with you as my escort."

There were two guards at the entrance to the armory. They had been informed of Abigail's arrival and admitted her without question. Inside, the air was thankfully cool. Abigail led Benjamin down the hall to the office door, which was ajar. Samuel was seated at his desk, writing in a ledger. He was in his shirtsleeves and his hair was untied. Though he appeared weary from his tasks, he looked up and smiled broadly.

"I trust you're hungry, Samuel," Abigail said.

She took the basket from Benjamin, and entered the office. The colonel got up, came around his desk, and without looking at Benjamin closed the door behind her.

Benjamin stood at attention in the hallway. Though his back was against the cool stone wall, sweat seeped out from beneath his hair, which was hard with tallow. He felt as though he was wearing a helmet beneath the heavy hat. A blister had developed on his right big toe, so he kept most of his weight on his left foot. The wooden door next to him was thick and he couldn't hear them in the office.

Outside, there was the constant sound of marching feet, small groups of men, stepping to the command of an officer. There was the clop of horses' hooves and the rattle of carts. There was also the murmur of voices and the clatter of utensils, which must be coming from a mess hall. The minutes were very slow.

When Abigail placed the basket on the desk and removed the towel, Samuel leaned over and took a deep breath. "Quahog pie," he said slowly.

"I wanted to make something special, since this may be the last time—"

He was staring at her, his eyes filling with anguish. "You're very kind."

"I don't have any wine, though."

"Ah." He tried to be cheerful. "But I do." She looked around the office. "It's down—it's down the hall," he said.

"Perhaps it would be more comfortable for you to take your repast there anyway?"

"Only if you'll join me."

"Really, I couldn't." She gazed up into his disappointed face. "When I cook, I tend to nibble, and I really couldn't eat another bite."

"Then you'll keep me company?"

She raised a hand and touched her hair a moment. "Of course I will, Samuel."

He replaced the towel, carefully tucking it in around the sides. Picking up the basket, he opened the door for her. She led him out into the hallway and turned left. Benjamin was standing at attention but she didn't look at him as she passed by. Samuel's private quarters were at the end of the hallway. When she was about halfway to that door, she heard Samuel's footsteps hesitate and then stop. She turned and watched him: he seemed perplexed, as though he'd forgotten something. He turned around and went back toward Benjamin slowly, passed by him, and pulled the office door shut. Then he came down the hallway, and when they reached the end he opened the door for her.

———

Benjamin remained at attention for several minutes. The door at the end of the hallway was closed and he could hear nothing from within. He kept thinking about the office door, how the latch had clicked when the colonel pulled it shut. It was a sound that reverberated off the stone walls.

There was a parade of soldiers approaching the depot. As they drew closer, it was as though he could see them through the opposite wall, advancing along the side of the building. They passed by him and continued down toward the colonel's chambers.

Suddenly Benjamin turned and put his hand on the latch to the office door, and he was about to raise it when the officer shouted a command and the marching soldiers came to a halt. Benjamin stood still, the latch in his hand. He considered returning to his position, standing at attention, but he couldn't move. The officer was saying something to his men, his voice muffled by the outer stone wall of the building. When he shouted, the men began marching again, and Benjamin raised the latch, stepped inside the office, and closed the door carefully.

He stood still for a minute, just listening. The sound of marching feet receded, but there were others in the distance, some seeming to come near. The office was tidy, illuminated by a lantern on the desk. There was a long oak cabinet with rows of drawers and, beyond the desk, another door. Benjamin picked up the lantern and went to the door. It was locked. On the desk there were only papers, a ledger, quills, and an inkpot. He opened the drawers and in the second one down on the right found an iron ring of keys. He unlocked the door and entered a long dark room. In the wavering lantern light he could see stacks of barrels, casks, and wooden crates.

For this, Madeira was required.

Abigail sat across the table from Samuel. He ate with grateful passion, complimenting everything, particularly the quahog pie.

Repeatedly, he asked if she'd reconsider joining him. Instead, she accepted a second glass of wine.

"There is great activity here tonight," she said, nodding toward the window, small and square, which was shuttered from inside. "They're beginning, your maneuvers."

Samuel nodded, chewing, concentrating on his plate.

"Earlier today, I heard there was much military activity at Boston Neck."

He drank some wine.

"You'll strike at Dorchester Heights, and then march out into the countryside."

As he wiped his mouth with his napkin, he asked, "Does that seem a sound plan to you?"

"I know nothing of military strategy, but only wish it didn't take you from Boston."

He leaned back in his chair. Clearly, he was discouraged by the prospect. "I wish—" He suddenly seemed ashamed. "I wish there was more time."

Abigail drank some wine.

The door to the hallway was behind her. She could hear nothing; didn't know if Benjamin was still standing there at attention, or if he'd gained access to the storeroom.

This was her idea. Weeks ago she had described the armory to James, not realizing that he would use such information as he formulated plans for this invasion. *Men will die soon,* he'd written in his letter. *We cannot stop it, but we must needs do all that we can to reduce their numbers.*

Thus, an invasion. An intimate invasion.

Behind Samuel, there was another door, closed. Certainly this was the bedchamber.

Rachel frequently spoke of intimate things, and often found humor in them. Once, laughing, she suggested *Like eating, it's merely a matter of commencing. The body succumbs, as to hunger.*

Samuel drained his glass, watching her. She finished her wine.

"More?"

Abigail glanced at the closed door again. It was made of wood planks held together with black iron strapping. She placed her empty glass on the table. "A little, yes."

There were barrels of gunpowder, casks of saltpeter; crates containing cannonballs for field guns and howitzers, each marked according to gauge: three-pounders, six-pounders, nine-pounders, twelve-pounders, eighteen-pounders. There was solid round shot that would skip through advancing troops, removing head and limb. There were shells filled with gunpowder and fitted with a fuse so, if properly set, the projectile would explode above the heads of infantrymen. There was case shot, which was packed with refuse—scrap metal, shell fragments, nails, glass, rocks—that burst forth from the disintegrating canister in a devastating spray of shrapnel.

Benjamin recalled the night at Colonel Barrett's farm in Concord, when he'd helped assemble the stolen British cannon. Barrett's men were at first wary of his knowledge. When asked how he knew so much, he merely said that boys in Boston had ample opportunity to observe the redcoats' artillery squadrons. There were constant drills: assembly, disassembly, transportation, loading, target practice. Heavier balls traveled faster and went farther, but lighter field guns, sometimes referred to as gallopers or grasshoppers, offered greater mobility for the exercise of a favorite tactic known as *in enfilade:* to flank a marching formation and rake it from the side, so that one shot could do more damage to more men.

Benjamin had never seen such a wealth of ammunition.

This was the stuff of empires.

The easiest solution was right in his hand: just drop the lantern in a barrel of gunpowder.

Samuel had brought the bottle of Madeira, which stood guard on the nightstand. They lay together on the featherbed, limbs entangled. Abigail had decided that she couldn't go through with it, but then, upon finishing her third glass of wine, she simply got up from the table and went to him. She sat on his lap as they kissed. They moved to the door, and then into the bedchamber. It was, as Rachel had said, a matter of hunger, of feeding. She was no longer frightened, she was no longer worried, and she might have been oddly giddy.

"What?" he asked, his face buried in her neck.

"Is this why they call it the armory?"

They both laughed.

He proceeded with laces and buttons.

Occasionally, she assisted him with a knot or snagged hook.

"There is order in everything," he whispered, "even this."

"Do we have time?"

"We have all night."

She pulled back so that she could look at him, risking a moment of clarity. "Then let's take our time. This is something I do not wish to rush into. Do you understand?"

"I do," he said. "I do."

Benjamin couldn't do it. Not that way, not with his sister down the hall.

He heard a noise but couldn't tell if it was a voice, a moan, a sigh. It might even have been laughter. It seemed to come from within the stone walls. He held still, and then he heard it again. A signal? A sign? He needed time and Abigail was giving it to him. To render this ammunition ineffective, he would proceed as planned.

He raised the lid of one of the crates marked *8 Pounders.*

XXIV

Acrost the Harbor

ABIGAIL WAS AWAKENED BY THE SOUND OF KNOCKING, KNOCKING on the outer door of Samuel's private chambers. Samuel had already pulled on a robe and was rushing out into the other room. When he opened the door, Abigail could only see lantern light streaming into the room.

"Pardon, sir," a man whispered, "I'm to report to you immediately."

"What time is it?"

"Nearly three bells, sir."

"Report *what* at this hour?"

"There has been activity observed by the guards, sir. Noises coming across the water from the direction of Charlestown."

"Noises?"

"Sounds, sir."

"Sounds. Do you mean voices?"

"No, sir. Shovels. Digging in the earth."

"Digging what?"

"We don't know that, sir. General Clinton was alerted to it, and he has left for Province House. He suspects it is the Americans, establishing a redoubt."

Samuel didn't speak for a moment. "It could be a farmer burying his cow. But we must take every precaution. What does General Clinton propose to do?"

"He will recommend to General Gage that we strike Charlestown at daybreak."

"I see. The plan, of course, is for us to strike south, at Dorchester Heights. This could be only a diversion."

"Yes, sir."

"On the other hand—" Samuel didn't finish his thought. "All right, that'll be all, Sergeant. I'll be out directly. And tell the soldier standing guard outside my office to wait outside this door."

"Yes, sir."

Benjamin had just returned to the colonel's office when he heard the heavy outer door open. He rushed out into the hall and could hear the sound of footsteps, though he couldn't see who was coming—there was a turn in the hallway up near the front entrance. He stood at attention outside the office, looking straight across at the opposite stone wall, and listened to the footsteps (boots: a long, determined stride) approach. The soldier strode by Benjamin, and at the end of the hall he knocked on the door to the colonel's private chambers. He was a grenadier, one of the British soldiers selected for his height and strength. They were distinguished by their tall fur hats, which made them seem even more imposing.

When the colonel answered the door, the two men spoke quietly.

Benjamin picked up phrases—something about digging, about a redoubt in Charlestown.

Suddenly the colonel shut his door and the grenadier walked swiftly back up the hallway. As he approached, Benjamin stiffened.

If he had to speak, the grenadier would immediately realize he wasn't British. The soldier didn't break stride, though as he passed Benjamin he said, "Colonel wants you down there by his door." He sniffed. "There's a lady to be got out of here." He continued up the hall, turned the corner, and left the armory by the front door.

Abigail dressed quickly. When she went out into the other room, Samuel looked at her in surprise, his mind elsewhere. "Something's happened?" she asked.

"Maybe. We're not sure." He came over to her and placed his hands on her upper arms. She didn't want him to touch her now, but when he drew her to him she didn't resist. After a long moment he let her go, but he looked at her with regret. "I'm sorry," he said.

"Don't be."

"But I am. I—"

"You're in a hurry now."

"I am."

"I should get out of the way."

"This isn't—it isn't what I'd hoped for," he said. "You deserve better than this."

"It's all right, Samuel." He looked uncertain, and she thought he was considering taking her in his arms again. She went to the door; he followed and opened it for her.

Benjamin was standing at attention outside the door.

"It's best that you go, yes," Samuel said. "He'll escort you home."

He put a hand on her arm, but Abigail didn't turn toward him. She stepped out into the hallway and began walking. Benjamin fell in behind her. She listened, waiting for Samuel to say something. The door was still open. He must be watching them.

When she had almost reached his office door, he said, "Abigail."

She stopped and turned around. Benjamin stood a few paces behind her. She looked past him, down toward Samuel, who had one hand on the open door. He merely looked at her.

"You will be careful?" she said.

Samuel continued to stare at her. His bathrobe was white, and it trailed to the floor. From this distance he looked like a boy, quite angelic. She turned and continued on down the hallway, holding her breath until she heard Samuel close the door, the sound of the latch falling in place with a sharp, metallic click.

They didn't speak until they had gotten through the gate and were well down the hill from North Battery. The city was dark, quiet, though somewhere in the distance they could hear the sound of marching feet and rippling drums. Benjamin was afraid to speak first. As they moved through the North End, he kept waiting for his sister to say something, but she didn't. They just walked, slowly because he was limping. When she was angry or nervous, she often fell silent. Since his childhood, it had always made him feel shameful, as though he were somehow responsible.

"You had enough time?" she said finally. He was surprised by her voice. There was no anger. Weariness, perhaps.

"Yes, I had plenty of time."

Then she did something that baffled him. She laughed. It was not her usual laugh, which he had always loved—there was something scornful and ironic about it. He was afraid to ask.

And she said nothing more, offered no explanation.

They walked the streets of Boston in silence.

At the moment, she didn't want to think. She wanted to sleep. She wanted to remove all her clothes, climb into the tin bathtub in the kitchen, and sit in hot water and drift off to sleep. But she couldn't. It wasn't possible, not in the middle of the night.

"What time is it?" she asked.

Benjamin seemed surprised that she'd spoken. "I last heard two bells."

"It's still so hot."

They walked on without speaking, until they reached Mariah's house.

"I should stop here," he said. "My clothes are here, in the shed."

"What will you do now?"

"Get out of this uniform, and these damned shoes. I must get to Charlestown to see what's happening. I will put my own clothes on, go down to the beach with a set of oars from Mariah's shed, and I will row her father's skiff across."

Abigail stopped walking. She looked at her brother, really for the first time since they'd left North Battery. "Do you think the Americans are building a redoubt there?"

He shrugged. "If they are, I'll help. If not, I'll continue on to Cambridge, take my orders from Dr. Warren. There'll be fighting somewhere. Soon."

She turned her head away. Suddenly she was afraid she might cry.

"Why don't you—you could come with me," he said.

"Across the water?"

"I could take you to Rachel. You could stay with her."

Abigail looked at Mariah's house. It was small, its shingles badly weathered. "She's in prison instead of me." She was startled by her own voice, how it trembled.

"That's not true," Benjamin said. "Neither of you deserves to be there. Why don't you come with me? I believe the best thing we can do for her now is fight. Just get in the skiff, and we'll be acrost the harbor—"

"No, no, I can't. I can't leave Mother and Father." Benjamin stared at her, and then nodded slowly. "And you must go quickly," she said, "before first light."

He looked up at the sky. It was a moonless night. "So many stars," he said. And then he turned toward Mariah's house.

316

"They're going to tear it down, for fuel. I overhead some soldiers. It'll be like Mariah, her father—they never existed."

"Benjamin, you must cross the harbor."

"I'd like to stay here and defend it, kill any redcoat that tries to take a stick of wood."

Abigail took his hand, much as she had when they were young, and they began walking again. "Hurry, Benjamin, while it's still dark."

It was a great relief to be wearing his own small-clothes. Though his foot was sore, he could walk down the beach, oars over one shoulder, the uniform tied in a bundle tucked under his other arm. Abigail insisted on seeing him off. When they reached Anse Cole's skiff, she helped turn it over and pull it across the kelp lines to the water. The moment when a boat suddenly becomes buoyant had always fascinated Benjamin. One moment the hull was heavy cumbersome wood, resistant to being dragged through the sand, and then, suddenly, it rose up on the surface of the water, light and maneuverable. Entirely another species. Anse Cole's skiff suffered from neglect, but she floated with ease, a low-centered, wide-beamed vessel. Benjamin climbed in and fit the oars in the locks.

Abigail stood knee-deep in the water, holding the transom. She stared at him in the dark. He said nothing. She said nothing. Then she pushed off and the skiff glided away from shore. He pulled on the oars, one, two, three times, and the boat moved easily through the flat water. His sister was a long pale figure. She seemed to rise up out of the dark plane. And then she began to move, not toward the shore, but toward him.

He stopped pulling on the oars.

"Go, Benjamin," she said. "It's all right." With each step she went deeper into the dark, her linen dress fanning out about her.

Carefully, he dipped his oars, but he could not pull.

She continued deeper, to sink, until she was up to her neck. Her hair came undone. She swept her arms before her as she swam toward him, a white form gliding through the black water, light and maneuverable. Entirely another species. She came alongside the skiff, and her hand slung over the gunwale, causing the faintest list.

"You've changed your mind?" he asked.

"No." There was the slightest laugh again, her voice odd, tremulous. "I'm cleansed now." Abigail's hand let go, and she swam back toward the beach.

Her dress, a white filament trailing in her wake, reminded Benjamin of smoke.

XXV

A Colony of Ants

AFTER ABIGAIL ENTERED THE HOUSE BY THE KITCHEN DOOR, SHE quietly climbed the stairs to her room, and there she removed her sopping wet clothes. She lay on her bed, naked. The air in the house was stuffy, and as the water dried she felt the salt encrusting her skin. She smelled of the sea. Quahogs, clams, periwinkles. She imagined how good an oyster would taste right now, how its briny liquid would wash away the stale Madeira that coated her mouth. She thought about how shellfish live burrowed under the soft muck near the marshes, six hours irrigated by high tide, six hours in the open air. Each clam had its own tiny breathing hole in the muck, its sole connection with the outside world. They were safe in their dark, cool, moist bed, their tender organs encased in a protective shell. Often when she was a girl, she had gone to the marshes with her brothers and other children. At low tide the muck was warm, and it covered their bare arms and legs. They would dig clams and fill their dreeners. Clams did not resist when pulled, by hand or raked up out of the silt. Once in the dreeners, they whistled and squirted water in protest. Sometimes, though, there would be a razorfish—a long thin shell, and they would escape. Abigail would feel the shell slip by her fingers as the fish pushed itself deeper into the muck, seeking the safety of the dark. It became a game. She would hold her hands over where she thought the razorfish was hiding, and then suddenly drive her fingers down through the muck; lacing her fingers together, she'd pull up. Often she'd only catch a handful of mud. But sometimes she'd catch the razorfish. Their shells were bronze-colored. They were inedible (Mother had made that clear the one time she found one in Abigail's dreener). James and Benjamin often liked to crush them. Boys liked to kill things that came out of the sea. Clamshells cracked open, to be fought over by seagulls. And horseshoe crabs, those armored monsters, were picked up by their hard spiny tails and left in the sand upside down, their rows of feet working frantically in the air as they struggled to right themselves before the seagulls got to them. When Abigail captured a razorfish, she would admire its blade-shaped shell, and then tuck it back in the divot and cover it up, safe once again in the darkness of the salt marsh. Her brothers thought she was daft, sentimental. James once said instructively (even in his teens he was destined to become a schoolmaster) *Everything here kills to eat. Nothing is wasted.* Abigail couldn't accept this as an explanation, and as she continued to dig she said *There is a difference between survival and cruelty.*

Benjamin was halfway to Charlestown, speeded by the flood tide, when he heard the churches in Boston ring three bells. There was some activity in the harbor, unusual for such an hour. Aboard the ships at anchor, voices gave orders. Lines groaned and creaked as they were hauled through block and tackle. And there were numerous small boats moving on the water. He saw their dark shapes, and if they were aware of him they seemed unconcerned, probably assuming that he was another boat conveying messages between the ships' captains. At one point he picked up the British uniform he'd tied in a bundle and dropped it over the side. As he closed in on Charlestown, he could hear the sounds that had alerted the guards in North Battery. Strange, how sound carried across water—it was faint, coming from up in the hills behind the waterside village: shovels and picks, digging into the earth.

He tied up at a pier and walked through the streets, quickly realizing that Charlestown wasn't quiet because it was the early hours of the morning, but because it had been evacuated. The only movement he encountered was when he came upon a dog tethered to a fence, its bark deep and baleful, resentful of the fact that it had been left behind. Then Benjamin was out of the town, climbing through pasture. He encountered no grazing livestock and assumed they too had all been driven off out of harm's way. The grass was often waist-high, and frequently he had to climb over split-rail fences. There were few trees and only occasional clusters of bushes. The hillside was open meadow, while overhead there was a brilliant sweep of stars.

Pausing for a moment, he looked east, across the harbor. The ships were dark forms, illuminated by only a few lanterns. Beyond them lay the dark peninsula of Boston. The black slopes of Trimount loomed over the city. The only lights were on Copp's Hill, the elevated brow of the North End, where the British had established their cannon. Often over the past few years, Benjamin had ventured up there and, being ignored as just another boy fascinated by such military precision, he would watch as the gun crews conducted drills.

He continued up the hill, which at times became quite steep. Above him, the sound of digging was constant, and when he was near the crest of the first hill he stopped walking. In the faint light he could see it, a dark scar in the earth: hundreds of men, perhaps a thousand, building dirt walls that ran in a wide V, its point facing the harbor below. Benjamin thought of ants, how they moved in such concert about their hill, lines moving in different directions, each with its distinct purpose. Digging, erecting, transporting supplies—it was the same with these men, who labored without the need of shouted commands.

He approached the redoubt from the side, expecting to be stopped and questioned, but there wasn't any guard—all the men were busy digging. So he moved among them, pleased that he looked as though he belonged. The entire time he'd been at North Battery, dressed in that ridiculous uniform, he'd expected at any moment to be found out as an impostor. But then, he wondered, why would these men not look at him in his small-clothes and at least suspect that he was here as a spy on a mission from the other side? Perhaps the most significant difference between both sides was in their garments. But they were too preoccupied, laboring through the night with a desperate sense of urgency, and they were not doing so only because of differences in clothing. He could imagine James, always the instructive schoolmaster, much like their father, saying *Sartorial distinctions are only representative of larger, more significant differences, such as questions of justice and liberty.*

And then Benjamin heard his name whispered. Down in a trench he saw Ezra, and, working beside him, Lumley. Each had a spade in hand, and they were filling boxes with dirt, which they passed up to men who sent them up to the top of the redoubt walls, where the boxes were emptied and then handed back down to be filled again. Again and again, all along the ditch, men moving the dirt. Ants, it was the work of ants.

Benjamin climbed down into the trench, and Ezra clapped him on the shoulder. "How is it that I always seem to find you wandering aimlessly on a hillside when things are about to get hot with the redcoats?"

"Could it be luck?" Benjamin smiled.

"Yours or mine?" Ezra studied him a moment. "What have you done to your hair?"

"What, you don't like it?"

Ezra laughed as he pointed at a pick lying on the ground. "Now, get to work."

Benjamin began to break the earth. They were all digging. There was no sound other than that of their instruments striking soil and rock, and the hard breathing that accompanied such labor. But then he came to realize that many of the men were also whispering, and they did not sound pleased. There were complaints about the command, about the lack of preparation, about insufficient ammunition, but mostly there were complaints about the lack of food and, especially, water. They were parched, and it was still night. Wait until the sun climbs into the sky and does its work. Yesterday was hot, and today was sure to be hotter.

"You see them," Ezra whispered as he dug. "Men and boys, they climb up out of the trench claiming they need a piss and such, and then they get across the Neck and don't return."

"They run away?" Benjamin asked.

"Can you blame them?" Lumley asked. "They know what lies ahead."

"He says we're doomed here," Ezra said.

"It's not always a matter of running *from*," Lumley hissed. "You've got to consider what you're running *to*. I ran away from the army, and now look where I am." He laughed with a snort. "Of course, we're doomed. When the British figure out what we're up to, do you have any idea what we're in for? There are cannon in Boston, there are cannon on every ship in the harbor, all aimed in this direction. This is not Lexington and Concord. They had no field pieces there, no howitzers, no mortars. We cannot hide behind stone walls in the woods like so many Indians. After their artillery soften up this hill, they'll send over the troops in longboats. If executed properly, it should be over by noon."

"I gather we are doing this to divert them from their planned assault to the south on Dorchester Heights," Benjamin said.

Lumley paused a moment and leaned on his shovel. "That's what you glean, is it?"

"You have to admit, Lumley," Ezra said, raising a full box of dirt up out of the trench. "It's a sound strategy. If the Brits are about to march out, we must needs divert them as best we can, make them adapt and change their plans."

"*Strategy?*" Lumley spat as though his mouth were filled with dirt. "You're dealing with the greatest war machine in the world, and you establish your fortress here, on Bunker Hill?"

Ezra pointed to the higher hill behind them. "That's Bunker Hill."

"No, that's Breed's Hill."

Ezra picked up his shovel again and drove it into the dirt. "You're an Englishman. What do you know about the hills of Massachusetts?"

"I have studied maps of the land surrounding Boston—"

"Accurate, are they?" Ezra asked.

"—and this is Bunker Hill."

"A hill is a hill, and dirt is dirt," Ezra said, sing-song fashion. "It's simple: this hill is where a farmer, named *Breed,* grazes his animals."

"It is simple: *that* dirt is higher than *this* dirt," Lumley said. "It's also farther away from Boston and the harbor—"

"I see," Ezra said. "You gleaned such crucial information from your maps."

"—and for every hundred yards, do you know what the reduced percentage in the accuracy of artillery is?"

Ezra stepped on his shovel and jammed it into the ground. "Perhaps that's the point, Lumley. Maybe that's our strategy. We *want* to be closer to them, so close they can see us claiming our turf. That'll bring them out of Boston and up this hill—whatever you want to call it." He looked at Benjamin, as though in search of someone reasonable who might intercede. "We have two commanders here. William Prescott, that fellow who has been patrolling the top of the wall, and then Israel Putnam, the old man from Connecticut who took charge of things on Noddle's Island. Remember how he climbed up out of that ditch and told the Brits to lay down their arms. Fearless, Old Put is. This be his doing, I tell you. The man has stones. You taunt the redcoats by establishing your fortress on the near hill—*Breed's* Hill—"

"Bunker Hill."

"Breed's Hill."

Ezra and Lumley looked as though they were both about to take a swing at each other with their shovels.

"Shut up," Benjamin said.

"If we're going to die for this mound of dirt," Lumley said, "we should at least call it by its proper name."

"Exactly my point," Ezra said.

"Both of you!" Benjamin shouted, causing them to turn to him, quite startled. "Shut up and dig."

He drove his spade into the dirt.

Then, as they leaned down to dig, they all—all the men in the trench—suddenly froze at the loud percussive sound that cracked out across the harbor.

The first shell rattled Abigail's bedroom windows.

Yet she clung to her dream. There was Ezra. Something to do with a carriage. It was cold, a winter's night, and he had his hand upon her thigh. His fingers were warm.

But then several cannon fired in rapid succession and she sat upright in bed, confused. Down the hall she could hear her parents stirring. There came another volley of cannon fire, and then it was silent.

In the distance church bells rang: four in the morning. Outside there was the sound of running feet. Across the way a window was opened and old Mrs. Pierce shouted, "What's that?"

"The British," a boy called as he ran down School Street. *"British cannon!"*

All the men had climbed up out of the ditch. From the top of the redoubt walls they could see flames and smoke pouring out of the side of one of the smaller ships.

"It's the *Lively,*" Lumley said. "Her guns may be too light to reach us."

"Imagine," Ezra said. "If we had been way back there——" He turned to point.

"They wouldn't even have bothered firing," Lumley said.

"What was the name of that hill?" Ezra said.

Lumley turned to him. There was a roar from the ship as several cannon were set off in rapid succession. They were talking, nearly shouting at each other, and though Benjamin was standing right next to them he couldn't hear what was said. And then came that whistling the balls made as they flew through the air.

Quite suddenly, beyond the dark hulking profile of Boston, the sky out over the Atlantic changed. At first Benjamin thought it was only a trick of the eye, an illusion. But, no, there was on the horizon the faintest shimmer. He looked away, up at the stars tucked in velvety black, and then gazed toward the ocean once more, and there, due east, there was no question now: first light.

The cannonballs landed in the meadow below the redoubt, each with a solid thud. One skipped up through the tall grass, like a stone hurled upon the water, and then suddenly to the left men were shouting. Some gathered in a crowd, while Colonel Prescott and Old Put shouted for the men to return to the ditch and continue digging.

In the confusion, Benjamin saw some men sprinting back toward Charlestown Neck. Others called after them, but they kept running. He went down into the ditch with Lumley—Ezra had disappeared. They began digging, frantic now. The guns were quiet, but the silence seemed even more threatening.

"He's run off, he has," Lumley said.

"I don't believe that," Benjamin said.

"When he gets to Cambridge, I hope he remembers to send us reinforcements."

Benjamin raised his pick over his head and drove it into the ground, striking rock. Lumley shoveled loose dirt into the box.

"It was a fellow named Pollard, Asa Pollard," Ezra said, pushing his way through the men in the ditch. "I'm a surgeon's apprentice, but he's beyond my assistance."

All the men stopped in their labor. "Dead, is he?" one of them asked.

Another said, "He's in the house not built by hands."

"Decapitated." Ezra picked up his shovel and jammed it into the ground. "Prescott ordered that he be buried immediately. No prayers. It's the right thing. We've much work to do." He threw dirt into the box and then dug deeper into the ground.

XXVI

Dirt, Stones, Straw, and Blood

ABIGAIL FOUND JOSHUA TIGGE IN HIS SAIL LOFT, SPYGLASS RAISED to his eye. Throughout the North End, crowds had gathered on roofs and in upper windows, any elevated place that afforded a better view across the harbor.

Joshua handed her the glass. "Our boys have guts, if they stay on that hill."

Then he looked at her. In her haste, she had pulled on the linen dress, which was wrinkled and the fabric stiff with sea salt. Her hair was undone, trailing well down her back. She peered through the glass. She could see the hills of Charlestown in the deep, clear light of daybreak. There was a wall of earth etched into the hill nearest the harbor; it looked like a scar in the green meadow and it was crawling with men, festering.

"It's just a victory to say to that old woman Tommy Gage we know your plans to march on Dorchester, but we'll determine where we'll engage you."

"What will the British do?"

"Thus far they've moved one of their ships up into the Charles River basin—see it, off to the left?"

"Yes."

"From there they can rake Charlestown Neck, challenging any reinforcements that might try to get out on the peninsula."

"The British will attack," Abigail said.

"Indeed they will, and as soon as possible, I would think." She handed him the glass, and looking through it he said, "But where will they land? They can't send longboats full of troops to the Neck, because there's a millpond dam there, blocking access to the beach. They could land at the wharves in Charlestown, but who knows—our boys may be waiting in every window, ready to open fire." He raised his other hand and pointed. "My guess is they'll land below that little mound, Morton's Hill, at the mouth of the Mystic, or go by it and up the river on the north side. They could easily flank the redoubt from that side. Holding the peninsula won't be easy, considering the lay of the land."

"I've never been there."

"To Charlestown?"

"Only as far as the clam flats." She returned the spyglass to him. He seemed incredulous. "I've only been out of Boston twice, Joshua." She dragged her fingers through her tangled hair. "And that was just to visit my mother's relatives in Roxbury."

As the sun rose up off the eastern horizon, Benjamin could see the open meadows rolling down to the water. The problem was evident: the redoubt could easily be flanked on either side. There was, down to the left, a spit with an old kiln on a mound called Morton's Point. The Mystic River ran by it, forming the northern border of the peninsula, and there was ample beach on which to land. To the right, the fields were open, broken only by occasional fences and a cart path, until the land leveled out at the village.

Benjamin, Ezra, and Lumley discussed this as they helped construct shooting platforms in the side of the fortification. There was little wood—only some planks that had been pulled from barns in the village—so they made rough steps by laying stones in the dirt and tamping them down with their boots.

"These rocks," Lumley said with a snort. "They may come in handy."

Ezra looked back toward Charlestown Neck. "If reinforcements do come, they'll bring ammunition."

Since the death of Asa Pollard, it seemed the two men had made a tacit peace. Benjamin also suspected that Lumley was impressed—though he'd never say it—by the fact that Ezra had not run off.

"If they bring ammunition," Benjamin said, jumping up and down on a stone until it burrowed in the dirt, flat side up, "I hope they bring me a musket to fire it with."

Ezra said to Lumley, "He's a good loader."

"Is he now?"

"I trained him." Ezra smiled, tamping down his own rock. "We practiced a full day, from Concord all the way back to Cambridge."

Cannons fired from one of the ships in the harbor. The British volleys had been sporadic, usually erupting in a cluster, and then there would be silence for minutes. The men continued to work and many didn't bother to look up, until they could hear the whistling balls approaching. Several more men had been wounded, but the worrisome news that came down the line was that one ball had smashed the two hogsheads of drinking water.

"Straw." Lumley shook his head, pointing off to the left. A group of men had been sent out to the north from the redoubt and they were gathering mown hay in the field and packing it into a fence that ran down toward the Mystic. He took his flask from his vest pocket. "Those boys are going to protect our left flank from behind a straw wall?" He hadn't offered any rum but now he did, saying, "It's just about finished. Can I buy you gentlemen a drink?"

Ezra hesitated.

"It's wet," Lumley suggested.

Ezra took the flask and tipped it up to his mouth. And then he passed it on to Benjamin, who finished the last few drops of rum, which burned all the way down to his stomach.

Ezra took the empty flask and returned it. "Thank you, Lumley."

"My pleasure." Lumley climbed down in to the ditch and began to gather more stones. "I hear that the fields of Vermont are full of rocks, but once they are cleared the soil is good for planting." He tossed a stone up to Ezra, who dropped it on the ground; and then another and another made flight.

"You were in Boston," Ezra said without looking at Benjamin.

"I was." Benjamin knew what was coming. He got down on his knees and with his bleeding fingers dug a hole, into which he eased one of the stones.

"How fares your sister?"

Benjamin kept working.

Ezra knelt next to him and also began digging with his bloody hands. "She is well?" When Benjamin didn't respond, he sat back on his haunches. "What?"

"I did what you asked," Benjamin said. "I said nothing to her about seeing you."

After a moment Ezra resumed digging. "You should not think that I don't care for Abigail. I do, truly. But—"

"But what, Ezra?" Benjamin rolled his stone into the hole. "But *what?*"

"There are circumstances that I, for which I am responsible—"

"Circumstances?" Benjamin stood up. "Don't *tell* me about circumstances." Using his boots, he pushed the stone deeper into the hole, which only aggravated the blisters on his feet. Disgusted, he slid down into the ditch and began collecting more stones.

Working next to him, Lumley said quietly, "Easy now, Benjamin, easy. We've a long day ahead of us."

The British bombardment continued through the morning. More and more Bostonians sought any place high enough to offer them a view across the harbor. Shortly after ten bells, Abigail left Joshua Tigge's sail loft, to see that her parents were all right. They were not at home, so she stopped at James's house. He was confined to bed and Mary said he was quite ill, probably due to all the activity in the city. The percussion of artillery was nearly constant, as was the beat of drums as redcoats marched through the streets.

When Abigail was at the front door with Mary, about to say goodbye, James appeared at the top of the stairs. He was wearing a sweat-soaked nightshirt, and he held the banister with both hands. "Last night," he said weakly. "How did it go?"

"Successful, I think."

James seemed too weary to stand another minute and he eased himself down until he was seated on the top step. "But at what price?" He seemed afraid to look at Abigail.

"The price that was required, James."

He glanced at her, stunned by the edge in her voice. "I'll never forgive myself—and to what end?"

Abigail laughed, surprising her brother and his wife. They watched her, wary. "There is nothing to forgive. It was my own choice."

"But—" James began.

"But it was something," Mary said. "You said so yourself. We did what we could."

"So little," he said.

Mary placed a hand over her enormous belly, looking wan and frail. Abigail helped her sit in the straight-back chair by the coat rack.

"And Benjamin?" James asked.

Abigail looked up at her brother. "He is away, with your letter to Dr. Warren."

"He crossed to Charlestown?"

Abigail nodded.

"I would venture our brother is still there then, digging in."

"I know," she said. "I fear this—I fear this more than anything else."

Quite desperate, James said, "I don't understand why the British are taking so long. I would think they would have attacked right at dawn. But it could be a feint, you know. They could be giving the appearance of going at Charlestown, while they send a force out the Neck—then they could march on Cambridge with no *real* opposition and surprise our army there and end all hope. In one day, take them down, and it could be over."

"They could, it seems," Abigail said, "but in the streets I see and hear nothing but reports of soldiers gathering down to harborside. Boats and barges are being prepared to transport them from Long Wharf and North Battery." James appeared skeptical. "Joshua Tigge thinks they are waiting for the tide. It will be high around three, and they will launch in the afternoon to take advantage of high water."

"Makes sense," James said, though he didn't seem relieved, only more distracted. "So much of Boston's history has been determined by the ebb and flow of the ocean." He was clearly invigorated by the thought of history, and as he struggled to his feet he added, "They may also suspect that our activity at Charlestown is a feint, that we actually plan to come at them from the Neck or Dorchester Heights. Regardless of what they think, they are in no hurry because there is no doubt about their military superiority." He daubed his eyes with the sleeve of his nighshirt, then he stood up, gripping the banister for support. "Where will you be?"

"I am returning to Tigge's sail loft. There's a good view from there."

"Well enough. You must take some food to Joshua." James disappeared down the hall and she heard the sound of the door close behind him.

Mary got to her feet slowly. "I'll fix a wallet for you to take to Mr. Tigge."

"Perhaps you should lie down too," Abigail said.

"I must tend to the children," Mary said, nodding toward the parlor, where several young faces gazed out at them. She made her way toward the kitchen. "Today requires imprecations to the Lord, and I find it easier to pray while I am doing something."

New England farmers know how to move earth and stone.

Throughout the morning, they continued to build their defenses. Colonel Prescott sent word to Cambridge to request reinforcements, though the courier had to travel the four miles on foot as no horse could be secured for the journey—which only fueled fears that the men building the redoubt were intended to be sacrificed in a lost cause. Furthermore, a sizeable group of men could be seen gathered on the far side of Charlestown Neck, but they did not cross to the peninsula, fearing bombardment from the British ship standing in the river beyond the millpond breakwall. They merely seemed content to observe the preparations.

There was little order in the redoubt. Like the others, Benjamin continued to dig. Word among the men was that General Artemis Ward, who was known for his caution and indecision, was laid up in Hastings House with gout. Lumley speculated that Ward would send few if any reinforcements, because the British activity on the harbor could be a ploy to distract the American army from the real assault from an expedition that would venture across Boston Neck. Late morning, four small field guns did arrive. After being rolled into position, they were fired once to open portals in the redoubt walls. The British shelling continued steadily on past noon. But the real concern was the lack of men, the lack of ammunition, the lack of food and water.

Benjamin was quite exhausted from the work, and from thirst. At one point, he paused to sit on top of the earthen wall. His eyesight had always been keen. Despite the billowing smoke created by the British artillery, he could see people in Boston, clustered on rooftops and in belfry windows. Specks of color. *Spectators.* He imagined that his family was among them, not knowing that he was here on top of this green slope. He was certain Abigail was there, somewhere. He did not want to think on the implications of last night, on her strange laugh after they left the North Battery. Most disturbing was the image of her treading water next to the skiff, saying that she was cleansed. He could often read his sister's moods, but at that moment there was something about her that he could not fathom. A sorrow, but also some kind of eerie joy. It was too far, too dark, too difficult for him to see what it was, what it had made her. She was changed, he was sure, but how he did not know.

And he wondered about Mariah, locked away in a prison cell. He had never seen her frightened, but couldn't imagine that she would sit within its walls and hear all the commotion outside and not be afraid. She would not know what was happening. No one would tell her. It was the not knowing that would drive her to distraction—that and the sense of isolation. She needed the harbor, the sky, the smell of the marshes at low tide. Since the night they had become lovers, he wondered at what she had said. *If my blood doesn't come in a month, it will be all right. You take my meaning?* He had said yes.

XXVII

Menarche

Along with the thunder of cannon, church bells rang constantly throughout Boston, giving this hot, sunny day a strange air of portent and festivity. When Abigail returned to Joshua Tigge's sail loft, the upper floor was filled with watermen and their families. The men and women crowded around the three windows that faced the harbor, while the food Mary had prepared was feasted upon by the children.

Sometime after one in the afternoon, barges and longboats set out from Long Wharf and North Battery, headed for Charlestown. It was an awesome spectacle: twenty-eight vessels lined up in two even rows and propelled by their oars, resembling scarlet bugs as they crawled across the harbor. Joshua estimated that there were at least fifty soldiers in each boat, their bayonets glinting in the sunlight. They were accompanied by barges loaded with supplies, horses, and field guns.

"Those grasshoppers will be set up at the base of the hill," Joshua said. "From several hundred yards they will be out of range of the American rifles, and they'll tear that redoubt to pieces unchallenged. A charge may not even be required."

Another old fisherman said, "I fought at Louisbourg, and I saw what cannon could do. Those Frenchmen that weren't killed and wounded were driven from the fort, many diving into the sea."

When the boats landed in Charlestown, the soldiers waded ashore and gathered along the beach below Morton's Point. Once empty, the boats began to return across the harbor. Over the course of the next hour it was clear that the British were in no hurry to initiate their assault. Perhaps, Joshua suggested, their mere presence would cause the Americans to flee. Though there were estimates that the first wave delivered some fifteen hundred redcoats to Charlestown, by midafternoon more troops were being ferried across the harbor. A small squadron marched into Charlestown, and soon the entire village was engulfed in flames. The thick plume of smoke drifted lazily across the peninsula, at times obscuring the redoubt at the crest of the nearest hill.

While everyone's attention was drawn to the scene across the harbor, a girl of about twelve took hold of Abigail's hand and looked up at her with imploring eyes. The girl's mother said, "Perhaps, Sympathy, you need to go outside?" The woman, heavy-set and missing teeth, stared at Abigail earnestly, as though trying to convey a tacit message.

"I'd be glad to take her," Abigail said.

Pointedly, the woman said to her daughter, "Attend to the lady now. You follow close behind, understand?"

Sympathy nodded. She let go of Abigail's hand, stepped behind her, and followed her down the loft stairs and outside. They walked up a path from the beach.

"You need to relieve yourself?" Abigail said. The girl had large moist brown eyes. Her wrists were thin as twigs. Something about her was awkward, embarrassed. "Go ahead," Abigail urged. "Go behind a bush there. No one will see."

"It be your dress."

"My dress?"

Sympathy looked away, toward the sail loft. Abigail took it now that her mother had orchestrated their departure. "On the back," she said, her voice barely a whisper.

Quickly, Abigail reached behind her and gathered the linen fabric. It was damp. She looked at her hand, which was smeared with blood. The air was filled with the thud of cannon fire, and church bells rang from near and far. She suddenly felt the heat of the sun on her scalp. "Thank you, Sympathy. I must—I must clean myself and change. Do you wish to go with me?"

At first the girl seemed uncertain, but then as Abigail continued up the path, the girl fell in stride behind her. When they reached Mariah's house, they entered the dooryard through the back gate. The place was already suffering from neglect—wood slats had been removed from the fence. The kitchen door was ajar. Inside, the house had been ransacked.

"Thieves," Abigail said.

"My father says the lobsterbacks will tear this house down because Mistress Cole is in jail," Sympathy said. "And she will surely hang."

When Abigail entered the parlor, broken glass crackled beneath her shoes. She stopped; the girl was barefoot. Abigail picked the girl up in her arms and carried her to Mariah's bedroom. The girl put her bare arms tightly around Abigail's neck and her smooth skin was warm. Abigail inspected the pinewood floor and, determining that there was no danger, put Sympathy down by the closet. There was an old seaman's trunk, which was opened; Mariah's clothing was spilled over the sides and was piled on the floor.

Abigail picked up a pair of shoes. "These may be a bit large but you'll grow into them."

Sympathy slid her feet into the shoes. As she walked about the room, the heels knocked loudly on the floor, causing her to giggle.

Abigail got down on her knees and sorted through the garments until she found a blue dress of light calico. There was a yellow scarf, which Sympathy picked up. She looked at Abigail, who nodded. The girl draped the scarf over her shoulders, dramatically throwing one end over her shoulder.

"It goes well with your eyes," Abigail said.

They went back into the kitchen, where there was a bucket of water. Abigail removed her white linen dress—Sympathy was surprised to see that she wore nothing underneath—and soaked it in the water, and then washed herself. "Do you understand what has happened?"

The girl nodded. She had remarkably long lashes, which snapped each time she blinked. Her stare was arrested, curious. "Mother says my blood will come anytime now."

"It's called menarche," Abigail said. "The first time can be alarming."

"And then I will grow them," the girl said, staring at Abigail's breasts.

"You will, and you will have a long, slender back and a high bosom that will give men and women pause." Incredulous, the girl laughed. "It's true, and you will learn how to walk, how to turn and move. You'll learn how to carry them." Abigail turned her shoulders, causing her breasts to sway, and, laughing, Sympathy mimicked her.

Abigail pulled on Mariah's dress and buttoned it up. "Your mother has told you what the blood means?"

"I am a woman, but as long as the blood comes every month I am not with child." She hesitated, her fingers playing with the end of the yellow scarf. "I don't understand if the blood is a good thing. Mother says it depends."

"Yes, it depends." Suddenly, Abigail seemed out of breath. It was hot in the house and the dress was snug in the shoulders and across the back. "It depends on whether you want to be with child or not." She placed a hand on her chest, inhaling.

Sympathy took Abigail's hand and led her out on to the back stoop, where the air was cooler. They sat on the step.

"It is painful?" the girl said.

"Sometimes."

"When our pigs mount each other, they squeal."

Abigail breathed slowly, deeply.

"It must hurt so," Sympathy said. "But my cousin Anne says not at all. Does it?"

"It depends."

Abigail leaned over, but when the girl placed her hand on her shoulder, she lifted her head. Then they were in each other's arms, and Abigail began to sob.

"I'm afraid," Sympathy said, crying, too. "I don't want the blood."

"I know. Neither did I."

Once landed, the British soldiers ate a leisurely lunch in the meadows down by Morton's Point. At six to seven hundred yards, they were well out of firing range from the redoubt. Many of them were sprawled in the grass, eating, smoking cigars and pipes, seemingly unperturbed by the constant cannon fire coming from the harbor and Copp's Hill. The village was completely consumed in flames, crackling and filling the air with black smoke, which at times nearly blotted out the sun. The shade brought slight, fleeting relief from the afternoon heat.

Benjamin watched the field pieces as they were being wheeled into place and prepared by teams of men, under the direction of officers, some of whom were on horseback. Equipment was still being unloaded from one of the barges, and the ammunition crates were carried up from the beach. Out on the water, longboats were returning with yet more soldiers.

"They are giving us time," Lumley said. "To run." He looked down along the wall, where men were still furiously reinforcing the redoubt. "I've never seen such confusion. Except for this fellow Prescott, no one's really in charge."

"He's leading by example," Ezra said.

True. Prescott spent much of his time striding back and forth along the top of the earthen wall in his shirtsleeves, white waistcoat, and broad-brimmed hat. He talked to men and he shouted orders, most of which were ignored. Men were constantly looking back toward the Neck. On the far side, the crowd of people had grown—Lumley estimated that there were at least two regiments—but because of the constant raking fire from the *Symmetry*, which stood in the river off the mill pond, few ventured across to the Charlestown peninsula. Several bodies could be seen lying in the road, taken down by grapeshot.

At one point, a couple of hundred men did cross the Neck, led by a tall thin man—word went through the redoubt that this was John Stark and his militia from New Hampshire. As they crossed the spit of land, the cannon fire from the *Symmetry* intensified, but Stark insisted that he and his men march across at an unhurried pace. The men in the redoubt cheered them on. A few of the New Hampshire boys fell, but most made it across and, after consulting with Prescott and Putnam, Stark led his men out to take positions behind the split rail fence that ran down the left flank toward the Mystic River.

After two o'clock, a horseman rode across the Neck, bringing another huzzah from the redoubt. Even from several hundred yards it was clear that the blond, finely-dressed gentleman was Dr. Joseph Warren. When he arrived at the redoubt, he met with Prescott, as well as several of his apprentices, who were setting up a field hospital farther up Bunker Hill. There was speculation that he would take command of the redoubt—the provincial congress had just granted him a military commission—but instead he removed his coat and accepted the use of a musket. When he joined the men along the embrasure, they greeted him with respect that bordered on reverence. He walked among them, pausing to talk with men as he went—many had been his patients, and he would ask after their wives and children.

As he approached Benjamin, Ezra, and Lumley, he shook hands with men all around.

"Still glad that you came over to our side?" he asked when he reached Lumley.

"I venture, sir," Lumley said, "that if you stand up on the ramparts, the advancing redcoats will be blinded by the sun reflecting off that satin vest."

The doctor laughed. "You know, I almost missed this occasion. All morning I was laid up in Cambridge with one of these headaches. Quite blinding it was, but I'd like to take a try with this musket. General Ward would surely join us, but he's got a bad case of gout."

The men had often heard about the general's gout, but coming from Dr. Warren it caused them to laugh like mischievous children.

When the doctor shook Benjamin's hand, he smiled warmly. "You got out of Boston just in time, eh?"

"Yes, sir. I rowed across this morning." Benjamin took a letter from his jacket. "My brother intends this for you."

"Thank you, Benjamin," the doctor said as he broke the seal on the envelope. "He is in good health?"

"Passable, sir."

"I see. Well, you wanted to fight, Benjamin. And now this seems to be our day." Warren became preoccupied with the contents of the letter as he moved on down the wall, still pausing occasionally to speak to men.

The men watched as the doctor moved on. Their faces were weary, covered with sweat and dirt. Yet they seemed encouraged, resolved.

Lumley gazed downhill toward the British soldiers. "They have a few such men, real leaders, but not enough. The way men are promoted, it's different. All too often a truly good officer will be bypassed. It has to do with, you know, breeding." Then he grinned. "It don't account for much with your lot, does it? Not a duke, a baron, or an earl among you. I suppose you think you're better off."

"It's what you came over for?" Ezra said. "It's what you're fighting for, is it?"

"Each of us, master of our own, and all that?" Lumley snorted. "Never work. You can't just eliminate things like greed and jealousy. There's always someone who's going to seek the higher place, the status of privilege." He glanced at Ezra and then Benjamin, a glint in his eye that seemed complicit. "If we were smart, we'd take our chances now in crossing that Neck. Get to the other side and just keep going." They stared at him, until he leaned forward and rested his arms and musket on the top of the wall. "I'm just saying it would be the reasonable thing to do, is all."

Upon the command of their officers, the redcoats had begun to fall into formation. Each man bore full battle gear, which Lumley said weighed about a hundred pounds. He was keenly interested in the field pieces, which would be fired before the soldiers advanced up the hill. There were two twelve-pounders situated on Morton's Point, which began erupting, belching a flash of fire and a plume of white smoke from their barrels. The smaller, mobile guns, however, seemed to be encountering considerable difficulty. Their crews struggled to get them across the swampy areas near the beach, and their wheels often bogged down in mud.

"Too many problems there, it seems," Lumley said. "It's not just the muck. Look at those men—they're not loading and firing. They should be doing so, even if they are stuck. Those guns should be doing most of the hard work here. We should already be torn to pieces, but those grasshoppers are silent. I don't understand it."

"Look there," Ezra said, pointing. "See how those men are going from one crate to another, opening them. And see that officer—he's livid."

"That's Colonel Cleaveland," Benjamin said.

Lumley shielded his eyes from the sun as he looked down the hill. "I believe you're right. He's the commander of artillery, but I don't understand what the problem is, why those guns aren't firing."

Ezra had turned and faced Benjamin. "You know that officer by sight?"

Benjamin nodded. "His men have discovered that they have the wrong shot, the wrong gauge balls." Lumley had also turned to look at him. "I switched them, last night."

Ezra and Lumley considered this, until Lumley finally whispered, "No. No, those crates would have been stored in the armory at North Battery, and the colonel—"

"How did you do it?" Ezra said.

Benjamin looked down the hill, where the phalanx of soldiers was slowly beginning to advance, moving through the tall grass in tight formation. "It was all because of my sister," he said.

"Abigail?" Ezra said.

"We went to North Battery and—" Benjamin paused. He wanted to look at Ezra but couldn't. "She provided a distraction while I worked on those crates."

Ezra was quiet for a moment. "A distraction."

"With the colonel of artillery."

They all stared down at the columns of redcoats. Along the redoubt, men had put down their tools and had taken up their arms. Though the two twelve-pound guns on Morton's Point roared away, sending balls into the hillside, the smaller field pieces were useless.

"What kind of a distraction?" Ezra asked.

Benjamin didn't answer.

Shortly after Abigail returned to the sail loft, the cannon fire from the British ships and from Copp's Hill ceased. The silence was so heavy, so frightening, that Sympathy would not let go of her hand.

Joshua Tigge finally said, "They're on the march," and everyone crowded toward the open windows. At first they were quiet, awestruck, but then some whispered *Good Lord* or *My God*.

Red phalanxes moved up the hillside with an undulating quality to their advance that reminded Abigail of how a flag might flutter in a slow breeze. Rags of smoke drifted across the sky, at times making it difficult to see across the harbor. Sporadic cannon fire could be heard from the small hill to the right of Breed's Hill, but smaller guns at the foot of the hill all were silent.

Joshua raised his spyglass to his eye and said, "There's some problem with their field guns. They should be peppering that hill right now."

Abigail looked for smoke from their barrels but saw none. "It's the ammunition," she said. Everyone turned and stared at her. "They have the wrong gauge balls."

"How do you know?" Sympathy's mother asked.

"They're the wrong gauge," Abigail repeated without bothering to look at the woman. "My brother Benjamin, he tampered with the cases."

Sympathy's mother said, "It's that officer you've been keeping company with, isn't it? He had something to do with artillery, I heard in market." Then she expelled a robust laugh. "They have the wrong *balls* over there, all right." Other women began to laugh, hysterically, defiantly. "She had *his* balls, so that little brother of hers could have at *theirs.*"

The women howled and chortled so now that the men became alarmed, even embarrassed. Some sought refuge by looking out the window again.

The men along the redoubt watched the soldiers come up through the tall grass, rising and falling with the uneven lay of the land. There were perhaps a dozen fences strung across the meadow, some wood, others stone. The soldiers were dressed in full battle gear, and their advance was ponderous, deliberate, but relentless.

Lumley scanned the field and said, "Looks different from up here, I tell you. Two thousand men, at least." He seemed impressed, even proud as he watched. "To our, what, seven, eight hundred?" Turning, he glanced back at the hundreds of men gathered along the higher brow of Bunker Hill. "And do you suppose those bastards will come down here and join us? They'd likely double our numbers, but it's safer up there, and there's an excellent view."

"Spectators," Benjamin said.

"There're always spectators," Lumley said. "And then there's us."

Well down to the left, standing on the wall, Colonel Prescott was continually shouting encouragements to his men. Other men who had been designated officers ran behind the men, telling them to hold their fire. Benjamin recalled hearing about the morning on Lexington Green, how one shot was fired—no one knew where it came from, which side had fired first. Prescott kept shouting. One man quipped, "Whites of their eyes, he says. How close is that?"

"You'll know," Lumley said. "The longer we wait, the better. And not all at once." He looked at Ezra. "I'll go first, and then you, right?"

"You weren't too keen on shooting at your countrymen last time," Ezra said.

"True." Lumley turned and looked at Ezra.

"Right," Ezra said. "Then you have first crack."

"And you," Lumley said to Benjamin. "Be ready to reload us quick." He leaned toward Benjamin and whispered, "And after they get off a volley, there will be plenty of muskets. Find yourself one."

Benjamin nodded.

Lumley looked up at the sky a moment, long enough that Benjamin did as well. "I always liked blue," Lumley said.

When the first line of British soldiers was less than a hundred yards from the redoubt, Benjamin could make out distinguishing characteristics—hair color, noses, mouths: they were no longer a row of soldiers, but men. Some were young, their skin marred with acne. He kept expecting them to stop upon command, take aim, and fire, but they continued to climb up through the meadow. The grass collapsed before them, a dry, crisp sound.

Down to Benjamin's right, one man said, "Lord, I'm thirsty."

Benjamin wondered if he was lightheaded from the lack of food and water. It seemed to give all that lay before him a rare clarity. He could now see brass buttons on the men's red coats. Each soldier was greatly burdened with backpack and cartouche box, and a Brown Bess fitted with bayonet. Each wore white belts, forming an X on his chest. Officers had silver plates about their necks, which glinted in the sunlight.

Lumley pointed off to the right. "See how they are coming up slower—the delaying action." And then he swung his arm over to the left, where the British were approaching the fence. "And there they are in the lead. That's where they expect to break through, then they will swing round and come upon the redoubt from the side."

When the front British line was less than a hundred feet from the redoubt, every musket was laid across the wall, but still no one fired. The soldiers were so close now that Benjamin could see sweat and dirt on their faces. With each step he expected someone to fire, but there was only a hard stillness. Everything seemed poised, while in the distance there was the squawk of seagulls on the harbor and the crackle of burning wood coming up from Charlestown village.

Then, off to the left, there was a single shot from behind the wood fence. There was shouting, and then the Americans opened fire, a burst of sparks and smoke all along the line. Benjamin had never heard such noise—it felt as though feather pillows had clapped over his ears. Soldiers in the front line fell by the dozen. They staggered, they sprawled, they turned in a circle and collapsed over each other in the grass.

Lumley had fired, and he thrust his musket in Benjamin's hands. As he tore open a cartridge with his teeth, Benjamin watched Ezra take aim and fire. The man he hit, an officer, fell to his knees and raised his head to the sky as if in submission, perhaps even in prayer, and then he lurched forward into the grass.

Benjamin worked quickly, without thinking, and then he handed the loaded gun to Lumley. Ezra gave him his musket, and

Benjamin began loading again. The smoke was overwhelming. Some of the British soldiers fired, but many who had not been hit began to move back down the hill, first tentatively, as though they expected to charge at any moment, but then more and more of them began to turn and run downhill. Still the Americans fired, their shots now random and sporadic. There was the sound of huzzas all along the embrasure. Some men tried to go over the earthen walls and take chase, but they were restrained.

As the volleys began to diminish, the soldiers lying in the grass could be heard: crying, moaning, screaming. Benjamin had lost track of how many times he'd loaded muskets, perhaps three, perhaps four times, all in a matter of a few minutes. The smoke lay heavy on the field, sounds were muffled, but the cries of the wounded British soldiers only seemed to grow louder.

XXVIII

The Second Assault, and the Third

IN THE SAIL LOFT, THERE WAS THE SILENCE OF DISBELIEF. NO ONE moved as the British lines broke and spilled downhill to the beach, leaving the green meadow dotted with red: fallen bodies.

"So many," Joshua whispered.

"They hardly got off a shot," another said.

Joshua raised his spyglass. "It's chaos—soldiers are wading out into the shallows for the boats. But officers are threatening them. Some have sabers drawn—pistols."

Then, there came the voices—from rooftops, church steeples, open windows voices rose up, swelling in the hot air as Bostonians cheered. In the sail loft, too, there was celebration. Men clapped each other on the shoulders. Women raised their hands. Sympathy's mother enfolded Abigail in her strong, heavy arms, nearly crushing her daughter between them. The jubilation went on for minutes. Abigail was pushed and passed from one to another, hugged, kissed, clutched about the waist and lifted off the floor.

Until Joshua shouted—not once, but twice—causing everyone to freeze. He stood at the window, peering through his glass.

"Our boys," a woman said. "Are they safe?"

"For *now*, they appear to be," Joshua said. "But the Brits are reforming their lines."

"It's not over?" the woman asked.

No one bothered to answer as they again crowded toward the open windows.

It did not take long—perhaps fifteen minutes—for the British to begin marching up the hill a second time. Their scarlet ranks were thinner, but they moved with the same slow determination as before. The formation, Joshua noted, was similar to the first assault, except that the left flank did not delay as before, moving directly on the redoubt. The provincials held their fire again until the redcoats were nearly on top of them.

"One hundred feet," a man said.

"Less," said another. "Eighty."

"Eighty?"

"Eighty. The distance from my barn door to the hay bales— I've walked it off."

The shooting lasted a good while this time. No one kept track, but it wasn't over in minutes as before. Some said twenty minutes; others thirty. There was, Abigail thought, an absurd obsession with measurements, of time, of distance. It was how the men came to understand what was happening. The women, for the most part, were quiet, talking amongst themselves, though a few prayed, their heads bowed, their lips moving. All the while, the shooting was constant. The smoke seemed to be emitting from the earth, a relentless shroud drifting on the faintest breeze, obliterating the view of the American defenses. The only certainty was that more redcoats lay on the hillside, dead and wounded. Men were dying. They were the enemy. They were the soldiers in red who had for years ruled the streets of Boston. Abigail felt neither elation, nor deliverance. That moment had passed. It was a hot afternoon in June, and across the harbor men were dying. She thought she might cry—some of the women were—but tears didn't come. She didn't feel that way, no. There was, really, only a curiosity, and a sense of clarity, and she suspected that for the rest of her life she would remember every moment, every detail, and that they would come back to her, alive as they were now, yet changed because they were recollections; they would be forever part of her, part of all of them.

And then it was over. Again British soldiers descended the hill, many running, running for their lives, until they were beyond the range of the American guns. Others staggered, wounded, and some bravely helped another down through the meadow, which was strewn with men.

This time there was no jubilation. Not throughout Boston. Not in the sail loft. Perhaps a weary relief. There was no question now: though the British had been repelled twice, the battle was not over.

Benjamin had a musket now, acquired from a man who had been taken down by grapeshot. Gaping wounds seemed to be everywhere: face, neck, chest. He might have been forty years old, and as he lay in the ditch at the base of the embrasure wall his eyes stared up at the sky in surprise and disbelief. His blood pooled in the dirt. All the dead were stripped of their weapons, no questions asked, and the wounded were taken up the higher slope to the field hospital on Bunker Hill.

The problem was ammunition. No one had more than a few rounds left.

There was no doubt that the British would attack again. The number of men along the wall had dwindled. Those who fled were ignored mostly, though some suffered curses as they ran off in the direction of Charlestown Neck. And still, remarkably, almost defiantly, there were hundreds of men gathered on the far side of the Neck who would not cross over to the peninsula.

And there was no water. Benjamin tried not to think about it, but he laughed when Ezra said, "One mouthful of water would make this all worth it."

His face was blackened by gunpowder. Benjamin looked about him. Lumley's face, too—all of them had darkened faces, which made their eyes seem overly large and white.

Dr. Warren walked along the top of the wall, speaking to the men. He had removed his coat, yet he still looked quite elegant in his white pants, shirt, and silk waistcoat. It seemed a pity that such garments had been soiled by dirt. He didn't seem to mind and, in fact, he appeared quite content as he passed by the men. He joked, he smiled, and when he reached Benjamin he paused and said, "You will need a bath when this is all over."

The men around him laughed, and one of them said, "If he don't drink the bath water first, eh?"

"I would prefer something stronger, thank you," the doctor said. "Madeira would do, though a tankard of ale would be just the thing with this heat. It's a bit warm for a bowl of flip."

There was more laughter, and debate regarding preferred beverages.

Dr. Warren dropped down on his haunches and spoke quietly to Benjamin. "Your brother." He patted his waistcoat pocket, which bulged with the envelope Benjamin had delivered to him. "I don't know how he does it. Hardly ventures from his house, always keeping his chamber pot close, and yet he has tentacles that run throughout Boston." He studied Benjamin a moment, his blue eyes humorous and conspiratorial. "I understand you had something to do with silencing their field pieces?"

"The balls," Lumley offered. "He and his sister, they tampered with their balls."

All the men burst into laughter. Except Ezra.

"You Lovells are a remarkable family," Dr. Warren said. "True Bostonians." Then, standing up, he nodded and moved on along the top of the embrasure, talking to the men as he went.

"A nice piece of benediction, that," Lumley said.

Ezra stared down the hill, pointing. "They've sorted out the problem with the ammunition by now."

It was true. The British were reforming their lines and their field pieces were being wheeled into position up the hill.

"I've got two rounds left," Lumley said.

"One, here," Ezra said.

"I have a little powder but nothing to shoot," Benjamin said.

They were leaning against the earthen wall. Some of the men were picking through the dirt for stones that would fit down the barrel of a musket: rocks, bits of glass, pieces of metal—anything that might be shot at the British with the little remaining powder. Lumley ran his fingers through the packed dirt and worked a stone loose. He held it up for inspection, as though considering all the facets of a rare gemstone. "That one ought to fit."

Benjamin took the stone and then began digging in the wall, looking for more ammunition. He found a rusty piece of metal, probably from a cowbell chain, and more stones.

"That's it," Lumley said. "Just ram the whole lot down and wait till they get close."

As Benjamin loaded his musket, he watched the redcoats start to move up the hill, slowly, as before. There was something different about most of them—and then he said, "Their haversack—they've left them behind."

"It's quite unlike the command," Lumley said.

"*Whot,*" Ezra said. "Not very sporting, I say."

Lumley laughed.

They watched the soldiers advance, stepping over and around the dead and wounded. The small field pieces were now firing, creating a sporadic rhythm and sending great white trails of smoke up the hill. Often the balls were off the mark, some passing

353

overhead, whistling, while those that landed short bounded up through the grass and slammed into the earthen wall, throwing up plumes of dirt. Down to their left, a man cried out when he was struck by a ball, which hurled him down into the pit, where he lay motionless.

Several officers prowled behind the men, shouting, *"Not yet! Wait! Wait!"*

At the back of the redoubt, there was a commotion. Some new men arrived—Benjamin didn't know from where—and they filed quickly through the narrow opening in the rear of the fortress. They filled in beside others, lying in the dirt.

"Got yours?" Lumley asked.

Benjamin leveled his musket across the top of the dirt wall. He was reluctant to look at any one soldier too long. "Not yet."

"There's still time," Lumley said. "Just wait long enough that you can't miss." Then he turned his head toward Benjamin. "You want to fire into a group. Fire low, for the legs."

"Right."

"After Noddle's Island I sorted out my problem," Lumley said as he cocked his musket. "Officers. I only shoot officers."

When the British were within a hundred yards, some began firing, though most continued to march uphill. The provincials held their fire. Lead screamed through the air and slammed into the earthen wall.

Benjamin sighted down the barrel of his musket. There were three men walking close together, hunched over as they moved through the swatches of flattened grass. They wore high fur hats: grenadiers. When they were within thirty yards, he could see their faces. They were all pale and lean, all young and broad-shouldered. The tallest of the three was in the middle. His stride was longer, and he appeared to be leading the other two. He was saying something to them.

To the left, there was a barrage of fire from behind the fence, and then the guns along the wall opened up. Benjamin looked at the three grenadiers. They seemed to understand that they were too close together and began to spread out.

"*Now*," Lumley shouted, and he fired his musket.

Ezra fired.

Benjamin's head felt thick, dull, and the gunshot seemed distant. He closed one eye, aimed at the middle grenadier's knees, and pulled the trigger. The musket had a powerful kick, slamming back into his right shoulder and causing him to slide a few feet down the angled wall. He crawled up and gazed down the hill at his three soldiers. Two were lying in the grass, one motionless, the other rocking back and forth. The tallest one was still coming on, limping. The right thigh of his white pants was streaked with blood. There were men lying everywhere in the grass now, crying out, screaming, and as the gunfire continued to pour into them, more soldiers moved up into the front ranks. The smoke from all the shooting made it difficult to see. Suddenly, as if ordered, the British who remained standing hesitated—except for Benjamin's tall grenadier. He kept coming, favoring his wounded leg. He was so close now that Benjamin could also see that there was something wrong with his left hand, which held the stock of his rifle. Fingers were missing and blood dripped onto his gaiters.

Some of the British soldiers began to move back down the hill, but still the provincials kept firing. It was hard for Benjamin to hear. His ears seemed stuffed. And the smoke only became thicker. Then he realized that the gunfire was diminishing. Looking down the wall, he saw that some men had put down their weapons. Some were hurling rocks into the meadow.

Suddenly, among the British soldiers, there was confusion. Officers had sabers drawn, threatening their own men. But they appeared stunned, disorganized, and while they were still being picked off some began to help their fallen mates to their feet. There was so much smoke that Benjamin could not find his tall grenadier.

He was aware of something new. Silence. The Americans were hardly shooting.

Turning, he saw that dozens were fleeing, passing through the narrow opening at the back of the redoubt. When he looked downhill again, he could barely see the British for the smoke. He wondered if they had begun to retreat. Perhaps both sides would abandon the crest of the hill—after all this, both sides would simply abandon the hill.

He looked at Lumley, and then at Ezra. He asked them what was happening, but he could barely hear his own voice. They both stared down at the meadow and shook their heads. They had put their muskets down. And they all waited.

Benjamin became preoccupied with working a stone out of the dirt. His fingers were raw from all the digging, black earth beneath his broken nails. The stone was gray, perfectly round, the right size. But it was pointless because he had no more cartridges. Beneath the divot left by the stone, he could see a rock and he began prying it loose with both hands. When freed, it proved to be the size of his fist, with a nice heft to it.

There came a sound from down the hill. It swelled, grew louder, and seemed to move. He could feel it—a rumbling in the ground, caused by pounding feet. And then they began to emerge from the smoke, soldiers shouting as they ran toward the redoubt. There was barely any gunfire from the provincials. Benjamin stood up, the rock in his hand. He threw it but he never saw it in the smoke. His grenadier was lying in the grass not ten yards from the base of the earthen wall. He couldn't get up and he had turned to watch the charge. It was a wall of men, with row after row behind them. They came up to the fallen grenadier, the first going around him, but then he seemed swallowed up and disappeared.

Someone was yanking on Benjamin's arm. It was Ezra, who pulled him down behind the wall and into the pit. Looking up, he saw Lumley, standing now, taking aim carefully, calmly, and just as he fired his musket soldiers poured over the walls. They used bayonets, running through men in their path. Benjamin was grabbed by the arm and shoved toward the back of the redoubt, stumbling over fallen bodies, boards, weapons, piles of dirt. The smoke was so thick that it was difficult to see the top of the wall. Men fell down into the pit, bleeding and crying out. There were few shots fired as they moved toward the small entrance to the redoubt. Dozens of men pushed to get through the narrow gap in the walls and Benjamin was crushed from all sides. Ezra kept pushing Benjamin ahead of him, and then suddenly they passed through the entrance and were outside.

Looking around, Benjamin shouted, "Lumley, where's Lumley?"

Ezra would not let go of his arm and kept pulling him away from the redoubt. There was shooting now, shots being fired by the redcoats lined up on the back wall, and, in the distance, there were groups of provincials who were firing up at them. Benjamin and Ezra ran until they were clear of the smoke, and then they stopped and looked back. The redoubt appeared to be smoldering, belching men from the cloud, many of them wounded, some being helped by others.

"Lumley?" Benjamin thought he shouted, though he could barely hear his own voice.

I don't see him, Ezra appeared to say.

He grabbed Benjamin's arm, but suddenly stood up straight, his body rigid. His fingers let go of Benjamin's, and then he fell forward in to the grass. Blood issued from a wound in his back, just below the right shoulder blade. Benjamin rolled him on to his side. The bullet had struck him in the chest, causing a smaller, neater wound.

Ezra's eyes were open and he appeared to be speaking. *Go. You must go.*

Benjamin took hold of both arms and yanked him off the ground. Ezra couldn't stand, and he began to fall, so Benjamin eased him down over his shoulder, and then began to walk slowly, following others on the path to Charlestown Neck.

In the early evening, Abigail made her way home. The streets were filled with stunned, horrified Bostonians, as well as hundreds of wounded soldiers who had been ferried back from Charlestown. Many redcoats used their rifles as crutches. They were bloodied, their uniforms torn and filthy. There were carts loaded with the dead. When the smoke had drifted off Bunker Hill, it was clear that the British had taken the redoubt; but there was nothing victorious about this army.

When she reached King's Chapel, she found Father sitting on the granite step, his back against a column. Dazed, he looked up at her and muttered something in Latin—she caught the word *clementia:* mercy.

"Where's Mother?"

At first he didn't seem to understand, but then he nodded toward the granary. "Do you know where Benjamin is?"

"Across the harbor, somewhere."

"He was on that hill, I'm sure of it. My son, taking up arms against . . ."

"Father, you must go home."

Confused, resigned, he said, "Perhaps you're right."

She helped him to his feet—he didn't resist. He made his way down School Street, relying heavily on his cane.

Abigail went to the granary and pushed her way through the throng of soldiers that were being herded into the building. Inside, the vast open space was filled with men. They lay and sat on the floorboards. There was a harrowing din. Men with gaping wounds and shattered limbs were crying out, moaning, screaming. There was the smell of dirt and gunpowder and blood. They were attended to by women mostly, but far too few, and there was little that was being done. Some distributed water from buckets. At the back of the building there were several tables where surgeons, their aprons smeared with blood, performed amputations.

Abigail found her mother, wrapping a soldier's head in a bandage. He had lost part of an ear. "Tear them up," Mother said, nodding toward the bag on the floor.

Abigail opened the bag and pulled out some of her dresses and petticoats. There was, sitting on the floor in front of her, a soldier, a boy really, who was missing several fingers on his left hand. His face was pale and fine blue veins stood out on his forehead. Abigail tore her petticoat, creating a long strip of white linen.

"Let's have a look at that," she said. The boy was reluctant, and holding out her hand she said, "What's your name?"

His eyes reminded her of a cat, observant, wary. "Liam, missus."

"And where are you from, Liam?"

"Newcastle."

"That's up north, isn't it?"

"Yes, Ma'am. On the River Tyne—near Hadrian's Wall?"

"It must be beautiful."

"Aye, it is." Carefully, he placed his wounded hand in hers, never taking his eyes off her as she began to wrap it in her petticoat linen.

With the help of others, Benjamin got Ezra to Winter Hill, where the provincials dug another line of defense. The field hospital had been established on the western slope. In the distance, beyond pastures and copses were the fine homes of Cambridge and brick buildings of Harvard College. Farm girls carried pails of water among the wounded and one of them offered Benjamin a tin cup.

"A surgeon will tend to you soon," he said, holding the cup to Ezra's mouth.

Most of the water ran down Ezra's chin. His face was pale, reminding Benjamin of the sand-side of a flounder. His shirt was slick with blood. "No matter," he whispered. "I need to tell you something. Something you must convey to your sister. Please, be my courier, but I haven't time to write a letter." His smile was weak. "So I'll have to tell you."

"You can tell her yourself."

"No," Ezra said. "Listen, I know I hurt her deeply, leaving Boston without full explanation. I made this terrible mistake, for which I am sorry."

"You shouldn't exhaust yourself talking."

Ezra ignored this. "That child my mother was raising in Concord?" he said. "You see, it's mine. There was a woman in Boston—she worked in a tavern—and she became pregnant. I was responsible. It was one night, an impulsive mistake, the result of too much ale. I am ashamed and completely at fault. Soon after, this girl tells me that she's with child, insisting that it can only be mine, and I believed her. She was horrified by this, and frightened—she was no deceiver. She said that her family refused to let her remain in their house. I was—I was devastated, Benjamin. I love Abigail, truly I do, and I couldn't bring myself to tell her of this situation. I was torn between love and responsibility, so I had no choice but to take the girl away from Boston. I just hoped that Abigail wouldn't find out, that she would forget me and . . . I took the girl to Concord, where my mother was with relatives." He coughed, and blood ran out of the corner of his mouth. Benjamin daubed at it with his shirt sleeve, until Ezra weakly pushed his arm away. "So we left Boston, quickly, and when the baby came, the girl, she died. So my mother is tending to the baby, and now her health isn't good. Please tell Abigail that this was not as I intended it, and that I hope she can forgive me. I wish only that I could have remained in Boston, with her." He looked once again at Benjamin. "You'll tell her? You'll explain it to her?"

"Of course."

With great difficulty Ezra reached down into the pocket of his trousers and produced a stone. "When we were digging on Bunker Hill I found this—too large for the barrel of a gun."

Ezra placed the stone in Benjamin's hand—it was white and smeared with blood from Ezra's fingers.

"An egg," Benjamin said, looking at Ezra. "It's a perfect egg."

"When you see Abigail, please give it to her."

Benjamin gazed down at the stone in his palm and said, "I will."

XXIX

Clementia

THROUGH THE NIGHT, ABIGAIL AND HER MOTHER TENDED TO THE soldiers in the granary. They returned home shortly after dawn. Their exhaustion was relieved somewhat by the fact that Father prepared tea as soon as they entered the house. The city was in even greater chaos than the night before, as though the real cost of the battle were just sinking in, and groups of drunken soldiers could be heard roaming the streets, and frequently there was the sound of breaking glass—bottles smashed and shop windows being broken.

Father had closed the storm shutters. They sat at the darkened dining room without speaking. The air was stifling, and though Abigail and her mother had washed as best they could, the smell of blood still clung to them. At one point Mother offered her daughter the faintest smile; it was one thing they would always share: blood.

"The tea," Father asked Abigail, "is it prepared all right?"

"It's fine," she said, and then took another sip. "The best cup of tea I've ever had."

Father appeared grateful, but then cleared his throat. "I went by James's, to see that they were all right, and I wondered if he might have some word of Benjamin. He hadn't."

After a moment, Mother asked, "How does he fare?"

"James?" Father said, breaking off a corner of his biscuit. "He's abed—has been for days. Excited, distressed. Says that Dr. Warren was killed. Bullet right in the head—in the cheek. He wasn't running away but facing them." He ate the biscuit. "That man stood up for what he believed in, I'll grant you that."

Benjamin accompanied the cart that was bearing several provincials, including Ezra, back to Concord for burial. When they stopped during the night to eat at a tavern in Menotomy, he learned that Dr. Warren had been killed. Various rumors were argued, some claiming that the doctor's body had been buried on Bunker Hill, while others had heard that the body had been taken to Boston, where it was on display for the ridicule of the British soldiers. Benjamin also wondered what had become of Lumley. It would be better if he had been killed in the battle. There was no knowing what the British military would do with him if he was captured.

The cart reached Concord in the early morning, and Ezra was delivered to the home of his relatives. While the women laid the body out in the parlor, Ezra's mother was overtaken with grief and had to be helped back to bed. Benjamin went out into the yard, sat down in the shade of an elm, and despite the crying and keening and prayers that issued from the open windows of the house he fell asleep.

Abigail was awakened by the sound of boots and hooves out in School Street, and then there was a pounding on the front door. Not a knock, but pounding.

She got up and left her room, buttoning her dress as she descended the stairs. In the hall, she saw her father standing at the closed front door, with Mother behind him. As he opened the door, Abigail moved back into the kitchen. She could see soldiers gathered in the street and behind them a white horse—Samuel's horse—prancing nervously. All she could see of Samuel was his boots, straining in the stirrups as he tried to control his mount.

She knew he was as angry with himself as with her. There must have been great embarrassment when his superior officers realized that the field cannon were useless. How could he explain bringing the wrong ammunition across the harbor? But his humiliation must be deeper, privately so. In his bedchamber, there was the moment when his hard member sought to press into her, his hand guiding it, but he went rigid, and from his mouth, hot against the side of her neck, he released a long shuddering sigh. She felt the desperation in his embrace, as though he were clinging to life, and then the warmth of his discharge spread over her thighs. Now he must know that she had deceived him, but she wished he knew, wished he could understand how difficult it had been for her. She was certain that he wasn't here to ask politely for an explanation. It was all beyond explanations now. There was no reasoning, and no regrets, not now. There was only survival.

Abigail rushed out the kitchen door and took the key off the hook, and then, raising her skirts with both hands, she ran outside to the back fence. She opened the gate and entered the alley, chased by the sound of soldiers swarming through the house. Boots clattered on the stairs. A bowl smashed in the kitchen. Her mother protested and then shrieked. Abigail sprinted down the alley toward the Latin School. It was a small building, which Father had kept locked since the British marched out to Lexington and Concord in April. All the windows, she knew, were latched. She could hear soldiers outside now, in the dooryard behind her house, coming through the gate to the alley.

She went to the side door of the schoolhouse and unlocked it. Once inside, she locked the door again. From a rear window she could see several soldiers coming down the alley. Quickly, she went up the aisle between the wood benches where for years her father and brother had instructed the well-to-do sons of Boston. When she was young, she would sometimes sneak into the schoolhouse in the early morning. She would hide in a closet where supplies were kept, everything from brooms and mops (the boys were expected to keep their schoolroom clean) to stacks of books in English, Latin, Greek, and French. There was a small window in this closet, and once school was in session she would sit beneath it with a book in her lap and listen to the lesson. This was how at times at the dining room table she would respond to her father and brother when they spoke, say, Latin. James thought it funny, a sign of how clever his little sister was, while Father found it suspicious—though she always suspected that his blustery veneer was designed to conceal his pride.

She slipped into the closet just as she heard pounding on the locked outer door—they were using the butts of their rifles, and it didn't take a minute for her to hear splintering wood as they broke the door open. Their boots knocked on the floorboards as they moved about the classroom and through the offices on one side of the building. She quietly made her way to the back of the closet, where books were stacked on a crate. There was a small space between the wall and the crate, and she sat there in the corner, her knees drawn up to her chest. She tried to slow her breathing as she listened to the soldiers.

But then she heard Samuel's voice, angry, demanding.

The others moved swiftly, running. Cabinet doors were opened and slammed shut. A pair of boots stopped outside the closet, and then the door was yanked open. Slowly the soldier walked into the small room, so dim that he knocked over some brooms and mops, their long handles clattering on the floor. He came to the back of the closet and Abigail looked up. His face was pale and the eyes that gazed down at her reminded her of a cat. He stared at her for a long moment, and then went out of the closet and shut the door. She waited. Samuel was shouting now, his voice impatient. The men continued to search, knocking books to the floor, causing a bust to crash (that would be Homer), but after a few minutes they were ordered outside and back into the alley.

Again, she was awakened by a sudden sound. Footsteps—not boots, shoes. Shuffling shoes, accompanied by the tap of a cane on the wood floors.

Father?

The light had changed and the closet was nearly dark: hours must have passed.

James?

She could not tell—they both frequently used a cane now.

The closet door was opened, and then silence. With her hands on both walls, Abigail pushed herself up from the floor in the corner and looked across the stack of books at her father.

"How did you know I was here?"

"I always knew. Where else would my girl learn Latin?"

"I was curious."

"You were brighter than most of the idiots seated out there in the benches." He left the closet and sat wearily in the first bench.

Abigail went out into the classroom. When Father took his hand off the knob of his cane to touch his forehead, his fingers trembled. "What is it?" she asked.

He turned his head toward the windows. Outside there was the sound of seagulls. "James," he said. "They arrested him. Apparently, when they killed Dr. Warren, they found he was carrying a letter, an encoded letter that they attribute to James."

"Dear God," Abigail said.

"How can a man in his condition survive prison?"

Father struggled to get to his feet, and Abigail helped him out of the schoolhouse and up the alley. "I cannot ascribe blame," he said as they entered the dooryard. "I'm overwhelmed by incomprehension." She expected Father to revert to Latin or Greek in his next utterance, but he continued in English. "The political aspects of this—I understand how this came to be. But our family." He paused, pulling his arm free of her grip. "How is it that our family became so divided?" He looked at Abigail then, his eyes welling up and his mouth quivering. "I'm responsible."

"No, Father."

"I brought this on. I know I did. I don't know what I should have done, but my failure goes back, it goes back years." He began walking toward the house, slowly. "I'd ask forgiveness, of all of you, but what good would it do, even if granted?"

"Father."

He paused but didn't turn around. Mother opened the kitchen door.

"Father," Abigail said. "You do not need to ask forgiveness, from any of us."

He stood for a moment, and then he stabbed the tip of his cane in the dirt and continued on toward the house. They were both so old, and frail. Abigail wanted only to go into the house, clean up the damage the soldiers had left behind, and help them up the stairs to bed. She began to follow her father, until Mother made a small motion with her hand, as though shooing away a fly that was hovering over the pie crust.

And then he appeared in the kitchen, standing directly behind her.

"Abigail." Formal, yet not unfriendly; it reminded her of when they had first met, when he had been so courteous.

"Samuel," she said.

"You have caused me—" He hesitated. "Great consternation. And embarrassment."

She merely stood there. Her feet seemed to be rooted in the ground beneath her.

"It makes me sad." He seemed uncertain, confused, even. She suspected that he had given great thought to what he might say, but now too many emotions, too many thoughts came together at once. "It could have been," he continued, "it could have been very different between us."

"I wish that were so," she said.

"Do you? Truly?"

"Yes. Yes, I do, Samuel."

There was something different about him, about his eyes. They were sad, hurt, even; but there was also an acceptance—or perhaps it was resignation—there that she'd never seen before, and it made her want to go to him, to ask his forgiveness and understanding. She wondered if they could still set things right between them.

He placed a hand on her mother's shoulder; it was gentle, loving even.

Abigail began walking toward the house, but then Samuel pushed her mother aside and stepped out through the doorway.

Father at first appeared uncertain. He glanced back at Abigail, and then again toward the house. And he raised his cane, causing Samuel to stop. "You'll go no further," he said.

"Sir." There was outrage in Samuel's voice.

He began to go around Father, until Father stepped in his path, shaking the cane even higher above his head. "Not another step, do you *hear?*" Father said.

Samuel appeared baffled, and then he looked angry. When he moved, Abigail ran back to the fence gate, and as she opened it she looked over her shoulder, to see Father and Samuel doing what appeared to be a ridiculous dance. Samuel would step to one side and Father would follow his lead; Samuel would step in the other direction, and again Father would do the same— back and forth, a strange sort of minuet that stirred up the dust in the dooryard.

Abigail turned her back on them both and ran down the alley toward King's Chapel. It was nearly dark, and chimney swifts darted above the rooftops. At the end of the alley, Beacon Street was packed with Bostonians and British soldiers, and she fell in with the throng, which was heading toward the Common.

There was a sense of urgency in the mob, a combination of joy and fear. Torches illuminated faces that were slick with sweat. There was the smell of ale and rum. Soldiers sang and whistled and some seemed to be barking at the sky. As they entered the Common, they joined hundreds of others who were gathered near the Great Elm. There were officers on horseback and a small drum corps. Four men were being trussed up, three in British uniform. The other was Lumley, who stood gazing out at the crowd, a noose about his neck. When the drums were quiet, an officer made a speech, saying something about cowardice and loyalty—it was difficult to hear because the crowd was so impatient and unruly. When the officer said "A traitor, a damned traitor who fired upon his countrymen at Bunker Hill," Lumley's eyes found Abigail in the crowd. He nodded to her once, and his stare appeared faintly amused.

The officer drew his sword, raised it above his head, and then swung it down. All four of the men were hoisted off the ground. Their bound bodies wriggled desperately. In the near dark, they resembled not men so much as insects, beetles suspended from their own filament. Their struggling sent the mob into a frenzy, and then one soldier hung in the air limp, but the others continued to dance and swing beneath their quivering branches, until a second, and then a third soldier became still. Upon seeing that Lumley was the last, the crowd broke into cheers and huzzahs, and still he would not be still.

Abigail had seen enough. She pushed her way through the crowd, and it wasn't until she reached Beacon Street that she looked back toward the Great Elm. Samuel was following her, seated now on his horse, which seemed to drift above the throng. As she rushed down the street, she realized that the crowd was still agitated, as though the execution were not enough. To the east, she saw that the sky was aglow. Groups of men ran toward the fire. Someone shouted that there was a riot at the prison on Queen Street.

When she reached the prison, the street was packed with people. There was no organization, despite commands being shouted by officers; all was chaos. The smoke from the fire made it difficult to see. Abigail could not locate Samuel astride his horse. She managed to make her way to the entrance, fighting against the stream of people, soldiers as well as prisoners, who were fleeing the building.

She ran through the stone corridors shouting for James and Mariah. Roof timbers roared and crackled loudly. Many cell doors were still locked. Arms and hands extended through bars as prisoners pleaded to be released. There were screams—women's shrill voices—coming from one wing of the building, and Abigail moved in that direction. Ahead, a wall collapsed, belching so much smoke that it was impossible to see. She covered her nose and mouth with her arm, but she could no longer speak. Everyone was running in the other direction, toward the entrance, and she could only continue by keeping one hand on the stone wall.

She came to a courtyard. Overhead, flames leaped into the sky. The fire was creating its own wind, and incredible heat, but here it was easier to see, and in the flickering light she found Molly Collins, lying on the cobblestones.

She helped Molly to her feet. "Mariah, my brother—do you know where they are?"

Molly's small face was black with soot, her eyes large. "Mariah," she said, pointing.

"Show me," Abigail said, grabbing her by the arm, "and I will help you get out."

Molly led her across the courtyard. So many women behind bars. Boston women, shouting, pleading, trapped in cells.

"She be kept separate, special like, away from us whores," Molly said, pointing at the end of the corridor.

There was a wooden door, with only a small barred window. Mariah's face appeared in the window for only a moment, and then timbers crashed down through the roof. Abigail was knocked down, her arm striking the stone floor hard. She seemed not to hear anything and she only wanted to sleep. It would be all right, she thought, to just rest a while. But she was lifted up by the arm and she cried out in pain. And then she realized that she was being embraced by both Mariah and Molly. They made their way back to the courtyard and entered a corridor. Walls had collapsed and there were dozens of women now, shouting, pushing. Abigail clung to Mariah and Molly as they were swept along with the others, while the building rumbled and disintegrated about them.

And then they were out, they were in the street. Abigail was dazed and her head hurt, worse than when she had struck the tree on Trimount. Mariah led both women away from the burning prison. As they turned a corner, Abigail looked behind them and saw Samuel astride his horse. He was following them, though his progress was impeded by the crowd.

Mariah took them through to the North End, using alleys and lanes. There was the smell of salt water, of low tide. When they approached her house, they could see the white horse in the distance, a faint smudge in the dark.

"Cleaveland," Abigail whispered.

Mariah pushed them back around the corner and down the path lane to the beach. Ahead of them was Joshua Tigge's sail loft. Skiffs and dories were pulled up on the sand. The three women ran to the boat nearest the waterline and shoved it down across the kelp and into the harbor, where it became light and buoyant. The water, salty and cold, felt good about Abigail's legs. She wanted to immerse herself in the sea; but, realizing that she was covered with blood, she only dipped her forearm and elbow in the water.

Then there was the sound of a horse's hooves pounding on the sand, and she saw Samuel riding along the beach toward them.

Abigail shouted, *"No! No more!"* And then, looking at Mariah and Molly, she said, "James, where's James?"

They didn't answer but only lifted her over the gunwale and into the dory. They climbed in, causing the boat to rock wildly, but then Mariah took up the oars. Abigail struggled to get up and sit on the stern thwart. In the bow, Molly said, "Pull, dammit, pull."

Abigail turned back toward the beach. Samuel dismounted his horse and strode purposefully out into the shorebreak, looking as though he might walk on the water toward them. Instead, when he was knee-deep, he drew a pistol from his holster, extended his arm, and took aim.

"Pull!" Molly screamed. "Pull with all you've got!"

Mariah groaned each time she dipped and pulled on the oars.

Samuel hesitated, lowering his arm slightly. He seemed to be saying something, speaking to her across the water.

"No," Abigail whispered. "I'm sorry, Samuel."

He sighted along the barrel once more, slow and deliberate, and then she saw the flash. His head seemed engulfed in white smoke. Out on the water, the report was small, harmless, lost in the vastness of the harbor.

Abigail slid off the thwart and fell to the bottom of the dory, crying out as her head struck the gunwale. She was unable to move, her cheek against the wood, staring back toward the shore. A hot, tearing sensation filled her breast, forcing her to gasp for breath. They were far enough out in the harbor that she could barely see Samuel, his pistol now at his side. He seemed tranquil and even satisfied, as though proud that he had executed such a fine piece of marksmanship. Beyond him, the sky over Boston was enshrouded in smoke, illuminated by the fire. The entire city appeared to be burning. She had never seen a sky so beautiful. By morning, surely, nothing would be left. As she closed her eyes, she heard the oars creaking in their locks, and Molly and Mariah, their voices frantic, but there was also the soothing sound of water trickling alongside the hull as it pushed out into the dark harbor.

EPILOGUE
April 1776

BENJAMIN DIPPED HIS OAR AGAIN AND LEANED BACK INTO HIS stroke. Now, after midnight, the air was dead calm, allowing the skiff to glide across Boston harbor, its wake curling ribbons of moonlight. He pulled in concert with the other oarsman in his boat, Dr. John Warren, Joseph Warren's brother, while Mr. Revere was perched on the stern thwart, one arm draped over the tiller.

From the bow, Mariah's uncle Joshua Tigge said, "Rocks to starboard, Paul."

"I see them." Revere swung the tiller a few degrees. "That smell," he said, looking at Benjamin, "don't you love it?"

The warm night air was heavy with the scent of low tide coming off the marshes.

"Always have, sir," Benjamin said.

"It's even sweeter this spring," Revere said, "now that the British are gone."

A month ago, Boston had seemed doomed. General Washington had ordered that cannon be placed on Dorchester Heights, where it could bombard the city. The artillery had come from Fort Ticonderoga, New York. In January, Benjamin had joined Henry Knox's detail that was charged with the task of hauling the fifty-nine British cannon back across Massachusetts through relentless snow, sleet, and ice. It had been a hard winter, and the three-hundred-mile journey took nearly two months. But once the weaponry was delivered outside of Boston, it provided George Washington, the new commander of the American army, with the means to liberate the city.

Or what was left of it. Benjamin had not been in Boston since the night before the battle at Charlestown the previous June. The siege had led to starvation and disease—every form of ague and flux, and, most feared, smallpox. Through the winter months, the British army, now under the command of General Howe, who, fittingly, was an illegitimate uncle of King George III, had become increasingly desperate and brutal. Buildings were continually razed for fuel. The Continental Congress had resolved that General Washington must do whatever was necessary to remove the British army, even if it meant the utter destruction of the Boston peninsula. Many provincials believed that firebombing it would be an act of mercy. Even John Hancock, who stood to lose substantial holdings in private and commercial property, agreed that the city must be won at all costs.

During the winter months, Benjamin had received only one letter from his father, delivered to Mr. Van Ee's house in Watertown. His report was unusually direct. James had been in prison since June, his health deteriorating. His wife Mary and the children were getting by as best they could—they had all suffered periods of illness. Yet Father still remained loyal to the crown (he had refused to see James in prison, though Mother visited their son frequently) and expressed bafflement at the provincials' desire for war and independence, neither of which he believed could be won. Benjamin was concerned by what Father did not address in the letter. There was no mention of his health, or of Mother's.

His hand, which like his voice had always been assertive and robust, was now shaky. Father acknowledged that he had heard that Benjamin had survived the battle at Bunker Hill, and he had sent the letter to Mr. Van Ee's, where, he understood, Benjamin now lived with his pregnant wife, the daughter of the fisherman Anse Cole. There was no offer of congratulations. Most troubling, perhaps, was how the letter concluded: *In Boston we are for the most part rendered Blind to the World beyond this Sorry Peninsula. We possess no news of Abigail and Pray constantly that you and she have been Reunited and are Safe and Well.*

"You're confident of the location?" Revere eyed Benjamin carefully, as though he knew that his thoughts had been wandering.

"I have no reason to believe I've been misled," Benjamin said.

Revere glanced up at the moon. "But you will not divulge your source?"

Perhaps Revere smiled—it was difficult to tell in such faint light. He seemed often to find things amusing, even when others did not. He was known to be difficult, some even suggested insubordinate, and he was no orator—that he would leave to his more eloquent compatriots—but his round, swarthy face was expressive, his large, dark eyes observant. His eloquence was in his hands, the certainty of his actions. This past year, since Dr. Joseph Warren had died, Benjamin often felt that Revere was being watchful, even protective of him.

"I prefer not to, sir," Benjamin said. "Doctor Warren always—"

"Yes, his instructions: mind your tongue," Revere said. "He was a good teacher." After a moment, he added, "And a dear friend. My wife and I have decided that our next child, if it is a boy, will be named Joseph Warren Revere."

Dr. Benjamin Church himself had removed the lead ball from Abigail's breast. It was lodged within inches of her heart. In July, the Continental Congress had appointed him Surgeon General, and, with the death of Dr. Warren, he was, along with John Hancock, the highest-ranking member of the Committee of Safety. Despite such duties, he visited Abigail several times a week and oversaw her convalescence personally. But by summer's end, there was much rumor and speculation about Dr. Church being in league with General Gage, providing him with invaluable information regarding the American troops. Yet he remained cordial with Abigail, devoted to her recovery, until the day that she inquired after the money she had given him on behalf of Rachel Revere.

"A hundred and twenty-five pounds, you say?" His eyes concentrated on the old dressing covering her breast. "I fear I have no recollection of that."

"I delivered it to your house in Boston, so that you could convey it to Mr. Revere once you left the city." As the dressing was removed, Abigail's flesh stung and she breathed in sharply through her nose. "Rachel gave it to me and I brought it to you. It was a Sunday morning, dense fog, and a woman left the house in a carriage."

He raised his eyes to her, curious. "A woman? Are you sure?" He attempted a smile. "Abigail, so much has happened during the past year, everyone is bound to misinterpret or misconstrue certain events."

"Your implication, then, Doctor," she said, "is that my memory is at fault?"

He finished changing the dressing and, without looking at her, said, "This is a serious wound. It is most fortunate that I didn't have to remove the entire breast."

Dr. Church never paid her a visit again, opting to send one of his assistants, who always claimed that the doctor's time was too precious. In October, he was first court-martialled by General Washington, and then brought before the Massachusetts Assembly on charges of consorting with the enemy. Though he vehemently defended his actions as attempts to mislead the British command for the benefit of the patriotic cause, there was sufficient evidence—ciphered letters, sympathetic ink, the confession of a young woman who admitted to conducting the letters to the British—that Church was sent to prison in Connecticut, where over the winter he developed asthma. The fall of one of the most influential leaders of the patriot cause was met with shock and outrage, but eventually a prisoner exchange was negotiated with the British command in Boston; however, at the last moment the agreement was abandoned. Though the proposed exchange didn't include Abigail's brother James (which Abigail thought would have been logical, considering that both men had been found guilty of similar charges), the idea of such an occurrence gave her hope, only to have such expectations dashed.

Abigail's recovery was difficult, and she might not have survived the winter but for the generosity of Mr. Van Ee. Not until February was she strong enough to venture outside for any considerable time. She had built up her strength by walking, first on the grounds about Mr. Van Ee's house, and then, more and more frequently, through the village of Watertown, with frequent visits to the house where Rachel now lived with the children.

"It will all come out," Rachel said. They were sitting by the stove in Rachel's kitchen. Outside they could see the children in the dooryard, playing in the snow. "Paul, Dr. Warren—none of them ever fully believed Dr. Church. The blood on his stocking, his so easily returning to Boston immediately after Lexington and Concord, and the missives—it has long been suspected that there was someone high up in the provincial leadership, perhaps even a member of the Committee of Safety, who has been feeding information to the British. I'm not surprised that it was our dear, sophisticated Dr. Church, who pens plays and liberty songs, and keeps an expensive wife in a country manor, and a mistress in Boston." Laughing, Rachel added, "It's preferable that you no long bare your breasts to him. He could never truly appreciate such rare beauty."

Though she blushed, Abigail laughed as well. "But, Rachel, a hundred and twenty-five pounds."

"It's a great deal of specie. And I suspect I'll never know what happened to it," Rachel said as she prodded the logs with the poker, bringing about a welcome surge of heat into the kitchen. "There are far worse things to lose than money." She closed the stove door and sat back in her chair. "You are recovering from more than that bullet wound. I can tell—"

"Tell? How can you *tell?*"

"Because you never speak of him, Abigail. It is your way."

"We were talking about specie."

"We were talking about loss."

Abigail gazed out the window. She bit her lip, but it couldn't keep her eyes from welling up, blurring the image of the children as they played in the snow. She knew Rachel was watching her and she turned her head away.

"Ezra left Boston," Rachel said quietly. "He left you."

"There was a reason. There had to be."

"Then remember him fondly, but you must allow your heart to heal, too."

Abigail wiped her cheeks with the palm of her hand. "And how do you do that?"

"Dwell not on the past. Think only of future plans."

When her strength finally returned, Abigail did make plans. At first, she thought she would join Molly Collins, who, like many Massachusetts women, had formed an attachment to the provincial army, providing assistance in caring for men who had fallen ill—as in Boston, disease was rampant in the military camps that surrounded the city. Molly had traveled to New York City with the army. In her letters, which were clearly dictated to someone (yet they still managed to retain the tone and spirit of her voice), she was adamant in the fact that she was not providing the American soldiers what she called the "old services." Abigail believed her. Molly was a changed woman. They all, it seemed, were changed, changed in ways that perhaps a year earlier none of them could ever have imagined. No one doubted that this would be a long war and there would be much to do.

Mariah, who had married Benjamin in January just before he went to Ticonderoga with General Henry Knox's detail, was expecting. She was also staying at Watertown, working in a tavern, and when she was close to term Abigail took her in to her own room at Mr. Van Ee's and assisted in the delivery of a baby girl. It wasn't until late February that Benjamin returned from Ticonderoga to see his wife and child, which they named Abigail.

On that first night at Mr. Van Ee's house, Benjamin sat before the fireplace in a rocker, his sleeping daughter in his arms, and he looked weary from the winter's journey. There was now something different about Benjamin. It wasn't just that he was exhausted. He was no longer the wild boy wandering Boston, living by the ebb and flow of the harbor tides. His gaze was distant, yet inward. He too was consumed by the war, by the difficulties that faced the provincials. As he spoke, his thoughts meandered, and Abigail realized that it was like so many conversations she'd had with their father. Benjamin talked about the importance of bringing the British artillery to Boston, of George Washington becoming the commander of the Continental Army. He talked about why the Americans must force the British to evacuate Boston, regardless of the cost to the city.

But then he stopped rocking in the chair. Hesitantly, he began to apologize as he gazed at the burning logs in the fireplace. Abigail didn't understand what he was saying; she worried that the strain of the Ticonderoga expedition had been too much for him. There was something odd about him, how he was scrutinizing her. He seemed worried, even frightened. Hesitantly, he took something from his vest pocket and held it out to her. Abigail leaned forward in her chair and gasped. Her entire body clenched like a fist. There was a pain in her breast—not the same as when she'd been struck by Samuel's bullet, but a wrenching pain that rose from within her heart.

The Egg?

Benjamin was still apologizing, saying that he didn't want to give her this until he felt she had recovered from her wound, that she was strong enough.

She craddled the Egg in her palm.

But it was a stone, a white stone, stained with blood.

"He dug it out of the ground on Bunker Hill," Benjamin said. "And he gave it to me just before he died later that day."

"Ezra," she whispered.

The keel scraped sand, and they shipped oars. The men climbed out into knee-deep water and then pulled the skiff up onto the beach. They removed their tools—shovels, a lantern, a wad of old sailcloth—and crossed the beach. To their left, the village of Charlestown was visible beneath a gibbous moon. Nearly a year after being burned by the British, new houses and buildings were under construction, presided over by an incomplete steeple, bound in staging. Once they reached the firm ground of pasture, they waded through tall grass that crackled beneath their feet and climbed over wooden fences. Dark, slow-moving forms—grazing cattle—littered the hillside. Benjamin led the way, a shovel resting on his shoulder, occasionally guiding the others around a cow pie. When they were near the angular, battered earthen walls of the redoubt, he paused and said over his shoulder, "East, now."

They descended toward the Mystic River, which bordered Charlestown Neck, until they could see a stand of trees by the brick kiln.

"Joshua," Revere said. "Light the lantern, and let's have a good look at this ground."

Though new spring grass had begun to sprout, there was evidence of digging—holes, numerous holes.

"Well, Mr. Lovell?" Revere asked.

Benjamin walked toward the stand of trees near the kiln, followed by John Warren, holding the lantern. When he reached the trunk of the tallest maple, Benjamin noticed that the bark had been gouged with knives.

"Lead balls," Joshua said.

"Souvenirs," said John Warren, "for posterity."

"For sale," Joshua said. "I've seen this in Boston, the sale of 'Bunker Hill balls.' Turns a nifty profit and certainly every ball is the genuine article." When Revere looked at him, he said, "Young Dr. Warren here is an idealist. I'm the cynic."

Revere turned to Benjamin and said, "Proceed."

Benjamin put his back to the tree, and then began to walk north, taking long, deliberate strides, counting to twenty, and then stopped in front of an oval-shaped mound of earth. The other men gathered around, and then John stepped forward, his shovel in both hands. "I hope to God you're right," he said.

"I do, too," Benjamin said as he stabbed the blade of his shovel into the dirt.

In March, General Washington had made his move on Boston. Benjamin again bid his wife and both Abigails farewell and rejoined the ranks. Under the cover of darkness and a storm that brought heavy rain and winds, thousands of provincials quietly—so quietly for so many—moved the Ticonderoga cannon into position on Dorchester Heights. The countryside was cleared of wood, and fascines were constructed—all the while, other provincial regiments conducted diverting tactics down near Boston Neck, as well as from across the Charles River. The result was that General Howe knew something was afoot, but he was unsure where it would come from—most British reinforcements were sent to the Neck. It was, Mr. Van Ee observed at his dinner table, like watching a shrewd chess game played in the dark of night. In daylight, when the weather began to clear, Howe was confronted with the fact that Washington had fortified Dorchester Heights to the south, with artillery in command of the entire Boston peninsula.

Bombardment from the heights would surely set the city ablaze. Abigail's father and mother were there; her brother James was confined to a prison cell there, his wife and children still in their home. Abigail had never known such an overwhelming sense of dread. And she had never seen it on so many faces. When she would venture from Mr. Van Ee's house, everyone on the streets of Watertown seemed lost in thought, fearing that the worst was about to happen. Trapped, the British would surely strike out, sending massive forces out the Neck, or perhaps ferrying them across the Charles—or both. Each day, the tension seemed greater. There were constant rumors and conjecture about sightings of troop movements, of ship activity in the harbor.

Until it was reported that the British were evacuating Boston. At first, there was disbelief, but for days there were clear indications that the ships were being loaded with troops and supplies, as well as with loyalists. Washington, perhaps most daringly, did nothing. He simply waited. There was looting throughout the city. What couldn't be stolen from homes and taken aboard ship was often destroyed. The river and harbor were littered with furniture, adrift on the currents and tides. The evacuation was a massive operation involving several hundred ships.

Rachel came to Mr. Van Ee's house with news about Samuel Cleaveland: he was responsible for loading the artillery aboard ship and in the process of doing so had lost several cannon, which inexplicably fell off of a barge and sank to the bottom of the harbor. "In the end," Rachel said with a laugh, "the man's simply incompetent. He probably thinks he shot and killed the beautiful, treacherous schoolmaster's daughter."

But Abigail did not laugh. "I don't wish to dwell upon Samuel. I only wish him God's speed in returning home. Rachel, what I did was deceitful."

"And necessary."

"It is nothing to be proud of. It's this war—in another time and place, he—"

"Now you only deceive yourself." Rachel ventured one more laugh, placing her hand over her mouth as though promising that it would be her last. "In war and love, Abigail, a man like that will always have the wrong balls."

It took the British ten days to evacuate Boston, concluding on March 17, St. Patrick's Day. His majesty's vast fleet left the harbor but remained in sight of the city, maneuvering in Nantasket Roads. Was this some trap? Lure the provincial army back into the city, and then return the ships of the line to the harbor and commence bombardment? Or perhaps they were only being cautious, waiting to intercept the troop ships that were expected to arrive any day from England? Then, after more than a week, the British fleet abruptly disappeared over the horizon. Many speculated that they would head south, and immediately General Washington began preparations to move a sizeable force down to New York City. But then there were reports of the British fleet, sighted off the coast north of Boston, apparently sailing for Halifax.

Provincials, led by the army, began to return to Boston.

But not Abigail. Thinking of Ezra, buried in Concord, she left Watertown and walked inland, against the flow of Bostonians who were journeying home.

The soil was loose, thawed now after the long winter months, but difficult.

"So many rocks," John Warren observed.

"Our beloved New England soil," Joshua said.

Benjamin's shovel struck something hard, but not stone. "There, now," Joshua said.

"Too shallow," Revere said. "The bastards can't even bury the dead with dignity. Go easy."

Benjamin and John continued to dig, carefully. First, they revealed a hand, then an arm in a frock coat.

John whispered an oath.

Benjamin paused and reached into the pocket of his leather vest, producing two folded bandanas. He handed one to John, and said, "You brought gloves, I hope."

John nodded, reaching into his coat pocket. They tied the bandanas around their heads to cover their noses and mouths, and then pulled on their gloves.

"You say there are two bodies?" Revere asked.

"That's what I was told," Benjamin said.

He resumed digging, going slowly now, pulling the earth away, exposing the form of a man curled up on his side. John gasped for air as he worked beside Benjamin. Revere stood close by, refusing to be pushed back by the smell. Finally, Benjamin got down on his hands and knees and took the body by the arm. John knelt beside him, and together they pulled the corpse free of the dirt.

Quickly, John scrambled to his feet, gagging, and then he lumbered off into the dark, where he hurled in the grass.

"Worms," Benjamin said.

"Some farmer, I'd say by that coat," Joshua said.

"Fifties, maybe older." Revere picked up the lantern and held it over the hole. "This must be Dr. Warren," he whispered.

"Can you tell?" Joshua ventured closer.

Benjamin reached down and with his hands began scooping earth out, exposing a shoulder, the skin bare. He continued to work, and eventually John came back and helped as best he could, but he was sobbing, and having great difficulty breathing. Still, they kept pawing at the hole, bringing dirt up, freeing more of the second body.

"All right," Revere said, finally. "This will require all of us."

He pulled on a pair of gloves, as did Joshua, and they all knelt around the hole. They reached down and took hold of a limb— an ankle, an arm—and slowly dragged the body up, everyone now gasping with the effort, and when it was there, lying on the ground, illuminated by the lantern, they fell away, rolling on the ground, repelled, coughing, and sputtering.

Several minutes passed while they regained their breath and composure. Joshua produced a flask, and each took a pull. The rum, hot and burning, cut through the vile taste in Benjamin's throat.

John picked up the lantern and crawled on his knees toward the body and began his inspection. "Shot in the left cheek," he said. "Bayonet wounds, chest and abdomen."

"Can you tell if it's him?" Revere asked.

"Impossible to say," John said. "They stripped him naked."

"And put him on display, I hear," Joshua added. "Then they sold his fine clothes."

"I can't say with certainty," John said, "if this is my brother." He looked out into the dark pasture. "He could be in any one of these holes."

"His teeth," Benjamin said. "Sir, didn't you—"

Revere nodded. "Last year I put two false teeth in Joseph's mouth." He took the lantern from Joshua and came closer. "Let's have a look then."

Carefully, Benjamin held the skull in both hands and pried open the jaws.

"There—those wires," Revere said, leaning close with the lantern.

"Are you sure?" Joshua asked.

"I can recognize my own handiwork," Revere said. "I fashioned those teeth, and secured them with wires. Gentlemen, this is our compatriot, Doctor Joseph Warren."

No one spoke for a moment, until Joshua said, "We take him back to Boston—for a proper funeral and burial."

"What about this other man?" Benjamin said, as he carefully lowered the skull until it rested on the soft earth.

"No knowing who he is," John said.

"He's a patriot," Revere said. "Bury him again, only much deeper, so that he honors this ground."

Benjamin picked up his shovel and, as he began digging, he couldn't help but think of Lumley, just up this hill on a hot June day, passing rum to him and Ezra before the British assault. He stayed in the redoubt when the others—those that could—fled. Certainly he intended to die there, at the hands of his countrymen. Instead he was captured, and Abigail had told Benjamin about how he stared at her in the crowd only moments before he was hung from the Great Elm in the Common. Where was he buried? Benjamin wondered. Traitors are seldom honored with a headstone. If he could, Benjamin would find Lumley, dig him up, take him north, bury him on a hillside in Vermont, and give him a headstone of New England granite.

Abigail returned to Boston in April, a few weeks after the British evacuation. She walked most of the way from Concord, though when she passed through the now-deserted fortification at the Neck she was riding in a wagon driven by Mr. Barnabas Tyng, who had years earlier matriculated at the Latin School. Mr. Tyng's wagon was filled with all of his earthly possessions, as well as his wife and their seven children. Tethered to the wagon were two cows and a vociferous mule. Abigail sat in a rocking chair, tied down next to a crate of chickens, the sleeping bundle in her lap.

The city was in ruins. Houses had been ransacked. There was evidence of disease and starvation. At the sound of chickens, people came out to the street. It was easy to tell that they were Bostonians who had endured the winter's siege in the city—they were gaunt and weary, and there was in their eyes something unsettling and true. They had survived, and there was nothing to stop them from salvaging their homes, rebuilding their lives.

There was something else. A woman Abigail knew from the Dock Square market gazed at her bundle, smiled, and then turned away in disdain. *I know where you got that from, your kind, consorting with the Brits.*

She would have to contend with that; it was inevitable.

When Mr. Tyng stopped in School Street, both the Lovell house and the school were shuttered. Abigail requested that she continue on with them. The wagon passed slowly through the streets, to the North End, and she got off at the place where Mariah's house had been. It was gone. Nothing left but a pile of chimney bricks and some lumber, much of it charred. At the back of the dooryard, however, the shed remained intact, and there was evidence that it was being inhabited: laundry strung on a line, a wood chopping block, an iron pot sitting on a fire pit constructed of rounded beach stones. She looked at where the house had been and realized that some of the lumber had been neatly stacked, and that there was a trench dug and the beginnings of a new stone foundation laid.

Abigail walked down the lane toward the beach, her bundle clutched to her shoulder. He was getting heavy, but she was pleased at the sounds he made while asleep. Strange, this language all his own, the sighs and grunts speaking to her of his needs and wants. At the end of the lane, the breadth of the harbor opened out before her, blue-black beneath a cerulean sky, and in the distance salt marshes and island pastures turning the palest green of early spring.

And there, down by the row of fishermen's shacks, she saw Benjamin with Joshua Tigge, working on a boat hull, the sound of their caulking mallets like a knock on an eternal door. Crying out, Mariah dropped the fishnet she was mending and began running along the beach toward Abigail. Then Benjamin came too, calling out, and his hat flew off as he ran, his long hair a flag in the breeze. But not Joshua, who sat down on the overturned hull, content with the business of packing his clay pipe with tobacco.

Mariah and Benjamin gathered about Abigail, clutching, embracing, and they all kissed and wept with joy. A baby, too, was crying, from a basket lying in the shade of the shack. "Time to feed our Abigail," Mariah said, laughing through her tears, as they started back along the beach.

The bundle stirred, and Abigail paused to open the blanket. Benjamin and Mariah leaned in close to see. "This is Ezra," Abigail said. "Ezra Hammond Lovell."

She put the child down and he began to walk toward the waterline, strands of kelp clinging to the bottom of his gown. Abigail followed close behind him, ready to catch him if he fell.

Each step was an adventure, precarious, determined. When he reached the water, he stopped and stared back at her, at all of them, curious, and then he squatted down and slapped his hands in the white foam as it swirled about his ankles.

Abigail lifted him up by his stout forearms. He loved this always, releasing silent peals of laughter. She waded out, dragging his legs through salt water. Turning side to side slowly, she pulled him through the small glinting waves and then up into the air, and then down and up again, and again, and again, until she gathered him, wet and shivering, to her chest. "Look, Ezra." He watched her lips as she formed the words slowly. She was convinced that when she held him in her arms, he was soothed by the feel of her voice, its timbre rising up through her breasts. "We're home."

On the shore, Benjamin and Mariah were clapping their hands.

Ezra didn't hear them—or the caw of the seagulls high over-head—but his mouth remained open with mute fascination as he extended his arm. He pointed, across the harbor, toward the islands, out to sea, and to the high clouds piled upon the horizon. It didn't matter where or in what direction. He was seeing it all for the first time.

ACKNOWLEDGMENTS

I wish to thank Northern Michigan University for the Peter White Scholar Award, which provided me with course release time and funds that helped me to complete this book. For their abiding commitment and enthusiasm, I am indebted to Claiborne Hancock and Jessica Case at Pegasus Books. Finally, I am deeply grateful to my literary agent Noah Lukeman, for his pugilist's tenacity and crystalline foresight.